Dreaming Southern

Dreaming Southern

Linda Bruckheimer

A DUTTON BOOK

DUTTON
Published by the Penguin Group
Penguin Putnam Inc., 375 Hudson Street, New York, New York 10014, U.S.A.
Penguin Books Ltd, 27 Wrights Lane, London W8 5TZ, England
Penguin Books Australia Ltd, Ringwood, Victoria, Australia
Penguin Books Canada Ltd, 10 Alcorn Avenue, Toronto, Ontario, Canada M4V 3B2
Penguin Books (N.Z.) Ltd, 182–190 Wairau Road, Auckland 10, New Zealand

Penguin Books Ltd, Registered Offices: Harmondsworth, Middlesex, England

First published by Dutton, a member of Penguin Putnam Inc.

First Printing, January, 1999
10   9   8   7   6   5   4

 REGISTERED TRADEMARK—MARCA REGISTRADA

LIBRARY OF CONGRESS CATALOGING-IN-PUBLICATION DATA

Bruckheimer, Linda.
    Dreaming Southern / Linda Bruckheimer.
      p.   cm.
    ISBN 0-525-94453-2 (alk. paper)
    I. Title.
    PS3552.R79425D74   1999
    813'.54—dc21   98-35761
                      CIP

Printed in the United States of America
Set in Minion
Designed by Stanley S. Drate/Folio Graphics Co. Inc.

To my mother
For inspiring all my fanciful dreams;
To Alex
For making them all worthwhile;
And to Jerry
For making them all come true.

Chapter One

Usually Lila Mae Wooten had to scream bloody murder before her kids would pay any attention to her at all. But she was desperately trying to turn over a new leaf, so she pushed the accelerator of the swamp-green 1953 Packard to the floor and smiled at them in the rearview mirror.

"Well, here it comes, kids—the Kentucky state line!" She had already told them five or six times that the state line was coming up very soon, but they still hadn't given her the type of response she had hoped for.

"Take a look at them tobacco fields and that blue grass . . ." she continued. "It might be years and years before you see 'em again, if ever—*if ever*." Lila Mae spoke very dramatically, arching her crescent eyebrows and sighing deeply. She was wearing a print housedress and simulated pearls, and her hair had just been tinted Polynesian Spice. Supposedly, it was the exact same color that Rita Hayworth used, but Lila Mae was afraid it was way too loud. "Come on, kids, it ain't right to just drive across like we don't give a hoot. . . ."

Determined to snag their attention come hell or high water, she said, "I swear there's an awful noise comin' from the trailer. Maybe I should pull over right before we cross the state line and double check." When that didn't work, she took a quick peek in the rearview mirror to see exactly what type of situation she was dealing with, then started to sing: "Oh, the sun shines bright on my old Kentucky home!"

Finally, Becky Jean stopped flipping the pages of her *Modern Screen* magazine and huffed, "We *heard* you the first time. What do you expect us to do, bawl our eyes out?" A pretty girl and the eldest of Lila Mae's four children, she had a heart-shaped, Miss America face and a rosebud mouth that was usually in one stage or another of smirk. Her caramel hair—flecked with gold and swirling around her shoulders—was styled in a perfect pageboy fluff, and she was wearing pink velveteen pedal pushers and ballerina flats. Looped around her wrist was a sterling-silver Speidel ID bracelet engraved: TO BECKY JEAN, LOVE YA, GLEN.

"Besides," Becky Jean said in a nonchalant drawl, "what's the big deal about a stupid old sign?"

"What's the *big deal*?" Lila Mae craned her neck and gawked into the backseat. "If this ain't your idea of a big deal, leaving the state you grew up in—probably *forever*—then I don't know what is. I swanee!" No wonder I have to exaggerate everything, Lila Mae thought, there's no way to get through to them kids normally.

"You act like we're moving to Mars or something," Becky Jean griped. Naturally, her mother, the queen of dramatic riga-maroles, wanted to depart Kentucky in a blaze of ceremonies and turmoil. The best thing to do when she was in a tizzy, which was fifty percent of the time, was to simply give her the cold shoulder. Shutting the *Modern Screen*, Becky Jean bent down and opened her cosmetics case, where she kept perfumes and dusting powders, two novels, half a dozen movie magazines, Tigress by Fabergé, and Can Can Dancer Red, a newly purchased lipstick the color of communion wine. Lila Mae said she'd better not catch Becky Jean wearing the lipstick unless she wanted to be taken for a brazen hussy, and she didn't want her daughter to wear the perfume, either, since she thought it would attract men like flies.

Locating the *Photoplay* with Natalie Wood on the cover, Becky Jean straightened up, made a sassy puff of a noise, and picked up where she left off. "What do you expect, anyway? Marching bands with tubas and trombones? Sheet cakes, confetti, tearful mourners?"

"Mouth off all ya want, Miss Smarty Pants." Lila Mae gave her a mournful warning. "Someday when I'm gone, you'll be sorry you didn't pay more attention to your heritage."

When they were mere yards from the state line, Lila Mae stopped the car, then took a deep breath and stared sadly at the crystal-white clouds and neon-blue sky. A chestnut thoroughbred galloped across a green meadow and a trio of Kentucky cardinals flitted past the last seasonal vestiges of crape myrtle. Swagged over the gently rolling hills of a horse farm were low, billowy vapors of Ohio Valley fog. Lila Mae gazed at the scene as if she'd never see another horse or bird or swatch of fog for the rest of her life.

Just when she started to get all choked up, she thought about Loretta Nutt, a woman who'd lost not only her beloved husband but all of her limbs in a horrible train wreck. Even with all that going against her, the woman had managed to raise six kids, worked full time in a dime store, and had even written an entire novel with a pencil in between her teeth! Lila Mae didn't know Mrs. Nutt personally, but she had read all about her in *Reader's Digest*. So, if a handicapped person could manage all that, then surely, Lila Mae thought to herself, she could handle a car trip across country with a few high-strung, smart-alecky kids.

Just thinking about the amazing woman gave Lila Mae a sudden gust of optimism. Jabbing the accelerator, she glanced in the mirror to see if she looked as good as she felt; then she tooted the horn several times and began to sing, her voice bellowing and vibrating like Ethel Merman's and her fist whipping the air like a spirited bandleader's. "Cal-i-fooorn-ia, heeere we come, riiiight back where we started from. . . ."

"Oh, great . . ." Becky Jean, her olive eyes smoldering, slapped her magazine shut and clamped her arms across her chest. "Here goes the singing again."

Since she was peeved at her mother in general—pretty much since she was born—everything Lila Mae did rubbed her the wrong way. Just keeping up with her mother's moods (Lila Mae was like a faucet with two settings, hot and cold) was impossible unless you were a mind reader. One minute she was like a high-speed mechanical doll, excited and animated, as she sang her favorite songs or pointed out interesting scenery. Then the least little thing would turn her rubbery. With a heaving sigh, her arm would drop into her lap with a dramatic thud, but if you asked her what was wrong, Lila Mae would insist with a world-weary sigh, "Oh, nothing." Then she'd continue her suffer-in-silence act, inching the car along the highway as if it was all she could do to keep from collapsing in a heap.

"Actually, I don't care if we *ever* make it to California. And at this rate"—Becky Jean noticed that they hadn't actually crossed the state line—"we won't."

"You'll thank me one day when you marry some big movie star." Lila Mae bobbed her head to punctuate each word. *"That—you—will."* She turned to Irene Gaye, her infant daughter, who was strapped in the seat next to her, and muttered, "Ain't that right, baby girl?" Irene Gaye had one white curl like the top of an ice cream cone, a constellation of chigger bites on her chin, and front teeth shaped like two small teardrops.

"Doretta Coombs visited Hollywood and she didn't see one stinkin' star." Twelve-year-old Carleen twisted her birthstone ring and wrinkled her nose at her older sister. "Not one!" She had glittery bleached-blue eyes and a face as golden and cheerful as a sunflower. Her straw-blond hair was pulled into a ponytail so high on her head and tight that it made her eyes slant. On her fingernails were chips of old pink polish, and cradled on her lap was a wrinkled grocery bag full of *Katy Keene* comic books. Zipping up her rose-red car coat, a Becky Jean hand-me-down, she poked their six-year-old brother, Billy Cooper, in the ribs and told him to quit hogging the backseat. "Heeeyyy—stop!" The boy elbowed Carleen right back, then socked her once more for good measure. With his pug nose splashed with paprika freckles and his chipped-front-tooth grin, he looked like Howdy Doody. Sliding his coon-skin cap across his burr haircut, he twirled the hat out the window, tracing figure eights in the air. "Goooodbyyyye, Keeentuuuuckyyyy!" Then he reached into his back pocket, slipped out a rubber dart, and loaded it into his gun barrel.

"This is no time for you to be shootin' that dern thing, unless you're trying to kill your baby sister." Lila Mae turned to her daughters for help. "Can't you girls handle that boy?"

Becky Jean popped Billy Cooper, who had looped his finger around the trigger. "Stop it, you little brat!" But Billy Cooper pointed the barrel at the windshield, winked one eye in a lop-sided aim, and pressed anyway. The rubber dart flew out, grazed Carleen's ear, bounced off the dashboard, and disap-peared into a heap of baby supplies and maps. The next dart skimmed Lila Mae's neck, did something to Baby Sister that caused her to slip and slide around, and ended up stuck on the windshield.

"Good lordy!" Lila Mae wheeled around to slug Billy Coo-per, blindly swatting the air with her fist. At the time she fig-ured she could control the steering wheel with one hand and her son, who had managed to dodge her, with the other, but the trailer was more than she could handle. She lost her grip and they ended up way over in the opposite lane. A chorus of honks, like off-key notes from a French horn, blasted a warning as oncoming traffic swerved to avoid the wayward Packard.

"WATCH OUT!" Becky Jean and Carleen let out an eight hundred–decibel yell. "WE'RE IN AN ACCIDENT!" Billy Coo-per screamed. Baby Sister rocked back and forth, gurgling and drooling and kicking her wrinkled legs. The glove compartment flew open, a Kleenex box zipped across the dashboard, and

Becky Jean's perfume bottles clinked together like pealing church bells. Worse, it started to rain, and the roads were slick.

"Good lordy!" Lila Mae gripped the wheel, turning it with all her might. "Stop, please!" she hollered, as if pleading with the headstrong car to obey her. But the Packard, swaying wildly, skidded into one lane, then another. After clipping past the Venus de Milo Figure Salon and narrowly missing the WEL-COME TO MISSOURI sign, they sheared the bark off a sweet gum tree and nosedived against an embankment. Finally, they shimmied to a halt in a rupture of dust and mud clods.

"Lord have mercy!" Lila Mae panted. "We'll be lucky if we don't end up corpses in the Harlan County morgue." She quickly surveyed everyone's condition and carefully avoided the dirty looks and wisecracks she was getting from the other drivers who were slowing down to give Lila Mae a piece of their mind. One angry motorist, petals of rain dripping from his eyelashes, lumbered toward her like Frankenstein's monster, stuck his big, round face against Lila Mae's window, and pumped his curled paw at her. His wife, who had curlicued bottle-brown hair, stood next to him, holding a tepee-shaped newspaper over her head and bunching her eyebrows together in a dirty look.

"Well, for cryin' out loud!" Lila Mae whipped around, sifting through the baby's diaper bag. "They act like I did it on purpose or something. And I'd like to know where that rain come from—that's what did it." She turned to Baby Sister, propped her up, and massaged her soft spot. "You okay, sugar? . . . Now, wouldn't it have been something if that boy had put the baby's eye out?" Still wheezing in anxiety, she tightened the straps on Irene Gaye's car seat.

"I swanee." Lila Mae's arms fell to her thighs as if they weighed two tons. "My nerves is already shot and we're hardly outta the state. I honestly don't know how I'll *ever* make it clear cross the country. . . ."

Although the nervous-breakdown reference was the signal that everyone should feel guilty for the way they treated their mother and totally responsible for any mishaps that occurred, Becky Jean simply murmured, "So what? Your nerves are always shot."

As for the heartbreak-of-leaving-our-home-state speeches, Becky Jean didn't know what to make of them. For years the shoe had been on the other foot. Lila Mae used to preach to her husband, "It's high time we got out of this pigsty," griping about the ugly Monopoly-board houses, the corroded Kelvinators strewn in front yards, the tufts of brittle dichondra growing on their neighbors' ratty property. Even the weather was dangerous: "Funnel clouds galore . . . one right after the other!" Conveniently, she'd pull out a magazine showing Californians wearing Bermuda shorts and Hawaiian shirts. In the dead of winter they'd be barbecuing steaks while their athletic, blond kids paddled around in the family swimming pool. Each house had its own palm tree, in every backyard was an orange grove, and every family was on a first-name basis with two or three movie stars. "Ain't that the life," she'd swoon. When Lila Mae wasn't looking, their father would wink at them. "They don't tell you anything about those earthquakes, do they now?" But to hear Lila Mae tell it, it was Kentucky, not California, that was Shangri-la.

Oh, it just irked Becky Jean no end that her parents were ruining her life with another wild goose chase. It was bad enough that she was missing her *Swan Lake* ballet recital and her chance to become prom queen, but she could also forget her dreams of ever being Mrs. Glen Buchanan. She envisioned the familiar scene: the amber glow of Glen's skin; his muscular hand that practically wrapped around her tiny waist; the long drives they took in his red-and-cream Chevy convertible with its radio blasting "Cherry Pink and Apple Blossom White"; and all those starry evenings when the sky above them was a dome of silver confetti and Glen, covered in the froth of angora from Becky Jean's sweater, would gaze at her with dewy moon eyes and gush, "You are a living doll!" It was only a matter of time,

Becky Jean mused, before Belinda Householder would get her mitts on Glen, mere days before they'd mount the swiveling vinyl bar stools at Klink's Drug Store, sharing a chocolate soda and snickering "Becky Jean who?" if her name happened to come up.

Even still, Becky Jean wasn't about to admit how upset she was, particularly to her mother. Opening the Blue Waltz cologne, she sprinkled the vanilla perfume on her finger, then rubbed it along the eggshell-white bone on her wrist, each pungent whiff reminding Becky Jean of her grandmother. She stooped down to retrieve her transistor radio and fiddled with the white dial, but all she could get was static. Planting the radio up to her ear, she listened to the faraway, blurry noises of her hometown station. Through the jumble of crackling buzzes and twangs, she could barely make out the sound of Doris Day singing "Secret Love."

Before it was too late, she removed her Evening in Paris compact and sneaked one last look at the reflection of Kentucky in the mirror. Through the fluttery vapor that rose from the highway, she watched the sugar maple trees with their chartreuse-and-burgundy leaves. They quivered and shimmered in the breeze, then became smaller until, finally, they were just one smashed clover-green blur on the horizon.

Chapter Two

Lila Mae's husband had told her to "make it snappy," and even suggested the best route to take, the highways he himself had driven to California a mere month ago. Roy, armed with NoDoz tablets, a steaming thermos of black coffee, and a determination to reach the Golden State in record time, had made the trip in three days. Although Lila Mae played along with him and even asked him dozens of questions to throw him off the track, she was bound and determined to take Route 66. She had read novels and seen television programs about the colorful, historical road, and there was no way she was going to miss out.

"If that man thinks we're gonna drive all the way across country and not see us some beautiful scenery, then he's got another think coming." Lila Mae snapped the last suitcase shut with a decisive click. "Let him zoom across country like heck on wheels, but that's not for us. . . . Ain't that right, kids?" Carleen and Billy Cooper were on the edge of their seats as Lila Mae told them spine-tingling stories about the Painted Desert, the mighty Mississippi, and the Atchison, Topeka, and Santa Fe railroad. She also informed them that Route 66 was the exact same path the pioneers traveled, so on top of visiting Indian reservations and souvenir shops, covered-wagon-shaped motels, and cozy cafes serving homemade cherry pie, the trip would be highly educational. One peep to their father, though, and Lila Mae threatened to clobber them.

The man at Arbuckle's Texaco station who checked the tires and changed the oil was nice enough to trace Route 66 on Lila Mae's map with a purple crayon. He had a broad, friendly face, a panoramic forehead like the windshield on a speedboat and he wore a pea-green uniform with a name patch that said BILL CORN. He smelled of gasoline and Wildroot Cream Oil and on his arm was a tattoo of a heart with JOANELLE inscribed across it.

"Hey, mister. . . ." Billy Cooper picked his nose, then took the gun from his holster, twirling it on his thumb. "Our daddy, he's already in California. . . . He seen some movie stars, too."

"He did? That's nice, son." The man patted Billy's furry head and smiled.

"Like who?" Becky Jean answered her own question with a know-it-all snap. "Just some woman with platinum blond hair and sunglasses who *looked* like an actress. He's nowhere near where the movie stars live. He's out in some dumb little suburb called—"

"Well, you don't have to tell the man our life story, for goodness sakes. . . . Can't you see he's busy?" Lila Mae reeled around and shot Becky Jean her bug-eyed warning stare. This meant the man could be a cold-blooded killer who would find out everything there was to know about the Wootens, chase them all the way to California, then stab them with butcher knives when they were least expecting it. "Why, he probably ain't got time for this nonsense anyway, do you, sir?"

Actually, Lila Mae was dying to tell *her* version of the tale, so she turned to Mr. Corn and said, "Some dear, *dear* friends of ours live in California. They been after my husband for just ages to move out there. Now both Roy and me, we was born and raised in these parts, so, naturally, we never dreamed of leavin'. You're not gonna believe this"—Lila Mae leaned forward and spoke confidentially—"but my mother was so protective of me, I couldn't cross the street alone till I turned sixteen. She had us kids so petrified of Winnie Ruth Judd that we couldn't hardly think straight. . . ."

"Winnie Ruth Judd." The man wrinkled his bushy eyebrows into two thoughtful waves. "I don't reckon I know Miss Judd."

"You don't?" Although Lila Mae reared back in disbelief, she was pleased to have the opportunity to fill him in. "Winnie Ruth was that cold-blooded murderess who chopped up her husband, stuffed all his parts in a brass trunk, and stored it in a train-station locker in Illi-noise."

Becky Jean's head dropped backwards with a snap and she groaned. "I'm *real* sure the man wants to hear about Winnie Ruth Judd. What's that got to do with California anyway?"

"Now, if Mr. Corn ain't interested, he can speak up, ain't that right?" Since the man didn't say a peep, Lila Mae continued. "Anyways, the trunk and whatnot stayed put for ages, but, as you can imagine, eventually there was some complaints about the godawful smell. That's when one of the train porters noticed red ooze foaming out of the locker."

"Well, my oh my." The man crinkled his face in disgust. "She sounds like a real doozie."

"Oh, that ain't all! The Judd woman got aholt of a razor or a lunch fork or some such, stabbed and killed a Joliet prison guard, escaped from her cell, and was on the loose. And there was no convincin' my mother that Winnie Ruth wasn't headed straight for Harlan County, Kentucky."

"Joliet, you say? The way I heared tell, they's nobody ever made it out of Joliet alive." Mr. Corn had seemingly discovered a hole in Lila Mae's story.

She looked at the man, her mouth a small puckered wreath, and said, "Now you can't go on what I'm a-tellin' you, because I kindly got some of the facts mixed up, but this is what I understand to be the case."

"You know what that means, don't you?" Becky Jean muttered. "That she made it all up. By the way," she announced with a victorious snort, "there's no such word as 'ain't.'"

"Oh, for heaven's sake, Rebecca Jean . . ." Lila Mae was afraid Becky Jean's one-hundred-mile-per-hour temper would leave a horrible impression on the nice man, so she pasted on a counterfeit smile. "She won a spellin' bee or some such, so now she's a big expert. Plus you know how teenagers are . . . they just love to embarrass the daylights outta ya. I got one who thinks she's the Queen of Sheba. Well, anyways, where was I?"

"Before you got sidetracked talkin' about that killer woman," Mr. Corn coached, "you was describing the house you grew up in . . ."

"Oh, that's right. Well, when Becky Jean come, we scrimped and saved and bought us a place on Pope Lick Road. We lived there until it liked to burst at the seams. Then I had me a case of cancer that shook us up pretty bad. I had to stop smokin' them coffin nails and they give me some cobalt treatments, but now I'm fit as a fiddle."

"You seem awful young for all that." The man squinted his glassy green eyes and took a closer look at Lila Mae, as if checking for some telltale signs that he had missed the first time around.

"Oh, they give me a clean bill of health a year ago. . . . But as luck would have it, Roy's health—that's my husband—took a turn for the worse . . . coughin' and gaggin' and what all. I tell you, Mr. Corn, the man almost coughed his lungs right outta his chest, I swear he did. His doctors said these harsh Kentucky winters would be his total, *complete* ruination." Lila Mae took a dainty gulp of Coca-Cola, then dabbed her mouth with the flowered handkerchief. "'Mrs. Wooten,' that doctor told me, 'if I was to let you stay in Kentucky, why, I might as well sign your husband's death certificate' . . . I swear that's what he said. So, we didn't waste no time. Roy said he'd go first, just to get situated while I stayed behind to clean up our affairs. I ended up sellin' just about ever' stick of furniture we own. But here we sit, rearin' to go. . . ."

What Lila Mae neglected to tell the man was that her husband's illness was no more than hay fever, that the real reason they were moving (or "skipping town," as Roy and Lila Mae called it when they thought nobody else was listening) was on account of a business deal gone sour. Roy Wooten had loaned his cousin Horace practically his last dime to manufacture Swat-A-Fly, a newfangled swatter that was subsequently yanked off the market by the Better Business Bureau. The promotional sketch, featuring "the Amazing, Revolutionary X-Tend-O-Arm," showed a man sitting in his bedroom reading a novel while smashing a fly in his kitchen seventy feet down the hall. Becky Jean had taken one look at it and thought something wasn't right. When she asked, "Why wouldn't the flies see that arm coming, the way they always see people?" Lila Mae said, "That's none of our concern. We're simply lendin' the man a little money to get his idea off the ground. Besides, I suppose *you* know more than the U.S. Patent Office!" Only after complaints by a group of irate customers, who said, "By the time the mechanical arm got where it was going, the fly was long gone," was the swatter declared defective. Naturally, Horace blamed the mix-up on his ex-girlfriend, who had drawn the sketch. He had also sent Lila Mae and Roy a letter from a P.O. box promising to iron out the kinks, but the end result was that the Wootens were flat broke.

As for the invitation to move to California, Charley Luckett was an old Air Force buddy who had simply told Roy, "If you're ever out my way, look me up." Luckett and his second wife, Helga, a Swede who barely spoke English, trained German shepherds and lived in the Garden of Eden Trailer Park in the San Fernando Valley. Becky Jean figured Charley would probably get the shock of his life when Lila Mae and Roy Wooten showed up some fourteen years later with their four bratty kids and a trailerful of beat-up, hand-me-down Ethan Allen furniture.

"What do you wanna bet the Lucketts don't even remember you?" Knowing that the best time to break the ice was in public, Becky Jean pulled out the Can Can Dancer Red lipstick and smeared two curvy lines across her lips. "You call them your dear friends, but *you* never even met them in person, have you?"

"Well, I've seen pictures, and we've talked on the phone plenty of times," Lila Mae, lobster red with embarrassment, said. "I swanee, Becky Jean—you make us sound like we don't have an ounce of sense. What must this poor man think?"

Becky Jean rolled her eyes at the man like she always did when she wanted to distinguish herself from her mother's scatterbrained ways. Curiously, though, most people seemed to be charmed by Lila Mae. Amid descriptions that put her one step away from haloes and harps—if not sainthood itself—Lila Mae's acquaintances would suggest that Becky Jean might even be jealous of her mother. "Nobody's sweeter than Lila Mae Wooten . . . *nobody!*" they would gush, stopping just short of adding, "Which is more than we can say about you."

"You don't know her like I do," Becky Jean sometimes felt like saying, although she couldn't come up with a smoking pistol since her mother had committed no real crime.

Anyhow, Mr. Corn was under Lila Mae's spell, ignoring other paying customers just to help her get her bearings.

Cupping her chin in her hand, she gazed past the sun, a lazy, orange disk, at some imaginary spot in the sky. "Everyone tells me, they say, 'Lila Mae, you should have your head examined to take a trip like that, especially this time a year, what with all the snowstorms and thundershowers—not to mention all them crooks on the loose.' They say I'll be lucky if we make it in one piece." She twirled a mahogany curl around her finger. Then she looked up at the man with her sparkly sapphire eyes and said, "What do *you* think, Mr. Corn?" as if he were the final authority.

"You'll make it just fine, ma'am." The attendant folded the map and patted the bumper of the Packard with his broad, sunburned hand. "Just fine."

"Mister," Carleen said, "you'd better show her how to drive this rattletrap. She'll crash it, sure as shootin'. She almost did already."

"Rattletrap? Why, I'll have you know I just had this engine overhauled. . . . And I'm a good driver." Lila Mae propped both hands on her hips and stamped her foot. "I am!"

Mr. Corn scratched his stubbly beard and nodded his head slowly. "Ma'am, I'm afraid your girl is right. There's a real trick to drivin' one of them things."

"There is? Oh, my." Lila Mae's eyes flew open and her hand clutched her throat. "W-what kind of trick?"

"Well, first off, take it easy with that gas pedal, little lady. I seen you pull in here, and you liked to skerred the livin' daylights outta me. . . ." Mr. Corn wiped his hands on an oily blue rag, then tossed it against a tool chest. "Yep, most important thing when you're hauling a trailer is to go easy and mind that brake. You jam that pedal too hard and you're gonna have yourself a jackknife."

Lila Mae was afraid to ask what a jackknife was, but she certainly didn't like the sound of it. She fetched her spiral notepad from her pocketbook, making Mr. Corn repeat everything twice so she could write down every single, solitary word of advice.

"Listen to me *reeeal* good now. *Never* slam on them brakes . . . just soft-pedal 'em. And this is important too: you be careful goin' over bumpy roads," Mr. Corn lectured. "When your car goes up, the trailer goes down and you can *disengage*."

"Disengage?" Lila Mae repeated quietly. "Oh, my."

Becky Jean glanced at their reflection in the gas-station window. The car itself was hideous enough—like Dogpatch on

wheels—but then there was the trailer hitched to the back, raggedy luggage strapped to the roof in a crooked, haphazard
heap, every nook and cranny of the car itself stuffed to the gills.
It would be a miracle if they got ten miles away, let alone all
the way to California.

"Best overall advice I can give ya"—Mr. Corn removed his
hat and scratched a plume of greasy hair—"is to slow down
and take it nice and easy. That way, you'll have yourself a real
safe trip."

"Well, sir, I certainly do thank you! Who knows, this information could save our lives."

Although Lila Mae almost sideswiped Arbuckle's flagpole
on the way out, she told the man not to worry, that she just
wasn't used to the car yet. She assured him that she was "pretty
good in an emergency." Then she waved like nothing had happened and promised to send the nice man a picture postcard
when they finally arrived in California.

Chapter Three

Since Lila Mae refused to drop off the face of the earth without saying goodbye to her friends and family, their first stop was to visit her younger sister, Clora Dee Dallas. The two women hadn't been on speaking terms for years, but Lila Mae was gung-ho about seeing her, sniffing into her hankie and sighing, "Poor, poor Clora Dee . . . who knows how long she'll be with us?" Although she made the woman sound like she was on her last leg, Clora Dee was simply down in the dumps because she'd caught her husband, Lyndon, carrying on with a cocktail waitress. Lila Mae claimed her sister, who had self-destructive tendencies, didn't have a friend in the world. "She is *desperate* for human companionship, and I just couldn't live with myself if something happened."

When she stopped beating around the bush—thirty minutes' worth of flowery, heart-wrenching excuses later—Lila Mae told them they had to get a move on if they expected to make it to Warrensburg, West Virginia, by nightfall. Becky Jean said, "Why are we going to Warrensburg when Clora and Lyndon haven't lived there for a year? They moved to Union Springs."

When Lila Mae said, "Union Springs, are you sure?" Becky Jean mentioned the Christmas card Clora Dee had sent them last year. "Don't tell me you can't remember. You spotted the return address and said, 'Kids, it looks like your flighty aunt still ain't settled.' "

Lila Mae said, "Well, I certainly don't remember anything of the sort. But, be that as it may, where in tarnation is Union Springs?" Although Lila Mae stamped her foot like there was some big conspiracy, she knew full well her sister had moved from West Virginia, but she put on a phony act, unable to admit she actually planned the inconvenient trip.

Deciding to play along with her mother (mostly because Aunt Clora had sent her a locket and jeweled bath beads for her birthday), Becky Jean checked the map, informing Lila Mae that Union Springs was in Alabama, two states over from West Virginia. Lila Mae, knitting her brow as if in deep, philosophical thought, said, "Just *two* states away, you say?" She still wanted to know what *kind* of states. If they were big, spread-out ones like Texas that took up a lot of space on the map, she just didn't know if they could swing it. If they were little bitty things like Rhode Island or Delaware, she figured a side trip from the original side trip certainly wouldn't spoil things.

After they had traveled for a day and a half and only reached Arkansas, Lila Mae turned to Becky Jean and said, "Is it my imagination or is it takin' forever and a day to get there?" She swore that the map was wrong, that it made Alabama look closer than it actually was. "You take a look at this, Becky Jean." She rattled the map at her. "Don't it seem like we shoulda been there by now?"

"Not with you takin' the scenic route, it doesn't." Just as Becky Jean suspected, Lila Mae couldn't drive five miles without veering to the side of the road for one thing or another. First it was Miss Maybelle's Candy Shop, where they bought licorice and horehound drops, and after that Harp Bros. Hardware Store, an establishment that displayed wheelbarrows, peat moss, and marble tombstones at the curb and an old-fashioned daguerreotype of Chester Cecil Harp I on a rooftop billboard. Lila Mae, who thought this might be a branch of the Harp family from Blue Lick Springs, Kentucky, chitchatted with a clerk, who told her it wasn't the same outfit. But she was thrilled when he told her, "You're not the first person who's thought that." As they were leaving, Lila Mae said, "See, it's a good thing we stopped. We got them extry batteries for the flashlight."

Nobody, Lila Mae included, had planned on visiting Cleopatra's Cut Hut, but, unfortunately, they made eye contact with the Negro boy with long, loose arms poking out of a moth-eaten jacket that was way too small for him who was standing at the road flagging down customers. Lila Mae said it wouldn't be polite to ignore the poor boy, so she went inside and bought Cokes from the vending machine and two cards of bobby pins from Idella Couch, the boy's mother.

After that she took pictures of the kids slouched against the Uncle Sam's Fireworks stand and even snapped an entire roll of Virgil Hicks, a mild-mannered mechanic with soft brown eyes who worked at the Phillips 66 station in Cuba, Arkansas. Hicks was eating an egg sandwich from a black metal lunch bucket when Lila Mae spotted him and asked if he'd mind posing in front of the Route 66 advertisement.

"I reckon that'd be all right," he said quietly. Then he carefully placed his lunch to the side and wiped his mouth with the sleeve of his blue mechanic's jumpsuit.

As cooperative as the man seemed to be, at first Lila Mae couldn't get the camera to work; then the sun was in the wrong spot; and then ("Wouldn't you know it!") a car parked right where she wanted to snap the photo. As a result, she had the poor man posing like a movie star. The kids made a "crazy" ring around their temples and pointed to their mother, just so the man wouldn't think they were as nutty as she was.

Right before pulling out of the gas station, Lila Mae noticed a little boy sitting at a folding table with a sign that said MINER-ALS & ROCKS—25 CINTS. Although the stones looked like the pebbles you find in driveways and flowerbeds, Lila Mae paid him for "hematite" and "chalcedony" and listened to the boy tell her, "That there's valuable merchandise . . . you won't find that elsewhere."

As if double-daring her kids to get angry with her, Lila Mae said, "I can't help it. That man reminds me of my poor, dead father, and that little boy is the spittin' image of Buster Smartt, a friend who died of leukemia at a very early age." From now on, Lila Mae assured them, there'd be no more dilly-dallying around. "I just had to get a few things out of my system."

Thinking two can play that game, they were traveling through Mississippi, snaking through an overgrown seam of an old plantation road, when Becky Jean hollered, "Stop!" Carleen said, "Wow, look at that!" and Billy Cooper said, "That's ritzy!" Becky Jean spotted a house that was partially hidden by vinery and hedges which she knew her mother wouldn't go for, so she told her to turn around quick, she thought she saw a lemonade stand back there, one with two little ragamuffin kids who looked like they hadn't had a customer all day or a square meal in weeks. Lila Mae said, "Oh, all right, just this once," and made a U-turn.

Even though Lila Mae had spent a good thirty minutes buying the hairpins and had taken ten jillion pictures of a mechanic holding a wrench, Becky Jean was supposed to look at the plantation in thirty seconds and not flip her lid when Lila Mae told her the camera was empty. As Becky Jean and Carleen edged along the old limestone fence and peeked through the catacomb of trees and shrubbery, Lila Mae stayed in the car, keeping the engine idling because she didn't want the girls to take all day and leaving the window open so she could add her two cents as a curbside tour guide.

"Them flowers next to the fence, they're called pink lady's slipper, that much I know," she yelled. "And the trees, them big ones, they're white oaks." They had lacy branches dripping with Spanish moss, and they draped to the ground in a swirl of dancing shadows and brushed the white curlicued settees and fountains beneath them.

In the background Billy Cooper was screeching, "Let's go! Hurry up!" and every minute or so Lila Mae would toot the horn. Becky Jean's eyes swiftly scanned the property—the fruit orchards, a gazebo, and peacocks roaming across the mossy grass. There was also an ornamental lake mottled with lilypads and black swans. And in the distance, past the alley of gigantic oaks and looking like a blurry dream, was the antebellum mansion.

"Look at that!" Becky Jean gasped to Carleen.

"Straight out of *Gone With the Wind,* ain't it?" Lila Mae, who couldn't even see the house, rhapsodized. "That's enough now, girls! Come on before they see us—come *on!*" Lila Mae, who was acting like Nikita Khrushchev was chasing them down, had spotted a little girl trotting around the property on an auburn horse. The girl, who with her champagne skin and blond hair waving down her back looked like a delicate cameo, came galloping toward the fence. When Billy Cooper yelled "Hey, little girl, what's your name?" instead of saying "My name's Susan, what's yours?" she gave them a poison dart of a glare and snapped, "You're not supposed to be here."

"*Come on, will ya?*" Lila Mae punched the horn. "These nice people don't want us hangin' around their property. For heaven's sakes, they'll probably think we're *vagabonds* or *field hands* or somethin'." Lila Mae wanted the girl to know it was a preposterous notion since she herself was joking about it. Under her breath, as she released the brake and prepared for a fast getaway, she was saying, "I could just crown you girls—I *knew* that was gonna happen."

"It's a free country, isn't it?" Becky Jean said. "Besides, that little prisspot was ten years old at the most. . . . You act like Ike and Mamie themselves came out and shooed us away."

Bouncing down the road, a coral-purple dusk streaking across the sky and bugs blinking past their windshield, they sang, "Oh, I wish I was in the land of cotton, old times there are not forgotten. . . . Look away, Dixieland." They passed Marvelle's Beauty Box, a lavender house with two women sitting under hair dryers on the front porch, and, at the edge of a rural town, the remnants of a small carnival. A corroded chain was strung across the Tilt-a-Whirl and a huge threadbare cloth thrown over the Ferris wheel. Across a tiny cottage was a faded banner with a crude painting of a man with oily, brown-veined eyes and a sign that said: THE GREAT SWAMI . . . DIRECT FROM EGYPT.

Carleen and Billy Cooper chanted, "Can we stop? Oh, pleeeasse!" but Lila Mae said, "Don't be ridiculous, everyone. It ain't even open. Besides, ain't you kids had enough commotion for one day?" When Lila Mae said that it did remind her of that "derned carnival setup in New Albany, Indiana, the one that should have been run out of business by now," Becky Jean and Carleen traded knowing looks.

Figuring that her mother probably felt guilty for the empty camera, Becky Jean got her to stop at a roadside fruit stand, where everybody else bought Georgia peaches and Becky Jean bought twelve postcards of several historical plantations in the area for one dollar. Long after everyone had forgotten about the mansion, when they were on the third stanza of "Dixie," Becky Jean spread the postcards on her lap, studying the curved staircases and crystal chandeliers and the tapestry furniture. In the entrance of one plantation was a portrait of a glamorous woman in an evening gown and beneath it was an onyx table and two Dresden urns; the grounds had sundials and a colonnade . . . all the ornaments she'd seen in movies and read about in novels.

Maybe someday, if things panned out, she would arrange American Beauty roses and scribble notes on parchment paper. In the afternoons, she would stroll the hallways of her mansion—her green taffeta skirts rustling softly—and point out minor housekeeping flaws. . . . Dressing for dinner, she'd sit at a vanity with cologne bottles and enamel powder jars. She'd be married to some Rhett Butler type, a man who would call her "darling," and from time to time he would sneak up behind her and slip some sparkly bauble on her neck or wrist. They would go dancing in the streets of Paris, France, and drink pink champagne while sitting on the edges of ancient Roman fountains. . . .

"Earth to Becky Jean . . . Earth to Becky Jean!" Lila Mae, slicing her hand back and forth like she was a beauty queen waving to the crowds, was trying to get her daughter out of a trance. "What are you up to? It's too quiet back there. Do you want one of these chili dogs or don't you? And don't disappear on me like that—I'm havin' a hard time readin' this map."

All along the rural Mississippi roads the weeping willows swayed and swished in the humid breeze. The moon, amber and full, darted behind shaggy brown clouds. Carleen said the sky looked like that monster wearing a huge, whirling black cape. Just like it was going to gobble everything up, Billy Cooper added. Then Becky Jean said, "Boy, I'd hate to run out of gas out here."

"If you kids is tryin' to scare the liver outta me, you're doin' a good job. This ain't as easy as it looks, you know. I need to keep my wits about me."

The night was nearly pitch black, and Lila Mae's neck was craned forward so that her nose was practically touching the steering wheel, and she was already imagining peculiar objects along the road, as she often did—only now, if she listened to Mr. Corn's advice, she wasn't even able to slam on her brakes if something *should* happen to jump in front of them and even if her eyes were playing tricks on her and the coiled cobra she saw earlier *was* only tire tread and even if Gila monsters (something she thought she'd spotted earlier) weren't even found in these parts, she still didn't know how in the world she was supposed to just keep going regardless. According to Mr. Corn, you had to wait for advance notice before you could stop for anything. And to top it all off, she wasn't sure she was on the right track.

Somewhere between Crystal Falls and Pine Grove, Becky Jean made the mistake of falling asleep, and when she woke up around midnight they were sitting in a filling station. Outside it was coal black and there were kudzu-draped trees towering over the small, lumpy road, and overgrown vines tumbling all over the place. When she lifted up, she saw a handpainted sign that said SWAMP TOURS. Becky Jean groaned, "Oh, no." When she rolled down the window, she smelled clammy, stagnant air and heard some strange bug and animal sounds. Off to the side was a faded billboard that said GIVE JESUS A CHANCE and a metal tub that said LIVE BAIT.

The gas station itself was dark, but inside Lila Mae and a man in a white uniform were curled over a road map. The man would turn the map to one side; Lila Mae would watch him for a minute, then turn it back around. Every once in a while Lila Mae would say, "Now accordin' to my calculations . . ." or "I certainly don't remember passin' by that bridge you mentioned . . ." or "Are you sure I ain't already been through King City?" Finally, after he'd figured out where Lila Mae wanted to go, the man said, "Here's your problem, lady—yep, here's your problem right there." He made a circle on the map and punched it three times. "See, you're in Loo-seana . . . you ain't in Mississippi. You been lookin' at the wrong map."

"Well, no wonder . . ." Lila Mae frowned. Then she said, "How do you suppose all that happened?" and looked outside at Becky Jean as if she were in on the mistake.

While the man was fixing the tire that had picked up a nail, Lila Mae said even though they were in the wrong state, if they *had* to get lost, it's a good thing it happened when and where it did. Not every gas station was open at that hour, and heavens! not every attendant would have been so observant. Normally, something like this would have gotten to her, but the older she got, the more she realized that most things happen for the best.

And what a nice surprise that Talla Bend, Louisiana, was one of those spots that you see listed in the "Off the Beaten Path" section of road maps. Why, they had even killed two birds with one stone! Yes, it was a good thing that she'd veered wrong in Ruby Creek.

The man had been agreeing with Lila Mae on just about everything—he'd already said "The Lord works in mysterious ways" several times—but when she said, "Sir, you don't think a jackknife or anything of that sort could have caused any of this, do you?" he said, "No, ma'am, if you had a jackknife, you'd know it. You just got lost."

Chapter Four

When, a few days later, they finally reached Union Springs, Lila Mae told the kids she would keep the engine idling, otherwise Clora Dee would probably lure them inside and talk their leg off. She rehearsed what she would say to Clora Dee if she got pushy. "After all," Lila Mae explained her position, "she's lucky we're stopping at all." If, for some unknown reason, Clora Dee wouldn't take no for an answer, it was up to Becky Jean to think of something. And by all means, nobody should mention that they'd already been all the way to Louisiana.

Clora Dee's two-story white farmhouse was situated on the fringe of a farm community in a brand-new housing development. There were two dogwood trees planted next to the brick entry posts, and a big sign that said DOGWOOD ACRES: A NICE PLACE TO COME HOME TO. Clora Dee's lawn was decorated with ceramic deer and whiskey barrels sliced in two and filled with huge, wild clumps of morning glories and bachelor buttons. There was a Halloween pumpkin propped on a bale of hay and a paper skeleton suspended in the front picture window.

Becky Jean kept hoping royalty would pop up somewhere in her background, but Clora Dee was anything but. In a high tide of emotion, the woman greeted them with a convulsion of whoops and hollers. She was wearing a red negligee as layered as a wedding dress and satin high-heeled slippers decorated

with red pompoms. Her hair, a goldfish-orange upsweep, undulated across her forehead and curved over one eye. In her
right hand was a frosted tumbler of bourbon. "Li-la! Li-la!" she
chanted.

"Well, Je-me-nee Christmas," Lila Mae mumbled, fiddling
around in the glove compartment as if trying to delay the inevi-
table. "The last time I seen her, she was normal—now she
could be a woman of the profession."

"Don't look at us." Becky Jean pleaded innocence. "You
were the one who wanted to visit your 'people.'"

Clora Dee clip-clopped toward them, her cocktail held high
in the air like an Olympic torch. "Why, I don't believe my
eyes!" she exclaimed, as if she'd been told they were dead.
"Come here and let me see all of you!"

"Well, ain't you the glamour puss!" Lila Mae exclaimed. At
close range, Clora Dee's face was caulked with shrimp-colored
makeup and her eyes were foggy little windowpanes.

"I said to myself, I said, Clora Dee, why should Lyndon and
the vixen be the only ones whoopin' it up?" The woman twirled
around like a music-box ballerina, modeling what she called
"the New Me." "I'm dressed for *fun!*"

"So I gather." Lila Mae looked her sister up and down.
When she told Clora Dee that they could only stay a few minutes, her sister assessed her through blue-mascaraed eyelashes
and scolded, "Now, you don't mean that, Lila Mae. You can't
tell me you drove for two days to spend ten minutes? At least
have one drinky-poo!"

Six hours later they were still trapped inside Clora Dee's
house, which—in contrast to the perfect Norman Rockwell
needlepoint exterior—was decorated like a jewelry box: tufted
red velvet furniture, gold frames, lamps with dangling crystal
icicles, and a cigarette lighter monogrammed CDD in crimson
rhinestones. The floors were covered in snow-white shag carpeting, and every few minutes Clora Dee would stagger across

the room, dig into her crystal ice bucket, and refill her whiskey glass. By now they'd heard a dozen of her where-it-all-went-wrong stories, every tale beginning with "When that business with Lyndon and the vixen happened . . ." Once or twice she looked at Becky Jean and Carleen and said, "I want you two girls to come live with me when you get older. It would do you good to get out in the world."

When Lila Mae stage-whispered, "Do something," Becky Jean reminded her mother that they had a pressing obligation. Lila Mae checked her watch and said, "Oh, that's right." But Clora Dee insisted on knowing what the appointment was, as if she wanted to be the sole judge of its urgency.

"Besides," Clora Dee pleaded, "you haven't eaten a bite, and you have to sleep *somewhere*, don't you?" She told Lila Mae she'd treat them all to dinner, which sounded okay until they found out the restaurant was actually a bar called the Topsy Turvy . . . as well as the scene of the crime. Clora Dee said if they were lucky, the kids could get a gander at their ex-uncle's face as Clora slugged the two-bit cocktail waitress who had stolen her husband.

To get the children on her side, Clora Dee reminded them that the next day was Halloween. "What kind of mother are you, Lila Mae, if you don't let your only kids go trick-or-treating?"

"Aunt Clora Dee's right, Mama," Carleen and Becky Jean and Billy Cooper agreed. "It's *not* fair." They wanted to have a juicy steak dinner at the Topsy Turvy; they wanted to meet the Vixen; and, obviously, they wanted to go trick-or-treating like everybody else.

Lila Mae said, "Oh, all right." She might as well let the kids get the Halloween festivities off their chest, but she put her foot down about the Topsy Turvy. So they had hot dogs and cherry Kool-Aid for dinner, which they ate from TV trays in the basement rumpus room.

Becky Jean was just settling into her rollaway bed thinking

that after Halloween they'd finally be on their way to California when, through the clatter of china coffee cups, a whistling tea kettle, and "The Jimmy Durante Show," Clora Dee and Lila Mae started reminiscing about old times. "You remember Jo Jo, don't you?" Clora Dee asked her sister. Becky Jean couldn't hear all the details, but apparently a woman named Jo Jo had been Lila Mae's best friend since grade school, and was some sort of important entertainer. "Well, I run into her about six months ago." Clora Dee said she never did understand why Lila Mae and Jo Jo split up, that everyone in Shepherdsville thought the Moonbeam Girls would go far.

"Shoot," Clora Dee said, "you two sung better than them Andrew Sisters. And I'm tellin' you, Jo Jo sure did perk up when she started talkin' about you and old times."

"She did?" Lila Mae's expression was a mixture of disbelief and awe. "Jo Jo *really* asked about *me*?"

"That's about all she *did* ask about. It would do her a world of good to see you, Lila Mae. She seemed to be on the verge of—of something *very* drastic."

By the time Jimmy Durante was saying, "Goodnight, Mrs. Calabash . . . wherever you are," Lila Mae was staring at the dripping prisms on Clora's chandelier with a game-plan expression on her face. "So, it's *that bad*, ummmm? Jo Jo's *really* at her *rope's end*?"

Knowing what a sucker her mother was for rescue operations, Becky Jean wasn't too surprised when, as they backed out of Clora Dee's driveway two days later, Lila Mae announced that they were making an unscheduled but very necessary stop in Duluth, Minnesota.

"Minnesota?" Becky Jean whooped. "That's up by Canada, isn't it? We'll *never* get to California."

Lila Mae asked the kids if it would make a difference to them if they were going to visit a famous singer. "Instead of drivin' through the same old boring states, we can drive through Tennessee, Illinois, Wisconsin, Iowa, and then Minnesota. That way, you can tell your new geography teachers about all the states you've been in."

"I know exactly what to tell my new geography teacher," Becky Jean announced and threatened at the same time. "But I'm trying to figure out what to tell Daddy."

It still hadn't dawned on them that the trip was as far out of their way as it actually was until they stopped off at a filling station to get directions to Minnesota. Lila Mae waved at the man pumping gas and said, "Sir, would you fill it up with ethyl, please? And could you tell me which road to stay on? We're on our way to California. One of these days we'll be a-takin' Route 66, but we're gonna stop off in Duluth first, and then—"

"Ladee, are you out of your cotton-pickin' mind? This is the wrong die-rection for Californy!" The whiskery man, sizing up Lila Mae through steel-blue eyes, chewed on a match, flipping it over and over with his tongue like he was twirling a baton. "Hellfire, woman. You cain't pick up Route 66 until eastern Missoura."

Lila Mae gunned the engine, flew into traffic, and snapped, "Well, who does he think *he* is? He sure didn't look like no Einstein to me." Besides, she told the children, he didn't have to be so rude about it. Lila Mae knew full well that Minnesota was north and California was west, and it was her business if she was going the wrong way.

"You say one word about this to you-know-who and you'll be sorry—I mean it now!" Lila Mae shook her finger. "You hear me, Becky Jean? While you're at it, this is a good time to memorize your state capitals. Do somethin' useful instead of readin' them cheap movie magazines and novels."

Although they still weren't thrilled about another side trip, Becky and Carleen unfolded the map and counted a grand total of nine new states they'd be visiting.

As they jingled through the country roads of Arkansas, they sang "I Get a Kick Out of You" and "Little Things Mean a Lot." They passed Bessie Mae Kidd's European School of Dance and a sign that said BEWARE: DO NOT PICK UP HITCHHIKERS. When everybody said they were thirsty, they crawled across a rickety metal bridge and pulled into Uncle John's, a roadside stand that sold cold apple cider and colorful chenille bedspreads displayed on the hoods of two cars. Within minutes, Lila Mae got to talking to the owner, a bone-thin young girl with hair that hung in loose pouches like cocker spaniel ears.

Rubbing her hand across a green spread with appliquéd flowers, Lila Mae—just as if she'd bumped into Rembrandt— shrieked, "You didn't make these *yourself*, did you, hon?"

"Yes, ma'am, I most certainly did." The girl had a high-pitched pierce like a child's squeaky toy and small, mongrel eyes that were runny and crimson-stained. Bunching up the hem of her gingham skirt, she swayed like a little girl, looking embarrassed and proud at the same time.

"Well, you have *talent*! My sixteen-year-old, Becky Jean, she's good in art, too. Her teacher told me she's got a high IQ. . . . My other girl, Carleen, she wants to be a nurse."

"Is that so?" The girl chewed her mangled fingernail and studied the two sisters.

One thing led to another, and before long Lila Mae was giving the girl, whose name was Imogene Virginia, pointers on how to effectively market the spreads. "You need exposure, hon!" When Becky Jean yelled from the car, "Why don't you tell her about those fly swatters?" Lila Mae yelled back, "That'll be enough, miss."

At noon, the young woman asked if they had eaten yet, and when Lila Mae said they hadn't, Imogene Virginia said she wouldn't feel right if she didn't make them a hot, home-cooked meal. Within no time, they were following Imogene through the crooked hills and dells of rural Arkansas, past a hand-painted REVIVAL TONIGHT sign, the K & K Eat Shop, and a flock of vultures pecking at a mass of feathers and green, maggoty flesh along the roadside.

"I wished she'd told us she lives in Timbuktu," Lila Mae

griped as she guided the Packard over the bumpy, twisting lanes. After what seemed an eternity, they turned into a grove of pinery and bumbled along a dusty trail, huge, phosphorescent beetles crash-landing on their windshield. Finally, they reached a dead end.

"Feast your eyes on that, would ya," Lila Mae muttered. The house was a ramshackle cabin perched on the bank of a rocky creekbed. Dead poplar trees lined the driveway, and the yard was littered with broken birdbaths, a rusty lawnmower, and a pickup truck on cement blocks. A tattered Confederate flag flapped across the pine porch railing. Lila Mae had to honk the horn to get a mangy dog to move aside, and there were stray cats running around every which way. In the air was the scent of stagnant water and horse manure.

"Whadja expect, the White House?" Becky Jean snapped. "Daddy's gonna kill youuuuuu."

"He don't have to know *everything*," Lila Mae threatened.

A gigantic, blubbery man with mossy teeth and a gourd-shaped head, who identified himself as Imogene's husband, Delbert, limped to the wooden gate. His ears, coiled like snails, were glued high on his cheekbones, and under his overalls there was doughy flab, rolling up and down like the ocean waves in a bad storm. When he walked, he seemed to be struggling to avoid his own body in order to get where he was going.

"What a tub!" Becky Jean piped.

Although Lila Mae was thinking the exact same thing herself, she said, "Now, just stop that! He's probably very *nice*."

The man went through a big, theatrical rigmarole as he flagged them onto the property, waving his hands officially, as if they were in a state fair parking lot.

"Thank you, Delbert," Lila Mae chirruped. "I sure do appreciate that." There was enough room to park fifty Greyhound buses, but Lila Mae gave the man her I-couldn't-have-done-it-without-you smile.

The man snapped the latch in place, turned a wooden knob,

then clicked a padlock. "Cain't be too careful these days. We got a state pen up the road apiece. Two fellas from the chain gang 'scaped a few days back . . . ain't caught 'em yet, fur as I know, anyways."

"Oh, my! What type was they?" Lila Mae grimaced. "I mean, what was they doin' time for?"

"I cain't say that I know." Delbert crinkled his entire face as if she'd asked him to solve the chicken-egg question. "I should . . . but I don't."

"Oh, probably just some rapes and robberies and murders and some other odds and ends," Becky Jean said very casually. It was a family joke, so Carleen and Billy Cooper howled, great sputtering coughs of laughter.

"Cut it out!" Lila Mae pawed the air to shut her daughter up. She was hoping Delbert hadn't caught on to her shenanigans, but he wrinkled his nose like a pig and oinked around the car, as if to see what types he was dealing with.

"Don't pay any attention to them. They're just kiddin' around." Lila Mae went on to tell the man that Becky Jean got her screwy sense of humor from her husband's side of the family and her daughter was just imitating her crazy uncle Merle.

She was counting on that being enough to satisfy the man, but he was thicker than a redwood tree. When he asked her, "So this Merle fellow's a *murderer*, you say?" Lila Mae said, "Oh, heavens no!" There was no end in sight to Delbert's confusion—every time she answered him, he asked her yet another question. So she simply started from scratch, telling him that Merle had tied the knot with a woman one day and left her high and dry practically the next. "The kids thought it was funny when their uncle—who's a real cutup, by the way—told everybody the split was on account of some rapes and suicides and affairs and some other odds and ends."

Lila Mae gave Becky Jean a dirty look, mad that she had to go through all that, particularly since the man hadn't cracked a smile. "Now you see, don't you, that everybody don't think it's all that hilarious. They don't know how to take you." In the meantime, Carleen and Billy Cooper still hadn't stopped giggling.

As trashy as Delbert and Imogene Virginia's yard was, it looked like a medical lab compared to the inside of the place. Dim and reeking of cat boxes and stale diapers, it was strewn with potato chip bags and half-eaten candy bars. In the kitchen sink was a heaping triangle of dishes, and on a metal stand was a black-and-white television with rabbit ears that nobody was watching. The sepia images of "Sky King" flickered against the white linoleum. In the breakfast nook were Eddie Joe and Arlen Moses, Imogene's twin boys, two wild toddlers who were shaped like Humpty Dumpty and had skin the color of rubber dolls. They belted one another in the stomach, fighting over a tiny, mewing calico kitten. Delbert, wielding a switch, told them to stop it right now, otherwise they'd "git a whoopin'."

"Aren't they just darling?" Lila Mae trilled. Behind their backs, she mouthed, "I feel so *sorry* for these poor people."

The whole episode just irked Becky Jean no end. Lila Mae had practically yanked the kids away from their own grandmother before they hardly said goodbye. All Lila Mae could talk about was getting on the road, staying on schedule. Becky Jean could still see her grandmother, a thin squiggle of a silhouette, standing on the dead brown grass between the cement strips of her driveway, hollow-eyed and sobbing, clutching the bouquet of dandelions Billy Cooper had given her and waving her wet lacy hankie for blocks and blocks.

Now here they were going out of their way to socialize with total strangers, Lila Mae, the empress of hospitality and goodwill, tidying up Imogene's house, pitching in to make deviled eggs and fried chicken for lunch. She even played tag and Pick-Up Stix with the two boys and gave job pointers to Delbert, an unemployed factory worker, who according to Lila Mae should have been running his own operation. Lila Mae was leading the poor man on, telling him he could be manufacturing his own lawn furniture and "advertising it on the television the way people do these days," when, in all honesty, Becky Jean thought his only hope was to contact the circus.

Why Lila Mae was acting like the head of Sears, Roebuck, Becky Jean did not know. What did she know about sales tactics except her limited experience at the church bake sale and her dealings with the Fuller Brush man? Plus, all the pointers in the world wouldn't help Imogene's spreads, which were as ugly as all get-out.

At six p.m., Lila Mae, buffing the last of Imogene Virginia's plastic dinner plates, placed the stack of dishes in a cupboard and folded the damp dishrag over the faucet. "Well, my lord." She glanced at the black-and-white cat clock on the kitchen wall. "Do you girls know what time it is? We'll never make it to Duluth tonight."

By now, Lila Mae and Imogene Virginia were arm in arm, strolling toward the Packard. "You know I'd take you with me if I could, dearie." She hugged Imogene Virginia, then patted her back like she was burping a newborn baby. Imogene Virginia said, "Miz Wooten, you just don't know how good you made me feel." Then she promised to write and to send as many bedspreads as Lila Mae thought she could sell.

Although she played along with the girl until they got to the car, the minute Imogene Virginia disappeared, Lila Mae hastily folded the lemon-yellow chenille spreads she'd just paid seventy-five dollars for and pitched them into the trunk. "I needed these like a hole in the head. . . . But she was such a sickly thing . . . and just as sweet as she could be! And, who knows, I might start me a little business when we git our bearings."

Later, though, as they crept along a dark, lonely highway, Lila Mae said, "Don't think I ain't plenty irked with myself, 'cause I am. I just keep gettin' myself in hot water, don't I?" Citing "willpower" problems, Lila Mae mentioned that it was probably on account of her upbringing, that her mother had told her to be ladylike and to always put herself in another person's place. "I just want you to know when I walked in that house I had no intention of stayin' more than half an hour. . . . Well, an hour at the very most."

When Becky Jean said, "You realize, don't you, that we're on our way to Minnesota and the same thing might happen there?" Lila Mae said, "This is completely different."

Driving beneath a midnight-blue, starless night, they sang "Ninety-nine Bottles of Beer on the Wall" and ate miniature Clark bars and Hershey's Kisses from their trick-or-treat sacks. They peeked in the window of Betty Joe's Cinderella Shoe Shop and stopped at Jimmy Pigg's Original BBQ Pit, where a man with one arm and a monkey hairline served them hickory-smoked sandwiches and peach pie.

When, at midnight, they finally reached the Minnesota state line, Carleen and Becky slugged their mother in the shoulder-blade and said, "All right, tell us more about this singer right now!"

It occurred to Lila Mae that she needed to build up the performer to keep the girls from blowing their stacks, so she started to bubble and chatter, hoping to whip them into a frenzy of excitement. But when she told them her childhood singing partner was somebody named Jo Jo Jenkins, a gifted performer who had worked with all the big-band greats, like Benny Goodman and Glenn Miller, they had a fit. "What a dirty trick! Whoever heard of Jo Jo Jenkins? She's a big noth-ing!" Becky Jean said the way the singer had been played up, she thought maybe it was Jo Stafford and Carleen asked, "Why can't it be Teresa Brewer or Patti Page?"

"Because I don't know them, that's why. But never you mind," Lila Mae lectured. "Jo Jo Jenkins is not only my best friend, she is the most popular jazz singer of her time. You kids don't know everything that's goin' on in the world." Then Lila Mae mentioned that she herself could have been an entertainer, too. "You probably heard Clora Dee talkin' 'bout what a good singer I was. . . . Dear me"—she chuckled and tsk-tsked, a rosy blush tinting her face—"I hope to high heaven Jo Jo don't get any ideas about us teamin' up again. Lordy!" She plucked at a stray curl. "What then?"

They spent the night at the Taj Mahal Motor Inn, a square building with an onion-shaped dome nailed on top and a curtain of beads instead of a front door. Lila Mae, a nervous wreck, who had already spent an hour on her own hair and makeup, made a huge stink about being presentable. She suggested that Becky Jean wear her tomato-red sack dress with a white, pearl-collared sweater and Carleen should put on her turquoise skirt decorated with 45-rpm records. Trying to turn Billy Cooper into Little Lord Fauntleroy, she unpacked his navy sweater and bought him a little bow tie at Woolworth's, but she was having a hard time getting him to cooperate. Jumping up and down on the sagging mattress, using the motel towel as a cape, he was singing, "Mighty Mouse is on his way!"

"Will somebody, and I don't care if it's Lucifer himself, stop him before he cracks his skull wide open?!" Lila Mae swirled around to inspect Becky Jean. "And put some decent clothes on, miss. What do you think this is, Ragpicker's Alley?" Becky Jean, her head dotted with pincurls, was still wearing rolled-up dungarees and a white shirt knotted at her bellybutton. "You heard me—stop standin' there and go git ready this minute!" Lila Mae said she was about to go off her rocker and she needed some privacy. Then she slammed the connecting bedroom door.

"What's *her* problem?" Becky Jean, suspecting something fishy, opened a slit in the door. At first everything looked normal enough, as Lila Mae rearranged bottles and tubes in her cosmetics case. But just when Becky Jean thought she had probably imagined things, her mother streaked to the bureau and hastily shoved a brown paper bag between the puckered satin compartments of her luggage.

Waiting until Lila Mae went to the toilet, Becky Jean tiptoed through the door and made a beeline for the suitcase. "Becky Jean Wooten!" Lila Mae hollered, "Git out of my things this very minute." Flushing the toilet, she flew into the room, her skirt still hoisted above her waist, and slammed the suitcase lid on Becky Jean's arm. "Who do you think you are, sneakin' in here like that?"

"Hey, that hurt!" Becky Jean shook her hand in the air and yelped.

"Well, don't go snoopin', then. How'd you like it if I went a rummagin' through your things?" Lila Mae wiggled around, adjusting her girdle.

"You do it all the time," Becky Jean accused.

"Well, so what. Somebody's got to keep tabs on you. And why are you standin' around here like we've got all day?"

Finally Becky Jean figured that Lila Mae was hiding those stupid *Confidential* magazines, the ones that featured stories about society women in cocktail dresses and chinchilla coats who cheated on their husbands and whatnot. All the headlines had exclamation points, just to get you all worked up over nothing, plus the famous people had black strips over their eyes so you didn't even know who they were. Lila Mae had joined a PTA committee to have them banned, and Becky'd even overheard her tell their minister that the magazines were "simply disgraceful and should be taken off the rack." As far as Becky Jean could tell, her mother read every single issue.

Lila Mae grabbed her toiletries, crammed the baby's diapers into the bag, and closed it with a grand-finale zip. She glared at Becky Jean and Becky Jean glared right back, but neither one of them said another peep about the paper sack.

After breakfast, they drove to a big brick building plastered with tattered posters of Stan Kenton and Gene Krupa. The small square windows were blacked out and covered with chicken wire, and over the double entry doors was a blinking marquee that said: THE FABULOUS KENNY GARDELLA! PLUS MISS JO JO JENKINS AND THE RAZZMATAZZ GIRLS.

A Negro man wearing an orchid shirt and striped suspenders informed Lila Mae that Miss Jenkins was rehearsing for a big show and couldn't see them right away. Lila Mae waited in the car, nervously smoothing the folds of her white crochet dress, reapplying her Ginger Snap lipstick and warning the children, "Put your legs together, Carleen, and Billy, straighten that tie. Now I might, just might, take you kids to the Dairy Queen if you don't act up. . . . By the way, I'd better not hear a peep out of you, miss." She locked eyes with Becky Jean. "And for goodness sakes, get rid of all that garbage—she'll think it's Ma and Pa Kettle outside."

When the stage door finally opened, the car shook with excitement. "Here she comes!" Lila Mae exclaimed, giving her hair one last fluff. "Here she comes!"

The Negro man held a Christmas tree–shaped mink in place while Jo Jo slipped it over her shoulders. The singer sauntered toward them, her hypnotic eyes—coal black and clotted with inky mascara—seemingly a thousand miles away. Everything about her was so exotic: the egg-yolk-yellow hair heaped on her head, the magnolia-white skin, her gold spangled dress, and the pointy maroon toenails. Wound around her neck was a long red chiffon scarf that fluttered in the wind like a wild flame. In spite of herself, Becky Jean couldn't stop gawking at Miss Jenkins. She also couldn't imagine that the glamorous singer and her down-to-earth mother were ever on the same wavelength.

"Why, Jo Jo!" Lila Mae rhapsodized, her eyes shining like flying saucers. "I can't believe it's really you."

With the smoke from her pastel-blue cigarette wreathing around her shoulders and without so much as an official hello, Jo Jo scanned the car until finally she muttered, "So these are Roy's kids. . . . I got me a little girl, too. She just turned six."

"Oh." Lila Mae craned forward. "What's her name?"

"Amy." Jo Jo flicked an ash off her cigarette, a gold bangle bracelet sliding up and down her arm. "I named her Amy."

"Why, I don't believe it!" Lila Mae panted, thrilled to establish common ground. "That's *my* favorite name, too, after Aimee Semple McPherson."

"If that's your favorite name, how come you never named any of *us* that?" Becky Jean gave her eyes one dramatic twirl in their sockets. "You sure had enough chances."

"As a matter of fact"—Lila Mae gave Becky Jean a you're-gonna-get-it-later glare—"I *almost* named Carleen that. How'd you like to be an Amy, honey pie?"

"Hey, ladee." Billy Cooper jiggled Miss Jenkins's mink sleeve. "My mama's a good singer, too. She's been practicing 'Red, Red Robin' and 'Rag Mop'."

"Billy Cooper Wooten!" Lila Mae's horrified face turned jugular-vein purple. "You know that ain't true. Why, I've not sung a note for years." In spite of Lila Mae's denial, she seemed willing to test out her talent if someone insisted. Maybe even audition as a razzmatazz girl.

"Wellll . . . so long, everybody." Jo Jo snuffed out her cigarette with the toe of her high heel, and then—just like that—the reunion was over. After a quick pirouette, she slinked back to the rehearsal hall. They watched, fascinated by the tick-tock swaying of Jo Jo's flapper dress as it brushed against her curvy calves. Waiting at the stage door was a cluster of fans, one of whom—a teenage boy—handed her an armful of red garnet dahlias and a slip of paper for her to autograph. She signed her name with a few lazy, dramatic scrawls, then patted the boy's head. When the Negro man opened the theater door for Miss Jenkins, a shaft of sunlight ricocheted off her gold bugle beads. Looking like an injured sparrow, Lila Mae stared, her forehead a plot of wrinkles, as the big iron gate finally whooshed closed.

When it was obvious that there wouldn't be any belated goodbye salutes from Jo Jo or any last-minute invitations to sing a for-old-times'-sake duet, Lila Mae cleared her throat with a quick, gravelly cough and jammed the silver key in the Packard's ignition.

It was dusk when they drove through the Minnesota countryside. The sky was pale, pale pink with tiny, glossy stars dotting it. The moon, an ivory crescent, hung over the Packard like a suspended hood ornament. As she drifted along the slim thread of highway, Lila Mae was paralyzed, her red hoop mouth and eyes frozen in an expressionless mask. Although they passed Jimmy George Bodine's Luncheonette and the Bingo Barn (which advertised FRESH CATFISH $1.49), the kids pressed their growling stomachs, afraid to complain. When the watercolor pastels of dusk melted into flat gray streaks, Lila Mae pulled the headlights on, rotating the knob on the radio until she located the sound of a misty, faraway station. Through a crackle of static, Frankie Laine was singing "That Lucky Old Sun."

When Lila Mae finally said, "If you kids is hungry, we'll stop up yonder for some hamburgers," Becky Jean thought the incident with Jo Jo was over. But like Old Faithful after it's skipped a few of the scheduled eruptions, Lila Mae finally exploded big time.

"Now, I wonder why Clora Dee made such a fuss about Jo Jo wantin' to see me? . . . Only two states above Missouri, my foot! She might have told me that they was medium-sized states, that they was nine hundred–some odd miles extry, and that when I drove all the way to heck and back that Miss Jazz Singer wouldn't even have time for a cup of tea. And how'd you like that crack about everybody being Roy's kids . . . as if I had nothing to do with it. And I'll tell you something else. Jo Jo Jenkins ain't even her real name. Her *real* name is Ethelene Gay Butts! Now how would it look if *that* got out?" Since she'd found a way to get back at the singer, Lila Mae's mouth was a triumphant little button.

Switching targets, Lila Mae suddenly turned on Becky Jean.

"And as for you . . . the next time you embarrass me in front of a friend like that, Miss Priss, you're in for a blisterin'. I don't care how old you is."

"Some friend," Becky Jean snickered. "Besides, I'll betcha anything she's a drug addict. Did you see the purple bruises on her arms?"

"Why, that's plum ridiculous!" Lila Mae scowled. "She probably just bumped into something."

"Inside her elbows?" Becky Jean exhaled a sarcastic little puff and told her mother she was living in the dark ages. Although she had a funny way of showing it, Becky Jean actually felt bad for her mother and hoped to convince her that the singer wasn't so great to begin with. "Don't you know what those marks mean?"

"No I don't and you shouldn't either! Where did you get so much information, anyway?" Lila Mae locked eyes with Becky Jean in the rearview mirror. "You didn't see that movie I told you not to see, *did you?*"

Becky Jean told her of course she hadn't seen *The Man with the Golden Arm,* even though she knew Lila Mae and her friend Haldeen St. Clair had lied to their own husbands and seen the movie three times. "While we're on the subject, my name isn't Miss Priss. I don't want to be called Becky Jean anymore, either. It makes me sound like a hick, so from now on I'm gonna call myself Rebecca."

"Well, you can call yourself anything you dern well please. You'd just better watch your p's and q's, or your name will be mud."

Carleen, folding Tiny Tears's diaper, said if Becky Jean was going to change her name, then would it be okay if she spelled Carleen with a K? "Would it?" she pleaded. "*Would* it?"

"Just hush all of you—*hush!*" Lila Mae hollered.

Through a window crack, a blast of chilly, fragrant air blew strands of hair across Becky Jean's face. A black dog with no tail zigzagged across the road, sniffing the pavement and finally scampering into the open doorway of the Wishing Well Laundromat. They drove down the highway in silence, only now and then passing a tavern or gas station, the wedges of orange city light disappearing in the blue-black dusk. Within minutes, Minnesota was just a cluster of dull lights miles and miles and miles behind them.

Chapter Five

After several weeks on the road, they finally reached Route 66. Chattering about the boll weevil and the Dust Bowl, Lila Mae told them romantic, tragic stories about the Depression. She promised Billy Cooper they'd stop at Meramac Caverns, where Jesse James hid out, and she made the kids pose in front of a dilapidated shack decorated with hubcaps and license plates. They stopped at Dairy Queens for root beer floats and cheeseburgers and at Pecan Joe's for date milkshakes. At an outdoor jamboree in Kansas, they listened to the fiddlers and banjo players and watched people of all ages dancing the Virginia reel and waltzing to "The Blue Danube." Lila Mae said, "Those were the good old days!" Every evening at sunset, she'd stop to point out the paint-box colors of the sky or the flying saucer clouds or the swaying, bare trees, which she said looked "like crys-chul chandeliers." All the while, she would tap the steering wheel as she sang a jazzed-up piano-bar version of "Get your kicks on Route 66."

Everyone was beginning to think the famous highway wasn't so great, but Lila Mae insisted on making a fuss out of the least little thing. "Oh, look at them flowers, kids!" She pointed to a meadow of large white blossoms. "Ain't they just beautiful? What *are* the names of them, anyway? They're not anthuriums, I don't think they're rhododendrons, either, and they're certainly not Queen of the Night tulips. . . . Well, darn it!" By naming so many flowers, she was hoping to get the kids involved in the process, but when she peered in the rearview mirror, Becky Jean was reading the "Debbie and Eddie: Splitsville?" story in *Photoplay* and Carleen was combing out the knots in Tiny Tears's coarse synthetic hair. When she added, "Well . . . whatever they are, when I'm dead and gone, I'd like them flowers on my casket," Billy Cooper pressed his nose against the back window, seeing what he could see.

Stalled by a roadblock near Amarillo, Texas, Lila Mae, her doomsday cap on, ordered her kids to "lock them doors! You never can tell what's going on!" The Packard crept forward a few feet at a time and the windshield wipers rubbed against the glass, water squirting first to one side, then the other. "With our luck, there's probably some maniac busted outta that prison nearby. . . . Who knows, it might even be that character they call Metal Fang—some foreign fellow who's killed dozens. I hear he might be loose. . . ." Lila Mae mumbled her predictions, a runaway train of disastrous notions tethered together by some logic that only she could justify. "This is all we need—to disappear on some lonely, godforsaken stretch of highway. They wouldn't even know where to bury us. . . . In some unmarked grave, I reckon."

"If he's a foreigner, then what's he doing over here?" Becky Jean gave Carleen a let's-see-what-she-has-to-say-about-this-one look.

Thrilled to be asked what she usually had to force on them, Lila Mae said, "Well, now, that's a good question. . . . You see, you just never know when and where them types'll pop up. That's what they're good at . . . foolin' you!" Then she retreated—as she always did after matters of this sort were settled—to the that's-all-there-is-to-it chamber in her head.

Coils of ebony smoke rose in the air, and green and red lights crisscrossed, creating X's in the sky. A squadron of fire trucks flew by, and the roar of distant sirens got louder until one ambulance and police car after another zoomed past them. Navigating through the traffic, blowing his whistles and pitching his hands through the air, was a policeman in a flapping yellow raincoat. Lila Mae, sticking her head out the window, said, "Officer . . . Officer, what's the problem?"

"Truck jackknifed." He waved her through, making small, impatient half-circles with his hand. "Keep going, lady. . . . Keep going."

"Did you hear that, kids? It ain't no escaped con, after all. It's a *jackknife!*" Lila Mae had one wide-open eye on the road before her and another goggle eye checking out the mess on the roadside. "That's exactly what Bill Corn warned us about. . . ."

Two trucks—one folded up like a half-open wallet, the other sprawled across two lanes, its big black rubber tires drooping over the jagged ravine—had spun out of control. Strewn across the pavement were crushed canned goods, orange rinds, and all sorts of smashed-up boxes and twisted metal. Hanging over the rubble were the vapors of burning rubber, chemicals, and spice.

When they jangled over a large bump, Lila Mae yelped, "Wha—what was that racket? Check to see if the trailer's still okay, kids. What about any, uh, dead bodies or anything like that? Tell me if you see something."

"Yep, I see the trailer *and* dead bodies—stacked sky high!" Becky Jean reported. "Look! There's some arms and legs and all sorts of other odds and ends."

"Now, don't give me that odds-and-ends stuff again. This is serious!"

"You wanted to know what was going on and we told you." Becky Jean and Carleen had their palms pressed to their giggling mouths. "Don't ask us anymore, then, if you don't believe us."

"You really mean it? Honest? Arms and legs and what have you? Lord, how I feel for their poor families—and here it is almost Thanksgiving." Yanking a Kleenex from the small cellophane packet, Lila Mae touched it to her nose and sniffled.

"Oh, what a holiday they'll have. I'm gonna say a prayer for them people. Girls, so should you. That goes for you, too, Billy Cooper."

The possibility that God would now be in on things, that Lila Mae would stop in some church parking lot, make them bow their heads as she said, "Dear Lord, please bless the families of them poor truck drivers in Texas—we don't know their names but, Lord, you do," was enough to trigger a confession. "Jeez," Becky Jean and Carleen said, "we were just *kiddin'*! We can't believe you really believed us."

"What do you mean, kiddin'? What in the *world* would make you joke about such a horrible thing?"

Even as Lila Mae asked them the question, she already knew the answer, and as irked as she was by her kids' quirky senses of humor, she was hardly surprised. Not that her own kin weren't lively or comical, but those Wootens (the ones her kids seemed to be taking after) were something else, always laughing their heads silly over mishaps and misfortunes—the more broken bones and crutches, the better. Congregating around a picnic or dinner table, doubling over, stomping their feet and giving their thighs hearty slaps, they'd howl about one kooky story or another.

And she was sure they didn't mean anything by it, since they were always the first to show up with food or offers to plow a farmer's field or look after their cows. And they actually got even more of a kick telling crazy tales about themselves . . . every single one of them involving slippery banana peels or the wrong body in a coffin.

When Lila Mae and Roy were newlyweds, Frank, his youngest brother, was in the hospital. Lila Mae offered to give blood, like everybody else, but her new father-in-law said it wouldn't be necessary, because, "fer one thing, we already got all the volunteers we need, and fer another, he needs *family* blood." Just when Lila Mae was feeling like an outcast, like she wasn't even good enough to donate blood to a dying man, he added the punch line: "Eighty proof!" They'd been in Frank's hospital room at the time, and Frank himself got to laughing so hard that he coughed up some tube in his mouth and they had to call the nurse.

In any case, Lila Mae had tried to raise her girls differently, but she could only do so much. Oh, well . . . at least the kids kept saying they were sorry; that was something. She made a mental note to have Roy talk to them before things got more out of hand than they were already.

To get their mother off the subject, Carleen and Becky Jean harmonized "Yellow Rose of Texas," and after that, "Your Cheatin' Heart," and Lila Mae joined in on "Tennessee Waltz." Becky Jean wrote in her diary that they'd now been in thirteen states, seven more than they had originally planned, and that they had memorized most of the state capitals. She mentioned that her mother was up to her old tricks, getting off the track, spending hours on end with people they'd never see again, but that they were having a good time anyway. As a postscript, she added that they were getting used to being out of school.

To make up for lost time, Lila Mae said, they would drive all night, so they stopped at Phil Hazlett's Standard station to visit the washroom and stock up on snacks. Carleen and Becky Jean bought Moon Pies and Nehi orange drinks while Billy Cooper got paraffin lips and miniature Coke bottles filled with dark syrup. Lila Mae changed Irene Gaye into her flannel pajamas and pulled off Billy Cooper's cowboy boots.

With a blurry harvest moon hanging in the sky, they drove deep into the Texas Panhandle. When they opened the car windows, they could hear the crickets chirping in the dark fields along the highway and the creaky swinging of a wrought-iron gatepost: LAZY L RANCH—REGISTERED TEXAS LONGHORNS. They gazed at the millions of silvery stars that tumbled to the ground like unstrung pearls. It had been hours since they passed another car. The only signs of life were the abstract profiles of the cacti, which in the metallic moonlight looked like strange, gigantic people. Everyone clapped their hands, singing "Deep in the Heart of Texas." It seemed to Becky Jean, as her eyes searched the ebony screen wrapped around them, that they were the only people in the whole wide world.

Chapter Six

It was Thanksgiving Day, and Lila Mae was way, way behind schedule. It was bad enough that her husband had expected them ages ago, but worse than that, he was probably worried sick, because he'd hardly heard a peep from them. Although Lila Mae had left one message with the desk clerk at his motel, and she kept meaning to call him personally, there never seemed to be the perfect moment. The one time she got up the nerve and called, she fibbed and told Roy that poor little Irene Gaye had the croup and they'd been slowed down on account of it. Even then, she claimed they were already in New Mexico. That had been days and days ago when they were just leaving Minnesota. Although she considered telling him the baby also had scarlet fever, which would have been worth another couple of days, Lila Mae was superstitious, petrified the baby would actually come down with it. Naturally, the longer she put it off, the harder it was to pick up the phone. As if that wasn't enough, she still didn't know how to break the news that she had somehow counted wrong and they were almost out of funds.

Bound and determined to make their Thanksgiving as traditional as possible, Lila Mae woke at the crack of dawn, first looking out the window of the Hitching Post Motel to see if the trailer was still connected to the Packard. Every morning she'd snap to attention, half expecting that someone had swiped it during the night, but "So far, so good," she muttered, dropping the panel of covered-wagon drapes.

After that she slipped on her tweed suit and black patent pumps, placed two daubs of Tabu on her wrists, then screwed on her pearl cluster earrings. Lila Mae had no intention of looking like a hobo on Thanksgiving Day.

Hoping to find a wholesome, home-cooked meal in a family setting, she asked the desk clerk at the Hitching Post Motel for a suggestion. The man said, "There ain't but one restaurant that's any count, and that's Lulu's Hot Spot." Although it was at least two hundred miles away, he promised that it was well worth the drive and that they wouldn't be sorry. But when they reached the place several hours later, it had flashing light bulbs framing the windows and an advertisement showing a scantily clad woman. In spite of the sign that said BEST DARN MEAL IN TOWN!, Lila Mae gunned the Packard and snipped, "Meal, my foot! That's a liquor bar or my name ain't Lila Mae Wooten!"

On second thought, Lila Mae said, just to be on the safe side, she would pop her head inside for an inspection. After all, the Hitching Post clerk had raved about Lulu's, and she probably shouldn't judge a book by its cover. Within seconds she marched right back to the car. "What kind of place would run out of turkey on Thanksgiving? And them waitresses weren't even wearin' any hairnets." Lila Mae said the hostess was nice enough to offer her some more suggestions, so she told the kids she'd be back in a jiffy. When, after fifteen minutes, Becky Jean went in to investigate, she wasn't too surprised when she saw Lila Mae squeezed into a booth with two other women and a small boy, drinking an iced tea and chatting up a storm.

"Dr. Shakespeare said he never seen a gallstone so big!" A woman with chipmunk cheeks and a crown of tangerine hair was making a large circle with her hands. " 'Bout the size of a grapefruit, he claimed."

"Is that true, Mama?" The woman's son had a yellow beak

nose, red cowlicked hair, and a long swivel neck, which made him look like a small woodpecker.

"Why, shore it is, son," the woman replied. "You seen it with yer own eyes, didn't ya, Chester Joe?"

"I had me a tumor the size of a orange, but a *grapefruit,* now that's *big,* honey." The other woman, with crossed eyes and one yellow bucktooth, swallowed a chunk of boysenberry pie. "Where the devil'd you put the thing?"

"Shoot, that ain't nothin'." The waitress, who was wearing a flowered handkerchief made into a corsage, ripped off the check and placed it facedown on the table. "My sister-in-law's got lupus so bad her blood's shootin' through her veins like it was a squirt gun."

"Law," Lila Mae said. "I feel downright lucky after listenin' to you all." When she spotted Becky Jean, she clapped her hand to her face, then took one last slurp of her iced tea. "Oh, there's my girl. . . . You two take care of yourselves, now. And you'd better let me hear from you!" Lila Mae slipped them her mother-in-law's address and wagged her finger like a strict schoolmarm.

"Okay, sweetie. And you be sure to call me if you ever come to New York." The woman with the grapefruit gallstone gave Lila Mae a bear hug. "I meant what I said about that job offer. You'd be good with people."

Lila Mae pushed the door open, fanned herself, and said, "My, that place was smoky, wasn't it?" Then she folded a napkin with a phone number on it and tucked it inside her pocketbook. "You know, that woman's eyes got as big as saucers when I told her I had cancer."

"That cancer story has already had more performances than *Gone With the Wind* and *South Pacific* put together. And, anyway, you were supposed to find out about restaurants." Becky Jean slammed the metal storm door. "We're out here starving and you're in comparing deathbed notes. . . . Talk about telling your life story. Plus, that's the stuff you said you were trying to avoid."

"It pays to have connections, young lady. You'll remember that one day when you're in New York and need a bed to sleep on."

As they coasted down the bumpy, desolate road, their last hope for food seemed to be Mabel's Country Pines. Signs, one right after another, said: ONLY TEN MORE MILES TO MABEL'S . . . FIVE MORE MILES TIL MABEL'S DELICIOUS HOME COOKING . . . BEST COFFEE IN NEW MEXICO . . . FOUR GENERATIONS OF SMID-LEYS TO SERVE YOU. . . .

"Did you see that? It says 'Home-Cooked Meals, Just Like Mom's.'" Carleen buckled her T-strap shoes and slipped on her coat.

"Well, that's more like it," Lila Mae chirped.

When the sign said ONE MORE MILE TO MABEL'S, Lila Mae told the kids to zip up their jackets, and even though there wasn't a car for miles, she stuck her hand out the window and signaled.

When they saw that after all that buildup, the cafe was shut down, Lila Mae, eyes like two boiling pots, slammed the car door and paraded up to the restaurant. A dead, gray branch crept its way across the porch; the wooden steps were pierced with termites; and the big metal MABEL'S sign—an elaborate, hand-painted portrait displaying the rosy-cheeked Smidley clan—was ventilated with bullet holes.

Marching up to a corroded wrought-iron chair, Lila Mae kicked it with her high heel. "This just takes the cake!" She paced in front of the deserted restaurant, flailing her hands like a trial attorney in closing arguments. "You'd think they'd have the common decency to take them signs down. Lord only knows how many starvin' people have been thrown off the track. I have a good mind to report them . . . don't think I won't." She also said she didn't blame the person who'd done that to the sign.

"My stomach's growlin'," Billy Cooper whined, and Carleen yelled, "Come on, Mama, let's go!" Baby Sister kicked her feet against the dashboard so hard that the cigarette lighter popped out.

The prairie landscape was bleak with dead, crooked trees and miles of hard, flat soil. The first faint traces of a white moon with gossamer clouds swimming across it appeared overhead, and a jackrabbit hopped across the road, disappearing in a grove of chaparral. Carleen pointed to a brick wall alongside the road. In crumbling white letters it advertised Thermos jugs and water bags, and there was a painting of a sweating skull with a warning: 700 MILES OF DESERT.

As if they needed to be any more down-in-the-dumps than they already were, every once in a while, Lila Mae would announce mournfully, "I can just picture your father carvin' a big, juicy turkey," or "Don't you wish we had some of my homemade pecan pumpkin pie?"

Miles and miles behind them were the deep green scallops of a mountain range and the remnants of a lonely, hazy dusk. A single silver light from a distant cabin flickered like a brilliant diamond. When the sky turned blue cobalt and the highway narrowed to two snaky lanes, Lila Mae punched the bright lights and dodged a tumbleweed.

When Becky Jean hollered "There's a place!" Lila Mae said, "You might give me some notice. I can't stop on a dime, you know." But she pumped the brake and swerved to the roadside.

Sitting on a plot of gravel, nestled in the dip where two mountains dovetailed together, was a small adobe cafe named the PowWow. It had a red blinking neon sign in the shape of a tepee and a curly ribbon of blue smoke twirling out of a plaster chimney. Dumped in an adjoining trench were a corroded tractor and the innards of a rotten mattress. Off to one side was a small corral with two whinnying Appaloosa horses.

"It don't look too bad, neither." Carleen pointed to a bubblegum-pink Cadillac with studded mud flaps.

"Oh, look!" Lila Mae exclaimed, snapping the car door shut. "It has crisscross curtains!"

It wasn't until they reached the front door that they noticed the Pabst Blue Ribbon sign and heard the blast of a jukebox playing "Hey, Good Lookin'." When they peeked inside the windowpanes just to get an idea of what to expect, they saw a woman with peroxide curls dancing with a tall, wafer-thin man. Lila Mae didn't know which one was worse: the woman, who with her shocking-pink skirt and harlequin eyes, looked like a hootchie-cootchie dancer; or her dance partner, who was spangled like a fancy show horse. There were red flowers on his shirt, and wrapped around his ten-gallon hat was a jeweled band. All over his outfit, sprinkled here and there, were turquoise medallions, and his cowboy boots were tooled in yellow roses and tipped in silver. Even the pistol strapped in a holster was pearl-handled.

"Look, Mama!" Billy Cooper tugged on Lila Mae's dress and pointed to the man. "Hopalong Cassidy!"

At the end of the song, the woman jumped on the man, giggling and wrapping her curvaceous legs around his waist. The cowboy swatted her rear end, tossed her high in the air, and brayed like a donkey. "Ride 'em, cowboy!" the woman whooped, then slid down his body like a fireman slips down a pole. At that, the man removed his shirt, held it over his head, and swirled it like a lasso.

"Dear me!" Lila Mae winced, just to let the kids know she didn't approve, but she pushed the door open anyway. "I don't care if they got burlesque dancers, we're eatin' here, and that's all there is to it."

The room was square and dingy, and a thick fog of smoke and bug spray hung over it. Along the walls were wooden booths gashed with hearts and initials, and in the middle was a checkerboard of green Formica tables. On each one, like a decorative corsage, were a ketchup bottle, napkins, and salt and pepper shakers. Stretched along the back was a quilted stainless steel counter with cardboard signs advertising the daily specials, and on the wall above the griddle was a framed, autographed dollar bill and a stuffed lizard.

Just to make sure it wasn't the type of establishment where all hell could break loose, Lila Mae swept her eyes across the room. Sitting by himself was a man with a seal-slick head jostling a pair of ruby-red dice who didn't look all *that* bad; at another table was a quartet of poker players—three men in denim and a sloe-eyed woman wearing a turban decorated with a garden of lavender flowers. Although Lila Mae said, "Who in the world does she think *she* is, Hedda Hopper?" that was no crime, either. As the card players sucked on their cigarettes, a man wearing an I LIKE IKE button placed the deck against the table and swooped it up dramatically. His nicotine-stained hands were a blur of movement, his emerald ring gleaming, as he shuffled the cards into a fancy arch.

"If we were gonna eat in a dump like this, maybe we should have stayed at Lulu's," Becky Jean said. "At least they had big leather booths and they didn't have a zillion bugs."

"I had no intentions of feedin' my kids regular food on Thanksgiving. Plus, you know dern good and well that I couldn't park there." After all this time, Lila Mae still hadn't put the rig in reverse, so she only stopped in places where she could make wide-swing U-turns or in spots that had a curb long enough to accommodate both the Packard and the trailer. "It ain't the Ritz, but it ain't all that bad, either."

Standing at the griddle and giving them an arctic once-over was a man with bronzed skin, hair that hung like black tinsel, and a sandpapery pink Christmas bulb of a nose. His menacing eyes—two bloodshot capsules that slipped from side to side—followed the Wootens as they filed into a booth. He extracted a lighter from a pocket of his buckskin shirt and ignited a Lucky Strike cigarette. When a fly zigzagged across the grill and circled once around his head, he picked up a metal sprayer, then pumped the handle twice, as if to get rid of the bug and the newcomers at the same time. Billy Cooper wanted to know why the man had long hair and was wearing turquoise bracelets. Lila Mae told him it was because he was an Indian.

A waitress with a stern, primitive face and jet-black braids marched toward them, menus in her fist. On her long, droopy earlobes were multicolored stones and silver hoops, and her fingernails were painted sloppily with blood-red polish. As she shuffled to their booth, her bosom undulated and her aqua gypsy skirt swished against her bare legs. When she was a foot away, Baby Sister pitched her rattle at the woman. Without formally greeting them, the waitress grunted and stooped down to pick up the toy. Then she set down their water glasses in a huddle.

"I bet she's an *Indian,* too," Lila Mae whispered dramatically. "She probably don't even speak English."

"Why don't you ask her? Maybe she'll send you some smoke signals." Lila Mae kicked Becky Jean frantically under the table, but Becky Jean said "Ow!" and kicked her mother right back.

When they were ready to order, Lila Mae winked at the kids as if to say "Get a load of this." Then, with a deadpan face, she said to the waitress, "We'll have five Spam sandwiches on white bread."

Fishing the pencil out of her black braid, the waitress wet the point with the tip of her tongue. When she started to write down the order, Lila Mae chuckled and touched her arm lightly. "I was just pullin' your leg, dear. We'll have three of your turkey dinners, of course." When the waitress didn't crack a smile, Becky Jean rolled her eyes so the woman would know she sided with her.

Carleen slapped the menu together and said she wanted a grilled cheese sandwich, but Lila Mae said, "Grilled cheese? You can eat grilled cheese anytime. This is Thanksgiving." Although Lila Mae looked at the waitress for support, the woman had spun around and was gone. "She's a sourpuss, ain't she?"

When the card shuffler dropped a nickle in the jukebox and selected "That Lucky Old Sun," the woman in the lavender hat fastened her cheek to the man's and they floated across the small floor. Closing her eyes and swaying to the music, Lila Mae sang, "That lucky old sun has nothing to do but roll around heaven all daaaaay!" while Carleen and Billy Cooper swayed with her.

In her head, Becky Jean also hummed along with the song, the song that reminded her of so many summer afternoons at her grandmother's farm. With the temperature over one hundred degrees and the air swagged with clouds of humidity, the two of them rocked on the porch swing, always with a pitcher of slushy pink lemonade at their side. As her grandmother batted away horseflies and grasshoppers, she'd look at the yellow-white sun and then she'd sing a spurt or two of the song that Becky Jean wasn't even sure she knew all the lyrics to.

Becky Jean could remember inhaling the aroma of the cascading honeysuckle and gazing at the ancient white oak trees and the red barn with the upside-down bouquets of tobacco. As her grandmother sang "Send down that cloud with the silver lining . . . ," she thought that the whole world ended at the rim of that farm, just as if the sky and earth and the sun themselves were her grandmother's exclusive property.

But now, in the smoky room with the poker players and flashy cowboys, the farm seemed so faraway that Becky Jean might as well be stuck on another planet. As she slurped her Coca-Cola, lazily swirling the straw around the glass, and listened to Frankie Laine, she stared beyond the muslin cafe curtains at the dusty, bug-spattered Packard. Behind it were a cap of platinum snow on the highest mountain and a golden moon that was bulbous and full.

When the waitress brought more Coca-Colas for everyone plus one beer, Lila Mae said, "I'm sorry, dear, but I don't drink any alcoholic beverages." When she told the woman she must have mixed up their order, the waitress told her there wasn't a mix-up at all, that Mr. Orin Hatcher, the gentleman across the room, was buying.

"Who?" Lila Mae stretched her neck forward and saw the man in the cowboy hat, the one who'd been jitterbugging with the flashy blonde. He looked up from his card game, a little worm of a smile crawling across his face, and gave Lila Mae a sly wink. "The very idea!" she puffed, turning neon orange.

"Mama," Billy Cooper flapped his hands at the man. "That's Hopalong Cassidy!" Lila Mae begged him not to egg the man on, but it was too late. In a quick limbering-up exercise, the man shook his legs—two long planks—then cracked his knuckles and hiked up his Levi's. The next thing anybody knew, he had scrambled to their table and slid into the booth right next to Lila Mae.

"Don't mean to horn in on you, ma'am, but it looked to me like you was itchin' to dance. . . ." The cowboy wore a silver and gold belt buckle with a bucking bronco on it and he smelled of spice cologne. His eyes—sky blue and watery—had tiny sand-colored moles that looked like cookie crumbs sprinkled across his eyelids.

"Oh, dear me," Lila Mae twitched, fingering the ruffle on her blouse and adjusting her tweed skirt. "Oh, heavens . . . I . . . I . . ."

Billy Cooper grabbed ahold of his mother's sleeve, yanking her toward him, and Carleen said, "She's tired, mister."

"She's also *married*," Becky Jean huffed, slamming her Coca-Cola down so hard that the ice rattled.

"I ain't gonna bite ya. . . ." Mr. Hatcher bumped his body playfully against Lila Mae's and smiled at the kids. "What's the harm in one little dance?"

"I ain't much of a dancer. And, besides that . . ." Lila Mae paused. "I'm in very poor health. . . . I—I really don't think I should. . . ." As if to verify the information she had just given the man, she took out her handkerchief and coughed, a string of loose, husky rattles.

"I suppose a gentleman should respect a lady's wishes. If she don't want to dance"—Hatcher set his beer bottle down with a decisive clunk—"then he shouldn't force her none."

The matter seemed settled, but that didn't mean Hatcher had budged. He told the waitress to bring everyone refills on the drinks, then he scooted closer to Lila Mae, draping his arm casually across the back of the booth. Lila Mae wanted to do something to dump the intruder, honestly she did, but the way he was situated (he was close enough to suggest intimacy, but at the same time neutral, so if Lila Mae made a stink, he could say, "It's just an arm stretched across a wood booth!") made it difficult—that is, unless she wanted to be outright rude.

Lila Mae could have clobbered Carleen when "Three Coins in the Fountain" came on. Right in front of the cowboy, the girl slipped and said, "Mama, that's one of your favorites, ain't it?"

"Well, now, are we gonna do somethin' 'bout that?" Hatcher angled his head at Lila Mae and rubbed his chin with his forefinger, the purple vein that ran up his bicep quivering with each movement. "Come on, it's Thanksgiving!"

When Lila Mae—with a coquettish shrug of her shoulders—said, "Oh, well, in that case . . . ," Becky Jean crisscrossed her arms and shot her mother the evil eye. It was absolutely absurd for a grown woman, particularly one who was married with four children, to be dancing with a complete stranger. The tide had turned, though. Hatcher, who had passed out packages of Red Hots to everyone, let Billy Cooper wear his ten-gallon hat and touch his pistol. Plus, he told Carleen she had the prettiest golden-blond hair he'd ever seen. He also promised them all a ride in his brand-new pink Cadillac.

As Hatcher and Lila Mae strutted to the dance floor, Becky Jean glared at them through narrow, accusing eyes. Another couple were dancing cheek-to-cheek, staring straight ahead, a hypnotic sheen in their eyes. Since they were clipping across the floor as smoothly as a cabin cruiser glides across a serene lake, Becky Jean figured Hatcher would be a copycat and her mother would be forced to trip the romantic light fantastic with the cowboy. But by the time they got situated, "Three Coins" was over. Hatcher dropped another nickle in the jukebox and selected "Mule Train." Lila Mae cast her eyes to the ceiling and muttered, "Of all songs . . ."

Even though Becky Jean tried to ignore the situation, Hatcher was making an absolute spectacle of himself. His legs—nimble and rubbery—moved up and down like they were on springs, and all the while he howled and made yelping prairie sounds. Lila Mae, who was being whipped around like a rag doll, was embarrassed to tears when one of her pumps flew off, but that didn't keep her from kicking off her other shoe and making a fool of herself when, a minute later, somebody played "Doggie in the Window." Hatcher and Lila Mae even started growling and arfing along with the song, managing to get the other remaining customers (Carleen and Billy Cooper included) in on things and turning the PowWow into a dog pound. If that wasn't bad enough, Lila Mae, for some unknown reason, decided to teach Hatcher the Charleston, knocking her knees together and slashing her hands across them at the same time.

"Not that . . ." Becky Jean groaned, and turned away. No amount of pleading would ever convince Lila Mae to stop doing that corny dance. Even Roy, who usually got a kick out of his wife's shenanigans, always told her that it looked ridiculous. But Lila Mae seemed to think the Charleston was her specialty.

Though Hatcher was giving it his all, you could tell he wasn't familiar with the dance, either. Finally, he saw an opening, so he grabbed Lila Mae by the waist and tossed her in the air. Becky Jean, who couldn't take it anymore, made a megaphone with her hands and yelled, "Our food is coming!"

Becky Jean figured that the man wouldn't quit until he was good and ready, but Hatcher, out of breath and coated with a membrane of sweat, was a perfect gentleman, sashaying Lila Mae right back to the table.

"Good luck with that trip of yours, pretty lady." He grabbed his brown beer bottle by its neck and gulped, his Adam's apple a scraping, bony hook. To get rid of him, Lila Mae scribbled some information on a napkin and slipped it to the cowboy. Although she was hoping to accomplish this on the sly, he made a big fuss, waggling the paper in the air and tipping his hat. "I'll hang on to this in case'n I ever get out Californy way."

"Mama's got a boyfriend!" Carleen and Billy Cooper chanted. "Mama's got a boyfriend—Mama's got a boy—"

"Oh, hush up, I have no such thing. . . . Well," Lila Mae grumbled from a side loop of her mouth, "he's no Fred Astaire, I'll tell ya that." In spite of her complaint, her cheeks were flushed and her spirits high. Becky Jean stared at her like a prosecutor waiting for a confession. "Well, what're you lookin' at?" Lila Mae took a gulp of the warm beer. "I couldn't very well say no, could I? He'd had a few nips, and who knows what kind of ruckus he'd create?"

"Is that why you told him your life story?" Becky Jean grilled her. "And what was that paper he was waving around?"

Lila Mae said all she'd done was given him their old street address in Kentucky with the wrong city and state. "I didn't want to be rude. Besides, if the Tri-State Credit Union and a slew of furniture stores can't track us down and Mr. Orin Hatcher *can,* then more power to him."

The waitress brought all four plates at once, each one balanced carefully in a row up her arm. "Well, look at you!" Lila Mae clapped her hands together and exclaimed.

When Becky Jean said, "Maybe someone should call 'The Ed Sullivan Show,'" Lila Mae waited until the waitress left; then she beat her fists against the table like it was a bongo drum. "I wish for once, just *once,* you wouldn't sass me every single, solitary time I open my mouth. There's somethin' called the art of chitchat that you don't know the first thing about.

Besides, if you don't quiet down, she's liable to boot us all out. So just *hush.*"

"Hey, how come *you* didn't order anything?" Becky Jean scowled. "You didn't already eat in that other restaurant, did you?"

"Don't be ridiculous. I just ain't hungry, that's all. . . ." Actually, Lila Mae was starving, but she was so low on cash she figured she'd just bide her time until the kids were finished, then she'd pick at their leftovers. In the meantime, she confiscated Billy Cooper's roll, cracked it open, and slathered it with butter. As she chewed on the doughy mass, her face turned flame red and she began to gag. She was flogging her arms around to call attention to her situation when, finally, Carleen and Becky Jean hopped up and beat her on the back.

"Lordy!" she croaked, coughing up a damp lump of bread and gathering it into her napkin. "I thought I was a goner." She studied the contents and said, "Look at this! Just what I thought."

"Hey, everybody!" Billy Cooper bobbed up and down, making a public proclamation. "She found a hair in her roll! Is it real long and black? I know who it belongs to!" By now, the other customers were curious and even the waitress had come to investigate.

"What seems to be the problem, lady?" The waitress, holding a dirty plate, shifted to one foot and pushed her eyebrows, two penciled tadpoles, together in a nasty look. "Said there's a hair or somethin'?"

To try to make up for her son's bad manners, Lila Mae wiped her mouth and shook her head in apology. "I found no such thing. You know kids. They ain't satisfied unless they're raisin' Cain. . . . The dinner is just delicious, dear. Just delicious."

Carleen said, "But, Mama, you ain't even eatin'." And Becky Jean said maybe they should get a refund or something, since the food wasn't that great.

When Lila Mae saw how peeved the waitress was, she tried to butter her up. "Don't listen to them. If it ain't a hamburger or French fries, it's no count. But I say there's nothin' like a home-cooked meal. I'll just bet you cooked this yourself, didn't you, dear?"

"Not exactly. It's my husband does the cookin'—that is, when he ain't drinkin' like a fish." A smile twinkled on the waitress's lips and she slid the bill under a dinner plate. "If you'uns want anything else, you just let me know."

"Well," Lila Mae stretched across the booth and wise-cracked, "I guess she speaks English after all, don't she?" As usual, the waitress was getting friendlier the closer it came to tip time. Lila Mae counted out seventy-five cents and left it on the table.

While she stood at the fancy brass cash register, she took out her coin purse and handed the waitress fifteen one-dollar bills. Waiting for her change, she glanced in the dusty glass display case, which held Prince Albert tobacco, Black Jack chewing gum, and coral jewelry displayed on square pieces of slick cardboard. Printed on them in fancy gold letters was DE-SIGNS BY JUANITA. When the waitress hit the cash register drawer to give Lila Mae her change, her back made a loud crack like a tree branch splitting. "Oh, dear Lord," she moaned, her legs crumpling as she clawed at the counter for support.

"Are you okay, hon?" Lila Mae rushed to steady the wait-ress, wrapping her hands around her shoulders, then lowering the hefty woman onto a wobbly wooden stool.

"Weellllll, yeeesss and nooooo," the woman strained to an-swer, as if it was actually her voice that was injured. "I had me some surgery a few months ago. They's a pin in my hip." The waitress massaged her leg as she scooted around on the bar-stool. "Ain't got over it yet, it looks like."

"A pin in your hip, I swanee. You shouldn't be on your feet, you *poor* thing." Lila Mae clucked over her like a mother hen, telling the woman she'd be happy to fill in for her if she thought that would help any. "Why don't you just take a break?"

"Try to tell *him* that." The waitress tipped her head toward the man in the buckskin shirt and turquoise bracelets, the one who'd gawked at them like they were from outer space. He raised his silver flask, taking a gulp of liquor that trickled down his cheek in a sticky, curvy track. "He'll kill himself with that stuff . . . if he don't kill me first."

"Is that your husband? I thought so." Lila Mae leaned across the counter and whispered confidentially: "Believe you me, I know a thing or two about poor health. I had cancer myself, I guess it's . . . oh . . . Becky Jean, how long has it been?"

"Come on, that's only the millionth time you've told that story," Becky Jean moaned. "You know *exactly* how long it's been."

"Why, that girl!" Lila Mae planted both fists on her hips. "You'd think I told our life story to every Tom, Dick, and Harry. You can't ask her a thing without gettin' your head bit off. Anything to make me look bad. It must be the age."

"Don't tell *me*. I got me a boy just about your girl's size. . . . He's back there in the kitchen. I gotta beat him to a pulp to get anything out of him."

"Goodness!" Lila Mae swiveled around and spotted the boy, a gangly teen with high, chiseled cheekbones and a brown-sugar complexion. He was leaning against a mop, smoking a cigarette. "Anyhow," Lila Mae said, setting her purse down on the steel counter, "it's been over a year now since they give me a clean bill of health. Some people think my doctor overdone the cobalt treatments, but I'm alive and kickin' and that's what counts."

"You don't say." The waitress slammed the register drawer closed, making all the change tinkle. "And you such a young and pretty thing."

"Believe it or not, my husband's allergies is the reason we're headed out west. Every stick of furniture I own is in that trailer

out there." Lila Mae, chin in her hand, stared melancholily
through the PowWow's front window at the Packard. The grill,
with its shiny chrome bars, resembled a big set of teeth frozen
somewhere between a smile and a grimace. "I had to sell pretty
near everything I owned, but I still got my good hutch and a
davenport—yes I do!"

"Well, you'll make it big again, honey." The waitress gave
Lila Mae's hand a supportive pat. "You just watch."

After that, Lila Mae and Juanita—by this time they were on
a first-name basis—were arched across the counter. Juanita
sliced them generous wedges of pumpkin pie, squirting curlicues of whipped cream across the top. Then she squatted down
on the stool with her feet wide apart and wiggled her toes in
her leather sandals. Holding a coffee cup with both hands, she
rolled it back and forth, staring into space as if she were talking
to everybody in general and nobody in particular. "Life sure
ain't fair, is it? . . . I got me a boy who's as strong as an ox but
as mean as a hornet. . . . Then again, my little girl's as sweet as
apple pie, but she can't even feed herself, she's so weak, weak
as a newborn baby. Ain't that just the way?"

"Oh, how very, very heartbreaking!" Lila Mae gushed.

The story got even more dramatic when Juanita told Lila
Mae that her little girl was in some special hospital, cooped up
in a lot of peculiar equipment—tubes and pulleys and buttons
and whatnot—and nobody, not even her parents (not that her
rotten father gave two hoots about visiting her), could even see
her without wearing a mask. Juanita said she'd give just about
everything she owned in the entire world to see her girl, the girl
she hadn't seen in *ages,* more often.

"Well, I'll just bet you would! You will someday, hon, you
will." Lila Mae patted Juanita's arm, one brisk slap for each
syllable. Becky Jean rolled her eyes and started playing an imaginary violin. Lila Mae stomped her foot and threatened Becky
Jean with a fist, trying to stop her rude daughter before Juanita
caught on.

When Becky Jean heard how drastic things were for Juanita, a twinge of pity snaked its way through her, but there wasn't much they could do about it. The world was crammed with people who needed help, and Lila Mae, who had no business acting like a one-woman Red Cross, had radar for them. Plus, Lila Mae always claimed she didn't want to get in over her head and she wished someone would stop her before things went too far, but she always said that *after* the incident was over.

"It's that good-for-nothin' lazy bum husband of mine. . . ." Juanita's eyes, whirlpools of hatred, turned to where the scoundrel was sitting. "Why, just look at him, won't ya?" The man, a halo of cigarette smoke suspended above him, had joined the poker game. "He can't even tie his shoelaces by hisself."

"You know why that is, don't you, hon?" Lila Mae announced conclusively. "The place would fold without ya. Why, you're the backbone of this whole operation."

Once again, Becky Jean was thinking, How in the world would *she* know? What her mother wouldn't resort to to make someone feel like a million.

"I don't mean to be braggin' on myself"—Juanita raked her fingernails across her scalp—"but I'm an artist, and I ain't got no business standin' on my feet, especially with my back all tore like it is. I should be out on the road sellin' my jewelry."

"Don't tell me them's *your* designs in that case?" Just as she always did when she encountered anyone who could draw stick men on a napkin, Lila Mae acted like the woman had introduced herself as Juanita da Vinci. "Do you really expect me to believe you made this jewelry *all by yourself*?"

"I wished I hadn't done 'em alone. I could use someone to give me a hand." Juanita opened the cabinet door and handed Lila Mae a lizard scatter pin, a mosaic of coral, mother-of-pearl, and turquoise.

"Why, this is just as cute as a button!" Lila Mae gushed. "Kids, isn't this just darling? There ain't a reason in the world why they couldn't sell like hotcakes. All you need is some exposure."

In spite of all the advice and buddy-buddy talk, Lila Mae, who might have been testing her new "willpower," zipped up the diaper bag and scanned the room for her kids as if she was ready to leave. But when Juanita perched the coffee pot over her cup and said, "Don't you want one more for the road?" Lila Mae fingered the straps on her pocketbook for about two split seconds, then said, "You know, I believe I will. Now"—she removed her clip-on earrings and massaged her bruised earlobes—"you just tell me more about that sick little girl of yours."

Seeing their mother was occupied, Carleen and Billy Cooper raided her purse for pennies and headed for the gumball machine. The baby was sound asleep, her mouth a tiny pool of bubbles and drool, as she lay on the booth. Little by little, the PowWow's customers were gone, leaving only the poker players. Once again, it looked like they were in it for the long haul.

Disgusted with her mother, Becky Jean decided that she wasn't going to stick around all night. Slamming the door of the restaurant, she sprinted across the dark highway and jumped into the car. She sat with her head pressed against the ice-cold window, flashing her mother dirty looks. She pulled out *Rebecca* and a *Modern Screen* magazine, thinking she would read, but it was too dark. She spun the dial on her transistor radio, but the battery was dead. Every once in a while, she raised her head up to see what was going on. She looked at the green iridescent clock on the dashboard. It was 10:30 P.M. when she dozed off.

At midnight or so, a dog began to howl and she heard the muffled wail and rumble of people arguing. Then there was a loud metallic racket, kind of like a garbage can rolling over. When she looked across the road, the restaurant was dark except for a blue triangle of glossy light from the Pabst's Blue Ribbon sign. Off to the side, though, there was a huddle of people crouched together like they were hiding. Next she saw a stooped but animated silhouette—she suspected it was her mother—creep to the PowWow's window and peek inside. Then that same silhouette darted around the corner, hands flying and arms flapping, and motioned to the cluster of human shadows. Then she heard a voice whisper: "The coast is clear! One—two—three—GO!"

As they galloped over the gravel and crossed the highway, Becky Jean verified that Shadow Number One—a form who had Baby Sister flopping on one hip and a big cardboard suitcase bouncing on the other—*was* her mother. Next came Carleen and a young boy whose identity Becky Jean couldn't make out. The two of them together were dragging a big, tattered steamer trunk. Billy Cooper was walking like a ring bearer on a tightrope, holding a single item at his belly button and taking one very careful step at a time. The waitress, bedecked like a coat rack, had a tote bag dangling around her neck and both arms clutching overstuffed shopping bags. She was kicking a suitcase forward with her left foot.

"I don't believe that woman." Becky Jean shifted around to get a better look. "This just takes the cake!"

The waitress pounded on the car door with her large round fist and yelled to Becky Jean, "Open up, Girlee!" When Becky unlatched the door, the woman pitched her luggage and bags into every possible crack and crevice, as if the Packard belonged to her.

"Hey," Becky Jean griped, "what's going on?"

Lila Mae, looking like a crazed jack-o'-lantern, pressed her face against the back window and narrowed her eyes. "I don't want to hear one peep from you, do you hear me, young lady? I have my reasons." Then she turned to Juanita and said cheerfully, "Now, you just put yourself right up there in the front seat, hon. Benny can sit in the back with Billy Cooper on his lap. We'll manage just fine."

Benny was Juanita's sixteen-year-old son, the one they'd

seen mopping the kitchen floor. He had stick-straight hair, the color of licorice, a rattail comb stuck in the waistband of his jeans, and a phone number scribbled on his hand in blue ink. His eyes, which he kept cocked toward the floor, were shifty little cinders that moved around like they were tracing geometric designs. At the time they didn't know he'd just gotten out of reform school.

"Daddy's gonna *kill* you!" Becky Jean was anxious to shake her mother up and at the same time inform the waitress of the possible trouble she was getting Lila Mae into. The fact that Juanita didn't seem fazed one way or another told Becky Jean something she needed to know about the woman. And, naturally, Lila Mae wasn't taking hints, either.

"Your father don't have to know everything, now, *does he?*" Lila Mae smiled at the waitress to let her know everything was under control.

The item Billy Cooper had been carrying was a mayonnaise jar. Swimming in a scummy liquid was a hairy mass that turned out to be a pickled tarantula. The minute he reached the car, he said "Yuck!" and pushed the jar at Benny. When Juanita said to Benny, "That's right, if *you* want it, *you* take care of it!" He said "Fine," and stuck it between his kneebones.

From the corner of her eye, Becky Jean noticed a naked bulb hanging from a chain inside the PowWow, rocking back and forth as if it had just been snapped on.

Benny muttered, "Uh-oh," then tapped Juanita on the shoulder and said, "Dad's woke up."

"Oh, my goodness," Lila Mae panted. "*Now* what should we do?"

"He don't scare me none." Juanita clicked the latch on an overnight case, nonchalantly patting her hair in place and spritzing perfume behind her ears. "That man's so plastered, he couldn't hit the broad side of a barn." She glanced at Lila Mae to see what was taking so long, then said, "That don't mean we gotta sit here all night, though."

It wasn't that Lila Mae didn't want to get the heck out of there, but she was so nervous she couldn't get the key to fit in the ignition. With Juanita's drunk husband—Ramon, she said his name was—screaming at the top of his lungs and threatening this and that and the other thing, it crossed Lila Mae's mind that this time she might have bitten off more than she could chew.

"Is your dad's rifle hid like I told you?" Juanita swiveled around and poked Benny in the chest. "You didn't forget, *did* you? If you did, I'll beat the tar outta you!"

Benny tipped his chin like a West Point cadet, held up his right hand, and said, "Scout's honor." He swore that he'd buried the shotgun in a dark, very hard-to-reach corner of the back supply room under a bundle of dirty tablecloths. He patted his coat pocket and said, "I swiped his pistol, too."

Everyone thought they were off the hook as far as the rifle was concerned, and Lila Mae even mumbled, "Thank goodness for small favors." All of a sudden, though, Juanita's eyes became smoky little disks. She wheeled around, slapping Benny with one hand, then the other, as if he had fainted and she was trying to get him to come to.

"Why did you lie to me, you little mongoloid idiot?" Juanita tugged on Benny's earlobe. "Now look!"

A barefooted, rowdy Ramon—his eyes like Jack Daniel's headlights—was staggering out of the PowWow. Instead of collapsing in a drunken heap like they all hoped, he waved his rifle around a few times, leveled it on his shoulder, and took aim. At the top of his lungs he yelled, "I'm comin' to git you, woman!" then, before anyone could bat an eye, he shot a piece of luggage right off the top of the Packard.

"*Somebody* help me get this GD car in gear!" Lila Mae boomed, and Billy Cooper panted, "Here comes a bad man, Mama!" Baby Sister was screaming—WAA-WAA-WAA!—her lungs vibrating, her mouth opening and snapping shut. The horses were whinnying, long piercing neighs, their hind legs rearing up and kicking the fence planks. Another shot cracked the air in two, rocketing over the Packard, and creating a showerstorm of rocks and dirt. Carleen, under an igloo of tented jackets, shrieked, "WE'RE ALL DEAD!" Becky Jean thumped Lila Mae's back and screamed, "WHAT ARE YOU WAITIN' FOR? GO! GO!"

Benny asked Juanita if she wanted him to shoot back and Juanita said if there was any shootin' to be done *she'd* be the one doing it. Then she told the kids to "duck!" and Lila Mae to "step on it!"

Sitting like a wax figurine—eyes trapped in place and skin ghostly pale—Lila Mae looked like a person posing for a portrait who'd been warned not to budge. When they had tried everything to get her going and nothing worked, Juanita finally swung one hefty leg across the baby, clamped her foot over Lila Mae's, and floored the Packard. Because it was in the wrong gear, it lurched and belched like a sluggish stallion. Even after Lila Mae got the car in first, everyone kept asking her if she was all right to drive, because she kept running the car off the road and she was so out of breath she was tongue-tied.

"You—you don't think he's still back there, do you?" Lila Mae panted, one jumpy eye glued to the rearview mirror. Juanita told her that more than likely the bum was staggering along the roadside trying to find someone stupid enough to pick up a drunk hitchhiker. "He'll be lucky if he don't end up smashed to smithereens."

They whizzed down a road as straight as a shotgun barrel, flying past cacti and tumbleweed, pink desert dust spraying from their wheels. Even when they were far, far away from the PowWow and the flat, granite prairie had evaporated and all around them were the crusty hills and cubic humps of another county, Lila Mae slashed through the landscape at top speed. Billy Cooper, still trembling, peeped through his shaky, open fingers, while Becky Jean and Carleen rested their chins on the backseat, keeping a lookout.

Regardless of what everyone said—that they seemed to be safe and sound—Lila Mae was worried about the menacing headlights that appeared and disappeared from sight. Just when she thought they were gone, she'd round a bend and—like a scene from an Ellery Queen murder mystery—the two silver beams would turn up once more. But Juanita told her that she was overreacting, imagining things. "Even if Ramon suddenly sobered up, how in the world could he catch us with that head start we got? On top of that, them lights is way too low for his pickup."

"How fast can them horses go?" Carleen asked. "He wouldn't be on one of them, would he?"

"Maybe he's hiding on the trailer," Becky Jean suggested. "What about that rattling we heard a while back? That didn't sound normal to me."

Suddenly Lila Mae thought of something that made her hit the brake. Years ago she'd seen a monster picture where a man with plugs in his neck and horns had hung on to the bumper of a car for miles. Not a soul knew he was there until the people were out in the middle of nowhere, and then the minute their guard was down, the monster planted his bloody handprint on the window and scared them all half to death.

"I didn't hear no rattlin'. And anyway"—Juanita turned to Becky and scowled—"that's ridiculous. Nobody can keep ahold on for over fifty miles."

Becky Jean made matters worse by asking Juanita if what she said was true, then how come Lila Mae's Samsonite train case was still sitting on the hood of the car. It had landed there when Ramon shot it off the luggage rack and it hadn't budged since they left the PowWow.

"Do you two realize you're scarin' the liver out of me?" Lila Mae hoped she got the point across to her daughter without being rude to the waitress. "So, I'll thank you to just *hush*. . . . It does make you wonder, though, where the derned police is when you're in a jam. Probably out on the highway somewhere eatin' jelly donuts and waitin' to catch someone goin' two mile an hour over the limit."

Later, when they passed through a small town, Lila Mae stopped the Packard in front of Vic Tanny Fitness and Tingle's Pontiac. She told the kids to look for anything unusual in the Vic Tanny reflection and she'd cover the showroom. She wanted to see if, against all the odds, Ramon was somehow dangling from the trailer.

While they were at it, Juanita told Benny that if he wanted to earn his keep (which meant he'd also be the first one clobbered if Ramon *did* happen to be skulking around), he should jump out of the car and grab Lila Mae's case from the hood.

Everyone fussed over the bag, acting like they should call *Ripley's Believe It or Not!*, and someone said, "Maybe Samsonite should know about this," as if the luggage had some features that even the manufacturers weren't aware of. Lila Mae, though, brushed debris away, muttering, "My poor, poor bag . . . my mother-in-law give me that." While no one noticed, Juanita grabbed the mayonnaise jar, looked left and right, then stuck it on the sidewalk in front of Vic Tanny's.

"We don't want to make no trouble, Lila Mae." Juanita wiped the sweat droplets off her neck with a woven hankie and sized up the damage on the case. When she patted her chest, Becky noticed that she had a cylinder of money tucked in the V of her brassiere. "This ain't gonna work. Just turn back and I'll face the music. You got your own life to live."

"Never you mind, hon. Where there's a will, there's a way. You'll see your little Rosita if it's the last thing I do. It just ain't right to let your husband run your life like he does." With her bottom teeth jutted out and her neck stuck forward, Lila Mae looked like a determined turtle.

Nodding her head and pinching her scarlet lips in thought, Juanita said, "I'll put that SOB back in the slammer before he knows what hit him, that's what I'll do."

Although Lila Mae was dying to ask Juanita what, exactly,

Ramon had been in jail for, she didn't think that would be polite. Plus, with her kids around, they'd embarrass her to tears with that odds-and-ends business. The Merle story had already come up once, and although Juanita had chuckled politely when Lila Mae told it to her, she hadn't seemed to get much of a kick out of it.

From a white paper sack, Juanita dug out pieces of peanut brittle, munching and humming and tapping her foot, just as carefree as could be. Unscrewing the plastic top on a silver Thermos, she poured steaming coffee and handed the cup to Lila Mae. Pretty soon she opened the glove compartment and stuck the map underneath the dingy yellow bulb. Hanging around her neck on a chain were her reading glasses, which she placed on the knob of her nose. Then, moving her ballpoint pen around from spot to spot, she chattered to Lila Mae about first one town and then another.

"Now, let's see here, Lila . . . we could swing over to Dawson, and then hit Clayton, but that'd mean we'd pass through Wheeler Park. It's one of them steep icy roads with hairpin turns and all . . . so we might be better off heading towards Questa . . . Then again . . ."

Benny draped his body over his mother's shoulder and peered at the map. "Hey! If we's going anywhere's near Colorado, I wanna go to Pikes Peak."

"Oh, Pikes Peak my foot!" Juanita swatted him off her back. "You'll be lucky if you see the light of day."

Colorado? Becky Jean knew they weren't supposed to go anywhere near Colorado. She kept waiting for her mother to butt in, but Lila Mae was acting like a chauffeur who didn't even have a say-so.

An hour later, they passed the ONE MORE MILE TO MABEL'S billboard, only this time the sign was on the opposite side of the road. Carleen said, "Mama! Mama! We're goin' the wrong way! There's that restaurant you was mad at."

"Restaurant? What restaurant?" Lila Mae creased her brows

together in disbelief. "We've only been to umpteen restaurants. Don't be such a busybody. Go to sleep, why don't you?"

Finally, Becky Jean whacked her mother on the shoulder and said, "Would you *pleeeease* tell us what's goin' on?"

Swiveling away from her daughter, Lila Mae said, "I think I'd like to hear me a little music, wouldn't you, Juanita?" Then she turned up the radio so loud that Becky Jean couldn't hear what the two women were cooking up.

Even so, she heard Juanita say something about Bismarck and something else about it probably being too far out of Lila Mae's way. For the life of her, Becky Jean couldn't remember where Bismarck was, so she elbowed Carleen, who was dozing. "Isn't Bismarck the capital of something? I forgot."

"North Dakota, dummy."

Although Becky Jean had a hard time picturing North Dakota on the map, she knew one thing: they didn't seem to be headed toward California at all. Her father, if he would even speak to Lila Mae again, would absolutely flip his lid.

When Lila Mae asked for something to nibble on—probably just to keep the kids distracted—Becky Jean unwrapped some meatloaf sandwiches from the waxed paper and passed them out. Carleen snuggled her Tiny Tears doll and Juanita took a long, heavy drag from a Lucky Strike. Benny wanted one, too, but Juanita said, "Oh no you don't. You're liable to set fire to the whole damn car." That's when she mentioned the part about Benny being fresh out of the Las Cruces Institute of Reform.

"Reform school?" Lila Mae gulped. "Whatever for? He seems like such a clean-cut boy."

"Huh? An 'incorrigible pyromaniac' is what that judge called him." Juanita jerked around, giving Benny a nasty once-over.

"Oh dear, what's that?" Lila Mae fussed. "There's a fancy name for everything these days, ain't there?"

"Yep, there sure is, but put plain and simple, he sets fires."

The words sprayed out of Juanita's mouth in an accusing spurt. "We send him to Vacation Bible School to help set him straight and he ups and puts a match to the curtains."

"Actually, that sounds like somethin' that could happen to just about anyone." Lila Mae claimed she herself had brushed against the stove in her favorite housecoat and set the sleeve ablaze, and that's as far as it went. "Now, you'd think, wouldn't you, they'd give a young boy like him the benefit of the doubt?"

"They done that three times already, but he's what you call a repeat offender. He'll never be any count."

For all anybody knew, Benny could have been a marble statue, sitting with one brown hand on each thigh, simply staring at the two braids pinned at Juanita's ears. It was only when Billy Cooper complained about his meatloaf sandwich, bringing up the subject of mayonnaise, that Benny suddenly puckered his brows in thought. Without saying anything, he moved his feet and looked around the floor; then he stuck his hands behind him and checked the backseat seam; then he tapped Juanita on the shoulder. "You've still got that jar, don't you?"

"Me?" Juanita shrieked. "I ain't got it."

"I give it to ya when I got this lady's bag. You took it from me, then everybody got out—I seen you with it then. Anyways, you never give it back."

"Well, it sounds to me like it got lost in the shuffle." When Benny said, "That was my homework," Juanita whispered to Lila Mae that he wouldn't be needing homework where he was going.

Out of a curious corner of her eye, Becky Jean gave him the once-over, wondering what Benny's real story was. He didn't seem so bad to her, not nearly as horrible as his mother was making out, but then again, she didn't know all the details. It occurred to Becky Jean that the Indian woman and her son were probably thinking the exact same thing about Lila Mae and her kids.

"P.U. Something stinks," Billy Cooper plugged up his nose

and puckered in disgust. Lila Mae told him it was probably the meatloaf sandwiches, but the truth of the matter was that Juanita had just removed her cardigan.

By now, everyone had loosened up, glad that the worst was over. "Ain't it funny, the things you think about when you're in a situation like that. . . ." Lila Mae sighed. "Me worryin' about that luggage that ain't worth but twelve dollars." She patted Juanita's knee and joked, "I guess we ain't ready to meet our maker after all, are we, Juanita?"

"No, *I'm* not. But my boy is." Juanita jerked around unexpectedly and belted Benny one more time, but he still didn't budge. When Juanita turned her head, though, this time he stuck his tongue out at her.

Suddenly, Lila Mae waggled her finger at her children's shadows in the rearview mirror. "This whole episode just serves you two girls right, you know that, don't you?"

"What in the heck did *we* do?" Becky Jean and Carleen, feeling innocent, looked at one another and turned up their palms in confusion. Lila Mae told them if they hadn't been telling tall tales about the big truck accident in Texas, none of this might have happened.

With a big curved sky—black and cold and studded with flickering golden stars and hazy planets—wrapped around them, they drove through town after town, passing Edgar Dill's Famous Luncheonette, E-Z Loan (TIRED OF BEING BROKE UNTIL PAYDAY?), and the TwiLight Drive In. Lila Mae seemed to be back to normal, because when they passed the theater, she said, "Oh, look—they're playin' *Come Back, Little Sheba* and *The Robe.* I still ain't seen either one of them."

Juanita and Lila Mae traded driving shifts so the other could doze. When it was Juanita's turn to rest, they pushed the front seat all the way back, and within seconds her huge, boxy chest was heaving up and down and she was snoring like a vacuum cleaner.

Although Lila Mae was pooped, as it turned out, she hardly

got one wink of sleep. Whenever Juanita took the wheel, she was either racing like a Kentucky Derby winner or putt-putt-putting along like a clunky parade float. As a result, Lila Mae spent most of her time slamming down on an imaginary brake pedal and hinting that if you happened to be going too fast and had to stop suddenly, you would be involved in something called a jackknife. "At least that's what I've been told by many *experts.*" Juanita simply said, "Is that so?"

In spite of a warning sign saying SLOW TO 15 MPH, she took a set of railroad tracks at fifty miles an hour, which made everybody's head hit the car roof. When a Studebaker—already going ten miles over the limit—wasn't going fast enough for the waitress, she slammed the horn three times, yelled, "Move it, you damned slowpoke!" then roared past the car.

With her hand tapping against her chest in an imitation of her heartbeat, Lila Mae glanced in the backseat, her jittery eyes circling around in their sockets, and traded nervous looks with the two girls.

Chapter Seven

At dawn, they stopped at Arroyo Grande General Store, a small country market with a fluttering American flag and a hog pen with a half-dozen oinking pigs. The owner, who had just flipped the OPEN sign when they pulled up, rolled up blinds and dusted mason jars as a blond spaniel scampered behind her. Claiming she was afraid the engine might die, Lila Mae kept the motor running while Juanita and Benny ducked into the shop to make a phone call; unlikely as it was, she was petrified that Ramon was still following them.

Across the highway a huge, dilapidated dump truck unloaded dozens of men, women, and children in a field. They were dressed in denim overalls, faded flannel shirts, and frayed straw hats that covered their faces. Within seconds, they had scattered through the rows of fruits and vegetables, their woven baskets perched on their hips, one arm circling the basket, the other picking the crop.

"How'd you like to be in their shoes?" Lila Mae cracked. "And you kids think *you* got it so bad."

Becky Jean, pressing her forehead against the frosty glass, had a pained, heavy heart as she watched the laborers—with their shoulders sloped and their leathery faces pinched—stoop over to gather the food. The workers looked cold and weary and exhausted already, and it was only five-thirty a.m. She also wondered if it was really okay for those kids to be doing that

80

type of work, since some of them seemed no older than Carleen and Billy Cooper.

When she noticed that Juanita and Benny had completely disappeared inside the store, she said—only half-jokingly—"Quick, now's our chance to get away."

"Rebecca Jean Wooten! Now, I have talked to you until I'm blue in the face, and I just don't seem to get through. You know as well as I do that we can't just leave the poor woman stranded like that. Besides"—Lila Mae saw the break-the-news-opportunity she'd been waiting for—"Juanita has some business dealings and I promised to help her out."

" 'Business dealings'? Where are they, the North Pole?" Becky Jean belly-flopped over the front seat and quickly swiped the map from the sun visor.

"What, may I ask, are you doin'? Give me that!" Lila Mae lunged for the road map.

"I'm keeping track of where we are for my new geography teacher, just like you told me." Becky Jean unfolded the map to see how bad the situation really was but mostly to shake her mother up. "We should tell Daddy, too, don't you think? We could call him *right now*."

"All right, Miss Smarty Pants." Lila Mae narrowed her eyes. "If you must know everything, Juanita has a sick little girl, a little girl who's so sick that it'll be a miracle if she lives to see the light of day." Then, swiping a glance at the general store, she said, "And anyways, we're low on cash—practically flat broke, if the truth be known. Juanita give me money to drive her to see her little girl, that is if she ain't already dead and gone. She's in somethin' called an iron lung. You kids wouldn't know what them is, since you're too busy readin' the funny papers and hanging around soda fountains."

Carleen asked if Juanita's girl was something like Mary Rose Lutes, the sick girl who used to live next door. Mary Rose hadn't been in the hospital, but she had a deformity and was

confined to a crib in a bedroom of her parents' home. Lila Mae
told her, "It's completely different but just as serious."

"Well, what *is* it?" Becky Jean insisted. "What's the big
mystery?"

To shut her daughter up, Lila Mae dug into the side pocket
of Juanita's tote bag and fished out a photograph, waving it
triumphantly in front of Becky Jean's nose. "Here! Now does
Her Royal Highness believe me?"

Becky Jean held the picture in her hand, staring at the
cracked sepia snapshot of the little Indian girl. Just as Juanita
had described, her brown nugget eyes were rolled into the back
of her skull and she was in some big metal thing with wires and
tubes and plugs hanging out of it. In the corner, written at a
diagonal in ballpoint pen, was "Rosita, 1958." She had to admit
that she was somewhat surprised. As unlikely as it would have
been for Juanita to exaggerate her daughter's condition, it
wasn't at all unusual for Lila Mae to get involved in some big
"illness" that was no more serious than a hangnail.

"Are ya happy now?" Lila Mae asked. "Well, are ya?"

"I'm not saying the girl's not sick," Becky Jean said. "But
why do *we* always end up in the middle of everyone's problems?
We're not the Salvation Army, *or* Greyhound Bus. And what
about the Grand Canyon? You promised you'd take us."

"Is that all you kids can think about, the Grand Canyon?
Your father made this same exact trip in three days and I can't
be stoppin' every five minutes for this and that and the other
thing. He'll have the FBI lookin' for us pretty soon, I reckon!"

"What about those caves where Jesse James hid out?" Becky
Jean needled her. "You promised Billy Cooper you'd take him
there, too."

"Them was way back five or six states ago, and they was
closed up for the night," Lila Mae huffed. "Why'd you have to
bring them up for?"

Billy Cooper kicked the seat in front of him and began to
cry. Becky Jean wrapped her arm around her brother and kissed

the top of his head. "You visit relatives you haven't seen in years and talk to total strangers for hours on end, and we can't even go to the Grand Canyon? Besides, you said this trip would be exciting and educational. 'Get Your Kiiiiicks on Rooooute Sixxx-teeee Sixxxx!' " She mimicked her mother's corny rendition of the well-worn song. "So, it's just not fair that we can't see one of the Seven Wonders of the World."

Although Becky Jean wasn't sure she had her geographical facts straight, nobody in the car questioned them. And it wasn't that she didn't feel sorry for Juanita and Rosita, but she couldn't help it—she *still* wanted to see the Grand Canyon. Turning to Carleen and Billy Cooper for support, she said, "We don't want to visit a stranger who's in the hospital, *do* we?"

Shutting her *Little Lulu* comic book, Carleen folded her arms tightly to her chest and copied her older sister. "Becky Jean's right. . . . We don't know that iron-lung girl from Adam."

"Not you too! I can*not* believe my ears." Lila Mae shook her head in disbelief. "Kids who don't care for the underprivileged and poor are no kids of mine. These people need *help*."

"We've done our share." Becky Jean reminded Lila Mae that they'd gone to at least four funerals right before they left Kentucky. If they had heard "O, Death Where Is Thy Sting?" once, they'd heard it a hundred times. "And what about Mary Rose? Who took care of her for months?"

"If I was you, I wouldn't be bringin' up that subject. You know what I mean, young lady."

"We want to go to the Grand Canyon!" They pumped their fists in the air and bounced up and down on their bent legs, and Billy Cooper even shot a few rounds of his cap gun. "WE WANT TO GO TO THE GRAND CANYON! WE WANT TO GO—"

"*Now* look what you've started," Lila Mae griped. "First of all, there's something called common courtesy. And you kids is gonna learn it, so help me Hannah! Second of all, we're gonna visit that poor little girl in the iron lung, no ifs, ands, or buts. Now . . ." Lila Mae paused. "Along the way, Juanita's gonna sell some of her jewelry. Sooo . . ." She wet her pinky finger and smoothed her arched eyebrow, peeking at the kids' faces in the mirror. "That means we'll be a-visitin' some *souvenir stands*. If you kids want to stay in the car, that's just fine and dandy by me."

"Souvenir shops," Becky Jean snapped. "I'll bet." She figured it was all a dirty trick to get them to shut up. Lila Mae would probably let them browse through some dumb head-dresses and tom-toms for as long as it took the souvenir shop owners to turn down Juanita's cruddy turquoise jewelry. Whatever it was that she had up her sleeve, though, Lila Mae managed to settle them down for the moment.

Finally, Juanita and Benny, plucking the strings on a pink bakery box, tapped on the car window and said, "Surprise!" As Juanita passed out chocolate cream donuts, putting each one on a small, round doily, she said she'd just called the St. Ignatius Memorial Hospital and ("Hallelujah!") Rosita was holding her own. The jubilant woman looked to the heavens in gratitude, clasped both hands together, and pumped them. "Course, that don't mean she couldn't take a turn for the worse, though. It just means I got a few days 'stead of a few hours."

Being that was the case, Juanita told Lila Mae, there was no need for her to be a fly in the ointment; she'd take the bus or hitchhike or something. "You and the kids should just go on your merry way . . . especially now that I'm goin' to Bismarck. . . . I *would* be happy to give you more money, but I know you got a deadline."

"Hitchhike? Why, you'll do no such a thing! Why, we wouldn't *dream* of leavin' you stranded out here in the wild blue yonder, would we, kids?" Lila Mae burned holes into Carleen and Becky Jean. "*Would* we?"

Since Lila Mae wouldn't accept no for an answer, Juanita caved in, and pretty soon it was all settled. Immediately the women turned the tables with their bright-side-of-the-situation and new-leaf talk, saying if they drove straight through, why, they could easily arrive in Bismarck in a day and a half with no harm done.

"But we want to go to the Grand Canyon, lady." Billy Cooper plunged over Juanita's shoulder and stuck his face next to hers. "Our mama won't let us."

Juanita creased her eyebrows and threw Lila Mae an unfit-mother look. "You mean you kids ain't never seen the Grand Canyon? Now that's a *pity*."

Benny, suddenly as animated as Peppy the Clown, joined in, telling them he even knew a secret way—a long, mysterious, winding road with caves and fossils and waterfalls and rock formations and gemstones and, best of all, ancient, sacred Indian burial grounds. "You ain't never seen anything like this place, ever before!"

"A secret way?" Carleen, her eyes shiny, goggly spheres, said, "Honest?"

"Benny, you just don't know when to shut up, do you?" Juanita grumbled to her big-mouthed son. "He'll build it up so much, you'uns are bound to be disappointed. . . ."

"Does that mean we're going?" Becky Jean pressed, her eyes switching from woman to woman.

"Mama, if Juanita says it's okay with her, is it okay with you? Pretty please? Pretty please with sugar on top?" Carleen joined her palms together like a cathedral, pretending to pray.

Finally, Lila Mae rattled her mahogany curls and sighed. "I suppose I won't get a moment's peace until I say okay."

"We're really going? Honest???" Becky Jean and Carleen raised their fists in victory and hooted in delight.

"Lordy, you don't have to break my eardrums! Yes, we're really goin' to the Grand Canyon!" Lila Mae hollered in one nonstop gulp. As if to seal the promise, Juanita turned around and snapped one round, brown eye in a wink.

The children stomped their feet, waved their arms in the air, and shouted "Yippeeeee!" with the enthusiasm of a Pentecostal congregation. "We're really going to the Grand Canyon!"

Suddenly, Juanita bent over and hunted through her tote bag. When she found what she wanted, she handed Becky Jean a trio of snapshots. "This here is *my* little girl, Becky Jean. Her name is Rosita." Swallowing a lump, her jowls settled in a sour crease. "I reckon she'll never be fifteen like you. . . ."

Becky Jean studied the photographs, pretending she'd never seen the little girl before. "She looks real sweet, Juanita. She's pretty, too. I'd really like to meet her sometime." Even though Lila Mae told them were was no connection between Rosita and Mary Rose Lutes, there was nonetheless something about the Indian girl that reminded Becky Jean of their next-door neighbor: maybe the small, hard crescent lines rimming their young eyes, or the sad shadow of death reflected in the very pores of their skin.

Even as she looked at the photograph of Rosita, the aroma of Mary Rose—flannel, talcum powder, and warm, curdled milk—and her haunting eyes, like the dead glass eyes of an antique doll, cleaved through her.

In the front seat Lila Mae was giving Juanita pointers on what to do for her daughter. Maybe she could set her up at home: "We had next-door neighbors that done that with their little girl. . . . Becky Jean even looked after her for a while. Course, I don't know your situation. I'm just sayin' there's other things to consider."

Wasn't it just like her mother to spoil the Grand Canyon and secret way excitement by bringing up Mary Rose Lutes? Surely there would have been a way for Lila Mae to discuss Rosita without mentioning their next-door neighbor? Did Lila Mae really think it was easy for Becky Jean to listen to all that without feeling sad? Any minute now her mother would shift from medical pointers to the unabridged version of how her daughter, try as she might to teach her manners and good breeding and to build her character, embarrassed her family and the church to tears, time after time after time.

Of course Lila Mae probably wouldn't tell Juanita the whole story: how the Sunshine Circle Girls, a group of teenagers who did good deeds in the community, had been hoodwinked into showing up at church one evening thinking they were planning Bethany Baptist's upcoming mother-daughter fashion show. Naturally, she wouldn't mention that the Sunshine Girls, who usually returned library books or walked an elderly person's dog, were supposed to be the cure-all for Irma and Jimmy John Lutes (the new Catholic family, which Bethany Baptist was desperate to convert). The Luteses needed a responsible young woman to stay with their little handicapped girl for two hours each day while Irma Lutes went to the market and post office and dry cleaners.

Becky Jean had made the mistake of raising her hand and asking, "Is it possible for *us* to go to the market for Mrs. Lutes and let *her* stay with the girl?" Immediately, Lila Mae had hopped up and said, "That'll be enough, miss!" But it was too late. The Sunshine Girls were already saying, "Yeah! That's a great idea!" Then Mrs. Weatherspoon, the minister's wife, got into things, thumping the podium and hollering, "Girls! Quiet! This is *not* a carnival arcade!"

Of course, Becky Jean hadn't meant it the way it came out; she was just looking for other ways to handle the situation. Before the evening was over, as the women placed chocolate chip cookies and strawberry punch on a banquet table and chitchatted about this and that, the Sunshine Circle Girls were asked to sign a clipboard and put down the days they would be available. Lila Mae made sure Becky Jean was the first name on the list. And nobody would have believed Becky Jean if she had told them she was going to volunteer anyway.

Before any of the Sunshine Girls showed up for duty, the neighborhood was atwitter. Lila Mae, who had befriended Irma Lutes, filled in all the details for her curious friends and family who wanted to know what they were in for. "Irma told me how she'd had a chance to do away with her—you know, put Mary Rose in a home somewhere but she and her husband, Jimmy John, talked it over and they kept her. I hear they even refused offers from the carnival . . . Irma said them promoters called day and night. I believe it's them same people who have that boy with the lobster claws for hands, I think they wanted the girl. It's not Barnum and Bailey but it's another big outfit."

Sue Ellen Sweeney said she had seen Mary Rose's pear-shaped head and it was "Bigger than a watermelon!" It was so enormous, she told them, that the girl couldn't even stand up, even if there weren't other things wrong with her . . . which, of course, there were. And then, after playing up the deformity as if it were a major sight, one that thousands would stand in lines wrapped around the block to see, Lila Mae had told her children that they should act like the girl was perfectly normal, that Mary Rose was like a dog who could sense what people were feeling and saying to her even though she couldn't communicate back.

Lila Mae probably didn't realize it, but every time Becky Jean heard Mary Rose's name, she might as well have been sitting in that small, humid bedroom with its tranquil lilac glow and the thin swatch of light under the door. She could still picture poor Mary Rose in the crib swathed in pink flannel, the mobile suspended over her bed, the prints of the Virgin Mary—hooded blue cloak, crucifix, transparent throbbing heart and all.

Lila Mae had been shocked when Mrs. Lutes called one day to tell her what a wonderful daughter she had, that the other church girls made Mary Rose feel uncomfortable. "Oh, they show up when they're supposed to and all that . . . but your Becky Jean, she even got her to smile." She was wondering if they could make some type of permanent arrangement. When Lila Mae hung up, she swung around—a puzzled frown on her face—and said to Roy, "Well, you won't believe what that was all about."

And Lila Mae didn't know that instead of talking on the phone or reading *Seventeen* magazine, as the other girls had done, Becky Jean would sing "Rockabye Baby" and read "Goldilocks and the Three Bears" to the little girl. She even brought animal crackers, which Mary Rose sucked on until the miniature lions and tigers became smaller and smaller. Becky Jean would turn the metal tab on the musical mobile, watching the little girl's wise, glazed eyes as they followed the dancing lambs.

Mrs. Lutes always brought Becky Jean a snack—tuna sandwiches and limeade—and every Friday she would leave with two five-dollar bills rolled in her palm. As Becky Jean turned the doorknob to leave, she'd swivel around, waggle her fingers, and whisper, "Bye-bye, Mary Rose." The little girl would open her tiny mouth and emit one small bird cheep.

One afternoon Becky Jean called to tell Mrs. Lutes she would be late and although she promised to be over in a few hours, she never ended up going. When Glen called and told her to meet him at Klink's for a hamburger, she was embarrassed to tell him she was supposed to visit the sick girl. She meant to call Irma Lutes to tell her something came up, but still she didn't know why she never did.

Lila Mae, pouncing on her the minute she got home, said, "Rebecca Jean Wooten! I hope you're happy with yourself. That poor little girl waited all afternoon for you. If I was you, I'd go over there this minute and explain. I ain't got the slightest idea what to tell the church people." Then she gave Glen, who was nervously jingling the coins in his pocket, some leftover nasty looks. She reeled around and closed the door with a disapproving slam.

Although Irma Lutes told Becky Jean she understood, she also mentioned that she happened to have had *very* important business to attend to on that particular day. She also said she'd call Becky Jean when she needed her again, but her arms were

woven across her concave chest and her eyes glowed with dis-
dain. Before she left, Becky Jean managed to waggle her fingers
and whisper, "Bye-bye, Mary Rose," but Irma Lutes had already wheeled the little girl's crib to the other side of the room.

Weeks later, when Becky Jean saw a mobile at Hutt's Five &
Dime, she paid for it out of her baby-sitting money, wrapped
it in soft, baby pink paper, and called Irma Lutes to see if it
would be all right to visit Mary Rose that afternoon. When she
heard the woman's hard, brusque voice, Becky lost her nerve
and hung up the phone.

Not long after that, Lila Mae got up from the dinner table
to answer the phone and after a few seconds, she stumbled into
the dining room and said, "Well, it looks like Mary Rose is
finally gone."

Quietly, Becky Jean dropped her fork, bunched up her napkin, placed it on the table, and excused herself. With her heart
booming, she leaped into her bedroom and fell onto her bed.
She dug her fingernails into the bedspread, gathering it into
messy swirls, and tore the lace off a decorative pillow. "I'm
sorry, Mary Rose." Her body sucked in one long, hiccough of
a sob. Then she took the scissors and threw them at her wall,
taking a chunk out of the plaster and rattling the pictures.

When her father pounded on her locked door and asked
what in the devil was going on in there, she told him that she
didn't feel well and to leave her alone. "Stop carrying on like a
screaming meemie, then!"

In the living room, Becky Jean heard her mother say, "Don't
that beat all?" Irma Lutes had told her that the service for Mary
Rose was private and that only very close family friends and
relatives were being invited. Lila Mae said, "That's funny, I
thought we *were* close friends."

Handing the picture back to Juanita and taking one last look
at Rosita's cadaver eyes, Becky Jean turned her head to the window and stared outside at the lonely, shadowy vista. As the kids
sang "On top of old Smoky . . . all covered with snow . . ." and

the red plains of New Mexico closed in on them, she shut her eyes.

*S*oon the sun began to rise, a buttery yellow glow rolling across the acres of desert. It swept across the sky, and like a blaze of metallic gold, it bounced off the road signs and the Packard's chromework. Low, fleecy clouds, like peach meringue, drifted across the sky.

Lila Mae cocked her head and assessed the weather situation through the top of the windshield. "Well, it looks like we're gonna have ourselves a beautiful day." Billy Cooper yawned and stretched his arms in the air while Carleen wiggled around and asked what time it was. Juanita, asleep in the front seat, made little smacking sounds with her lips. When Lila Mae tapped her arm and told her they were almost there, she popped up like a jack-in-the-box and gripped the dashboard, looking confused.

At the Silverado Cafe, they bought hot coffee, chocolate milk, and glazed donuts and took their picture standing next to a wooden Indian. Before long, they were all nestled in their little cubbyholes, passing around sweet rolls, snapping their fingers and tapping their feet, singing, "If I knew you were comin', I'd've baked a cake, how'dja do? how'dja do? how'dja do?"

Chapter Eight

Twenty miles outside Springer, New Mexico, they approached a huge billboard for CHIEF FEATHERHORSE'S TRADING POST. Scattered across the sign were clusters of Indian symbols and paintings of handwoven rugs and jewelry and tomahawks. Every five miles, they'd pass another sign with a picture of the chief—a majestic, spectacular profile of a man in warpaint and a rainbow-hued headdress, with a backdrop of thunderhead clouds and a slogan proclaiming him "the Friendly Indian." Lila Mae slowed the Packard and asked Juanita if that was the place.

"Yep, that's it, all right." Juanita rubbed a powder puff across her face in big, sloppy circles, then smeared her violet lips together. "You get your stuff together now, Benny. We're almost there." Earlier, Juanita had told Lila Mae that selling her jewelry was just one reason for stopping at Chief Featherhorse's. She was actually hoping to dump Benny there for a while. But now she had changed her tune. "Ha!" she snorted like a horse, and clicked her compact shut. "Who am I kiddin'? I got as good a chance of them keepin' the boy as Mr. Louis Armstrong has of waking up a white man."

"That's your uncle?" Billy Cooper gawked at the enticing billboard and quizzed Benny. "What a lucky dog."

"Yeah, what's so great about it?" Benny frowned, a crooked sneer.

Although Becky Jean was excited about the possibility of getting rid of one of the intruders, she was upset that they might not go to the Grand Canyon by the secret road if Benny wasn't with them. Now she didn't know if the trip would be botched up or what.

They pulled into the gravel parking lot in front of a long cement building emblazoned with red, yellow, and green zigzags and crowned by a trio of stuffed buffalo heads. Strange plants shaped like abstract pinwheels shot up here and there, and a big painted sign that said YOU ARE HERE! CHIEF FEATHERHORSE GENUINE SOUVENIRS ran across the rooftop. Framing the front door were a totem pole, a carved wooden Indian, and a stray dog sniffing at a melting Popsicle.

In a weedy adjoining lot was a dilapidated shack with a wrinkled tin roof that said LIVE POISONOUS RATTLESNAKES. A group of teenagers—four guys in black leather and ducktail hairdos and three girls with beehives and yards of crinoline—stood in front of it. The girls licked strawberry ice cream cones while the guys tried to pick the lock on the snake cage.

Lila Mae marched Billy Cooper over to the snakes so he could see the cardboard shingles with descriptions that said:

WESTERN DIAMONDBACK RATTLER—EASILY IRRITATED

EASTERN DIAMONDBACK—TEMPERAMENTAL

BLUE RACER—AGGRESSIVE

She let it sink in for a minute, then wagged her finger at the boy, saying, "Now, I don't want you anywhere near them snakes, you hear? See that sign? It says, 'Do Not Touch Glass.'" Lila Mae tapped her fingernail against the window four times and stared at the teenagers as if to lecture them, too.

Billy Cooper, his face a tiny, moody oval, kicked a dirt clod and muttered, "All right."

"I mean it, now! You aggravate them poor snakes and they'll just break right out and come *git* you!" Lila Mae lurched forward and stomped her foot when she said "git." Billy jumped backwards and flinched.

Anxious to test their mother's promise about souvenirs, Becky Jean and Carleen were already inside sizing up all the possibilities—vats of rose quartz and citrine geodes and flinty arrows, metal stands caressing glass beads, and racks of fringed suede skirts. Lila Mae studied the round glass pie dish at a lunch counter where the waitresses wore buckskin skirts and headbands with red feathers. Billy Cooper was panting, running up and down all the aisles desperate to locate Chief Featherhorse, while Benny stood at a glass container with arrowheads, which said, ALL ITEMS IN THIS CASE IS GENUINE INDIAN ARTIFACTS. He slipped the top off, rubbed the rocks together, and in no time had sparks flying from two arrowheads.

Juanita grabbed Billy's arm and said, "I gotta big surprise for YOU, sonny boy!" Planting her hand over his eyes, she guided him down dusty, narrow aisles to a dingy cubicle in the back of the store. She removed her sweaty palm and pointed to Chief Featherhorse, standing in front of a brass birdcage. He threw a handful of seed to his parakeets, wiped his hands together, then stooped down to smile at Billy.

"Billy Cooper," Juanita said officially, her hands making curlicues in the air. "I'd like you to meet Chief Featherhorse."

The chief tugged at the string on Billy's cowboy hat and said, "Hi there, little boy."

Something definitely didn't seem right to Billy Cooper. The Indian chief on all the billboards had burnished skin and coffee-black eyes, his hair hanging in a flowing, velvety blanket down his back. He was wearing an elaborate feathered headdress and a beaded jacket. *This* man had greasy, stringy hair and skin that was waxy, like the fake fruit sold in Miss Maple's Gift Nook. To top it off, his stomach drooped over his stained Levi's like a wrinkly kangaroo pouch, and his eyeglasses were held together with electrical tape.

"You're not Chief Featherhorse," Billy Cooper snarled.

"You're not even an Indian." Then he doubled his fist and socked the chief in the leg.

Thinking maybe it would make a difference, the chief grabbed his headdress, which dropped to the ground like a bridal train. He put it on his head and said, "There!" wheeling around like a fashion model. But Billy Cooper, his arms kneaded across his pounding chest, didn't budge. Finally Featherhorse threw up his hands in the air and said, "I'm sorry, little boy."

"Billy Cooper Wooten!" Lila Mae, suddenly wise to the situation, swatted Billy's behind. She yanked him up by one arm and let him dangle like a fish from a hook. "Juanita, Mr. Featherhorse, I am just beside myself with embarrassment!" She gave Billy Cooper's arm one final jerk and his behind one departing punch. "You go sit outside . . . you hear now?"

"Kids'll drive ya crazy, won't they?" Juanita sighed. "If I had it to do all over agin, I just don't know. . . . Oh, well, let's get this business over with."

The two women waddled through the store, toting Juanita's jewelry in deerskin cases. They hoisted them on a glass counter and began unfolding pouches, piece by piece. Juanita lined her necklaces and bracelets up like tin soldiers, but Lila Mae arranged hers in what she claimed was a more "fetching" sunburst design. When they'd emptied all the bags, Juanita elbowed Lila Mae, crossed her fingers for luck, and whispered, "Here goes."

The chief, sticking his bifocals on the tip of his bumpy nose, peered at the silver beads and squash blossom necklaces and wide turquoise bangles. His eyes jittered from piece to piece as Juanita nervously arranged and rearranged it all, waiting for the chief's reaction. When he asked her to quote him some prices, he cupped his hand to his ear and said "*How* much?" as if he couldn't possibly have heard right. Then he asked Juanita to tell him the amounts once more (just to see if she had the nerve to quote the same outrageous price twice), and Juanita fell into the chief's trap, telling him a lower amount on each item. Even then, he said the prices sounded "awfully steep." When she reminded him that everything was handmade, he simply muttered, "Um, I see . . . I see."

In any case, they were getting nowhere until Lila Mae got a bright idea. She snagged a lady who was milling around the postcard carousel and asked her if she could give her a hand with something. The middle-aged woman had more puckers and creases than Winston Churchill, but Lila Mae trilled like a canary and said, "Miss, would you mind modeling this earring for Mr. Featherhorse? I wouldn't do it no justice. I'm afraid aqua just ain't my color. . . ."

The woman clipped on the earrings reluctantly, then she looked into space with a stony expression; tapping her hand impatiently with an unpaid postcard. Lila Mae twisted and turned, stroking her neck as if in deep thought. Finally, a friend of the woman's placed her forefinger on her lip and said, "You know something, Verna? Those suit you."

Jumping on the bandwagon, Lila Mae said, "Don't they, though?"

"Do you really think so?" Verna pursed her persimmon lips and studied herself. At long last, she removed the turquoise hoops and dropped them into the chief's hand. "I know I shouldn't. . . ." She opened her coin purse defiantly. "But I'm going to anyway."

Before long, more customers were snooping over Juanita's shoulder as she unwrapped piece after piece. Lila Mae waited for Verna to leave, then recruited another elderly woman—this one with a dowager's hump—to model a different pair of earrings. "My! Don't you look pretty!" Lila Mae exclaimed. The woman wore glasses as thick as the bottom of a crystal tumbler and all you could see were two blurry orbs, but Lila Mae said, "Juanita, would you lookee here at her *beautiful* eyes! This turquoise matches them perfect." She told yet another woman— this one sporting a thick brown mole with a coarse hair curling out of it—that a coral necklace brought out the radiant color in her cheeks and the ginger tones of her lustrous hair. The woman, who was a real fussbudget, kept saying, "These prices are higher than a cat's back!" but in the end, she bought two silver bangle bracelets for her granddaughter and a tourmaline ring.

The chief licked his wide, flat thumb, flipping over each dollar, one by one. "Now, ain't that somethin'!" he exclaimed. "Over five hundred dollars, just like that." Slipping Juanita the cash, he scribbled the name of another shop up north that would probably buy more of the jewelry. She tucked the money in a cove at her breastbone and adjusted her bodice. "Looks like you shoulda left that rascal a long time ago, Juanita," the chief said. "Probably just as well . . . let's face it, he'll end up back in the tank."

Lila Mae had her ear cocked, still itching to know what Ramon had been in for. With all the references to tanks and slammers, it seemed like Juanita wouldn't mind her asking. Maybe Lila Mae would get up her nerve one day.

At the lunch counter, they snacked on cactus juice and pistachio nuts, and since Juanita had promised Lila Mae some traveling money, Lila Mae, in a weak moment, told the children they could each spend two dollars. With her money, Becky Jean bought a locket and a miniature cedar chest with a cactus blossom and "New Mexico" stamped on it, and Carleen chose an Indian doll with glassy black eyes, propped on a heart-shaped stand. Billy Cooper tried to talk Lila Mae into a hula hoop, but she said, "That's all we need!" She told him he could buy one of the hoops anywhere, so he got a rifle and a tomahawk instead. When the kids made fun of Lila Mae for trying on an embroidered blouse and beaded squaw moccasins, she said, "When in Rome . . . !" In the postcard section, which sold cards from all over the country, Lila Mae bought a desert scene from Needles, California, which she planned to send to Roy, just so he'd think they were farther along on their trip than they really were.

Juanita and Benny didn't buy anything, because they were saving their money for a fresh start. But Lila Mae felt sorry for Benny and asked him if he wanted a gun, too. "No, ma'am," he replied, "I want me a toy rattlesnake," so Lila Mae bought him one.

"That's awful nice of you, Lila Mae. Say thank you to Mrs. Wooten, now, Benny." Juanita slugged him in the back for a response.

"Thank you, ma'am." Benny traced circles on the linoleum with the square toe of his boot, then he and Billy Cooper took off with their loot.

"You know, I believe that's the most polite boy I've ever met," Lila Mae remarked. "I really believe he is."

"It's not often that you find a hoodlum with good manners," Becky Jean curled her hand over her mouth and whispered to Carleen.

"You girls better not be cookin' up anything," Lila Mae warned. "I mean it."

Chief Featherhorse gave Lila Mae a special discount on the souvenirs and even threw in Benny's rubber snake. When it came time to pay for everything, though, Lila Mae reached in her pocketbook but came up empty-handed. "Hmm, that's funny. . . ." She knitted her eyebrows together and dug inside once more, this time setting each item on the counter. "Well, there's that rose lipstick I been huntin' for," she muttered, placing the fluted gold tube on the glass case and extracting Necco wafers, Irene Gaye's rattle, a wadded-up Kleenex, and an ancient address book held together by rubber bands.

"Now, where do you suppose that wallet is?" she sighed, rummaging around once more. This time a stray safety pin stuck her finger. "Ow!" she squealed, sucking the bead of blood and shaking her hand in the air. Practically in tears, she once again pawed frantically through the disheveled contents for the billfold, turning her pocketbook upside down. "It just ain't here! . . . *Now* what am I gonna do?"

"Retrace your steps," Juanita advised. "That's what I do when I misplace something."

"Let's see. . . ." Lila Mae scowled at the ceiling, rubbing her lips in thought. "I had it at Lulu's, that's the last time I honestly remember seein' it. Then I paid at your place, but I took that from my change purse. And you got the donuts at the Silverado. You know what?" She snapped her fingers. "I'll bet that cowboy at your restaurant lifted it. Yes, I'd say he's got it."

"What cowboy?" Juanita replaited her hair, then tucked a silver-and-coral comb behind her braid. "You mean *Orin?* I don't think it was Orin took it. Orin's a good man."

"I'm a good judge of character, too, and I didn't see it comin'. Although—" she paused, her eyes like suspicious searchlights as they rolled from side to side "now that I think of it, it did seem awfully fishy that he come on so strong, gettin' all palsy-walsy with the kids and then *poof!* he's gone." Lila Mae said, "Yes!" it was all coming back to her now. "He also set his ten-gallon hat down right over my purse—that give him plenty of chances to slip my wallet out . . . practically in front of my eyes!" Lila Mae said she was an absolute featherbrain not to have seen it coming. She made a cradle with her hands and buried her face in it, her mood shifting from anger to desperation.

"I don't know." Juanita squinted in thought. "I'd say my boy took it before Orin . . . I really would."

"Benny?" Lila Mae shrieked in mock horror. "Heavens! He'd be the *last* person I'd suspect."

"He don't steal," Becky Jean whispered in Carleen's ear. "*Fire's* his specialty."

"What are you two up to? If you girls is hidin' that wallet, just give it back to me this minute!" Lila Mae stamped her foot and turned to Juanita. "They ain't happy unless I'm at my wit's end."

Becky Jean said, "Don't look at *me*."

"I'll get to the bottom of this." Juanita snatched the money from her dress to pay for the souvenirs and told Becky Jean and Carleen to check the Packard. "Now, let's go find that little juvenile delinquent!"

They marched up and down all the aisles; they checked the bathrooms and even asked the waitresses if they'd seen the boys, but nobody had. A man shoving his arm through an alpaca sweater said he'd bet they were outside, where everybody else seemed to be. Lila Mae said, "You know, I thought it was kinda empty in here," and asked Juanita what in the world she supposed was going on out there.

There wasn't a soul in the parking lot itself, but a huge, noisy crowd was gathered around the rattlesnake cages. Lila Mae and Juanita bumped into a man wearing a shirt decorated with cigarette labels who stuck both hands up like a stop sign and said, "Ladies, I wouldn't go over there if I was you. Some foolish boys are horsin' around and about to cause trouble."

Lila Mae hoped against hope that it was those teenagers who'd been fiddling around with the locks, but she had already spotted Billy Cooper. Standing with his head smashed right against the glass, his face was a distortion of flattened, ghoulish features. His thumbs were stuck in his ears and he was wiggling his fingers at the snakes. She could see Benny, too, jiggling his rubber snake in front of the cages and making loud, godawful hissing noises. Nobody could believe their eyes when, out of the clear blue sky, Benny grabbed the sides of a container and began to shake it.

Lila Mae pounded her fist to her breast and exclaimed, "Heavens to Betsy!" Juanita growled, "Those little idiots! I'm gonna wring Benny's neck." The women zoomed toward the dense, restless crowd, bulldozing their way through the platoon of bodies like twin Sherman tanks. They were hoping to yank their boys away like it never happened; but just when they got to the fringe of the group, they heard a creaky bump of a noise.

Before they could blink, the door of the container flew wide open. "Oh, lordy, Juanita!" Lila Mae clawed her friend's sleeve nervously.

"If them things bust out and get to crawlin' around, we'll all be goners." Juanita told Lila Mae to hurry up and get her kids and she'd find the chief. "Where's Benny???" She hit her bosom, shaded her eyes, and spun around like a carousel, looking high and low for her son. "Oh, where *is* he? He was just *here!*"

"Billy Cooper! Carleen Raye! Becky Jean! Who's got the baby?!" Lila Mae screamed. "Where the devil are you??" She started to run left, then right, then left again, her arms circling like a windmill.

Out of the corner of her eye, Lila Mae could see what seemed to be dozens of huge, speckled, grotesque snakes. They looked like poisonous vacuum-cleaner hoses as they crawled down the sides of the open container, jumping to the ground, going every which way. People were screaming and shrieking and scrambling for cover.

"Billy Cooper!" She chased after her son, huffing and puffing. "Git over here!" She grabbed his sleeve and they skidded toward the Packard, but it was locked and she couldn't find her keys right away. She circled the car, rattling each doorknob, but it was drum tight. "Oh, I could just brain you, young man! Now what do we do?"

Some man in coveralls, whom Lila Mae didn't know from the man in the moon, honked his horn and motioned her to jump in his Plymouth . . . *fast.* The man, who said his name was Lucky O'Dell, had corn-kernel teeth, a whitish-yellow beard like a billy goat's, and clutched a bag of chewing tobacco.

"Thank you, sir! Thank you!" Lila Mae shoved her son into the backseat and slammed the door like he was a shirt being thrown into a clothes dryer. "Now, Billy Cooper, you—you stay right where you are with this nice man and don't budge. I gotta find your sisters."

"Lady," the man tugged her arm, "git in here right now or you'll be sorry."

"But I cain't, sir, I got other kids." Lila Mae jerked away, leaving the man holding her empty coat sleeve.

"What are you gonna do, woman? Go out and git yourself bit??" Reaching across the car, he yanked her inside, then barricaded the door and pointed to a spot right in front of them. "You got three rattlers just a few foot away from ya! You sure ain't gonna do your kids any good dead!"

"What should I do, Mr. O'Dell?" Lila Mae, inside the car but with her hand curled around the doorknob and her head spinning in confusion, tried to size up the chaotic situation. "What should I do?"

"You think I ain't got kin here, too?" Mr. O'Dell pointed to a woman with long, spidery limbs. There was a pompom of burnt orange hair peeking out of a paisley scarf, and she was crawling up a ladder to join a small group on the roof. "That there's my wife, Earlene." Lila Mae couldn't tell for sure, but she thought it was the woman she and Juanita had sold an abalone scatter pin to. "Ma'am, your kids'll turn up, too. Now you stay put! You're a derned fool if ya don't!"

By now everyone was dashing for cover, hopping on car fenders and overturned trash bins. Two cars even collided while trying to make a fast getaway, and a panicky woman attempting to escape on foot bolted across the highway, leaving her dumbfounded husband holding two paper cups with hot coffee.

Presiding over all the ruckus was Chief Featherhorse, who stood on the roof of his fancy Buick, one arm up in the air like the Statue of Liberty, the other fist holding his hatchet. "Keep calm, everybody!" he shouted. "Keep calm! Just stay where you are. . . . Nobody move!"

Lila Mae fidgeted, her heart crashing against her chest as she fiendishly scanned the crowd. "'Western diamondback rattler, easily irritated' . . . like heck! If that ain't an understatement, I don't know what is," she wisecracked. "They got no business displayin' animals like that."

With his hatchet swaying like a pendulum and with his own safety ensured, the chief barked his orders to everybody else. "Just stay where you are! Help'll be here!" When he spotted a couple of snakes coming his way, he threw his ax but didn't hit anything. "No need for alarm!!"

"No need for alarm, my foot!" Lila Mae chortled sarcastically. "I'd like to see his idea of an emergency."

"Boy, ain't that the gospel," O'Dell piped in.

Lila Mae wasn't saying this just because her son had started the whole mess; actually, the situation could have been a lot worse. Not that it was over by a long shot, but it wasn't like the snakes were attacking people right and left, either. In fact, some of them had seemingly vanished into thin air. What she was really worried about was the location of her family. She didn't know how in the world she'd ended up in one spot and all the others somewhere else. By now, she didn't even know what had become of Juanita. At the moment it was the least of her concerns, but there was also the underlying problem of the missing wallet and lost money—every cent she had to her name.

"Well, whatdya know?" O'Dell pointed his pipe toward the entrance. The waitress who'd served them cactus juice was crooked over the top of the totem pole. She had heavy, ink-black hair gathered in a horsetail and cat-eye glasses with rhinestones in the corners. Her arms were wrapped around the pole like a koala bear and she was kicking and screaming for dear life. A long, slimy snake was milling around the base of the pole, like a creature you'd see in the jungle, coiling up and lurching out in every direction. The waitress screamed, "Help me, somebody! Help me!"

"Just hold it!" The chief told the waitress not to budge, that it only egged the snakes on. When she continued to squirm, he threw the woman a schoolmasterish glare. "I said . . . just stay put!"

"Stay put? What's that nincompoop waiting for?" Lila Mae griped to Mr. O'Dell. "And tell me, please, what that poor woman's supposed to do?"

"You see that snake going after her? Now that there's one of yer blue racers," O'Dell said. "They'll chase you just about all over tarnation. You turn around and go after *them* and they'll run the other way!"

"Dear me," Lila Mae fretted. "Why don't somebody tell the poor woman that? Although . . . I don't know that *I'd* slide down and chase the snake. You never know when it turns out to be one that don't do what it's supposed to do."

Mr. O'Dell said he had an idea and told Lila Mae, if she didn't mind, to trade places with him. "I'll stick my head out the winder and you just do what I tell ya. We're gonna git that ugly critter and I ain't whistlin' Dixie." In the background was the first faraway wail of a siren and the deep, sputtering chortle of fire trucks.

Since it wasn't her own car, she told O'Dell she was a little concerned that she might not know what was what, but the man said, "Cars is like people, they all got the same parts." There was an accelerator, a steering wheel, a clutch, and a brake, and that's all she had to know.

When the chief spotted the rescue mission in action, he yelled, "You, lady—stay out of this."

"Well, what is *that* all about?" Lila Mae asked indignantly. "Believe you me, Mr. O'Dell, he sure wasn't tellin' me to get lost when I was sellin' expensive jewelry right and left."

O'Dell, leaning out the window from the waist up, directed Lila Mae, making hand signals and telling her to go a little more to the left or a little more to the right. She went forward, then back, then forward again. A couple of times she had to stop and ask him, "What was that again? I forgot." Once, when she could have sworn the car was in reverse and it wasn't, she floored it and instead of going backward, they lurched forward, accidentally barging into the totem pole. The waitress squawked and pedaled her feet and the chief, who seemed more concerned about the totem pole than he was about the woman in trouble, screeched, "Watch it! That's valuable!"

O'Dell told Lila Mae a few more times ought to do it, so once again she clicked the gear in first, then reverse, then first again, the car undulating and rolling up and down like a caterpillar. At long last, Mr. O'Dell said, "I think we got her! Yep, that just about does it!"

A round of applause sputtered through the crowd and several volunteers helped the woman as she shimmied off the pole to the ground. An Abe Lincoln look-alike with a beard that came to a sharp V tapped on Mr. O'Dell's window and said "Good work" to Lucky and Lila Mae, and a boy with rooster-red hair and trophy-handle ears said, "Thank you, lady, thank you."

Although she tried to play down the heroics, Lila Mae's voice had a happy lilt to it when she said, "Oh, come on now. Anybody could have done it," to a group who said there was just no telling what would have happened to the waitress if someone hadn't taken charge.

Billy Cooper, still coiled in a ball in the backseat, suddenly started to sob. "Oh, hush," Lila Mae scolded him, and tugged at her disheveled skirt. "You started all this. You'd just better hope your sisters are all right." O'Dell turned his head while Lila Mae rolled up her snagged copper stockings, which were in a wilted lump around her ankles. "You hear them sirens? How do you know the girls ain't already *dead*? You git bit by a rattler like that and you might as well pick out your coffin!"

"Now, now." Mr. O'Dell patted Lila Mae's shoulder gingerly. "I'm sure your sisters are fine, son." He opened a box of Chiclets and shook out a piece of gum for Billy, who was dazed and sheet-white, his heart pounding like a wild puppy dog's. Without blinking, he stuck out his hand and took the gum.

It seemed like an eternity before Lila Mae finally spotted Becky Jean, but there she was, jostling Baby Sister on the curve of her hip, inside the store, right where Mr. O'Dell said she'd probably be. The infant—her little gumdrop eyes shining brightly—played pattycake with a young girl in braids, slapping her hands together like a trained seal. Then Billy pointed to Carleen, who was with the group on the roof. So were Benny and Juanita, only Juanita was flat on her back. One leg was dangling over the side like a charm hanging from a bracelet, and two people were fanning her. Lila Mae groaned, "This is all she needs. She's already got a pin in her hip." Sirens were moving closer, the high-pitched whines and the guttural roars clashing like a discordant duet of sopranos and baritones.

Mr. O'Dell removed a pack of Lucky Strikes, tapping out one cigarette. "I seen a couple of snakes head for the bushes a minute ago but"—he cracked to Lila Mae, and struck a match against the sole of his shoe—"with a dozen of 'em things jumpin' around, two don't seem so bad now, does it?" He massaged his yellowish beard thoughtfully.

"Well," Lila Mae said. "I suppose that's one way of lookin' at it."

A racing caravan of police cars and ambulances slammed into the souvenir shop's parking lot; then, a minute or so later, fire trucks rumbled to a quick stop. Men with whistles and megaphones, moving quickly and robotically, scattered through the crowds and ordered everybody to move inside the store.

The firemen, who'd been sidetracked by Chief Featherhorse, were heaving and hoing, straining to straighten the precious totem pole. The chief, eyeglasses perched on his nose, the plumage of his headdress cocked forward, inched his way around the circle, inspecting the pole for damage. Spying something unusual, he drew his eyes into investigative slits, rubbed his finger across a nick, then flapped his hand in disgust at Lila Mae.

Inside the souvenir shop, the restless crowd milled around, taking sips of complimentary coffee, comparing notes and answering questions being asked by several police officers. A lawyer named Joe Guy Wellins passed out business cards, and a young Indian boy from a rival souvenir shop down the road slipped several people flyers for Indian Bill's and assured them that this sort of thing wouldn't have happened at the other establishment. Lila Mae began rehashing some of the details with Lucky, talking loudly to see if anyone else in the crowd agreed with her.

"I just thought of somethin', Mr. O'Dell, and you tell me if you agree with me, and be honest now. I wouldn't be displayin' them snakes if I didn't know the first thing about the upkeep of the animals, would you?" One couple—a petite man with pink, manicured hands and a pencil moustache and a woman with a hawk nose and nervous black eyes—stepped forward, seemingly interested.

"And who told him to throw that hatchet around like he done?" Mr. O'Dell nodded his head with a stubborn jerk. Lila Mae thought the situation should be reported. A buzz of agreement spread through the heavy, edgy crowd and the man with the feminine, groomed hands said, "That's right!"

"What are they, running for political office or something?" Becky Jean, in a sputter of sarcasm, muttered to Carleen and anybody else who happened to overhear her.

The lady on the totem pole, whose name was Roselle Peet, sided with Lila Mae and O'Dell even though she worked for Chief Featherhorse. She told them they just couldn't imagine how much sleep she and the other waitresses had lost over this very situation. "Oh, we told the chief all right—time and time again. We knew . . . we knew! Didn't we know, Birdie?" Roselle Peet straightened her jeweled glasses and looked to the second waitress, a woman with a stack of shoe-polish-black hair and Maybelline eyebrows, to verify their premonition. Birdie nodded and said, "They wuzn't a day that wint by that we didn't complain. We wanted to report it, but they was nobudy to tell. He's the boss."

Roselle Peet mentioned that she just couldn't live with herself if she didn't do something for Lila Mae to show her appreciation. While she was digging in her pocket, she kept saying things like "You are an angel from heaven!" so it seemed like she was going to offer Lila Mae a reward. Instead, she pulled out a frayed business card. "This ain't much, mind you. But my husband, Thomas, owns Peet Brothers Funeral Parlor, and if you ever need his services, you just tell him you saved Roselle's life and I guarantee ya, you'll git the works!"

"Well, this is just as sweet as can be, but, honestly, Roselle, you really don't have to do this." Lila Mae made a rolling motion with her hand, trying to get O'Dell in on things. "Here's the brains behind the operation, the man who should *really* get the special rates."

O'Dell kept shaking his head and saying, "Oh, no, that's okay," but Lila Mae just wouldn't give up.

"Now, Lucky!" she preached, her finger cocked in the air. "I don't wanna hear another word about it."

Although Becky Jean didn't have the same size audience as Lila Mae, Carleen agreed with her when she pointed out that maybe the man didn't even *want* funeral services. "Yeah, sure, like everybody's going to bend over backwards for a casket discount! And to top it off, they have to die in New Mexico!" Carleen agreed. "They do, don't they?"

What Becky Jean really didn't understand was the big-deal aspect of it. "She ran over one stupid snake and acts like a four-star general or something. All she did was talk up a storm and make some more friends while we were scared out of our wits."

Juanita pressed an ice pack to the pulsating mound on her forehead, her eyes assessing Becky Jean. "You shouldn't talk about your mother like that, girlee."

"Oh, hush up. You ought to talk," Becky Jean puffed under her breath. One minute Juanita was clutching Benny to her bosom and thanking God and the next she was doubling him over and kicking his behind. And Becky Jean couldn't wait to see Juanita's reaction when she found out that her son had swiped Lila Mae's wallet. Becky Jean thought she spotted it in Benny's jeans pocket when he hunched over.

They were just about to leave when a policeman split away from the crowd and flagged them down. The officer—a roseate, fleshy square of a man with a billy club wigwagging from his waist—placed his grubby paw on the crook of Lila Mae's arm and said, "Oh, no you don't, ladies. You're comin' with me."

"Yeah, and who's gonna make us?" Juanita, her chest thrown into a billowy mass, took a step forward, as if she was about to raise the roof.

The officer flicked his silver medal with a dense fingernail. "I'm the deputee shuruff, so I reckon I am." He had eyes as colorless as ice cubes and a long, thick blade of a nose that seemed to sniff rotten air all around him.

"Let me see what this is about, Juanita." Lila Mae shooed the huffy woman away, figuring she could sweet-talk their way out of it. She pulled the deputy to one side and told him tear-jerking stories about her husband's serious medical condition and Juanita's daughter, a sickly thing whose days were numbered, who, for all anybody knew, could actually be dying at that very moment. For good measure, she added that she herself was none too healthy, having just gotten over a case of cancer. But the man was a tough nut to crack. He kept saying, "Uh-huh, I cain't do that." Once, she got her hopes up when she happened to mention to the officer that she was from Kentucky and he exclaimed, "Well, what do you know? I've got kin in Egypt, Kentucky!"

"You don't say?" Lila Mae perked up. "Now, I never been to Egypt myself, but I heard they's some fine, fine people and beautiful country down that way, if it's the Egypt I'm a-thinkin' of."

"There ain't but one Egypt, I'll grant ya that." At long last, the man's sour squiggle of a mouth turned to a smile.

"You know, I might even have some connections down

there—I believe I do." Then she told the officer that he looked like a man with a good head on his shoulders, that he should ask Mr. Lucky O'Dell and Roselle Peet what happened and they'd vouch for her. "They'll tell you there's no need to turn this into a big song and dance. It was all just a silly accident."

"That might very well be," replied the officer, "but it's actually up to Chief Featherhorse if charges are pressed. I'm just tryin' to round up the troublemakers."

"Troublemakers?" Lila Mae squalled in disbelief. "Oh, the chief liked me fine and dandy when I was sellin' jewelry hand over fist. Now I'm a *troublemaker*?"

"Ma'am, this don't have anything to do with *your* character. This is about your *boys*."

"Hell!" Juanita barked. "We might as well get this over with."

Chapter Nine

One thing led to another and they were wedged in the car on their way to Crumpler and Rose, an attorney's office several miles down the highway. Against the pink-purple foothills were sandstone mesas and Spanish Colonial missions and Indian pueblos. They rattled over a set of railroad tracks and tumbled down a steep hillock. Spread before them like a haphazard scattering of building blocks was a colony of bungalows and filling stations and St. Mercy of the Angels Catholic Church, where Lila Mae stopped the car and asked two elderly women draped in black lace mantillas and crooked over hickory canes where the law office was. Lila Mae speeded up, then slowed down, checking each block for the right address.

Finally, she spotted a two-story, flat brick building with a faded brown awning and cement urns holding wild, dead groves of hollyhocks. A bronze CRUMPLER & ROSE shingle swung from a bracket at the front door. Their mouths pursed in grim little rosebuds, the odor of onions and leaking gas hanging in the air, they climbed a shadowy staircase to the second floor.

Behind the milky glass door of the lawyers' office was a reception area decorated with dented venetian blinds and adjustable bookshelves. Hanging on the wall were certificates in black metal frames and an oil painting of four bulldogs playing poker. A skimpy philodendron plant sat on a brass magazine stand and a beam of sooty twilight drifted through a transom.

A receptionist with Mamie Eisenhower bangs and a big, elastic circle of a mouth sat at a gray metal desk shuffling papers and tapping a pencil. The green plastic nameplate on her desk said: MISS JEWELL RUTH BLODGETT. She told them to have a seat and Mr. Crumpler would get to them.

Lila Mae snatched a magazine from the fan-shaped clusters of *Argosy* and *Life* on the coffee table and leafed through it, her head quickly jerking from one side to the other. "I know a little boy who won't be gettin' a visit from Santee Claus this year." Her mouth was a fleshy little ring that twittered, and her eyelids had a high-and-mighty arch as she turned each page loudly and dramatically. Billy Cooper, his legs wrapped around him pretzel-style, wiggled around and traded furtive glances with his partner in crime.

Squatted on a chair, her arms plaited around her bosom, her eyes focused on the wooden ceiling fan, Juanita lectured her son. "I hope you're satisfied with yourself, mister. . . . If I was Miz Wooten, I'd dump the both of us the first chance I got." Benny propped a lit cigarette into his mouth, but she growled, "Give me that" and crushed it in the glass ashtray. Finally the receptionist told them they could go in.

Leon Crumpler wore a parrot-green sports jacket with wide lapels, his slick, tan hair rolling across his head in tiny wrinkles. He had pointy, canine teeth and a long, narrow smile that stretched to his earlobes. As he danced around the room—one hand pressed to his chest like Napoleon Bonaparte—he waved his pudgy fingers in the air and tossed around a slew of fancy words to describe "the sitch-ation." He explained to the women that it was a pretty open-and-shut case, since there was a civil code that had been violated, a code that would ordinarily call for an automatic prison term of ten years. He paused for effect and lunged forward. "Now that's a fact."

"Ten years!" Lila Mae jumped up. She told Crumpler that

it just didn't seem fair, that the boys were just horsing around like boys do. "The way I see it, it was the chief's fault for havin' such a slipshod setup. Why, my kids got better locks on their school lockers than he had on them cages!" She bobbed her head defiantly and studied the man to see what type of impression she'd made on him.

Mr. Crumpler paced back and forth, locking his hands tightly, kneading and rubbing them together. His sandy eyebrows were knitted shut, making one somber slash. "I know what you're saying, don't think I don't, *but*"—the man did a quick spin on one heel—"be all that as it may, Mrs. Wooten . . . and, again, I'm not saying you don't have some good points"—he stopped and scratched his brilliantined head— "but, ma'am, the sitch-ation just ain't that simple. The police is gonna make a stink. Now that's all there is to it." He let the bad news saturate for a moment; then he told Lila Mae and Juanita that being the boys were minors, he could probably get them off for a "price."

Crumpler spread both hands on his desktop and leaned over his marble pen-and-pencil set. "I'd say eight hundred ought to cover it." He looked anxiously back and forth at the two women and licked his dry lips.

His partner, Hiram Rose, had a shrub of carroty hair and triangular sideburns that grew to his jawbone. On his hands were patches of wiry red hair, and one foot, wearing a big, black wing-tipped shoe, hung loosely from his bony ankle and thumped against the white wall. He sat on the windowsill pinching a cigarette between his thumb and forefinger. He moved it nervously in and out of his rubbery lips, blowing smoke toward the acoustical ceiling.

"Well, what's the verdict, ladies?" Rose said, his jawbone twitching. He opened the window a few inches, flicked the cigarette butt out, then slammed it shut. "We ain't got all day."

Chin in hand, two fingers pointed to his temple, Crumpler

fixed his foxy gleam on the women and said, "That's right. The po-leece'll be bustin' in about any time now."

With her bosom bubbling up and down, Juanita took a deep breath, which she released in an angry puff; then she unbuttoned the top two buttons of her sweater, reached for the sweaty roll in her bosom, and slapped down eight one-hundred-dollar bills.

They marched to the parking lot like soldiers, settling inside the car in a muffled swish of depression. Juanita—her braids loose and her forehead dappled with dents and scrapes—adjusted the stained brassiere strap and slammed the souvenirs against the dashboard as if all their troubles had started with the necklaces and dolls and rubber toys inside the bag. Then she slid the seat back in one swift zip. Benny, as if trying to stuff himself into a container too small for all his parts, pressed his arms around his chest and tucked his legs underneath him, slipping farther into the corner.

Dressing her face up in a pleasant smile, Lila Mae tried to puncture the tension with small talk. "Well, I suppose things did get carried away, but my goodness! It ain't like you run into two dozen rattlers ever' five minutes, is it? And another thing . . . Who told the chief to throw that hatchet around like he done? Why, I'd just as soon get bit by a snake as get all chopped up by one of them things, wouldn't you?"

When Lila Mae checked the rearview mirror to see if she was getting through to anybody, Carleen was humming to herself, making her plastic doll dance on her lap like a marionette, while Becky Jean, trying to block her mother out, was riffling through her makeup case, wondering what in the world had happened to her bottle of Cutex Fire Engine Red nail polish.

"And, you know what else? I never knew how them snakes operate, did you?" Lila Mae moved the wheel with one hand, making theatrical hoops with the other. "I always thought they just took off and chased you till they caught up. But did you see the way they can stay put and lurch out at you? They's practically no gettin' away from 'em! Why—"

"Benny Featherhorse." Juanita's eyes erupted like two volcanoes. "You pull another stunt like that and it'll be the last one. I stood up for you this time on account of Billy Cooper. But no more!" She slashed her hands through the air in an X. "Don't mess around with me, young man. *You know what I can do.*" Fanning herself with the road map, she blew air into her own face. "And hand over that wallet that you stole from Mrs. Wooten. Becky Jean seen it in your back pocket." She mechanically extended her arm into the backseat and wiggled her fingers. "Come on—*hand it to me.*"

"I ain't *got* no wallet." Benny scowled at Becky Jean. "The onliest wallet I got belongs to *me.*" Although Becky Jean felt guilty for turning him in, it wasn't her fault that he stole it in the first place. But there she was in cramped quarters, hemmed in by his sad, smoky gaze.

"Well, then, let's take a look." Juanita snapped her fingers. *"Now!"*

"Go on, take it. There ain't nothing in it anyhow." Benny leaned forward and slipped a billfold from his back pocket.

It was hand-tooled and it smelled of nicotine, cheap leather, and chewing gum, and Becky Jean saw right off the bat that it didn't belong to Lila Mae. She started to say something, but Juanita was already digging through it like a mad dog searching for a bone. And what if Benny *had* swiped Lila Mae's wallet, threw it away, but kept her money?

Burrowing her fingers into compartment after compartment, slot after slot, at first Juanita didn't come up with a thing. Finally, she let out a triumphant snort and said, "Well, well, well! What have we got here?" like she'd found gold bullion. Everyone waited for the unveiling of the "treasure," but all she pulled out of a small zippered pocket were two sticks of Juicy Fruit gum, one Camel cigarette, and one match. The wallet didn't have any money in it, either, except for a lone one-dollar bill.

"See!" Benny yelled. "I told you!"

Although Juanita kept hunting, the only other thing that turned up was one glossy black-and-white picture of Benny's sister. The photo of Rosita was small and torn, and in it she wore a white starched blouse with a Peter Pan collar and a knitted sweater. Her sad, buggy eyes—magnified by thick glasses—stared straight into the eyes of the person looking at the photograph.

"Give me that." Benny vaulted across the car for the picture, pressing it to his chest.

"Here, take it." Juanita threw Benny's wallet back at him. It bounced off the top of his head, but he scrambled to catch it. "I'm sure you've got Mrs. Wooten's wallet somewheres," she mumbled.

"Why don't I just pull over and we'll look through the car?" Lila Mae swerved to the roadside. "So much has been goin' on, I swear, I can't keep anything straight." She tried to remain calm as they checked coat pockets and sun visors and hand luggage one more time.

Under the circumstances, Lila Mae would normally be a raving lunatic—she had less than twenty dollars to her name—but she didn't want to make Juanita feel worse about the situation than she already did. She couldn't resist making a few cracks about what a fool she'd been to let Juanita's "cowboy friend" bamboozle her, but Juanita didn't suggest that they report the incident or track the man down or anything. Since they were kind of on the lam from Ramon, that could be tricky anyway. The end result was that the money was *gone*, period.

"We'll think of somethin'," Juanita consoled her. "Sell more jewelry, that'll do it."

Billy Cooper, his eyes small, wounded gashes, said, "I'm sorry . . . Mama." Carleen sat quietly, her hands neatly crossed on a stack of *Katy Keene*s. Becky Jean—absentmindedly rubbing Irene Gaye's gums with a teething biscuit—stared into the distant lights of a tiny town, her face illuminated by a bar of golden light.

Tucking her hair behind her ear, she removed her diary key from the long, thin gold chain around her neck, scanning the last few days for highlights. She scribbled that there'd been a lot going on lately, jotting down: "rattlers," "PowWow incident," "reform school," etc., etc., planning to fill in all the gory details later.

Creased in the pages of the diary were the postcards of the Southern plantations, which she'd been planning on sending to her grandparents and her father, maybe one to Glen, too. As she looked at the pictures, it seemed like years—not a month or two—since she'd been home. She realized that the farther away they drove, the less she liked the landscape. Although the scenery was pretty—the thunderheads, the camel-hump mountains and flame-red skies—and she even enjoyed tiny towns strung together with the quaint cafes and wigwam-shaped motels, she didn't like the hardness of it all. Everything seemed to have its own specific space, like the black outlines in a coloring book. It was nothing like what she was used to, where everything bashed into and overlapped the next thing. The vinery coiled around trellises . . . and the bundles of honeysuckle trailed into the oleander, which were covered with the same moss that crept onto the stepping stones . . . which were dusted with the Spanish moss from the oak tree that hung over it. And all of it was a landing strip for the cicadas and fireflies and praying mantises.

Maybe she was being dramatic, and maybe, as her parents told her, she should just "hold her horses" until she saw things with her own eyes. And even her friends, most of whom would be thrilled to move to California, said, "I'll trade places with you, pleeease!" But how could her parents guarantee anything when they didn't know themselves? She had already stood by and watched them make other mistakes, unable to do anything about it. How did she know this wasn't one more of their nutty schemes?

Pressing her head against the damp window, Becky Jean stared into the terra-cotta dunes of an Indian pueblo and the notch of orange lights from an upcoming town. She could hear the spooky rattling of a rusty windmill as the wind blew it first one way, then another. On a distant butte sat a white wooden cross.

Huddled by the roadside, dressed in burlap, their colorful woven baggage at their feet, was an Indian family who looked up at the Packard and waved. Becky Jean quickly opened the window and waved back, but as they traveled farther down the road she wondered if, after all, the Indians were in trouble and were actually flagging them down.

Overhead was a colorless crescent of a moon. From some invisible spot beyond a crooked mountaintop came the lonely wail of a coyote. Becky Jean took a heavy, rumbling breath and carefully replaced the cap on her fountain pen.

Chapter Ten

The topaz plains slipped away, and wrapped around them was a dirt-brown wilderness of broken chain-link fences and towers of blinking maroon lights. Factory smokestacks, like giant cigarettes, pointed skyward; plumes of exhaust billowed in the air, leaving a metallic trail and a bitter odor of burning chemicals.

In Alamogordo, Lila Mae stopped at the Blue Swallow Motor Court to call her husband. They drove through a grove of birch trees with white painted bands on the trunks and parked in front of a stucco cabin that said OFFICE. Propped in the window was a sign saying: GUS AND BETTY ANNE FRIZZELLE, PROPRIETORS. Everybody jumped out of the car to stretch their legs while Lila Mae rang the small silver bell on the counter and asked the Frizzelles, who were nestled in Naugahyde recliners watching "I Led Three Lives," to use their pay phone. Without looking up, Gus Frizzelle pointed outside to a booth near the motel laundry room. Storm clouds and a bolt of lightning rushed across the deep purple sky. Becky Jean, looking straight above her, felt one raindrop splash against her forehead.

Dropping a nickle in the slot, Lila Mae was a nervous wreck, jumping from foot to foot and licking her lips as she placed the collect call to Roy. The kids weren't making it any easier either. They milled around right outside the booth, determined to get in on things, making her even more agitated than she was already. When the operator said, "Go ahead, please," Lila Mae twiddled with the lace trim on her blouse. "Roy? . . . Roy? Is that you? . . . It's Lila Mae . . . your wife!" She didn't have the luxury of telling him all the normal things, such as "I miss you" and "I can't wait to settle down," since those comments would just trigger the very topic she was trying to delay. So, in a voice dripping with fake excitement, she rambled about this and that, hoping by the time Roy got a word in edgewise, he'd have so many head-spinning details to digest that the disappearance of his wife and kids, seemingly into thin air, would be the last thing on his mind.

But finally her husband couldn't take it anymore. He said, "Lila Mae, cut the small talk and tell me where the devil you are and when, exactly, you are planning on arriving in California." Before she answered, he said, "I hope to God you're not on another one of your wild goose chases—that's what it sounds like to me."

"Roy, honey . . . now, don't git on your high horse till you hear what I'm goin' through. This trip sure ain't no picnic, I'll tell ya that. But now, we . . . we should be there by the . . . the, uh . . . the end of the week." Lila Mae crossed her fingers as she lied. Besides, she thought to herself, she didn't say which week their arrival would be at the end of.

"What on *earth* is taking you this long? . . . I did it in three days—not that I expected you to do it that fast, but Jesus H. Christ! And by the way, what's the deal with this COD crate that was delivered to me at the Foothill Auto Court?"

"Crate?" Lila Mae shrieked in surprise, thrilled that for the moment, the attention was off the trip itself. Plus, for once, he seemed to be implicating her in a so-called crime of which she was completely innocent. "What crate?"

"It's some huge box that's addressed to Lila Mae Wooten, and it cost me a pretty penny, that's all I know. . . . I haven't had a chance to count, but it seems to me like there's seventy-five or eighty bedspreads in it."

"Bedspreads?" Lila Mae squawked. "Now I *know* there's a booboo. Why on earth would I order bedspreads when we hardly got a stick of furniture to put 'em on?" She added that she didn't know the sender, an "I. V. Foote," from Adam.

Just to make it more believable, and just so Roy would think she was trying to cooperate in getting to the bottom of the mystery, Lila Mae covered the mouthpiece and shouted, "Kids, we don't know anybody by the name of Foote, do we?" It didn't ring any bells with Becky Jean, but Carleen said, "Yeah, we do, Mama. What about that lady Imogene Virginia?"

As reality chiseled its way to the surface, Lila Mae turned paste white and gulped. "Roy? . . . Roy, honey . . . are you still there? . . . Well, now that I think of it, yes! yes! I did meet a party by that name, but for cryin' out loud, I told that girl, I said, 'Don't you *dare* send me a *thing* till you hear from me!'" Lila Mae wagged her finger in the air at the imaginary Imogene Virginia. "'I've got to get situated out there first,' I told her. . . . 'Don't you go sendin' anything to California till I got my bearin's.' . . . Boy," Lila Mae chortled, "she's got gall, I'll tell ya that. Never mind, though, I'll set that little sneak straight."

"How straight can you set her, Lila Mae?" Roy asked. "I'm already out several hundred dollars. We don't have a dime to spare and you're out buying accessories. What are you thinking?"

"Roy, now don't, don't get mad at me so fast," she pleaded. "I am at my wit's end. . . . Besides, who ever heard of someone acceptin' a package like that without knowin' what was in it?"

"How did I know you didn't run off and leave something valuable in a motel or somewhere? Then I'd never hear the end of that."

"If that was the case, I'd'a told you!"

"When, during one of your yearly phone calls?"

Although Lila Mae felt like cussing him out, she realized that at the rate they were going, she and Roy wouldn't be on speaking terms, and since she still needed to butter him up, she was forced to change her tune. So she started using expressions like "be that as it may," "in any event," and "when everything is said and done." Then she said, "Uh, by the way, honey, I'm a-runnin' a little short. You just might have to wire us some money to a Western Union somewheres. . . . It's, uh, on account of unforeseen expenses." She told him that there'd been an "incident" and she'd had to pay Leon Crumpler and Hiram Rose, attorneys at law, a sizable sum to get Billy Cooper off the hook.

When Roy asked, "Hook? What hook are you talking about?" Lila Mae stuck the receiver to the baby's ear and before he could say another word, she said, "Say hello to your daddy, Irene Gaye." Carleen was feeding her sister applesauce from a little glass jar. Irene Gaye blew bubbles with the mashed fruit and clapped her hands together like crashing cymbals. Lila Mae could hear her husband yelling, "Lila Mae! Pick up, Lila Mae!" But she wasn't about to get her head bit off. Racing off like a bat, she let the phone bob and weave in midair then told Carleen to talk to her father and tell him that she had some "female problems" and was nowhere to be found. She marched to the car and tried to look occupied with important business, shuffling through papers, sorting dirty laundry, all the while monitoring the phone booth situation.

Billy Cooper confiscated the phone and panted, "Daddy! Daddy! We're going to visit a girl in an iron lung, and Mama, she—she did the jitterbug with this cowboy who gave us candy then swiped our money. . . . Oh, and guess what else? We're takin' a secret way to the Grand Canyon with an Indian named Juanita." As if that wasn't enough, he added that Juanita's drunk husband tried to shoot them and they almost got bitten by rattlesnakes. "Daddy wants to talk to *you* again, Mama." Billy Cooper hopped around in an Indian rain dance and yelled for Lila Mae, "MAMA, DADDY WANTS YOU!"

"I'll just bet he does, little blabbermouth." To avoid another confrontation with her husband, Lila Mae slammed the door of the Packard and headed for the motel's laundry room. "I ain't talkin' to him now and that's all there is to it. There ain't much he can do about it, neither, since I'm *here* and he's *there*."

Pretty soon Carleen showed up with a message from her father: Lila Mae was to " 'get back in the car, stop horsin' around, and drive straight to California, or else.' . . . Uh, he was also sayin' 'hell's bells' a lot, too."

"Oh, he said that, did he?" Lila Mae, goose-stepping to the car, haphazardly tossed the diaper bag in the backseat and scooped up Carleen's comic books and flung them underneath the seat. A recent issue of *Confidential* magazine tumbled to the ground, but Lila Mae simply plopped it down on the front seat as big as you please.

Opening the trunk, Lila Mae collected a hunk of garbage, threw it in a waste can and slammed the trunk lid shut, all the while mumbling through her teeth like a ventriloquist, "If he thinks it's so easy, drivin' across country with four rowdy kids and a loadful of furniture, then why don't *he* do it? . . . I'll gladly change places with him . . . Footloose and fancy-free, lollygaggin' around a motel room swimmin' pool and God only knows what else."

Grabbing a whisk broom, Lila Mae went to town on the car's upholstery. "And another thing," she griped, debris and dust clouds exploding in the air. "If he wanted me to get to California any faster, he should have give me airplane or train tickets. I'll just git there when I git there. Rome wasn't built in a day, dammit." Lila Mae told everyone to excuse her French, then she threw the whisk broom into the glove compartment and slammed it shut.

"Maaama," Becky Jean scolded, throwing her eyes toward the motel office. The Frizzelles—two round, curious heads eating Fig Newtons—were peeking from behind their burlap curtains to see what the commotion was all about.

Although Lila Mae knew full well that driving across country had been her bright idea, it still didn't seem like she and she alone had made all the decisions that got them where they were. And she knew she was making Roy's silly crime of accepting a COD crate worse than her crime of all those things Billy Cooper told him happened. But for one thing, when those incidents were all bunched up like that, with no explanation attached, she just didn't know where to start in defending herself, and for another, the COD package was the only thing she really had on Roy. So she had to turn it into a big deal. Plus, there was her general tendency to get illogical during an argument and to conveniently blame the other person.

"Are you in hot water?" Juanita returned from the laundry room, wringing out a pair of socks.

Normally, Lila Mae would write everything down on paper and it never looked as bad as she imagined. This time, though, she suspected her troubles would look ten times worse in black and white. Bending back each finger one by one, Lila Mae began counting. "No job . . . friends who beg us to move out there who are nowhere to be found . . . a bad check for some furniture we sold . . . not a penny in our pocket with six mouths to feed. If all that sounds like hot water, then I guess I'm in scaldin'. And that don't even count the attorneys' fees I owe you, or that totem pole."

"By the way, you never did tell me what kinda business your husband's in." Juanita wrapped the socks in a white towel and patted them dry.

"You ever hear of the lazy-bum business, Juanita?" Lila Mae folded a pair of khaki pants. "Well, that's what my husband's in. . . . Roy don't see it that way, of course. The way he tells it, he's an idea man. Oh, he gits the idea all right, but then he sits on his can like King Tut and don't do a GD thing about it."

"Why do you always make it sound like he doesn't even have a job?" Becky Jean asked. "Just so you know, Juanita, he's in the construction business, but he's got lots of stuff on the side. He plays instruments; he can fix anything—cars, appliances. He can even build a house from scratch." Of course there was that fly-swatter fiasco, plus some business with a cure for baldness, but it wasn't the time to bring all that up. "But at least he didn't sit in a car and flirt with someone like you did while we almost got killed by snakes."

"Flirt with that man, my foot. Why, he ain't even my type!" Although she didn't mean the "type" reference the way it came out, Lila Mae made it sound like there was such a thing. "It was all Mr. O'Dell could do to keep me from jumpin' out of the car. Tell 'em, Billy Cooper." She tapped her foot and waited.

Billy Cooper gulped and said, "I—I dunno."

"Oh, I knew I'd never hear the end of this!" Lila Mae clamped her hands to her hips, a blue cotton shirt in her fist. "The next time Her Royal Highness tells the story, I'll be havin' a T-bone steak dinner and a vodka martini in Tahiti or somewheres while they got chewed up by snakes."

"Well, it almost happened." Becky Jean knew she was exaggerating, but she was frustrated and nervous. They were floating in the middle of nowhere, not even close to being in California, stuck with people they hardly knew, one of whom was a teenage boy who thought he was John Dillinger. When she'd mentioned the gun to her mother, Lila Mae, who was scared stiff of Billy's cap gun, simply said, "If you went through what that poor woman has gone through, you'd carry a gun, too."

As usual, Lila Mae's fabricated threats were worse than the real ones. A gun-toting stranger in their own car was no big deal. It was the devastating fire that *could* wipe them off the map, or the FBI's Most Wanted criminal who *might* pounce on them from behind a tree trunk somewhere, that was the real problem. It was impossible to count the number of times Lila Mae, wild-eyed and hysterical, forced them to sit on feather pillows during electrical storms because she was dead certain they'd be electrocuted. Then, as they sat there cross-legged reading magazines and drinking Coca-Cola, with the thunder rocking every floorboard and shingle in their house, to calm

Billy Cooper or Carleen, she'd tell them that there was nothing to be scared of at all. She'd make up fairy tales about the silly monsters that were up there fighting and making a bunch of racket.

Then she'd stage weekly fire drills because she could feel it in her bones that their house would someday burn to a crisp. She'd even pound on the bathroom door and remind anybody taking a bath that "all it takes is a teacup of water to drown, just one teacup!" According to her, even Metal Fang—a person who, if he *did* exist at all, probably had never stepped foot in the United States—was out to get them. When Becky Jean said, "Well, *I've* never heard of Metal Fang," and accused her mother of making him up, Lila Mae said, "Won't all of *you* be surprised when we *do* run into him!"

Some of what Lila Mae said *was* true. They did live hand-to-mouth, but their father promised them that someday, when things panned out, they'd have a big stone house with wall-to-wall carpeting and air conditioning and four-poster beds. Lila Mae could go on big shopping sprees, buying Prince Matcha-belli perfume and ermine-trimmed coats, Lily Daché hats, duchess satin cocktail dresses by Don Loper. Becky Jean would finally have cashmere sweaters in every color, her own private telephone, and maybe even a flashy red Corvette. Dozens of Madame Alexander dolls would sit on Carleen's shelves, and flounced party dresses would hang in her closet, and for Billy Cooper there would be a brand-new Schwinn bike and cowboy hats and Red Goose shoes.

Becky Jean could just picture her father now, lying on his back on some motel divan, his fingers locked behind his neck, a wide grin on his face as he ate pretzels and watched "The Honeymooners"—what Lila Mae called the life of Riley. As for the "lazy bum" reference, when she was mad, anything was liable to tumble out. More than likely her father was thrilled to be off the hook for several weeks. Finally some peace and quiet with no bicycles and television sets and washing machines or cars to repair.

When Lila Mae told everybody to speed up the tempo, she didn't have all day, Becky Jean told her it was her own fault they were in such a hurry. "We should have been in California weeks ago."

"Ain't she just the sweetest thing you ever laid your eyes on, Juanita? I wouldn't have dared talk to my mother like that." Lila Mae glared at Becky Jean and shook her head, wondering where she'd gone wrong with that girl. Oh, Carleen was no angel, and Billy Cooper could be plenty sassy, too, but Becky Jean was another matter altogether.

When Becky Jean was growing up, Lila Mae used to make excuses for her whenever she was fussy, explaining to friends whose daughters were obedient little cherubs wearing white gloves and Mary Jane shoes that Becky Jean "needs a nap" or "hasn't eaten a bite today," or that "the poor little thing had her booster shots and the doctor warned us she'd be cranky."

Then there was that Mother's Day when Lila Mae was in the hospital. Becky Jean bought her mother a music box and wrapped the gift herself. The staff wasn't supposed to allow anyone under sixteen into the cancer ward, but they slipped Becky Jean, who was only ten at the time, in to see Lila Mae anyway. Still, after all that trouble, when Roy said, "Becky Jean, honey, ain't you going to give your mother her gift?" she said "Here!" then tossed the package on the hospital floor like she was pitching horseshoes.

The nurse had slapped Becky Jean's hand and said, "Now, you be a nice little girl—your mother will get well just as fast as she can." She told Lila Mae that Becky Jean was probably just mad at her for being sick.

When Lila Mae said, "Mad?? I've never heard of such a thing," the nurse told her that she had taken a course on how the mind works, that Becky Jean's behavior was only natural and Lila Mae shouldn't let her little girl upset her. Someday, the woman promised, she'd outgrow that attitude and they'd probably be very close.

Although Lila Mae and Roy kept assuring each other that Becky Jean was just going through "phases," as far as Lila Mae could tell, each phase was worse than the last. Shrugging his shoulders in defeat, Roy said, "I just don't know what it is with Becky Jean. It's like she has some ferocious, barking dog living inside her."

For the life of her, Lila Mae just didn't know how that worked. When Becky Jean was born, she and Roy had lived in a rooming house with paper-thin walls, and the other boarders—a few dozen tobacco workers, men who slept in thin, hard cots in an attic dormitory—got up before dawn and were asleep by seven-thirty p.m. Their landlady had said she ran a tight ship and had warned Lila Mae that she'd have to keep that baby quiet, that she had other tenants to be concerned with, otherwise "you'll have to find other quarters." So Lila Mae, naturally, picked Becky Jean up the minute she cried. Although she didn't think the reason was all that simple, Lila Mae wondered if that could be it.

*G*reen, turbulent storm clouds hopped across the moon, making it appear and disappear. Raindrops, large, clear polka dots, started to plop here and there on the windshield. Lila Mae turned on the wipers and found herself singing "Ol' Man River." She said she didn't know why, but it was just about the saddest song she'd ever heard.

Billy Cooper and Carleen dozed, their mouths petite open rings and their heads collapsed together. Juanita assembled more jewelry, opening her legs to make a little cradle with her skirt to hold her hodgepodge of stones and clasps. As she hummed along with Lila Mae, she threaded a long steel needle and flossed some wire. Picking up a coral bead, she knotted the strand with her teeth. "Ol' Man River, dat Ol' Man River . . . He jes' keeps rollin' . . ."

A bittersweet orange moon hung over the fields of black contours. They passed Deke's Camp, a curio shop with rusted buggy springs, and animal skulls strewn across it like broken chunks of a necklace. Lila Mae turned on the radio, which came on with a snap of static, and Les Paul and Mary Ford were singing "How High the Moon." Nobody seemed to know just where they were going. When they came to a fork in the road, Lila Mae turned the car to the left, then—for some reason— quickly swerved to the right.

Chapter Eleven

The plan was to detour and drop Benny at reform school, which was just outside of Truth or Consequences, New Mexico, only they hadn't broken the news to Benny yet. Juanita promised the girls fifty cents to keep him occupied, which meant whenever there was a telltale road sign they were supposed to point to something interesting on the other side of the highway and see if they could get him to look at it. Carleen tried to get him to read *The Bobbsey Twins in the Deep Blue Sea*, but Juanita told her it was "way over his head."

They had a close call when Lila Mae spotted a sign and cracked, "Truth or Consequences—ain't that some name for ya? It's like they knew that reform school would be there someday." Juanita shushed her and the girls started singing "Sixteen Tons" as loud as they could.

In the meantime, Benny was getting the royal-carpet treatment. They let him smoke as much as he wanted and even stopped at Buster's All-You-Can-Eat, where he ordered a New York strip steak, a short stack of buckwheat pancakes, biscuits, and red-eye gravy. Juanita even stopped nagging him every five minutes.

They passed a vacant lot strung with naked light bulbs and red plastic reindeer stuck in the ground. A sign decorated with mistletoe said, PRITCHETT AND SONS XMAS TREES. Huge lumps of evergreen trees were tied together and piled on the ground, waiting to be propped up.

Stalling the car for a moment, Lila Mae sized up the Christmas tree lot and shook her head. "I can't believe my eyes, can you? Them decorations get earlier and earlier every year. Seems like we go from skeletons and pumpkins to turkey to Santee Claus in no time at all. It's all a person can do to keep up."

Well, Juanita reminded her, it wasn't all that early, it was already the first of December. "I guess it is, ain't it?" Lila Mae's face drooped at the realization that they'd left Kentucky in October.

She just wondered what kind of Christmas they would have this year. Her kids always made a long list of gifts they wanted: dolls that wet their diapers, train sets, petticoats, radios, mechanical toys, and everything else they saw advertised. Becky Jean even wanted a ruby ring and fur sweater one year! Lila Mae wondered where her kids got the gall to ask for all that, especially when they knew full well how hard it was just to make ends meet.

At dusk, Juanita glanced at her watch and announced that she could use a little something to wet her whistle, adding that if they were where she thought they were, the Firebird Inn was only a few miles down the road. She said it wasn't in the best area, that sometimes "a colored or two" was there. Lila Mae told her that didn't bother her one bit, that she'd had a Negro cleaning girl, Vernelle Swanson, who worked for their family for years. "I thought the world of that girl," Lila Mae gushed.

"Mama . . ." Carleen looked confused. "If that's really true, then how come you always lock the car door every time you spot one?"

"Now you know that's not true, Carleen." Lila Mae looked at Juanita to see what effect it had on her. "It's *not* true at all!"

The Firebird Inn was connected to the Mission Auto Court, a chain of boxy motel units that sat in the shape of a horseshoe on dark, hard-packed dirt. Surrounding it were saguaro cacti, the ruins of adobe huts, and two rusty gas pumps. Lila Mae parked the Packard underneath the fluorescent lamp illuminating a Stopette deodorant billboard. A hive of dragonflies circled the bulb.

Juanita suggested they gussy themselves up, so they rummaged through cases of jewelry, swagging turquoise and coral necklaces across their bodies like Christmas tree garlands. Throwing a strand of agate beads over her head, she nodded toward a small bungalow where a bony old Negro man sat on a mint-green glider. "What'd I tell you? Right off the damn bat, too."

Sitting there on the porch, the looped cord to his radio draped through a window of his unit, the man seemed harmless enough. He was wearing soiled brown gabardine trousers and cracked leather shoes. His hair—a matted gray pelt—looked like one big piece of fuzz from a lint trap. Lila Mae opened her car door a crack, and the sounds of Mahalia Jackson and the scent of eucalyptus and night air bombarded her.

"Hello there, ladies!" The man, who had high, protruding cheekbones and haunted, moon-shaped eyes, swatted a bug against his thigh and turned down the radio.

Juanita warned Lila Mae that they should just keep to themselves, but Lila Mae'd already said, "Why, good evenin', sir. Now, doncha turn that music down on accounta me. I just love Negro spirituals."

With that, the man turned the radio up full blast and pulled his faded brown sweater around his shoulders. "Gettin' kindly cool, isn't it?"

"You can certainly say that again." Lila Mae bobbed her head dramatically. "I'm on my way to California, though. It's supposed to be nice and sunny there, even in the winter. . . . The way I'm goin', I'll be lucky to get there by summer. These kids got me goin' to the Grand Canyon first."

He told her she wasn't going anywhere with that "car

a-smokin' like it is," then pointed a knotty, quivering finger to the grillwork.

"What do you mean?" Lila Mae turned her head upside down to examine the hot, smoky vapor that oozed out of the engine. She could also hear a noise like a hissing tea kettle. "Well, th-that just can't be." Lila Mae stamped her foot. "I just had this engine overhauled. Now what'll we do? We got no place to stay, and me with all these kids. Oh, dern it all, anyway! Just dern it all!"

The man slipped a flannel cap over his head and scratched his ear. "Now, now, don't get all stirred up. . . . It ain't all that bad, ma'am. She probably just needs some water." He told Lila Mae he was a retired mechanic and he'd be happy to take a look at it for her—that is, if she wanted him to.

Juanita turned to Becky Jean and said how did they know he wouldn't fiddle around with some part of the engine and charge them a bundle to fix it or, worse yet, pretend to fix it, then leave them in a big mess somewheres? "Coloreds is like that," she announced.

But Lila Mae, looking at him with pleading, hound-dog eyes, said, "Oh, sir . . . would you? Would you pleeeasse?"

The man put his two frail arms on the glider and hiked up his baggy trousers, which were bunched up at the waist and cinched with a black leather belt. Barely lifting his feet off the ground, he scuffed his way to the car and fumbled for the hood latch. When he opened it, a cloud of black smoke shot up and swirled around and both of them jumped back and coughed.

"Well, good night!" Lila Mae exclaimed, one hand to her chest, the other fanning the air in front of her. Even the colored man said, "Holy Toledo!" When a few small flames squirted out, he said, "Sweet Jesus!"

It took five minutes, but they finally got the fire out and the engine cooled off. "You been runnin' her a little hard, I 'spect," the man said. "Don't worry, ma'am, I'll doctor it up for ya." He kept tapping the radiator with his thick, ridged fingernail and flinching until finally he unscrewed it with his handkerchief.

"You're probably wonderin' how you got yourself into this mess. I just can't tell you how much I appreciate this, though." Lila Mae studied his every move, as if she were watching an Academy Award–winning movie. "If I don't get to California soon, you can just change my name to Mud or Miss. My husband's pretty sore at me. I wouldn't put it past him, and I wouldn't blame him, neither."

"Californy, you say? I ain't been to Californy myself, but my wife's kin, Regina and Oscar, they been." He jerked his head backwards, gesturing to the bungalow. Standing in front of the window was a thin woman in a crepe dress decorated with white magnolia blossoms, assembling an ironing board. "They been there, oh, two or three times, I believe. . . . They tell me it's sunny pert near *all* the time."

"That's what we're countin' on. . . . My husband's got allergies so bad I thought he was gonna up and die on me, I swear I did. My girls, though, you think they care about his health? Huh! I told 'em what Dr. Gibbons said, that he might as well sign their father's death certificate if we stayed in Kentucky, but they just rolled their eyes and said, 'Oh, Mama,' like I was fibbin' to them or something. I am so tired of them rollin' their eyeballs every time I say somethin' that I can't hardly see straight."

"Kids is like that. They think of themselves, period." He nodded to punctuate his point and smiled. He had a big, crooked gold tooth.

"You can say that again. They blame me all the time for exaggerating. . . . That's the only way to get through to 'em, though, I swear it is." Lila Mae propped her elbow on the car and peered at the radiator. "All them girls worry about is boys, boys, boys. I got one girl, the big one over there, all she talks about is her boyfriend, Glen. She's scared stiff some other girl's gonna get him. Why, if he's such a Casanova, then it ain't meant to be, but she claims we ruined her whole life. Don't that just beat all, sir? Carleen, that's my other girl, she's not as bad, but she still does her share of complainin'."

"My boy"—the man pulled out a long metal stick and checked the oil level—"his name's Marvin, he liked to drove my wife and me out of our skulls, always wantin' somethin' . . . cars, motorsickles, you name it, he wanted it, just like we was Rockerfellers. So I know a thing or two about that."

"You know what I think?" Lila Mae cradled the radiator cap for the man. "I think if there's any gripin' to be done, *we* should be the ones doin' it. Look at me, for example—I had to sell just about everything I own to pay for movin' expenses."

"I sure am sorry to hear that," the man said.

"Oh, I've still got me a couple of decent pieces of furniture. They ain't much to speak of, and I cain't say that I really wanted 'em when I got 'em, but now they mean the world to me. . . . You see, when my mama died, I wanted her pearls, and, well, being the oldest, I know she would of wanted me to have 'em."

"Well, of course she would of. . . ." The man stopped what he was doing. "Now don't tell me you didn't end up with 'em?"

"No sir." Lila Mae gave the man a sad, weak smile. "I didn't. Clora Dee, my sister, was cryin' and poutin' and, well, it just wasn't worth the trouble, so . . . I—well, I—I just took the furniture instead." A cloud of melancholy skimmed across her face. "I was seventeen at the time and needed credenzas and hutches like a hole in the head. And—you won't believe this— after all that big to-do, Clora Dee don't even know what become of the pearls! I still got Mama's furniture, though."

"Well, ain't that too, too bad." The man wrinkled up his face in disgust. "Now, you should of had them pearls, the way I see it."

"I ain't even told you the worse—and not too many people know this." Lila Mae locked eyes with the man. "We even come up with instructions where . . . Mama had it all spelled out, you know, that I was supposed to get the pearls. But Clora Dee, she looked at Mama's letter and she said, " 'Why, there ain't nothin' official about this paper at all.' And that's what the lawyer told us too, said it should of been drawn up proper or some such. . . . Now you tell me, how did a girl Clora Dee's age know that? A fifteen-year-old girl?"

The man said, "Official or not, it still don't seem right that she got 'em."

"My husband, Roy's his name, he said to me, he said, 'Now, Lila Mae, can't you just let bygones be bygones?' But . . ."

When, a few minutes later, Becky Jean heard her mention train-station lockers and Winnie Ruth Judd, she said to Juanita, "You better shut her up. She'll be telling him everybody's life story if you let her. She might even invite him along."

When Juanita tapped her watch and signaled to Lila Mae, the man told Lila Mae to go on and have herself a good time, to just leave the ignition keys and he'd fill the car up with gas and oil.

As they walked away, Lila Mae whispered, "Me and my big mouth. I hope I didn't hurt his feelin's when I mentioned Negro spirituals. Everybody's so touchy these days."

"I hope he don't mess with that car, that's what I hope," Juanita wisecracked.

"Oh, I don't think so," Lila Mae mused. "He seems awfully nice."

The Firebird was shaped like a cement cube, with low ceilings and creaky, warped wooden floors. The room, which was meat-locker cold and bathed in shiny royal blue light, had a long, blue, mirrored bar against the wall. Suspended above it was a blue neon sign with a bare-bottomed woman sitting in a martini glass that said, BOTTOMS UP! Clinging to the air was the heavy smell of fried hamburgers, cigarettes, and dime-store cologne. In the corner, a fluorescent jukebox was playing "Goodnight, Irene."

Two servicemen sat on a red leather booth with tiny cigarette burns, sipping tankards of beer, blowing smoke rings across the table at one another, and plucking at wads of stuffing from the gashed upholstery.

In another booth was a girl with a cascade of yellow hair, dressed in red ruffles and white lace like a box of Valentine candy. On her head was a sparkly paper tiara, and she had a smeared varnish of red lipstick and black mascara going every which way, like a beauty queen who'd been in a bad accident on the way home from the pageant. She was sitting on the lap of an older man with one crossed, shapely leg bobbing up and down—the heel from her spike shoe completely missing—as she toyed with his silk necktie.

When the man spotted Becky Jean, he patted his other leg and invited her to join them. "Come on over here, sugar pie." The man had rubbery, Donald Duck lips and thick, capped teeth like piano keys. "Bambi here won't mind, will ya, doll baby?"

"Don't you *dare* go over there." Lila Mae jerked the tail of Becky Jean's print blouse, tugging her in the opposite direction. "That girl is a lady of the evening," something she said Becky Jean would end up looking like if she didn't ease up on the makeup. "And look at him, actin' like the Sheik of Araby. Who knows what's in his ole head?"

"Are you kidding?" Becky Jean made a "crazy" face at her mother. "*You're* the one we have to watch."

Juanita headed for the bar, where a man with a greasy brown pompadour and a square, dimpled chin poured drinks. The sleeves on his white T-shirt were rolled like a donut, and there was one cigarette cocked behind his cauliflower ear. Without looking up, he said, "What can I get you ladies?" He picked up the brandy snifter stuffed with one-dollar-bill tips, then swabbed the bar with a smelly, Clorox-dipped dishrag.

Lila Mae said she wanted to try a Tom Collins and Juanita ordered a Grasshopper. They made the kids sit in a different section, where they ate hamburgers with Bermuda onions and drank orangeade. Billy Cooper wasn't hungry, so he bought a pack of candy Chesterfields and sucked them until they became brittle daggers.

"Excuse me, ma'am." A man with a haircut like a newly clipped shrub tapped Juanita on the shoulder. He wore a plaid jacket, tasseled loafers, and a class ring. "You're Juanita Featherhorse, I believe."

Juanita frowned and looked him up and down. "Yes? Do I know you?" Lila Mae was afraid he was a plainclothesman who'd tracked them down, but the man extended a beamy hand and introduced himself as Budger Hellman, someone who had done business with her at the PowWow. "I'm the Pepsi-Cola distributor. I sell you your soft drinks, remember?"

"Well, well, well, what do you know?" When Juanita patted the chrome bar stool and told Hellman to have a seat, Becky Jean slugged the table and fumed, wondering just how long it would be before Lila Mae was teaching the man a thing or two about the Charleston.

Just as she supposed, in no time at all the trio were carrying on. Juanita tossed a drink down her throat, slammed her glass on the bar, and the bartender automatically refilled it. As if preparing to get down to brass tacks, Hellman rolled up each shirtsleeve, slid his flat palms back and forth, then ordered a dry martini with an olive bobbing in it. Clinking their glasses toward the neon sign, they giggled, "Bottoms up!" Luckily, Lila Mae seemed to be nursing the same Tom Collins, but Becky Jean kept tabs on her anyway. Becky Jean heard Juanita say to Hellman, "Yes, but you'd better not tell my husband you saw me." Hellman shut his mouth tightly and pretended to zip up his lip.

Somebody got the bright idea to play "The Bunny Hop," so Lila Mae, Juanita, and Budger organized a happy-go-lucky cable of dancers. Suddenly everyone in the place had grabbed the person in front of them and they were weaving in and out of the tables and chairs. Naturally, Hellman had his mitts wrapped around Lila Mae and was trying to take playful nips out of her ear. So far she had been successful in warding him off. Juanita was shaking like Gypsy Rose Lee, her bosom jiggling like a loose pillow and her necklaces and bracelets jangling and jingling as she hopped and kicked and wiggled. For someone who supposedly had a pin in her hip, Juanita certainly wasn't doing that badly, Becky Jean thought.

"I bet we ain't goin' to the Grand Canyon," Carleen said, but Becky Jean, her bloodhound eyes tracking her mother, said, "I'll bet we *are.*"

The shiny black pay phone made it tempting to call her grandmother. At this hour, she was probably doubled over her sudsy sink washing the supper dishes. Or it could be that she was finished cleaning, that she was moisturizing her hands with rosewater, ready to turn on the television or pick up her embroidery basket, wondering why in tarnation she hadn't heard from her grandkids. Maybe her grandmother could take some of the cash in the White Owl cigar box underneath her brass bed and bail them out like she always did when they ended up in another jam. If she called, it would worry her grandmother sick, and she had her hands full as it was. Four or five farm hands, each old alcoholic bum worse than the next. Plus a husband who was in a Jim Beam stupor ninety percent of the time, mixing up buckets of outlandish paint and slapping his concoctions on toys or power tools, even automobiles and living-room furniture. Becky Jean decided to leave well enough alone.

Next the frisky customers were rearranging tables and chairs to make room for the Mexican hat dance. Assembling in a wobbly, slaphappy line, they clapped hands and clicked heels to the mariachi beat. Lila Mae, mimicking a flamenco dancer, was clacking imaginary castanets in the air, and Hellman, pie-eyed and rowdy, had clipped on Juanita's dangling earrings and was thumping a white dinner plate like it was a tambourine. Another couple—this one a barrel-chested man and a tall, thin, blond woman with a haystack hairdo—were doing their own thing. The woman looked like an upside-down broom as she circled around the floor, one hand holding her partner's index finger, her other hand whipping her eyelet petticoat back and forth like a matador's cape. The man stood in one spot like a human maypole around which the frisky woman revolved.

But Juanita, who'd been the ringleader of the ruckus, suddenly clutched at her squash blossom necklace, her medicated, bloodshot eyes slipping to the back of her head. She stumbled around like a sleepwalker, knocked over a wooden chair, then collapsed to the floor in an inebriated, higgledy-piggledy lump.

"Dear me!" Lila Mae shrieked, quickly gathering her kids together and shooing them toward the door. Benny, sitting at a Formica table in the luminescent blue ring of the jukebox, squeezed his arms across his ribs and refused to move. Lila Mae staggered toward him. "Bennnnnny!" she cajoled, steadying herself on the table's rim. "Benny, come on now, sonny boy. Your mama's not so well, so we're leavin' now."

"I ain't goin' back to that reform school." Benny, jerking his head defiantly, double-dared Lila Mae to do something about it. Then, as if to remind them of his "specialty," he rolled a Firebird napkin into a ball, struck a match, and tossed it into the ashtray. He picked up another match and started over, watching the ashtray bonfire with one eye and Lila Mae with the other. "And you can't make me!" Suddenly, he sprinted to the men's washroom and fastened the latch.

"This is all we need." Lila Mae clopped behind him, beating her fist on the door. "Now what? . . . Come on, Billy Cooper. See if *you* can get him to come out. He *likes* you."

After hemming and hawing and threatening and refusing, Benny finally said yes, he would unlock the door and come out, but only if Lila Mae *promised* to take him to the Grand Canyon with everybody else. "I'll even call my pa and tell him to come git me if you don't!" Just so Lila Mae would know he meant business, he let out a bloodcurdling, dish-rattling scream.

"Oh, heavens! Don't—don't do that." Lila Mae chewed her lip and paced in one straight line, then—mostly so she'd have help with making the wrong decision—asked Becky Jean what in the world they should do.

With Benny along, they'd be sure to take the secret way to the Grand Canyon, so Becky Jean said, "What can we do? We don't have much choice," which they really didn't. Juanita would be peeved, but Lila Mae would cross that bridge when she came to it.

With so much going wrong, Lila Mae supposed Juanita's prediction about the colored man had been right all along. As nice as he seemed, he was probably a seasoned confidence man sitting on his porch waiting for some stool pigeons to come along. By the time she opened the door to the Firebird, she was in a state, figuring there'd be an empty spot with a few telltale oil drippings and a rubber tattoo where the Packard's tires used to sit. He and his wife would be long gone, already in another state, howling in laughter and looking for a nice place to set up housekeeping. With the way she'd built up the heirloom furniture, it was no wonder.

But, much to her surprise and relief, the car was next to the entrance, just where the man said it would be. The man himself was planted next to it like a Buckingham Palace guard. "Here I am, ma'am . . . right here." He waved her down.

Juanita, snoring like a buzz saw, had to be lugged outside by three people. Lila Mae figured the two servicemen would have been the first to pitch in, but they, like Hellman (who, without even returning Juanita's earrings, had sped away in his Plymouth), were long gone. In the end it was the beauty queen and her sugar daddy who couldn't have been nicer. The man with the thick teeth said, "Ma'am, let me help you with that," and the girl said there was no reason why Norm couldn't hold one end while she and Lila Mae held the other. The "ends" the girl was referring to belonged to the tablecloth that they turned into a hammock to handle Juanita.

The colored man tried to tuck the hem of Juanita's skirt inside the car, but she reared up long enough to say, "Hey, what's the big idea?" Lila Mae could have died when Juanita actually slapped the man's hand like she was swatting a pesky gnat. Lila Mae tried to make up for it by telling the man, "She probably thought you was one of them soldiers makin' a pass at her."

"See here, ma'am, let me show you what I done." The man snaked his finger across the jungle of parts.

Although Lila Mae couldn't make heads or tails of anything, she studied the labyrinth of hoses and rods and springs with the determination of someone searching for a precious lost item. "Sir, do you realize that if it wasn't for you, we could have been stranded somewhere? I had *no* idea the engine had problems. I just thank you *so* much," she said. "It just kills me that I can't give you anything extra for your trouble . . . but"— she stopped in embarrassment—"to tell you the truth, I just don't have it. . . . Juanita here has been helpin' me along." She told the man to give her his information and she'd be sure to send him cash when she got on her feet.

"No . . . no." The man shook his head back and forth. "You seem like a nice lady, and your kids are gonna need that money. Before you take off, though, let me show you a picture of my little grandbaby." He bent forward and slipped out a wallet, tobacco brown and curved with age, from his hip pocket. "Ain't she somethin', now?"

"Just as pretty as a picture . . . ain't she, kids?" The girl, whose name was Donetta Jo, had eight or nine pigtails popping out of her head like weeds, each one snapped shut with a yellow barrette shaped like an airplane.

The man told Lila Mae that Donetta Jo was Marvin's little girl, that his son had already "up and left the baby's mother," but he was hoping to see his little granddaughter once in a while, anyway.

"It's been a year ago since I seen her . . . but I—I got my fingers crossed . . . You know, ma'am?" The man bowed his head and clutched his cap. "The boys, they disappear on you

. . . but you got your daughters, and I reckon they stick around
. . . least that's what my wife says, anyways." The man's mouth
quivered in a halfhearted smile. "Well"—he slammed the hood
down and patted it gingerly—"that oughta do it. . . . You folks
have yourselves a safe journey, now. I'll—I'll be seein' you real
soon."

In the moonlight, the man looked like a pearly black lava
statue, his arms dangling limply, his milky brown eyes fixed in
place. He waited as Lila Mae fiddled with the car seat and
slipped the key in the ignition. When Lila Mae turned on her
headlights, he raised his arms slowly, shielding his eyes. Then,
just before they sped away, he shook his hand, the pink palm
moving slowly, very slowly, back and forth like a windshield
wiper. "I'll be seeing you. . . ."

As Lila Mae rolled through the parking lot and stopped at
the edge of the highway, she raised her eyes and looked into
the rearview mirror. The man was a mere stencil against the
blue-black sky. "Oh, I know you'll think I'm crazy . . ." Lila
Mae sighed, "you really will, but . . . that man reminds me of
my poor, dead father."

"Are you tipsy?" Becky Jean yelped. "That's what you said
about that mechanic back in Arkansas! *He* reminded you of
your father, too." Anyone who could change oil or handle a
whitewall tire reminded Lila Mae of her father, and this one
wasn't even the right color.

"I know. Oh, I know," Lila Mae fretted. "There's just a
quality about him . . . or somethin'. He looks like life has kicked
him around some. . . . I hope he knows how much I appreciated
his help. I just hope he knows." As she looked over her left
shoulder, waiting for a stream of cars to pass, she rolled down
the window several inches. Then she reached her left hand out
and moved it back and forth one more time, hoping the colored man saw her last goodbye.

With the speedometer barely touching twenty mph, Lila
Mae told the kids to get settled for the night, that they had a

long haul ahead of them. Every once in a while she'd stray over the center divider, then quickly swerve back. The car behind her honked and then flew past them. A raindrop or two hit the windshield. The moon was crystal white, with the troubled shadows of earth reflected on it, and tissue-paper clouds floated across. Lila Mae, her head crooked to one side, stared at the hood decoration with a faraway gloss in her eyes. "Fairy tales can come true . . . It can happen to you . . . if you're young at heart," she sang softly. "You can go to extremes for impossible schemes . . . You can laugh when your dreams fall apart at the seams . . ."

Normally Becky Jean would have asked her mother to "pipe down, please" and Carleen usually went along, but Becky Jean raised her finger to her lips and shushed Carleen so they could listen. It wasn't often that they heard their mother's voice alone, and Becky Jean sometimes wondered how many of those high notes her mother could reach, or if she could do much more than carry a proper tune. It was always so hard to tell with the voice of Rosemary Clooney or Patti Page twisting and tangling with Lila Mae's, rescuing her, if need be, from sharps and flats. But her voice was clear and beautiful all by itself.

"And if you should survive to a hundred and five, look at all you'll derive out of being alive! And here is the best part, you'll have a head start . . . If you are among the very young . . . at . . . heaaaaart. . . ." Stringing out the last note, Lila Mae gazed at some fanciful spot in the black crystal space surrounding them. Becky Jean wondered why the song seemed so sad with such happy, upbeat lyrics and why her mother had tears in her eyes.

Just inches behind them, a three-story truck tailgated the Packard, its huge headlights bouncing off the trailer. The chrome grillwork looked like hungry fangs about to gobble them up. Behind that truck was a column of trucks. In a sour serenade of sound and light, the impatient drivers kept honking their irritating horns and flashing their blinding golden headlights. But Lila Mae didn't seem to know the trucks and cars were even there. As she sat with her fingers wrapped around the steering wheel, she seemed to be melting, getting smaller and smaller, until she was a mere puddle inside her brown wool coat. With hypnotized eyes, she turned on the windshield wipers with a slow, mechanical motion and wiped the foggy window with a tissue.

As she drove farther and farther away from the flickering blue lights of the Firebird and toward the sheer black sky, and long after the cars and trucks had streaked by them, leaving them all alone on the highway, Lila Mae realized that she hadn't even caught the colored man's name.

Chapter Twelve

After all that commotion about taking the secret way to the Grand Canyon, they didn't end up going that way after all. Lila Mae and Juanita convinced everyone they'd never arrive at a decent hour if they detoured, and Juanita claimed that it would be better to go *after* they visited the canyon itself. Lila Mae rationalized, "That way we can take our time and enjoy the scenery."

The kids asked Benny to tell them one more time about the secret way. How many waterfalls were there? Could you see the burial grounds from the road? And would they be able to stop and explore the caves?

They streaked up the mountain, past the terraced rock dwellings of the Zuni Indian pueblo; they waved at the Smokey the Bear statue and followed the signs for Grand Canyon National Park, finally turning onto a two-lane highway. Caravans of cars and trailers passed them, their bumpers spackled with Grand Canyon decals, their dashboards crammed with souvenir ashtrays and coffee mugs. They rolled past picture-postcard landscapes—alpine forests and skies with coiled clouds shaped like pink seashells—climbing higher and higher and higher into the crown of juniper trees and rocky cliffs. Opening the windows, Becky Jean and Carleen put their whole faces into the wind, sucking in the crackling, cold air and the aroma of pine cones.

Finally, they spotted a small painted signpost that said, GRAND CANYON, 8 MILES. Carleen pretended to pluck a banjo and began to sing, "She'll be comin' 'round the mountain when she comes. . . ." Juanita, Lila Mae, and Billy Cooper joined in on "When she comes." Even Benny whistled along and said "Toot! Toot!"

Becky Jean didn't know if it was because of the secret-way excitement or what, but all of a sudden, visiting the Grand Canyon itself wasn't that thrilling. She still wanted to go, if for no other reason than to prevent her mother from having a conniption fit. But she'd seen so many photographs and television shows that she already had a pretty good idea of what to expect. Like Carleen and Billy Cooper, she couldn't wait to see the Indian burial grounds and gemstones and caves and the hidden ancient rock formations.

Barreling into the parking lot, Lila Mae set the brake and everyone jumped out. Carleen and Billy Cooper clasped hands and skipped and hollered, "Last one there is a rotten egg!" so everyone broke into a wild gallop.

Assembled at the railing, Billy Cooper crowed "Cock-a-doodle-doooooooooo!" and Carleen yodeled "O-da-ladee, o-da-ladee, o-da-ladee—who!" Lila Mae, her hand to her chest in a Pledge of Allegiance pose, hyperventilated, shaking her head in awe at the rocky phenomenon before her. "Oh, what a sight," she drooled. "I wouldn't have missed this for the world." She dropped a nickle in a slot of the brass telescope for a closer look.

"Well," Becky Jean said, "you sure changed your tune about this place, didn't you?" She hung over the railing with her lip curled in confusion. "That's it??" Like so many other places that had been built up in travel shows and magazines, the real thing was a big disappointment. Oh, it was pretty all right, and there was no denying that it was enormous, but she'd expected it to be blinding, kaleidoscopic colors—emerald green, amber, flaming orange. The sight before her was nothing more than a big, jagged, beige hole. She was already thinking about Carlsbad Caverns, Old Faithful, Mount Rushmore, the Petrified Forest, and other sights she wanted to see. Why, she was more excited about those plantation houses in the South than she was about the Grand Canyon.

"What's wrong *now*?" Lila Mae unpeeled her eye from the telescope. "It's always somethin' with you, ain't it?"

"I wish we could ride the mules I've heard about," Becky Jean pouted. "They go right down in the canyon." She remembered all the travel pictures of campfires and marshmallow roasts and paddling rafts.

"Don't start that." Lila Mae shook her index finger three times. "Did you hear that, Juanita? Becky Jean ain't satisfied to just *look* at the Grand Canyon like other folks—she wants a donkey trip on top of it."

"My boy's no better." Juanita told them to take a look at the little nincompoop. Benny was snubbing the Canyon altogether, tottering on the guard rail, swinging his feet from side to side. "He's been begging for one of them heleecopter rides. What do ya make of that?" Juanita gestured to the Grand Canyon Skytours helicopter that hovered midair on the opposite side of the gorge.

After fifteen minutes, the kids were raising such a ruckus to leave that Juanita and Lila Mae—saying it's a darn shame that they had no life of their own—decided they might as well go. Lila Mae sighed. "Oh, well . . . I guess we can't stay here all day," and took one parting look through the telescope.

"I need a little belt for the road." Juanita unscrewed the Thermos and took a slurping, gurgling gulp of whiskey. Then she handed the liquor to Lila Mae.

"Ooooohhhh, noooooo, that episode at the Firebird left me a little green around the gills."

Juanita assured her that in no time at all Lila Mae would "build up a resistance to it"—which, Becky Jean said, was exactly what she was afraid of.

They bought Drumsticks from a wooden cart, and Lila Mae flagged down a foreign fellow—who Becky Jean said looked like Metal Fang and Lila Mae said looked like a person who knew what he was doing with a camera—to take their photograph. The man had a tall, gauzy turban on his head, and perched above his mouth was a moustache shaped like a musical note. He was fiddling with a tripod and a camera with an accordion lens when Lila Mae asked if he'd mind taking their picture.

She posed them in a semicircle, arms hooked around one another. Lila Mae spoke to him very slowly, enunciating each syllable. "Sir . . . make . . . sure . . . you . . . get . . . that . . . sign . . . in . . . the . . . picture." It said, GRAND CANYON, LARGEST CANYON IN THE WORLD.

Then there was a wild stampede to the parking lot, everyone hopping around like Mexican jumping beans, beating the windows and doors, hollering for Lila Mae to hurry and open up. Juanita asked Lila Mae if she had enough film for the camera because "they'll be plenty of pictures to take." Becky Jean reminded Billy Cooper and Carleen about their plan to bury something inside the caves, then draw a treasure map. "You didn't lose those crayons, did you?" she asked. Carleen, her Crayolas in hand, had already written HIDDEN TREASURE on a sheet of white paper. She said maybe someday they could come back and find it. When Billy Cooper asked if he could meet some "real" Indians, Benny switched looks with his mother and said maybe.

"My lord," Lila Mae cracked, "a day or so ago, nobody didn't even know the secret way existed, and now they won't shut up about it."

Becky Jean said, "Let's sing songs," so they sang "Davy, Davy Crockett, King of the Wild Frontier!" at the top of their lungs. After that, they started singing "Ninety-nine Bottles of Beer on the Wall," but Lila Mae said, "Anything but that, please." So, instead, Billy Cooper began to sing: "See you later, alligator—After while, crocodile . . . See you later. . . ."

"I can't say that I care to sing that one, either. It's a sore subject . . . ain't it?" She traded glances with Becky Jean, but her daughter just said, "A little bit, I guess," and continued to sing her lungs out with everyone else.

Although Becky Jean was playing it down now, it had definitely been a big deal the night before Roy was leaving for California. Lila Mae and Roy had been carrying on in their rumpus room with the alligator song on the record player. Lila Mae had been jitterbugging, her forefinger making tiny circles in the air, her crepe skirt fluttering around her: "See you later, alligator . . . dah-dah-dah-dah-dah!" she'd sung. "After while, crocodile . . . dah-dah-dah-dah-dah!" Roy had wielded an imaginary trombone and hopped around, his skin glazed with perspiration. They'd been having themselves a grand ole time until Becky Jean, who was supposedly at a movie, showed up. "What's this, Arthur Murray?" She stood in the doorway, a stiff mannequin. "Do you two realize how utterly ridiculous you look, cha-cha-cha-ing like a couple of I-don't-know-whats?"

Roy continued to twirl Lila Mae and simply panted, "Oh, hi, honey. How was the movie?" But Lila Mae was peeved no end. Snatching the needle from the record, she snapped off the machine. "You got a way of hornin' in when people is just havin' themselves a little fun and makin' them feel like gibbering idiots."

For days they didn't speak, and whenever Becky Jean saw her mother coming toward her, she'd jump back and turn sideways so Lila Mae could pass, just like she was afraid of getting germs if they happened to brush one another.

"See you later, alligator—After while, croco—" Lila Mae hummed along. She told Juanita she "hoped that song don't know somethin' we don't know."

They crept down the wisp of a highway, a dark yellow sun overhead, scanning the landscape for a telltale opening. Lila Mae stuck her arm out the window, motioning for the cars stacked behind her to pass them so she wouldn't miss the turn-off when it finally appeared. Soon, though, Juanita yelled, "Slow up!" and pointed to a small dirt pathway between a corridor of sagebrush. "This is it. . . . At least I believe it is."

"You gotta have good eyes to spot this, I'll tell ya that," Lila Mae snickered nervously, craning her neck forward to get a better look. The strips looked more like two John Deere tractor marks than a road. In the middle there was a row of tall, ratty weeds, and a bunch of rocks were scattered here and there. Swooping down to feast on the carnage of something hidden in the sagebrush were two vultures. A lone saguaro cactus stood near the entrance, one prickly limb jutting out like the arm of a hitchhiker. "I really don't know. You—uh—just can't hardly see it at all, can you?" Lila Mae hesitated.

"*I* can see it," Becky Jean insisted, rolling her angry eyes. "You have to be *blind* not to." Carleen said she could see it too. "What'd you think? There'd be a big neon sign showing everybody the secret way?"

"COME ON!" Billy Cooper kicked the front seat so hard that Lila Mae's head snapped forward and her chin hit the steering wheel. "LET'S GO!"

"For cryin' out loud, everyone! Give me a minute!" Lila Mae guessed they had a point about the neon sign, so she downshifted the Packard, reached her arm out, and made a left-hand-turn signal. "After this," she announced to the kids, "I've had my fill of sightseein'. So don't go gettin' any more bright ideas about goin' here or goin' there. This is *it*—ain't that right, Juanita?"

Lila Mae had been half hoping everybody would change their crazy minds, but they were just as gung-ho as ever. So, if they still wanted to take the secret road, then Lila Mae was just going to keep her mouth shut and take the derned thing. It didn't pay to argue, anyhow, especially when she always caved in. She just wasted her time fighting when she could have spent the time doing what everybody wanted her to do all along.

They were hardly off the main road when Carleen wanted

to know where the waterfalls were, Becky asked about the gems—how did they know one semiprecious stone from the other—and Billy Cooper said he couldn't wait to see the burial grounds—how much farther were they? "We'll git to 'em," Juanita assured everybody and made a dribbling motion with her hand. "Just hold your horses now."

It wasn't until they were several miles back in the middle of nowhere that Juanita suddenly swung around and poked her finger in Benny's chest. "This better be *it,* Mr. Know-It-All. I ain't been through this way but once."

"*Now* you tell me," Lila Mae grumbled.

"Yeahhhh . . ." Benny chewed his lip and scowled, swiveling around in all directions and checking the view from every window. "It *don't* look right, does it?" Lila Mae stopped the car and asked if they should just forget it, which would have been fine with her. The Packard was bouncing across the lumpy road like a rickety covered wagon, and it was all she could do to just steer. It was colder than she thought it would be, too. Here and there were sheets of hard, yellowish snow.

"Wait a minute!" Benny suddenly hopped up. "I think this *might* be the way, after all. . . . Yeah, that peak over there looks like Deadman's Cave. That's where Dad and me went deer-huntin'."

Benny pointed to a mountain way, way in the distance. It had a cap of snow that drizzled down the side like the icing on a coffee cake. "Yeah . . . yeah . . . I—I *think* this is it. . . . See the mountain?"

"I *see* the mountain plain as day." Juanita grunted angrily and furrowed her penciled eyebrows together. "But if this is the road that leads to it, then I'm a monkey's uncle."

Billy Cooper and Carleen giggled hysterically, but Lila Mae told them to shut up, that it was no laughing matter.

"Huh!" Juanita snorted. "Pretty soon we'll see the moon a-comin' out, too. Maybe we should drop in for a little visit while we're at it."

Gauzy pink film curled through the mountain peaks and a flock of umber birds darted across their path. Lila Mae steered the Packard forward, one impossible inch at a time. They passed an abandoned, decomposed car, its parts flung in the air like confetti—the steering column here, a rusty fender there, the backseat imbedded in the ground beak-first. Lila Mae figured the stray whiskey bottles, which were in the midst of all the litter, meant that only drunks would dare to take this route. At least the car remnants told her that humans had been through there since the Stone Age.

A distant radio station played the last few notes of a classical piece. The announcer said, "And that was *Rhapsody in Blue* by Mr. George Gershwin. Now we bring you several minutes of uninterrupted musical pleasure. First, Tchaikovsky's Symphony Number Four performed by the New York Philharmonic and after that, Van Cliburn will play Rachmaninoff's Piano Concerto Number Three in D Minor."

Billy Cooper asked if they had to listen to that stupid stuff. He wanted to sing more songs, so he and Carleen slapped their knees and warbled a few feeble notes of "She'll be comin' 'round the mountain when she comes, when she comes. . . ."

When Becky Jean looked through the back window, a dome of black, serrated storm clouds rushed across the sky and a whistling wind slashed tree branches and snapped up loose fragments of the landscape. She leaned forward and tapped her mother's shoulder. "It's getting dark and it looks like there's a storm coming. So, maybe we should . . . should turn back. It's not that important. We can go another time."

"This is a fine time to tell me *that*! All I've heard this whole damned trip is the Grand Canyon this and the Grand Canyon that. . . . I take you there and even *that* ain't enough. So . . . WE'RE TAKIN' THE SECRET WAY COME HELL OR HIGH WATER!"

The truth of the matter, Lila Mae thought to herself, was that she couldn't turn around even if she wanted to. The road,

if you could call it that, was no wider than your average banquet table, with a mountain of granite on one side and a Baby
Grand Canyon on the other. When you turned the car one way,
the trailer went the other way, and there wasn't enough room
for her to make a mistake. If she had to guess, she'd say there
were mere inches on either side. The only other thing to do was
to back out all the way, which would have been ten miles,
maybe even more, but if she did that, it would be the first time
she'd ever operated the car and trailer in reverse. Plus, slowly
but surely, the road was getting narrower and steeper.

Juanita told Lila Mae to stop the car someplace so they
could get their bearings. So Lila Mae and the kids watched from
behind the windshield as Juanita and Benny stood on the fringe
of a lofty cliff. Moving like lazy Susans, they put their hands
over their eyes like awnings and squinted around. First Juanita
would point in one direction and Benny would shake his head.
Then they'd turn the other way and pucker their lips in confusion. The wind lifted a tuft of tumbleweed into the air, bouncing it across the ground like a rubber ball. Juanita, fighting a
flyaway skirt, her braids swinging east and west, wrapped her
arms around her chest, while Benny jumped from leg to leg
and hugged himself to keep warm.

"Hell!" Juanita zipped across into the front seat and
slammed the car door. "He don't know where we are. It's my
fault, Lila. I shoulda knowed better than to trust that little
lamebrain. If I was smart, I'd leave the numbskull out here—
that'd show him."

Lila Mae said Juanita shouldn't blame herself, that they were
all in this together. Besides, her kids had been like broken
records with the secret-way stuff. "It's my fault, too, Juanita,
for givin' in to 'em."

Having said all that, Lila Mae still didn't know what in the
heck they were going to do. The road was tricky, too. Just when
she thought she was crazy for going another foot, the path

would string you along with a patch of gravel or something that made you think it was a real road, after all.

Lila Mae wondered if she should just bundle up, change into her navy flats, walk up ahead, and see with her own two eyes what was there. Juanita had had so much to drink, she was flopping around like a slippery fish, and Lila Mae certainly wasn't going to let her kids out of her sight. Benny volunteered to go, but you couldn't trust him as far as you could throw him. He'd come back and make it sound like the Pennsylvania Turnpike was just ahead. Lila Mae sat there in a tearful daze, wondering what on earth she should do.

"Did you read the map wrong, Mama?" Billy Cooper leaned over Lila Mae's shoulder.

"Map? *What* map?" Lila Mae placed her palms on her eyelids and held her aching head. She told the girls to "please! please! please!" give Billy Cooper something to occupy himself so he wouldn't be pestering her. She needed to get her wits about her. "My nerves are shot, completely shot!"

"I see London, I see France . . ." Billy Cooper bobbed up and down and pointed to Carleen's hiked-up skirt. "I see Carleen's under—"

"Didn't anybody hear me?" Lila Mae shouted. "Shut that boy up before I go STARK . . . RAVING . . . MAD!"

"Listen to me, little boy." Juanita lowered her voice a gruff octave and poked her finger at him. "You stay right where you are and do what your mother tells you."

After racking her brain, Lila Mae didn't see any other choice but to keep going, at least give it another mile. So she reached down and released the parking brake. "Are you gonna mind your sisters this time, Billy Cooper?" When she spun around to give her son a quick, I-mean-business look, her foot slipped from the brake. As she groped for the right pedal, she mistakenly touched the clutch instead. By the time she removed her foot—only a split second later—the road dipped and the car began to shimmy.

"Hold on, everybody!" Lila Mae warned, a stinging tightness gripping her throat.

"Look! Look!" Billy Cooper hollered, pulling the trigger on his cap gun and firing at a deer parked in the road. Its enormous brown velveteen eyes were fixed on the Packard. "It's a deer. It's Bambi!"

"Kids . . . kids!" Lila Mae jammed the brakes, her heart hammering. They rocked up and down like a teeter-totter, first the car, then the trailer. She clung to the wheel, trying to steady it, but she hit a slab of ice. "Oh! Hold on, kids!"

"What are you doing?" Juanita, stirring from an alcoholic haze, shoved her foot against the floor. Carleen screeched, "STOP! . . . PUT ON THE BRAKES!" Billy cried, "MAMA, PLEASE DON'T CRASH!" Becky Jean cried, "DO SOMETHING—FAST!"

But, try as she might, Lila Mae just couldn't get the Packard to stop. As she pumped the brake, they seesawed up and down, the car and trailer, in a deathly duel with one another. As they zoomed toward the ledge, Lila Mae turned the wheel sharply: the tower of granite on one side, the bottomless pit on the other. Her mind was in a free fall; a kaleidoscope of rocks and trees and gray sky swirled before her, spinning like a haywire roulette wheel. There were the muffled shrieks of her children, which seemed to travel from some murky, remote planet. One high unison scream stabbed the air. Then the car collided— snout first—into a bank of thorny rocks.

When Lila Mae opened her eyes, she sat for a moment, her chest one wild, throbbing heartbeat. She whispered, "Don't . . . don't anybody make a move." Very slowly she turned her head. Everybody seemed to be in one piece. Behind them was a sheer drop into the canyon; staring them in the face was a wall of stone. The car shivered and creaked as if it hadn't come to a complete halt. "This car could tip right over the side."

"My back. My poor back." Juanita grunted in pain. "It's surely broke." Benny—dreamy-eyed and woozy—wrapped his hand around his neck, rolling his aching head. Becky Jean, her body a pincushion of pain, felt an open trench on her chin and blood drip, drip, dripping into her lap. Carleen—her front tooth loose and both arms skinned—threw her arms around Becky Jean and whimpered. Billy Cooper, his arm seemingly out of its socket, rubbed his shoulder and sobbed, "My arm, Mama! My arm hurts!"

"The baby!" Lila Mae panicked. "Who's got the baby?" A dead-silent Irene Gaye was on the back floor, a tiny ringlet of flesh. She was pink-faced and clammy, and everything about her looked lopsided.

Carefully slithering out of the car, Lila Mae slipped the children, one by one, from the Packard. At first she was thrilled that she could walk at all, but as she limped around, a scalding pain jumped through her body like a lightning bolt, attacking in unpredictable spots. Beneath her mangled stocking was a bloody hollow, one that frightened her to even look at. Her head was a pounding mass. When she pressed her palm to her temple, she discovered an imprint of blood and panicked.

"Give me that damned gun!" Lila Mae snatched Billy's cap gun and pitched it into the air. "You girls was supposed to be watchin' that little demon! . . . How many times do I have to tell you that???"

Carleen staggered around, chin to her chest in shame. Becky Jean held the baby, planting little kisses on her spume of whipped-cream hair.

"Now what are we going to do?" Lila Mae moaned. Juanita's passenger door was crumpled like a candy-bar wrapper, and the windshield looked like the landing strip for a baby meteorite.

The trailer was another matter altogether. Lila Mae didn't know if the situation was called a disengage, a jackknife, or what, but it had landed at a very odd angle. The back was sticking up higher than the front, shooting into the air like a dislocated limb. Worse, one wheel stopped at the very perimeter of the canyon, a canyon so deep that Lila Mae had to turn away when she looked into it. It seemed to her that the very air that sifted through their lungs was enough to make the car tumble into the gorge.

Lila Mae grabbed the baby from Becky Jean, feeling the pitter-patter of her little pebble heart as it thumped against her chest. Billy Cooper ran to Lila Mae, flinging his arms around her legs. She could feel the tiny, delicate circle of his rib cage. "Mama, is that deer okay?"

"Billy, son, you're hurtin' my leg." Lila Mae winced in pain and fidgeted away. She told him the deer was just fine, that she'd seen it run off with her own eyes. Actually, everything had happened so fast, Lila Mae didn't know if she'd hit the animal or not. Since there wasn't any fur or blood on the car bumper and she couldn't see an injured deer itself, she supposed it was okay.

A small plane flittered above a remote mountain range. "Look!" Lila Mae, at first stunned, finally jerked off her jacket. She flapped it high above her head and yelled, "We're here! We're over here!" Becky Jean and Carleen waved their arms like flags and Billy Cooper screamed, "Hey, mister! Come get me!" But the plane, already in the last few steps of a dance recital, moved farther and farther away. "Well . . ." Lila Mae shrugged her shoulders and heaved. "I don't know what we're goin' to do, but we can't stand here like bumps on a log."

Benny said their only chance was to dig the car out of the puddle, and that they needed something to wedge between the tire and the ground—a flat rock or plank of wood. "I also need a rope and a crowbar and maybe a hammer," he said matter-of-factly, as if he were sending someone to a hardware store for supplies.

"Yeah, and I'll take a Scotch and soda while you're at it," Juanita barked sarcastically.

They searched high and low for rocks or wood or anything that would work. They eyed one single tree. Dead and growing so close to the unguarded canyon rim that the roots were exposed, it had a few puny twigs at the very top.

Finally, Lila Mae, her zombie eyes focused straight ahead, wobbled to the car and unwrapped a gray quilted furniture pad from the luggage rack. She asked Benny if a leaf from her dining-room table would do.

Even though Lila Mae followed all of Benny's instructions—releasing the emergency brake the way he said, and pressing the accelerator just the way he told her—nothing happened: the tire just made a grunting sound. When Benny hollered, "Do it again! Harder!" she rammed the pedal all the way to the floor. Little by little the leaf slipped loose, and finally, when Lila Mae gunned the engine, it catapulted through the air.

"Stop! Stop!" everyone hollered. "It's getting deeper . . . stop!" But she didn't hear them, and the wheels just kept spinning and spinning and spinning like sinking cartwheels.

"*Now* what?" Lila Mae stared at the back tire, a scrap of rubber drowning in quicksand.

"Don't worry, Mama," Becky Jean assured her. "We'll make *something* work." Lila Mae, though, was irked that out of all the people who had given her "important" advice about this and that and the other thing, *not one single soul* had warned her about spinning her wheels.

"If you was stuck somewhere, then how, pray tell, would you get out if the wheels weren't a-turnin'?" Her frantic voice crescendoed into a high squeal. "Bill Corn might have told me that! Damn that man, anyway!"

Her eyes—furious, fiery capsules—crashed around and sized up the surroundings. "Caves and waterfalls, gemstones and Indian burial grounds my foot!" she hooted. Everywhere you looked were rocks, rocks, and more rocks. There wasn't a bush or sprig of greenery to be found, nothing but dirty gray boulders and one dead bare tree. As for the cliff and the rock formations, even they were strange, knife-sharp and pointed like the turrets on a spooky Gothic castle. Lila Mae kicked a front tire and rubbed her pounding head.

If only there was a way to disconnect the two vehicles, Lila Mae thought. Chances were that during all the tugging and pushing, the whole setup would skid right off the side. And even if they did successfully disconnect the trailer, the Packard was smashed right up against the rocks. She'd have to back up, something the trailer wouldn't give her room to do.

Benny said he could start a fire—a big, explosive fire. That way, people would see the smoke. "People?" Lila Mae asked. "What people?" Benny said a fire would keep them warm, too. If they set fire to the brush (not that Lila Mae or anybody else could even *see* brush, let alone any *dry* brush), it could get out of hand in no time and cause trouble, at least according to Benny. "Uh . . . a mattress would be perfect."

"But I—I ain't *got* no mattress. I sold ours to Naomi Adcock," Lila Mae moaned.

"Come on, Mama," Becky Jean and Carleen urged. "There's all sorts of stuff we can use." They scoured the car, dumping a waxy hamburger wrapper, old newspapers, a crumpled Firebird Inn napkin, and *Kiss Me Deadly*, a Mickey Spillane paperback, into a grocery bag. Into the jumble of items, Lila Mae threw the envelopes from all Roy's letters, the ones he'd sent her when he was overseas. Carleen handed Benny some Popsicle sticks, but Becky Jean, trying to lighten things up, said, "Wait, we might need them for gravemarkers." Lila Mae pleaded, "Come on, Becky Jean, honey. Ain't we in enough of a pickle without all that?"

Carleen said to take her *Katy Keene* comic books and Becky Jean volunteered *Forever Amber* and *Wuthering Heights*, two library books she had never returned. There was also the *50,000,000 Elvis Fans Can't Be Wrong* album cover. Taking a last look at the multiple Elvis figures dressed in the gold sequined suit, she handed it to her mother.

But Lila Mae said to put their comics and records away for

the time being. "I've got me some magazines I'm done with. . . ." Lila Mae separated the different issues of *Confidential*, putting the one about Tallulah Bankhead's secret life and another one about the Roberto Rossellini–Ingrid Bergman affair in a special pile. As she sized them up, the picture of Estes Kefauver wearing a coonskin hat at a wild party caught her eye. "Gee, I ain't seen this one," she muttered. Suddenly, though, she pushed them toward Benny and said, "Oh, just take all of 'em."

"Mama!" Carleen pointed to the small red object nestled between the magazines. "Look!"

"Not now, Carleen . . . I need to get my bearin's."

"But, Mama!" Carleen insisted.

"What is it, Carleen? Didn't I tell you— Why . . . why, that's my wallet!" Lila Mae gasped. "I—I reckon I musta stuck it with my magazines. Well, I'll be."

"A lot of good it does us out here," Becky Jean muttered.

"But still"—Lila Mae's hands landed on her chest in an X— "at least now we know what *really* happened to it."

"I told you, ma'am." Benny, his face a mask of sadness and relief, turned to his mother. "I tried to tell everybody."

"Well, no hard feelin's, I hope. Becky Jean didn't mean a thing by it, did you, hon? And in my heart of hearts, I knew all along that cowboy probably wasn't the type to steal, but you know how upset a person can—"

"Shush!" Juanita held her hand in the air. "I hear something."

They could see another plane in the distance—a metallic, motorized bug, its engine clacking like a broken lawnmower. On its belly was a ruby-red light, rotating like a search beacon, circling the cliffs and folds of the mysterious gulleys below. Becky Jean thought it might be one of those tourist helicopters.

"Quick!" Lila Mae said. "We gotta try again. Call attention to ourselves!" They rummaged through their cases, pulling on bright red and blue sweaters and yellow knitted caps—swiftly, the way Lila Mae used to dress her kids when they were late for school. Flinging his arms high in the air and limping back and forth, Billy Cooper waved his Davy Crockett hat and chopped his rubber hatchet through the air in Z's like Zorro with his sword. Juanita twirled her petticoat and the turquoise Gypsy skirt in the air, shaking them like cheerleading pompoms.

The helicopter came closer and Juanita told Benny they didn't have time to light no fire. "Go get the gun and make some noise!" Benny rushed to the car, cocked the pistol, and shot a few rounds into the sky. They sounded like a convulsion of backyard firecrackers. Then he whooped, "I think he's coming!"

"MISTER! MISTER!" Billy Cooper screamed, and Carleen and Becky Jean crawled on the highest boulder, flailing around a striped bedsheet, calling to the plane to please come get them. "HERE! OVER HERE!"

The helicopter suddenly jittered around like a reckless hummingbird. Like an entry at a fancy air show, it did a few more grand-finale loops—and then it took off over the pointed cliffs. "WE'RE HERE! COME OVER HEEEEEERE!" they all shrieked and screamed, and listened to their own hoarse voices boomerang back to them. When it vanished, they stood like statues, staring at the string of violet exhaust smoke.

"Whoever was drivin' that thing should be reported," Lila Mae snipped. "It don't seem like all that daredevil stuff would be safe, does it?"

"That's a good sign, though, Mama . . . don't you think so?" Becky Jean patted her mother's shoulder. "Two planes like that so close together. *Somebody* will see us."

"I—I hope you're right, honey." Lila Mae figured if the planes could see them at all, they probably looked like a swarm of lively, colorful insects—stupid ones at that.

Thunderheads—glowering, rumbling thunderheads— scudded in slow motion above them, the kind of clouds Lila Mae had lived with her entire life, clouds that used to frighten the whole family to death, clouds that would cause her to yank her kids out of their wading pool or to fly around the house closing windows and doors.

She could even visualize her worried mother looking up at the sky, standing on the steep banks of a Kentucky mountainside, her print skirt whipping around her legs, the first sheets of rain hammering her face. She'd scream, "LILA MAAAEEE! . . . CLORA DEEEEEEE!"

Sweeping across the canyon was a cyclonic pillar of copper dust and leaves. "Look, Mama!" Billy Cooper pointed. "Up in the clouds, there's a bad monster wearing a cape!"

"I see it, hon, I see it. . . . Come on, everyone!" Lila Mae hollered over the storm. "Let's get a move on!"

Loud cracks of thunder shook the car, and the rain fell in stinging needles. Situated as they were in the humid capsule with a door that wouldn't quite close, and tilted at such a peculiar angle, they were almost flat on their backs, staring at the car ceiling, like they were in the back row of a movie theater. Plus there was the snarl of comic books and stiff, black banana peels, pacifiers, and soft-drink bottles . . . like a messy, upside-down drawer.

Wiping her elbow against the foggy glass, Lila Mae looked through the small, irregular circle. She said she'd never seen it pour like that, that it seemed like there was some invisible demon out there rattling things up. Pretty soon, with their luck, she supposed, something preposterous like a hurricane or typhoon would hit.

"We're lucky it ain't snowing," Juanita added. "It usually is this time a year."

The kids, wrapped in makeshift bandages and tourniquets from Lila Mae's white blouse, their wounds dabbed with Tussy cologne, were yoked together. They snuggled in the chenille blankets that Lila Mae bought from Imogene Virginia and the towel that Lila Mae found out Billy Cooper had swiped from the Wagon Wheel Motel in Catoosa, Oklahoma.

Nobody said a peep about food, but Lila Mae found herself thinking about the moldy hamburger bun, the lemon wedge, and the sooty cough drop that they'd discovered underneath the seat. Carleen traced the outline of the Hershey bars that were stuffed in the flannel pocket of her car coat, wanting to surprise her mother later.

"Your brother-in-law . . ." Lila Mae suddenly chuckled. "He'll have himself a heck of a time collectin' for that totem pole with me stuck out here in no-man's-land."

"What was it he said?" Juanita spliced her eyebrows together. "There were damages or somethin'?"

"Damages?" Lila Mae wailed. "Try twelve hundred some odd dollars. He even wanted it right on the spot. I told him, I said, 'Mr. Featherhorse, I just don't have that kind of money.' Now, that sounds steep, don't it, Juanita, even if it *was* a collector's item like he claims. . . . Mr. O'Dell said it didn't look like no antique to him." Lila Mae said she'd just have to pay for the derned pole on layaway or somethin'.

"Speaking of Mr. O'Dell," Juanita said, "you didn't happen to mention anything to him about where we was headed, did you?"

Since she hated to disappoint them, Lila Mae, with a ray of phony optimism, said, "You know, I just *might* have!" But then she added, "When you think about it real good, I doubt if J. Edgar himself could find us!" Although everyone chuckled, Becky Jean included, Becky Jean was actually thinking, Isn't that great. We've done such a good job of getting lost that we managed to outsmart the nation's top investigator.

Lila Mae honestly couldn't visualize spending the rest of her life on the secret road, but for the life of her, she didn't know how they'd get out of the godforsaken place, either. It would take days and days before anybody really missed them, and even then, nobody would know where to look or who to ask. Lila Mae was mostly to blame. She had complained to Juanita again and again how Roy tried to keep tabs on her and how ridiculous it was for a grown woman to report every single, solitary little twist and turn she would be taking. Now she could just clobber herself for not informing Roy of their every move. That postcard she sent to Roy from Needles, California, certainly wouldn't help matters any, either. Lila Mae wondered if she *had* mentioned anything to Mr. O'Dell, after all—not that she could bank on him being in on a rescue mission. She also thought about that Negro man at the Firebird Inn. Juanita had shushed her up before she could give him enough concrete information to be of any help, but who was she kidding? The mechanic wasn't any more of a possibility to come to their aid than Lucky O'Dell.

In those split seconds when the lightning turned the pitch-black night into daylight, Becky Jean fingered the gold-tinted edge of her diary pages. Here and there were margin notes and doodles where she had written "Mr. and Mrs. Glen Buchanan" and "Becky Jean Buchanan." Scotch-taped to another page and embalmed in cellophane was one brittle, yellowed petal from a gardenia corsage.

Although she wanted to write something—a letter to her father or her grandmother—it was too dark, and she really didn't know how it would even get to them if something did happen. And she wasn't sure if she should report all the details exactly the way they occurred or be a chip off the old block and exaggerate everything the way her mother would do. While it would be nice for them to have an accurate account of the trip, she was tempted to add some ornate descriptions, the type she'd read in her Emily Brontë and Daphne du Maurier novels. Then, if worse came to worse, somebody might discover the diary and realize that the lives of some colorful people had been nipped in the bud. Although she tried her best to stay calm, she began to think dramatic thoughts.

She remembered a movie she had seen, a movie about people who were trapped in an airplane that was about to crash. Scanning the trapdoors and secret passageways of their lives, each person racked their brain to remember all the bad deeds they'd done and all the people they'd apologize to if they had it to do all over again. Becky Jean thought about the tube of Golden Frost lipstick she'd swiped at Hutt's Five and Dime and the time she cheated on her algebra test. And there was the fancy homecoming dress—a suds of pink tulle and ivory chantilly lace—that she insisted on buying even though she knew full well that her parents could hardly pay the mortgage. And, of course, there was Mary Rose.

There was also that business with the carnival in Indiana. Never in her wildest imagination had Becky Jean thought it would become such an ordeal. But now that she looked back, it was just one more attempt to shake her mother up, for what reason she didn't really know.

It had certainly started simply enough, with the visit to their cousins' house in Indiana and the trip to a traveling carnival. Becky Jean decided that instead of going on the rides with everybody else, she would save her money for the fortune-teller, a woman named Doreena the Amazing, who had a setup at the far edge of the carnival.

So while her sisters and brothers and cousins rode the Cobra and the Wild Maus, Becky Jean paid five dollars and waited in a long line as people went through the red velvet theater curtain of a raggedy tent and exited through a plastic flap on the side. When it was her turn, she stumbled through the darkness until she spotted a glow-in-the-dark face. Although Doreena looked like a typical fortune-teller—greasepaint eyebrows, a red sequined shirt with pirate sleeves, and a gold kerchief tied at the nape of her neck—she suspected the woman was a fake. All she did was wiggle her jeweled fingers across the crystal ball; then, every once in a while, she'd roll her eyes to the back of her skull and go into a "trance."

When Carleen asked her what Doreena said, Becky Jean snatched a strand of her sister's cotton candy, let it melt in her mouth, and said, "Oh, not much—just that I'm high-strung, my favorite color is green, my boyfriend's name is Glen, and some other odds and ends. Oh yeah—she said I was probably going to die young. But don't tell Mama the last part. She'll be *reeeeal* upset."

Becky Jean hadn't meant anything by it—she had gotten into the habit of jolting her mother whenever she got the chance—and she certainly didn't think her sister would take her seriously. But Carleen had burst into tears and immediately told Lila Mae, who gasped in horror. "Oh, honey!" She had grabbed Becky Jean and squeezed her for five minutes, then threatened to report Doreena, saying, "I ain't gonna let that woman get away with that, nosireebob!"

Becky Jean told her ten times that she'd just been kidding and that the woman was a fake, anyway. Lila Mae said, "Of *course* she's a fake!" But all afternoon she fussed over Becky Jean and gave her long, sorrowful looks. And then, after the carnival, when they were bunched around the dinner table with tureens of fried chicken and mashed potatoes and the assortment of relatives, talking about gravy that didn't turn out the way it was supposed to, Lila Mae finally said, "Well, *we* had quite a scare, didn't we, Becky Jean?"

For weeks, Lila Mae would beat on the bedroom or bathroom door, saying, "Becky Jean, hon, are you in there? Is everything okay?" as if Doreena the Amazing's prediction had already come true.

Sitting there as they were, complaining about the totem-pole expense and thinking about Doreena and wishing she'd said goodbye to Mary Rose and reminiscing about the nice colored man who wouldn't take dime one for his work, Becky Jean didn't think it was possible that they'd simply wither away or disintegrate. But try as she might, she didn't know what they'd come up with or what her mother had in mind. When Carleen asked Becky Jean if she thought everything would be okay, Becky Jean said, "Of course," but when her sister pressed her for some specific solution, all she said was, "*Something* will happen."

From time to time, a troubled sliver of a moon and the faint blue imprint of Venus appeared through the clouds. Two glowing, devil-red eyes were suspended in the air. The animal stared into the night, then crawled down the rocks and disappeared. Lila Mae dozed, dreaming that she was tumbling, tumbling, tumbling. Juanita twisted and turned in her small space, her mouth open in a noisy snore. She exhaled in three quick bursts like the smoke from a train whistle.

Carleen said she heard spooky noises and wanted to know if they could turn on the Packard's radio, but Lila Mae said the battery would run down and then where would they be? Becky Jean turned on her transistor, but it was already dead. It sounded like the hollow noise you hear when you put your ear up to a seashell.

*A*ll the next day they waited for the weather to change. Early in the morning the sky was a clear canopy of lilac. Then charcoal clouds raced across it, flashing black dragon shadows against the ground. Then it rained for hours on end, metal-perforating bullets that seemed to cut right through the car.

Lila Mae had woken up early, thinking she'd just have to march right back from where they came. It wasn't like they were lost or anything. She kept thinking how simple it would all be: just get out of the car, turn her body to the right, and start walking until she reached the highway. With each ear-splitting crack of thunder, Lila Mae's hopes would plunge. And she was so dizzy that the landscape seemed to shift and slide and turn like a merry-go-round, and she'd have to press the network of veins at her temple so that everything didn't go fuzzy. Then there was her leg. It was bruised and double its normal size, a sausage-shaped slab that she could hardly move. In all honesty, she didn't know if she could walk a few yards, let alone all those miles. Juanita said it could be at least twelve, maybe more, and Lila Mae had no idea how many hours that would take.

Then there were the kids. Weak and dreamy, they all seemed to be shrinking before her eyes. Billy Cooper's forehead was radiator hot, and Carleen frantically clawed her dress and said, "Mama, what if you don't come back?"

Lila Mae was plenty aggravated at herself. Over the years she'd seen so very many movies with people in predicaments of one sort or another and she'd be the first one to be peeved at the characters. She'd elbow Roy and gripe, "Now, why don't she just swim ashore? Them waves don't look that high to me," or "Don't tell me them hikers couldn't tell one trail from another."

Now she knew how tricky it could be. Everybody was sick or hungry or injured, and every time Lila Mae mentioned something about one of them going for help, Juanita would shake her head and whinny, "Oooooh, nooooo yooou dooon't!" Then she'd bring up that pin in her hip. Lila Mae even doubted that the woman who'd written that book holding the pencil in her teeth could handle this mess.

So they waited and waited, praying the storms would end. They sang a song or two and leafed through magazines. Lila Mae read a *Betty and Veronica* comic book and the "I'm So Happy I Could Die" article in *Photoplay* about Lana Turner and her third husband. When Becky Jean picked up a *Confidential* magazine Lila Mae scowled, then she said, "Oh, all right, just this once." So Becky Jean read "The Secret Sex Life of Li'l Abner" and "Six Days and Nights with Tallulah" and studied the photos of Al Capp and Betty Grable and Miss Bankhead, who was sipping champagne from a peau-de-soie slipper. Carleen waggled her eyebrows like Groucho and said maybe they should read Becky Jean's diary if they wanted to read something *really* entertaining.

Lila Mae said they could turn on the car radio for a moment to see if they could catch the weather report. She rotated the knob back and forth, the noises skidding together like one quick slide of a harmonica. "When you want music, all you git is news and weather. When you want news and weather, all you git is GD music. Oh, well . . ."

"Mama!" Carleen, like a magician pulling a rabbit out of a hat, plucked the treasured chocolate bars out of her pocket. "Look what I got . . . trick-or-treat candy!" Lila Mae smiled wanly, caressed Carleen's cheek, and told her what a good little girl she was to have saved it. Then she split it into little nuggets. Billy Cooper, who had three candy Chesterfields left, cracked them into powdery slivers and passed them out. When they found a small packet of ketchup, they smeared it across the stiff hamburger bun and divided that up. They were saving the Red Hots and Alka-Seltzer tablets until later.

"Pretty soon we'll be roastin' lizards and cockroaches and snakes and some other odds and ends." Becky Jean sighed.

Late in the afternoon they heard a hum. Rising from behind the mountain was a tiny black speck. Slowly, Lila Mae stretched her neck and screened her drowsy eyes. She peered at the sky, her heart pitter-pattering.

As the raspy engine noise came closer and closer, Lila Mae pleaded, "Come on, everybody!" They hobbled out of the car and moved around, wiggling their arms halfheartedly. The kids called out "Over here!" and Juanita, her lips to the liquor flask, looped one arm in the air. It floated lazily and haphazardly, like a leaf falling to the ground.

But Benny moved quickly. Dumping the contents of the paper bag onto the ground, he slipped the Firebird Inn matchbook out of his pocket. One, two, three, four, five, six, he counted. He removed one match. One miniature flame popped and crackled to life. A thin stitch of smoke drifted into the air. But Benny was too quick to add the envelopes, and with one rapid blanket of a move the fire was gone, just a circlet of marshmallowy ash.

Benny said if they were going to attract any kind of attention at all, they'd have to start a big fire, a fire much larger than that.

"You cain't even get a *little* fire going!" Juanita cursed him, her eyes two black pools of hatred. "What'd they lock you up in that reform school for if you didn't know what you was doing? Now that you could *finally* come in handy . . ."

Overhead there was a variegated sky—dancing pink light and a hedge of gray clouds. Lila Mae figured they had mere minutes before it started to storm or snow.

Gathering her mouth into a bitter rosette, Lila Mae limped to the car, silent. She unsnapped her black handbag and dug into a zippered pigeonhole. Standing at the trailer door, she clutched the cold padlock in her fist and inserted the brass key. She opened the door, then reared back. It seemed an eternity since she'd seen her cherry dresser and mahogany table and the lamps with the raw silk shades. And there was the oak hutch, the very one she'd just told the colored man about. As she stood breathing in the strange odor of cedar and lemon furniture wax and mildew, she rubbed her hand across a walnut table and touched the cinnamon wool fabric on a dinette chair.

She opened a dresser drawer and discovered Roy's blue plaid shirt. Pressing her palm against it, she let it linger there as if she were touching Roy himself. She told the girls that all that stuff she'd said about their father, she didn't mean it. "You girls know that, don't you?"

Juanita, snooping through Lila Mae's things like a cheap-skate at a rummage sale, finally burrowed into the davenport, her skirt rippling around her like a giant flower petal. She re-moved her huarache sandals and rubbed her toes against the gold tapestry of Lila Mae's living-room couch. She opened her Thermos and took a nip of cold coffee.

"Make yourself right at home, why don't you?" Lila Mae mumbled, her eyes resentful, puffy little cracks. The fabric was already threadbare, the springs were shot, and it was the very least of Lila Mae's problems, but that wasn't the point.

They set down the furniture every which way, moving silently and nimbly, keeping their eyes on the gathering clouds.

Benny, sizing up the possibilities, pulled out the brocade drapes etched with chartreuse palm leaves. They had been folded carefully, still with the hooks in them, and stored inside a Bacon's Dry Goods box. He shook them out, then neatly arranged them in a pile, ladling one musty panel on top of the other.

As Benny stared at one spot on the ground, he scratched the crown of his head and cleared his throat. "Uh . . . Mrs. Wooten, I got your highly flammables right over here; then I put your slower burners on this here side. You take a look and tell me if they's any valuables you want me to hold off on. . . . Uh, make it quick, though, ma'am—it's a-fixin' to rain or snow, and I gotta keep this material dry."

"I don't know where this day went, do you?" Lila Mae turned away, rubbing her crossed arms and gazing absentmindedly into the sky. Benny flinched and shifted from foot to foot. When he tried to press Lila Mae for an answer about the highly flammables and the slow burners, she made a flipper motion with her hand and said, "Whatever . . ."

Before long the sun, a bloodshot orb, would once more be sinking behind the black clouds. Lila Mae wondered why it had to wait this long to stop raining. Why oh why oh why?

Carleen and Billy, their tiny sparrow shoulders shaking, were fastened together, and Irene Gaye was manacled to Becky Jean's shoulder, while Becky Jean slumped against a rock and swayed. "Patty-cake, patty-cake, baker's man, make me a cake as fast as—"

"I'll bet you wished you was in sunny California now, doncha, hon?" Lila Mae was thinking about how much Becky Jean loved hot, sticky summers. She'd spent hours on end in their backyard with her movie magazines and bottles of Coca-Cola. Spreading a colorful towel on the ground, she'd coat her body with a concoction of baby oil and iodine, her fingers splayed open to dry her tangerine nail polish. Sometimes she'd bake until her shoulders were blistered and her legs were tar black, and if anybody happened to get within six feet of her, she'd rear up and snap, "Could you *please* move, you're shading me!" Once Roy peeked out their kitchen window and told Lila Mae to take a look at their daughter, that she looked like a corpse, all brown and still and rigid. "If I didn't know better, I'd think she was a goner."

"Well, good night, Roy," Lila Mae griped. Her husband could casually joke about things like that, but Lila Mae was superstitious, afraid that saying it made it happen.

Unscrewing the bolts on the oak hutch, Benny disconnected the mirror, removing the drawers. He cautiously propped the glass against a boulder. You could see reflections of the sky and little chips of glittery light, like the drops on an aurora borealis crystal, fanning across the canyon.

Lila Mae, heavy lidded and dizzy, stood away from the car, sinking farther into her brown woolen coat and feeling sick to her stomach. She wished she could pitch in, but her body was nailed to the ground, and the small screen in her head was playing scenes from long ago and far away. She thought about the overturned canoe on Lake Cumberland when she, who couldn't swim, was just a desperate bobbing head floating in the corona of debris; and the straw hats and bangle bracelets and the long silk scarf that she could see swirling through the water as she drifted farther and farther away. And the lifeguard who finally rescued her and her cousin Maudelle and who, right in the middle of saving them, hollered at them, too. "What made you two ninnies think you could handle a *canoe* of all things?"

She remembered the Thanksgiving years ago when she was practically a newlywed and Becky Jean was just an infant: the house garnished with odds and ends scraped together from her family, the embroidered cloth, the stalks of delphinium, and the platter of turkey and the china bowl with cranberry sauce and one bottle of Kentucky bourbon. Lila Mae wore a purple

orchid corsage and the taffeta dress she'd made from a Butter-
ick pattern, the sort that ladies' magazines suggested the perfect
hostess would choose.

It was the first time Lila Mae had ever cooked Thanksgiving
dinner by herself. In spite of reading all the instructions on the
package, Lila Mae forgot and left the giblets bag in the turkey.
Worse, she'd also accidentally put sugar instead of salt in the
stuffing.

"Law." She shook her head slowly back and forth.

"What's so funny?" Becky Jean asked.

"Oh, I was just thinkin' about the time I made a real mess
of Thanksgivin'. I mistook sugar for salt in the stuffin' and ruined the turkey to boot! Your grandmother Wooten, you know
how she is, she pulled me aside and said, 'Why, Lila Mae,
honey, they ain't supposed to be no sugar in the stuffin', and
you was supposed to pull all them spare parts out!' But . . . how
was I to know?" Lila Mae hunched her shoulders, taking a deep,
melancholy breath. "I was a young girl then . . . nineteen at the
most." She dragged her toe in the ground, making a squiggly
line in the soil. "Well, anyways . . ."

"I don't remember any of that, do you, Carleen?" Becky
Jean grimaced.

"Well, why would ya, honey?" Lila Mae said. "You weren't
even walkin' then, and Carleen, she wasn't even born. Didn't I
just tell ya that?" Lila Mae smeared a tissue across her runny
nose, stuffed the wet Kleenex in her pocket, and glanced in
Benny's direction.

Above them were rolling black clouds gathering to the center of the sky. All the way at the top, as far as they could crane
their necks, was a tiny puckered opening, where a crown of
iridescent light and silver clouds had collected. All the sunlight
in the world seemed to be concentrated in that one spot. It
looked like the only safe, happy place in the whole universe.
"That's the little spot where God lives," Lila Mae's mother always told her daughters. Whenever the storm clouds gathered

closer together and the sunny spot got smaller until the sky was pure black, her mother would say, "Well, girls, looks like he's closed up shop for the night."

Benny, holding the spine of the hutch in the air, paused for a moment, then crashed it against a rock. When the chest split in two, he took the largest pieces and smashed them again.

"I never realized how chintzy my mother's furniture was, did you?" Lila Mae stared at the transparent water tumbling down the cliff. "You'd think they'd build something like that to last, but they don't, they just don't."

Taking the loosened slats, Benny added them to the pyramid of furniture. He made a torch from the newspaper and dragged one more match across the striker. He watched the yellow teardrop flame as it blinked and trembled, then throbbed to life. It inched its way across the surface of a silk lampshade, leaving behind a charred stain. Then it caught the hem of the chartreuse drape. Taking the bottle of Arpège, the last cologne Roy had given Lila Mae, he jiggled until it was golden and foamy. Finally, a garden of gusty flames and a steeple of billowy smoke curled and coiled high into the air.

Quickly, and one by one, he added the dining room chairs, and then the bedposts, and after that the cherry table, to the highly flammable pile.

Benny said he needed somebody to help him move the gold davenport, that it was next. Then he picked up the matchbook and struck one more match.

Chapter Thirteen

When the man from the Marathon station finally got to them, he parked his truck yards and yards away. Switching off his headlights, he swung his two gangly legs over the side and hopped to the ground. He stood for a second to get his bearings; then he draped a yellow rubber raincoat over his head. He pulled a flashlight from inside his jacket and guided the silver beam in large triangles. Spotting the cluster of people, he trotted toward them, his high black rubber boots carefully avoiding lagoons of mud. When he was several feet away from the Packard, he stopped and he revolved around very, very slowly.

"Mercy, mercy me," he grimaced, scratching the back of his leathery neck. It was heavily creased in diamond shapes like the patterns on a scored ham. "What in the *world* made you folks come all the way out *here?*"

Slinking across the sky was the misty white cloud of the Milky Way. One wide spear of frosty moonlight gilded the canyon. Lila Mae sighed, her shoulders sagging, her eyes smoking in exhaustion. She gave the man a weak flicker of a smile and murmured, "Well, sir . . . that's a long, drawn-out story," although she knew he couldn't hear her.

But the man rubbed his loose orange flap of an ear and pressed them for an answer. "Didn't *nobody* tell ya where the highway was?" Becky Jean, in a flash of rolling eyes, muttered,

"Can't we please just get this show on the road?" But Carleen, her skin goose-pimply and her long blond pigtails dripping wet, gathered the Wagon Wheel towel into a shawl over her shoulders. She squinted in confusion and said through her chattering teeth and narrow blue lips, "What do you mean, mister? Ain't this the secret way?"

Lila Mae in Her Old Age

Los Angeles, California

L ila Mae had been trying for weeks on end to find out if her next door neighbor was dead, but she didn't know how to go about it. The woman, whose name was Rose, had come down with some exotic, crippling disease and supposedly had been on her last legs for a couple of years. During that time, Lila Mae usually spotted the neighbor in the early afternoon taking her daily walk with her heavyset Norwegian nurse. When Lila Mae hadn't seen Rose for a few days, she would get suspicious and be on the lookout. Each day she would peek through the fortress of eucalyptus trees that separated their property. Just when she least expected it, she'd spy the nurse's big white rubber shoe on the cement step, then the round gray tip of Rose's cane, and realize it had been a false alarm. This time, though, it had been a whole month, the weather had certainly been warm enough to go outdoors, and still there had been no sign of her dying neighbor.

Even more mysterious was the fact that several weeks back Lila Mae had seen dozens of cars parked in their neighborhood and oodles of strange people going in and out of Rose's house. Many of the cars even had out-of-state license plates. Grabbing her binoculars, Lila Mae had tottered over her curlicued balcony and craned her neck through the greenery, hoping to get a better look. But she still hadn't seen a soul she recognized. This made her all the more suspicious that Rose had died and the strangers were actually relatives from out of town who'd come to pay their respects and offer condolences to her husband, Sid. She sized up the crowd, looking for family resemblances, but all she could see through Sid and Rose's living-room picture window were the backs of sport coats and the tops of women's heads.

The other possibility was that Sid and Rose had thrown a party of some sort and hadn't invited Lila Mae. This was beyond her, since Sid always went out of his way to chat with Lila Mae whenever she weeded her herb garden. And, before Rose fell ill, Lila Mae would see the couple swinging their tennis racquets over their shoulders, Rose in her white pleated skirt, her nest of hennaed hair pinned at her neck, and Sid with his wavy, mercury-colored hair and the Grecian bas-relief profile. They always bent over backwards to toot the horn on their red Mercedes and wave. Plus, their tree trimmers often clipped her trees free of charge—and once Sid and Rose even asked her to have dinner with them at Sven's Swedish Smorgasbord. So, if they invited that many people—and it looked to Lila Mae like it was way over one hundred—then she certainly figured she'd be one of them.

Besides all that, Lila Mae couldn't remember the couple *ever* giving a party, period, even when Rose was healthy. Why would they throw one now that Rose was worse than ever? Plus, that still didn't explain Rose's strange disappearance.

Then one August morning Lila Mae got a lucky break, although at the time that seemed like a strange thing to call it. The aroma of smoke and a shaft of chartreuse light shooting through her shutters woke her up. Cranking open her bedroom windows—blazing one hundred degree heat choking her nostrils—she peeked through the flowering lemon trees and across the cypress treetops and cottages of the Hollywood Hills. Whipping along the crest of Mulholland Drive, mere miles from Lila Mae's home, was a tower of ferocious, blood-red fire clouds.

"Oh, dear me!" Lila Mae's heart palpitated in fear. Quickly, she sprinted from room to room, sideswiping armchairs and tables as she clicked on the radios and televisions, searching for Eyewitness News. "Can't be all that bad, yet," she cracked. "They're still runnin' pantyhose and aspirin commercials."

Sliding her feet into her bedroom slippers, she wrapped her satin quilted robe around her and scurried to her back porch to size up the situation.

From the brow of her rugged hillside, Lila Mae's brick cottage sat like a watchtower with a bird's-eye view of the hills surrounding her. Through the thick gold mist that obscured the sun, she surveyed the plots of purple ice plant and trailing bougainvillea, all the patterns wedged together like crazy quilts. Buried under the canopy of Italian pine and palm trees were the terra-cotta tile roofs of the houses that sat haphazardly, sometimes perched at the top of rolling fields of English ivy or nestled in overgrown vinery at the end of curvy driveways. For miles around her she could see the emerald and amber hills that rose and peaked and dipped against the apricot sky.

On clear days, she could even see across the steep gulleys, through the spiky leaves of the yucca plants, to the stone slabs leading up to the old Houdini estate. Another fire had already taken that house years ago, but at the cap of the hillside, the remnants of chimneys and the foundation were still embedded in the ground.

Here and there, her neighbors were tottering on their tiptoes, binoculars glued to their eyes, as they stretched to view the flames. Behind the fretwork of their iron gates and with their palm trees swaying like pompoms, Gary and Lorraine Lippman were hustling to assemble the pump and hose that connected to their swimming pool, armed to fight the fire if need be. Henry Alter Booth, a stick-thin musician with alabaster skin and ink-black hair who kept odd hours, stooped to pick up his newspaper. He gaped into the smoky sky with a what-gives? expression, then scratched his unkempt head. And Josephine Avery, the schoolteacher with the pagoda of butterscotch hair who lived in the Santa Fe adobe, was arched over her garden hose, spraying her succulent plants, her teardrop rear end swaying under the caftan. Yanking a dead palm frond from the ground, she waved it in the air at Lila Mae.

"Here we go again," Lila Mae, hands cupped around her lips, shouted across the gulch between their houses.

Josephine, entwined fingers raised in the air, hunched her shoulders, and yelled back, "What can we do but keep our fingers crossed?"

In the background, barreling through the twisting, narrow lanes of the Hollywood Hills, moving closer to Lila Mae's area, was the percussion of sirens and squealing tires and the shrill pierce of ambulances. Lila Mae lunged over the wooden picket fence that separated her patio from the bluff that sloped down to Sid and Rose's property. Usually Sid was the first one to hose down the terraced ivy and the manicured flower gardens or to activate the sprinkler system on his roof. Yet there was still no sign of him or Rose. For the life of her, Lila Mae just couldn't imagine what was going on over there.

A gust of wind slashed through the canyon, decapitating the bundles of lilac and newly planted wisteria and lifting up Lila Mae's black iron patio furniture as if it were scraps of paper. A white ceramic flower pot tumbled down the driveway, and the hummingbird feeder swayed back and forth like an out of kilter pendulum. "Well, gee whillikers . . . this is just what we need!" Lila Mae complained. "Hurricane-strength winds." She gathered her robe, which was billowing like an unruly parachute, holding the hem in one tight knot. With her other hand, she flipped the hose spigot around and around, but with all the fire hydrants working overtime, the water ran out in a thin trickle. Waving the nozzle back and forth, she examined the pitiful damp lines in the pavement. "A lot of good this does me!" she muttered, tossing the hose to the ground.

At the base of her driveway, Henry Alter Booth's boy whizzed by on a skateboard, cuddling a big loud stereo to his ear. Garbed in baggy black pants with heavy silver chains roped around him, he was a carbon copy of every other kid: a junior chain-gang member. "Hey, little mister," Lila Mae murmured to herself, "you're about to get your britches burned." Well, what can you expect from a boy raised by beatniks? The stereo was blaring a silly old tune, one that Lila Mae's kids used to sing all day long and one she hadn't heard for ages: "See you later, alligator . . ." Lila Mae hummed along. "After while, crocodile . . . See you later, alliga—" Through the shaggy tree branches, which shielded her property from the street below, she could see the boy, his shaved skull notched with Egyptian hieroglyphics, maneuvering down a crooked driveway, the skateboard clapping time with the song.

Coiling the hose on the grass, she smeared her hands against her robe, making two dusty tracks, then went inside to fix herself some raisin toast and corn flakes.

When it came to most things, Lila Mae was usually afraid of her own shadow. But since she'd been through the fire business so many times in the past, at this point it was beginning to seem like a dress rehearsal for a production that was doomed to cancellation. The first blaze, a legendary holocaust that demolished thousands of acres from Griffith Park to Laurel Canyon, had come within a few blocks of her home. Paralyzed with fear, she'd filled all of her luggage and pillowcases with her precious belongings, ready to flee. She had boarded the sheriff's evacuation van with her neighbors and spent the night in the Red Cross shelter, only to learn the next day that the fire had changed its course and missed them completely. Over the years, there had been so many hours of waiting for the next evacuation notice followed by even more hours unpacking and rearranging everything.

Because of so many false alarms, it was hard to believe anything would truly threaten their area. But, it *could* happen, Lila Mae reminded herself—it very well could! The canyons and high winds were a combustible combination—so tricky that the fire could jump around, blowing embers hundreds of yards away. And it had been so bone dry that even the tiniest ash could ignite a completely different blaze. Lila Mae could see flames licking the hillside just a few miles away and spears of oily black smoke shooting into the sky. And on the news, reporters stood next to cyclones of fire, interviewing hysterical people with boxes and infants who were running from their burning houses, homes that had seemed perfectly safe an hour before.

But all she could do was stay tuned and wait until the firemen and police penetrated the area to tell her what was what. When the time came, the officials would cruise through the hilly labyrinth, like General Schwarzkopf orchestrating his troops, barking emergency information through a megaphone about the location of the fire, the wind patterns, and evacuation procedures that might be necessary.

While the tea kettle boiled, she collected her magazines and newspapers, putting them in a pile. Although she preferred reading them in the exact opposite order, she had the stack in a save-the-best-for-last arrangement. So, on top was the *Los Angeles Times,* next came *People,* and after that, her tabloids. She noticed that one of the latter had a juicy article about the poor beauty queen who was murdered and a man who was facing a prison term for killing some exotic squirrel.

Taking a sip of English Breakfast tea, she unfolded the newspaper, scanning the front page of the *Los Angeles Times.* As usual, the paper had hundreds of articles containing heartbreaking or earth-shattering news, fifty pages of advertisements for computer paraphernalia, and one "Local Fireman Rescues Kitten Stuck in Tree" story. On the front page alone, there was a horrifying article on the ozone hole, plus the headline story detailing a drive-by shooting. The incident left twelve innocent bystanders dead, including two honor students, a beloved clergyman, a missionary couple fresh from their honeymoon, and Helena Blankenship, a forty-year-old woman who recently survived bone cancer only to be gunned down by hoodlums. Flanked by their attorneys, Lorene Blankenship and Leon Dorr, relatives of the slain cancer survivor, said, "The cowardly thugs who did this to Helena must be brought to justice." Sometimes Lila Mae wondered if the papers made this stuff up, or if it was pure coincidence that every dead person turned into a hero or heroine. Naturally, to balance things out, on the back page there was a human-interest story about Victor Raymond Poole, an armless bowling champion who shoved the bowling ball down the alley with his foot.

"Oh my." She sat upright, adjusting her glasses and whacking the newspaper in the center to straighten it. Some fellow, one James E. Starrs, a professor of forensic sciences, was reexamining the Lizzie Borden murder story. Starrs even claimed the hatchet introduced into evidence during Borden's trial was not the murder weapon at all! The professor was about to use radar to determine if the skulls of Miss Borden's father and stepmother were still intact, and he even planned to exhume the craniums for proof. "Well, how do you like that . . . Lizzie was framed!" Lila Mae, on the edge of her seat, devoured each syllable, but, after a dramatic buildup, she was shocked when the professor said, "It would *still* not tell us who the murderer is."

"What kind of stunt is Starrs tryin' to pull? If Lizzie didn't do it"—Lila Mae slugged the table—"then he's got to tell us who did!" That's the very same thing the papers did with the Black Dahlia murder, writing about it every few months even though there'd been nothing new to report since the 1940s. Oh, it just irked her no end.

Lila Mae folded the paper, looking around the kitchen as if there was something she should be doing. But she didn't know what. Outside her window, flitting through the filigree of her herb garden, were a pair of brown quail. "Bob Whiiiiiite!" they whistled. "Bob Whiiiiiiite!" Transfixed, Lila Mae stared at the pink-cheeked Olympic athlete pole-vaulting across the corn-

flakes box, her eyes scanning the nutrition chart with its cholesterol and fat gram information. "See you later, alligator—After
while, crocodile . . ." Her feet jittered around as she cleared the
table. Smoothing the creases on the linen tablecloth, she then
rinsed her cereal bowl and arranged it in the dishwasher. Her
lace curtains needed to be hand-washed, but what good did
it do to clean them with so much grit and ash flying around?
On the small silver pad at her telephone she wrote: "Clean
curtains."

The African violets on her windowsill didn't look too hot,
so she pinched off the crisp, dead leaves and tossed them into
the garbage. After that she changed the scummy, lime-green
water in her crystal vase and readjusted the clumps of Queen
Anne's lace and cabbage roses. Since nobody had contacted her,
she picked up the phone to see if she still had service and she
got a dial tone. "That's funny . . . I'd'a thought someone would
have called by now."

Time to make the bed and tidy the bathroom, she thought.
So she did the usual, making the bed, fluffing the petit-point
pillows on her armchair, shaking out her scatter rugs. On her
vanity was a small community of cologne bottles and jars. Although most of them were as old as Methuselah, many of them
had been gifts too. Swishing the damp cloth to clean the
smoked-glass top, she moved the containers around like chess
pieces: the square, tailored bottle of Chanel No. 5, the urn-
shaped glass of Shalimar, and the Eiffel Tower steeple of White
Shoulders perfume. What else is there to do? she wondered.

As she bobbed along the hallway on her way to her living
room, she noticed that the frames in her den were uneven.
Crouched on the cushions of her gray couch, she reached up
and straightened Leona Helmsley's autographed picture, making a mental note to come back with the Windex. The photo
was hung dead center in her grouping of celebrities to whom
she'd sent letters of support in their troubled times—H. R. Hal-
deman, Jean Harris, Michael Milken, Patty Hearst, even Lau-

rence Powell, a police officer involved in the recent Rodney King beating. Oh, her kids rolled their eyes every time they spotted a new eight-by-ten wood-tone frame, and Becky Jean even told her she was nuts, that someday one of the criminals would get out of prison and hound her. It was true that she had gotten rather chummy with the police officer after he sent her a form letter to thank her for her kind note. It was addressed "To Whom It May Concern" and ended with "Very truly yours, Laurence J. Powell," but his last note—one of dozens—started "My dearest Lila Mae" and was signed "All the best, Larry." So far Becky Jean didn't know about the correspondence with the policeman, and that's just the way Lila Mae intended to keep it. And it certainly didn't mean the man was going to pounce on her if he was imprisoned and then released.

Helicopters—a squadron of four or five—were cutting across the area, searching for stray embers that could ignite new fires. The sky was dark and heavy, a choking auburn blanket that covered the sun and filled Lila Mae's lungs. Just to be on the safe side, she gathered together the shoeboxes and suitcases that held her irreplaceable items. Through the years, they ended up in one convenient spot, just in case she had to make a fast getaway. Lugging the first batch of cardboard boxes outside, she set a lopsided stack on the ground, and from the huge jailer's key ring on her wrist, she pulled out the trunk key and fiddled with the latch.

"Oh, my gosh!" Lila Mae thumped her chest. There was Sid! In between a lacy elm-tree branch, blanched by a column of sunlight, were the ripple of his silver hair and the curve of his bare, sunburned back. He was on bent knees, unraveling a cable of garden hose. "Hey!" she hollered, her heart skipping beats. "Hey, Sid!"

Pivoting around, Sid placed his hand in a salute position to block the sun. "Oh . . . Lila Mae. Hi there." He brushed his dusty palms together briskly, his voice booming through the battlefield of canyon noises. "Isn't this something?"

"It sure is!" Lila Mae screamed back, her heart doing a lively minuet. She set down a cardboard box and smoothed her robe, wondering if she was a disheveled sight. "How is everything?" Just then, like a John Philip Sousa marching musicale, the caravan of fire engines and police cars careened around the curve. They belched and tooted and groaned until the roar was so deafening that it shook the very ground on which they stood. Cupping his hand to his ear, Sid joggled his head in confusion. Lila Mae repeated, "I said, HOW IS EVERYTHING?"

"Fine . . ." Sid shrugged. "Considering." Lila Mae figured it was as good a time as any to get the lowdown, so, taking small side steps, she inched down her steep driveway, still gripping her robe. The first thing she'd do is apologize for the way she looked, and after that she'd talk about the fire, and then she could say something vague like, "And is everything taken care of with Rose?" But when Lila Mae looked up, Sid was standing next to his perforated wall of organized hammers, drills, and wrenches. He gave her a hasty wave as he ducked farther into his garage. In a seizure of rattles and squeaks, the automatic garage door rolled down and Sid disappeared, one inch of him at a time, behind the corrugated metal wall.

"Well, shoot." Lila Mae stood with one hand pressed on her narrow hip. Now she didn't know if Sid meant "Fine, considering the fire" or "Fine, considering Rose's recent death." Oh, it just peeved her no end that those fire trucks and every other emergency vehicle in the city popped up at the exact moment she finally had a conversation going. "Just my luck," Lila Mae fumed. Oh, well . . . if they *did* have to evacuate the area, sooner or later Rose would be forced out along with everybody else. "Lord," she guffawed to herself. "What a price to pay, havin' my house burn down just to find out if my neighbor is still alive. Have I gone off my rocker? I think maybe I have."

When she snapped on the television for an update, every channel featured their top news anchors on the air and had dispatched dozens of reporters to the fire scene. So far, hundreds of acres had been scorched and hundreds more were threatened. One reporter, Phoenix Arnett, a tanning-bed victim with a Julius Caesar toupee, was determined to get his point across to the TV audience. He stuck his microphone toward the fire, which sounded like a thundering stampede of elephants. Then the camera—inching across the once-lush terrain—showed the black, brittle skeletons of shrubbery and cacti and the silhouettes of stoves and lawn furniture, all trapped in hot, gurgling embers. The most tear-jerking image was the crying toddler sucking her thumb and holding a toy bunny by a long, pink, floppy ear. Then there was an ancient couple named Talmadge who were wearing striped pajamas and holding a shabby Yorkshire terrier puppy. They'd lost their sixty-year-old Spanish villa plus a menagerie of strange animals that they weren't even licensed to keep. The camera showed close-ups of a bunch of open cages, and the reporter told residents in the area to be on the lookout for monkeys, mandrills, peacocks, and other exotic animals that could be roaming around.

The assortment of reporters, festooned in fireproof raincoats, their pompadour hairdos blowing wildly and rivulets of sweat trailing down their cheeks, heaved in excitement as if they were soldiers in a war zone. They'd wave their arms toward the various spots where the fire had raced down hillsides and swallowed up entire housing developments. And just to make things ultradramatic, they always stood under a hive of helicopters or next to walls of fire. Danny Phillman, a slick reporter with a clump of Clairol-blond hair and shifty eyes, cradled a small rubber doll with singed hair left behind by Guadalupe and Horatio Alvarez, an immigrant couple with three small toddlers who were now homeless. "This tragic, tragic fire that woke Los Angeles up before dawn and has already flattened thousands of acres and over one hundred houses is showing NO SIGNS OF LETUP!" the man, practically in tears, hollered into the TV camera.

"That's good news for you, ain't it, pretty boy," Lila Mae

barked to the television screen. Even though the news reports referred to "these heartbreaking, tragic events" and all the reporters looked like they'd lost their best friend, they didn't fool Lila Mae one bit. They got their kicks from scaring people to death, wanting them to believe that no matter what they did or where they were, they were doomed. When they got desperate for legitimate material, they'd dream up horror stories about tragedies that *could* happen, playing up deadly this and killer that. To hear them tell it, commonplace items such as air-conditioning systems and stadium bleachers and dishwashing liquid and hot tubs were first-degree murderers who were out to get you. Why, even the bacteria found on an ordinary toothbrush could do you in, at least according to Phillman's last exposé! So after weeks of reporting counterfeit tragedies, the fire finally got them off the hook.

Every time there was a disaster, it was no wonder that Lila Mae would get phone calls from friends all over the city and country. Whenever she picked up her phone, they'd pant, "Lila Mae, is that you?" like they didn't expect her to be alive or Los Angeles to still be there.

All things considered, it was only her kids who were nonchalant and unpredictable in emergencies, especially when it involved Lila Mae. Hopping from one extreme to another, most of the time they made her feel like she was the weakest, most vulnerable person in the world, someone who couldn't be trusted to make the smallest decision by herself. If they picked her up for dinner, Lila Mae would open the door and one of them would say, "Is *that* what you're wearing? It's cold outside, you know," or if she happened to buy an appliance that went on the blink, they'd gawk at her and say, "Whatever possessed you to buy a Kenmore instead of a Maytag?" or some such.

Then when catastrophe struck, they'd shift into another gear and treat her like Hercules, a pillar of strength who was so self-sufficient and indestructible that a fire that not only had the whole city scared stiff but was within striking range of Lila

Mae's property was no big deal at all and they didn't even need to call her, let alone pitch in to help.

As ashamed as she was to admit it, she used to count the hours until they were grown up and out of her hair. Oh, she loved them to pieces; they were the engine that kept her life chugging along. But enough was enough. For years, she was like an octopus, her tentacles extending north, south, east, and west. Sixteen hours a day she was bent over washing machines or ironing boards, four barnacles clinging to her arms and legs. If she didn't have a baby shackled to her hip, she'd be hemming a dress Becky Jean needed "right now!" or gluing the plumage on Carleen's majorette uniform or concocting a costume for a play. The school would send home a note saying, "Your child will be playing the part of . . . ," and naturally it was always something utterly absurd, like a cauliflower or a chest of drawers.

Even when she went to the bathroom, someone would pound on the door to inform her that they were looking high and low for a wool cardigan or baseball glove or arithmetic homework and Lila Mae should hurry up and do whatever she was doing in there and come help them find it. Once, when the kids were running around like wild animals and she couldn't take it anymore, she even screamed, "You're just like insects buzzin' around rotten fruit! Just get out of my hair for a while!" They just yelled right back, "We'd rather be insects than rotten like you!"

Lila Mae winced, just thinking of all the hateful things they'd said to each other over the years. Oh, sure, they'd always apologize to one another, sometimes popping corn or going out for ice cream cones, eventually chuckling about how hotheaded they all were, trying to reel the person out of the sewer in which they'd just been dunked. But the damage had already been done, the insults embedded in some secret hiding place of half-healed wounds.

Now that they were grown up, and Lila Mae had taken a

few unbridled trips to shopping malls and an impromptu drive to Montecito, or after she'd watched a few Miss America pageants without being interrupted or had her fill of reading the tabloids without being called a nincompoop, twenty years' worth of pent-up desires were out of her system. And now, after so many years of yearning for peace and quiet, she was ensconced in a cozy little home with her flower beds and birdbaths, right where she always thought she wanted to be, with nobody to look after, wondering why in tarnation the phone wasn't ringing off the hook.

By late afternoon, the only people who had called were her friend Dixie, who wanted to know if Lila Mae was still planning on driving her to the market, a computerized sales message soliciting lower mortgage rates, and Olive, her ninety-year-old mother-in-law. "Lila Mae, honey, is that big far anywheres near you? I had me a time gettin' through on the phones yes I did." The woman seemed to be shouting all the way from Kentucky to California. "You're okay, ain't ya?" When she said, "I reckon the girls is there with ya, though," Lila Mae was too embarrassed to tell her she hadn't heard a peep from them, so she fibbed and said they were racing over and they'd be there any minute.

Finally, Lila Mae decided to make a few calls of her own just to see if there might be something unpredictable about the phone service after all. Although she reached Carleen right off the bat, the conversation, which began with a bang—"Mom! I've been trying to get through. . . . Are you okay? I was so worried!"—ended with a whimper. She told Lila Mae that she hoped she'd be all right and to let someone know if she had to evacuate so they could keep tabs on her. With Carleen living in San Francisco, that's about all she could expect from her. But where in tarnation was Irene Gaye? Deciding not to stand on ceremony, Lila Mae picked up the phone, visualizing the familiar atmosphere at the other end of the wire: the ether black room strewn with empty cigarette cartons and a "dinner" table with open potato chip bags, skillets, and saucepans—food containers and cooking utensils that were also the dishes. Irene Gaye—sluggish and disoriented, her voice fraught with irritation—said she didn't know about the fire since she was still in bed. "What *time* is it, anyway?" she griped, her snapping-turtle personality coming to life. To her credit, she did ask Lila Mae if she wanted "us" to come get her—"us" being her and the viperous boyfriend Lila Mae despised—but Lila Mae figured her daughter's offer was as counterfeit as the WILL WORK FOR FOOD signs the street-corner hobos held up to motorists. Try to take 'em up on it and see how fast they refuse, Lila Mae thought.

In any event, nobody got as hysterical as Lila Mae thought they should, and it wasn't until that evening that Becky Jean even called her back. (If Becky Jean wasn't interested in her mother's welfare, Lila Mae would have thought, if nothing else, she would be concerned that maybe the house itself would burn to the ground, since, after all, it belonged to her!) It was true that her daughter was out of town, but what kind of excuse was that, since she *always* seemed to be out of town? And even after she knew about it, she was still very casual, only saying, "Mom, did you call me? I got some scribbled message about a fire or something. I guess the new housekeeper took it."

"Haven't you been watching television? There's a fire all right . . . more like an *inferno!*" Lila Mae's voice rose several hysterical octaves. "Dozens of houses have been burnt to a crisp, and all those acres above the reservoir . . . *gone forever!* There's some old couple who had a zoo in their backyard. Someone reported monkeys and ocelots running wild in the streets!" Lila Mae cradled the phone on her shoulder and squirted lemon furniture polish on a walnut end table. "When people I haven't heard from in years call me all panicky and I haven't heard boo from my own kids, it makes me wonder. I even heard from your grandmother!"

"Can you believe, at her age? She is *amazing*. How in the *world* did she know about a fire in Los Angeles?"

"She's just up on things, I suppose." Although Lila Mae shared Becky Jean's views on Olive, her mother-in-law's mental agility wasn't the topic she had in mind for the telephone conversation. "Where are you, anyway, New York? You be careful when you're there." Since Lila Mae had never been to Manhattan, with everything she'd read in the papers about the goings-on, she was always afraid her daughter would be shipped back in a pine box. Even though she knew that telling Becky Jean to watch out—like *all* the advice she had ever given her—went in one ear and out the other, she still had to get it off her chest.

"Mom, we've been here for over a week. . . . You knew that." Becky Jean covered the phone, barely muffling what seemed to be a secondary conversation she was carrying on in the background. Lila Mae knew it was too good to be true that she would have her daughter's undivided attention. More than likely, she was flapping her hands at this one to do one thing and mouthing an order to another, running back and forth like those performers who spin plates . . . just to make sure the three-ring circus didn't grind to a halt.

"Wouldn't the fire department evacuate you if you were in any danger? What about the Bancrofts? Have they left the area?"

"Huh! You certainly asked the sixty-four-thousand-dollar question. I haven't seen hide nor hair of either one of them for weeks. Well, actually, I *finally* saw Sid this morning, if you can call it that. . . . But I'm not even sure Rose is still alive, the poor woman. You know, she's been *gravely* ill. She has something wrong with her central nervous system or some such. . . . I'm *sure* I mentioned it."

"I guess I remember something like that."

"It's a miracle Rose has lasted this long, especially since I was made to believe she only had months to live. If she's gone, I should send a bouquet or a casserole or something, don't you think? But can you imagine if I did that without concrete evidence? And try as I might, I just can't seem to find out a thing—not a thing! I even called the *Los Angeles Times* to see if the obituary department could trace Rose's name, but the man said, 'You must be kidding, lady.'

"I told him, I said, 'All you ever hear about these days are those darned computers and modems, how they're supposed to tell you everything and then some. Yet I want to find out about one simple death and it's like pulling teeth.' "

"It sounds like you're making a big deal out of nothing. Don't any of the neighbors know?"

"Nobody knows a thing, not a *thing*. It's all so secretive. . . . Hold on a second, hon." Lila Mae hopped up, then dashed to the mirrored armoire and wiped another smudge. "Why, I'm even lucky I know who my neighbors are, the way things are going in this world. This would have *never* happened in Kentucky, you know. Why, everybody would have nursed Rose right up to the end, I'll grant you that."

"Hey, I've got an idea. Drop Sid a note asking him if they'd watch the house while you're on vacation. Maybe you'll get lucky and Sid will say, '*I'd* be happy to watch your house for you, but Rose can't, because she kicked several weeks ago.' "

"Now just stop it, Becky Jean. This is no laughing matter." Lila Mae pressed the remote control on her TV volume, her forehead creased in curiosity. "Well, look at this. . . . They're interviewing some woman who's got a strange bird in her back-yard. She said it landed on her stepladder at eleven o'clock this morning and it hasn't budged since. It looks like the cockatoo that belonged to that Talmadge couple. . . . Well, I'll be darned."

"Mom, did it occur to you that Sid or Rose might be peeved at you for something?"

"Well . . ." Lila Mae made a prune face. "Not really." In all honesty, she couldn't think of anything that would have offended the Bancrofts, and Sid had seemed perfectly fine that morning. If they *were* snubbing her, Lila Mae figured, it was Rose's doing. Since her illness, the woman, who used to be a slash of animation and energy, was a wet mop. Her groomed, burnished hair of old was now stringy and rat gray and it hung from her droopy head like a weeping willow. As she sat in her wheelchair tearing holes in a damp, crumpled tissue and balancing a *Sunset* magazine on her lap, Lila Mae and Sid chatted about this and that. Once Sid, in a candid moment, told Lila Mae that despite outward appearances, Rose had always been a stick in the mud, illness or no illness.

"If I didn't know better, Mom, I'd think you had your eye on Sid."

"Becky Jean, that's *not* so!" This was a recurring theme with Becky Jean, and one that embarrassed the daylights out of Lila Mae. Plus, nothing could be farther from the truth. But if Becky Jean was picking up on something, maybe Rose did, too. Lila Mae decided to make a point of playing up to Rose—that is, assuming the woman was still alive.

"Mom, wouldn't it be something if Rose has been alive all this time, but dies in the fire?"

"Rebecca Jean! Now, that isn't even funny! Lord!" It was all Lila Mae could do to keep from giggling, but she didn't want to egg her irreverent daughter on. She jerked her sheet with a loud crack and folded down the bed. "Put Ava on the phone if she's there."

Ava, her twelve-year-old granddaughter, had a sweep of cottony blond hair and eyes as bright as blue Christmas ornaments. She was cheerful and twinkly (much more so than Becky Jean had ever been—which really wasn't saying much!), with a seashell-pink complexion and an exquisite little mouth that was like two flower petals pressed together.

Although Lila Mae adored Casey, Carleen's little girl, it was Ava who made her heart soar. It was also Ava who loved to sing along with Lila Mae, while Casey, one evening when Lila Mae was doing a very frisky version of "I'm Gonna Wash That Man

Right Outa My Hair" and rubbing her scalp at the same time, had snapped her hands over both ears and said, "Ooooh, shuuut up, Gramma!" Since the girl was only five at the time, Lila Mae had laughed it off, but, who knows, maybe Lila Mae secretly held it against her. Actually, it was the type of reaction Lila Mae figured Becky Jean's daughter would have come up with. If she didn't know better, she'd have said her two grand-daughters were switched at birth.

And, while Casey was more of a tomboy, Ava was so lady-like! Lila Mae and Becky Jean had attended a Mother's Day tea presented by the Bel Air Ladies Cotillion, and Lila Mae spent the entire time beaming at her exceptional granddaughter. In her lacy, parfait-colored dress, a strand of graduated pearls, and silk gloves, she sat on a damask Chippendale settee. In front of her was a tea table with silver kettles and strainers and porcelain waste bowls and one tiered confection tray with triangular cu-cumber sandwiches and pastel bonbons. As Ava expertly poured and distributed the tea and smeared a dollop of Devon-shire cream on her scone, Lila Mae defied anyone to make the distinction between her granddaughter and English royalty.

Ava's father, who was long gone, was a peculiar fellow, though, a scientific type who'd talk your leg off about physics or something that you couldn't make heads or tails of, then clam up during ordinary chitchat. When Lila Mae asked Becky Jean why they'd divorced—in record time, no less—all she said was, "He just wasn't my cup of tea." Lila Mae would have loved to ask Becky Jean when that dawned on her, but, naturally, she wasn't going to press her for details. Might as well try to pry open Fort Knox with a hairpin. In any case, that was yesterday's news since there had been two more husbands since him. Not that Lila Mae was an expert on such matters, but if she had to guess, she'd say Becky Jean's current husband, David, was it. If this one doesn't work," Becky Jean had joked, "just call me Zsa Zsa!"

"Grandma, you'll never guess what!" Ava exclaimed. "We

went shopping at Bloomingdale's. I got a Barbie Dream House, a patent leather purse, and new shoes. You'll never believe it—they're a grown-up size ten."

"Good gracious, honey." Lila Mae chuckled. "That's a real clodhopper. You must be growin' like a weed."

"After that we went for spaghetti and meatballs in an Italian restaurant where a famous gangster was killed." Ava stopped for breath. "Oh yeah, then we visited an apartment building called the . . . uh, what is it, Mom? . . . the Dakota, to see where John Lennon, a singer, was shot."

"For heaven's sake, Ava." Lila Mae wondered if all that wasn't a bit excessive for a twelve-year-old. She couldn't say too much, though, because she herself had taken the little girl to the Charles Manson–Sharon Tate murder house. She'd even promised to drive her by the Menendez brothers' place, but they hadn't gotten around to it yet. Actually, they had already gone there once, but after Lila Mae pointed out the telltale features of the English Tudor mansion, including a description of the interior layout where Kitty had been eating ice cream when The Mishap occurred, and made a hugh fuss over the eerie, spooky atmosphere that was "so thick you could cut it with a knife," Ava saw the real house—a Spanish villa—on the news that night. When Lila Mae checked further, she realized that she'd had the correct address but the wrong street.

"Ava . . . honey . . . you come visit your grandma when you get back, okay?" ("That is, if I'm still in one piece," Lila Mae murmured.) "I guess you better put your mother back on the line, okay, sweetie? I need to tell her something."

"Okay . . . love you, Grandma."

"I love you, too, Pumpkin . . . I love you, too."

"I'm back, Mom. . . . Is everything all right? Ava said you sounded very sad."

"Well," Lila Mae sighed, "the fire and Rose and whatnot got me to thinkin'. Here today, maybe gone tomorrow! And you're so busy, the last thing you'd want to do is clean up my affairs.

. . . So, I thought it would be better if I handled all my own funeral arrangements."

"Mom, don't tell me we're on the funeral-arrangement kick again. You act like you're planning the coronation or something. You're not sick or anything, are you? Is there anything you're not tell— Oh, shoot, hold on just a second, that's my other phone—fifty jillion people working here and nobody *ever* picks up the phone."

Before Lila Mae could say a peep, the phone clicked and she was listening to "I Left My Heart in San Francisco." She almost started singing, but the last time she did that, Becky Jean came back unexpectedly and caught her singing "Swaaneeee, how I love ya, how I love ya, my dear old Swaaaneee!" at the top of her lungs. "Mommmm!" she'd huffed. "That's so corny. Do you *have* to sing?" So, now Lila Mae didn't do it anymore, even though she sometimes dangled for ten minutes and listened to dozens of her favorite songs in the process.

It crushed her to think that her singing irritated her daughter to that degree, but she supposed it didn't surprise her all that much. Although the situation was one hundred percent better now than it ever had been, for as long as Lila Mae could remember, Becky Jean had seemed embarrassed by her in general. Right in the middle of a conversation with a total stranger, her teenage daughter couldn't wait to put her on the spot, even correcting her English: "It's not 'I seen' . . . it's 'I saw'!" or some such.

Naturally, when they moved to Los Angeles, it just got worse. Since Becky Jean had decided to scrub away all the unappealing traces of her background, she seemingly expected the rest of them to do it also. One evening at the dinner table, as everybody was talking about this and that, Becky Jean suddenly announced, "In case you don't know it, we all sound like a bunch of stupid hicks, and it's time to do something about it." According to her, they were one step away from Li'l Abner and Daisy Mae. If they wanted to get ahead in the world, then they'd have to spruce themselves up. Lila Mae knew Becky Jean was right, that she had the family's best interests at heart, and Lila Mae had tried her best to erase the "Kentucky twang" and to stop saying "Well, I swanee," but still, every once in a while she'd slip up. An interview Lila Mae had seen with an Italian opera singer pretty much summed up her sentiments. The singer had been in the United States for twenty years, and on top of speaking perfect English, she also spoke four other languages. But when the journalist asked the woman which one she was the most comfortable with, the singer said, "Well, I have to admit that I still dream in Italian." So, after all these years, Lila Mae was the same . . . still dreaming in Southern.

You'd never get her to admit it, but Becky Jean seemed to be peeling back the veneer of sophistication, drifting back to her roots. More and more often, Lila Mae heard her say, "As crazy as all get out" or "Come hell or high water" and "Well, I'll be darned!"—quite a change from the fancy five-syllable words that nobody could ever make heads or tails of. There were other signs: the Johnny Cash CDs sitting in an organizer on the floor of her Range Rover, the trip she and Carleen recently took to Kentucky.

Supposedly the girls wanted to visit the Kentucky State Fair, where they planned to stock up on handmade quilts and baskets and other Kentucky crafts for a guest room Becky Jean was redecorating. But Ava told Lila Mae that was hogwash. The two sisters spent the first week dragging Ava and Casey all over tarnation, taking hundreds of photographs of old houses and trees, looking up friends, and searching high and low for Wesley Davenport's Five & Dime, Joyce Hogg's All You Can Eat BBQ, and Klink's Drug Store, where they were particularly excited about locating some woman named Miss Cherry, who had lilac hair and who used to serve them fountain Cokes and French fries.

Most of the places were long gone, but they did find the BBQ restaurant, which was now called The Original Joyce

Hogg's. Miss Hogg had sold her award-winning recipe to a franchise, and the establishment had become a chain of glossy fast-food restaurants scattered through the South. Klink's had been modernized ("beyond recognition!" Becky Jean griped), but at least it was still standing. As for the waitress, the woman behind the counter had scowled and said, "Oh, honey, Miss Cherry died ages ago."

Lila Mae could see her daughter stalking into a store or restaurant, sizing it up with a hey-what's-going-on-here? expression on her face. She'd roam around, hopping mad that people had the gall to die or that the establishment hadn't frozen everything in place so she could come back to enjoy now what she didn't appreciate then.

As for the state fair itself, Ava said they finally got there, but they never even went near the crafts building! Instead, they made a quick pit stop at an old-fashioned cotton-candy kiosk, then made a beeline to the sideshows, where they spent several hours visiting tents with sword swallowers, Shenille the Snake Woman, and King Carno, the Amazing Two-Headed Monster. Ava told Lila Mae that Shenille was a rook, that she was just a regular woman wearing a scaly leotard, and the so-called monster was something floating in a pickle jar. She even said Becky Jean thought about reporting the situation to the management, if for no other reason than to get some free tickets, but when Carleen said, "You're acting like Mom," she dropped the matter. Nonetheless, Lila Mae was pleasantly surprised when she learned that instead of going on one of those exotic trips, Becky Jean had spent her vacation in rural Kentucky.

Oh, well . . . She moved her cloisonné vase around to see if it might look better in between the silver box and her Waterford cut-crystal candy dish, then pushed it back again.

"Are you tired, run-down, or just plain exhausted?" the television announcer asked. A haggard woman with a triple row of bags under her hound-dog eyes dragged a vacuum cleaner over her living-room rug. "Then call this number for Energy

Plus!—the new, amazing, food supplement. Not available in stores. Order now and you'll receive this free cookbook. . . ."

"Well, shoot!" Lila Mae fretted. "I meant to tell Ava that ten was Jackie Kennedy's shoe size, too." It was something she'd read in a magazine once, and even though Lila Mae often forgot her own clothing sizes, for some unknown reason, she never forgot what size shoe Jackie wore. Lila Mae thought it might be nice for Ava to know she had something in common with a great lady, so she jotted it down on a small pad so she could mention it to Becky Jean when she came back on the phone. While she was at it, she put another item on the list— the name of that darned movie that had been driving her crazy for several days. As usual, Lila Mae knew everything about it— the soldier with hooks for hands, the Academy Awards it had won—but for the life of her, she couldn't remember its actual name. Maybe Becky Jean knew what it was.

Picking up the gold-foil box of candy, she popped a chocolate-covered cherry into her mouth, realizing that she'd have the entire top row eaten by the time Becky Jean materialized. At least the music—at the moment the theme from *The Poseidon Adventure*—assured her that she hadn't been cut off altogether.

It was no coincidence (at least that's what Lila Mae thought) that every single solitary time she tried to settle her affairs, a ringing phone or doorbell—even a 5.0 earthquake once— would interrupt. On the rare occasions when her kids weren't saved by the bell, they'd simply moan and groan and say, "Oh, Mom . . . do we have to discuss funeral arrangements right now?"

Although Lila Mae didn't believe it was the case with her own kids, her friend Tootsie Polk had said, "My daughter'd stick me in a shoe box if she could get by with it!" The comment did make Lila Mae wonder exactly what type of setup the kids would pick for her if left to their own devices. She just hoped that her unsentimental brood would come up with more than her name, rank, and serial number.

At the rate she was going, she'd never get anything squared away. Time after time, Lila Mae had lost golden opportunities, letting the kids avoid the subject until the "perfect" moment arrived. She had invited them all to Easter dinner thinking that surely somewhere during the four or five hours they'd spend at her home, there would be an opening. After they had eaten their baked-ham-and-sweet-potatoes dinner, Lila Mae set a lemon meringue pie in the center of the table and poured coffee from a silver pot, waiting for an opportune lull in the conversation.

At exactly 6:00 P.M., she turned on the television, knowing full well that the evening news would include information about the Trudi Buzler case. Buzler, an Athens, Alabama beauty operator in a coma, was at the center of a life-support controversy that had dominated the news for several days. Sure enough, Lila Mae snapped on Channel 4 and there was the familiar high-school-yearbook photo of Buzler, with her ghoulish Cleopatra eye makeup and her ebonized hair piled high on her head in little petals. It looked like a dripping ice cream cone.

"Not that again!" Lila Mae slipped her family a sly glance to see if they were paying attention. Good, she thought. Little by little, they were all focusing on the scene in the Athens Community Hospital. The corridor was a Tower of Babel as a gaggle of reporters and photographers snapped pictures and poked microphones in the faces of various family members.

"I know my Trudi!" Sue Ann Buzler, the matriarch of the Buzler clan, was parked on a waiting-room bench, hands planted on her knees in a sumo-wrestler squat. She had flamingo-pink skin and a fountain of dishwater-blond hair with one wavy cluster that sprang forward and grazed the bridge of her nose. "She's a fighter, she is!" Trudi's common-law husband, a wiry tobacco worker named Buster Allan Reedy, squared his beagle eyes at the camera and, as if auditioning for a role of some sort, said, "Well, I beg to differ! Yes, she's a fighter all right, but that girl's got a good head on her shoulders. You tell her both sides of it—you know, that she'd be a vegetable and all—and she's gonna tell ya, 'That ain't for me.' " They continued to bicker and battle, expressing conflicting views and second-guessing what the woman would want them to do if she had a voice in the matter.

"Boy oh boy," Lila Mae sighed. "I sure don't envy Trudi's family, do you? Bein' totally in the dark like that. Why, she should have left 'em somethin' to go by!"

Nelson, Carleen's lawyer husband, who always had a briefcase full of expert opinions and preconceived notions, at least was on the right side this time. He said, "Twenty years ago, it was unheard of, but now almost everybody has provisions in their wills. The overwhelming majority advocate the disconnection of life support."

"I know what I'd do." Carleen cast her vote. "I'd pull the plug. It's one thing to have a heartbeat, but you also have to consider the quality of life."

"That's my sentiment, too," Nelson added. "After all, if I can't *do* anything . . . why live?" After everyone else had their say, Becky Jean, beginning with a little squirt of acid, said, "You guys are defeatists." After she snared everyone's attention, she told them a miracle cure story about Bobbette Killgallen, an amazing woman from Marietta, Georgia, who had been in a head-on collision, was in a deep coma for months on end, and—to get to the heart of the matter—defied all the experts. "Specialists the world over had thrown up their hands in despair—even the woman's family stopped visiting. Then"—she paused dramatically, as if she were reading a fairy tale to a young child—"one morning a nurse entered the room expecting to find the same old blob, and lo and behold, the woman had *completely* recovered."

To boot, the woman was currently running her own outfit, a multimillion dollar cosmetics business called BobbCo. "Can you imagine if you had decided to pull the plug on your husband or child and they suddenly snapped out of it?"

"Where'd you hear that one?" Carleen said it sounded like one of their mother's tabloid stories, and Irene Gaye said, "So what? That's just one example in thousands."

What it boiled down to, when Becky Jean further explained her position, was that she wanted to be kept alive *at all costs,* even if she was just a head with no body, like some bust in a museum, and even if it involved every tube and contraption in the hospital and took every red cent her family had to do so! "I'm just telling you what *I'd* want."

Everybody just stared at Becky Jean—they were actually waiting for her to tell them she was just joking—until finally, Carleen and Irene Gaye rolled their eyes and said, "Fine, then."

Lila Mae could hardly believe her luck, thinking any minute it would be her turn. And contrary to what they probably believed, she wasn't going to talk their leg off or bore them to tears. With them avoiding it the way they had, they probably thought it was going to be some long, drawn-out affair. But she'd fool them by making it short and sweet, and when it was over they'd be thinking—although they'd never admit it—Well, that's all there was to it . . . we should have done that ages ago.

When the momentum had reached a high pitch, the reporter said, "We'll be back in just a moment with more on the Trudi Buzler case." But during the commercial break, Ava snatched the clicker, switched channels, and pretty soon, instead of discussing Lila Mae, they got caught up in an "I Love Lucy" rerun. Naturally, it was the chocolate-factory episode, everybody's favorite, so they insisted on watching it for the jillionth time. Lila Mae, fists perched on her hips, shook her head. "I don't know what you all see in that one." Although it was beside the point, she preferred the one where Lucy tried to steal the answers to a quiz show so everyone would think she was a genius, and that other one when she got the loving cup stuck on her head. She shot the laughing hyenas a dirty look.

When she confiscated the remote control and flipped it back to the Buzler report, everybody said, "Hey, what's the big idea?" Normally Lila Mae would have caved in, but she surprised them all by sticking to her guns. Not that turning the show back on did her any good. The conversation took an unexpected turn for the worse when David, Becky Jean's husband, who seemingly hadn't been the least bit interested in the Buzler case, turned into Mr. Chitchat. He said, "You know, it's all hypothetical. . . . How could a person tell if they wanted the plug to be pulled until they were faced with the decision? It's just one of those issues that you can't intellectualize."

Irene Gaye chimed in, "You're probably right. Last week my friend Lori Gainer was held up at gunpoint—*in broad daylight*. Two blacks came out of nowhere, pointed shotguns at her, and told her to hand over the keys to her Porsche." Instead of following the criminals' instructions, Irene Gaye's friend screamed to high heaven; the robbers got cold feet and vanished. "Lori never dreamed she'd respond that way. See, you just don't know until you're in the situation."

"I wouldn't hand over my car keys either, and I don't even drive a Porsche," Carleen mused.

"You'd better," Becky Jean lectured. "You might not be as lucky as Lori. Besides, it's not worth getting clobbered for a car."

"Uh, that's funny talk for someone who just called us defeatists!" Carleen snorted.

Try as Lila Mae might to get the conversation back to unplugging plugs and associated events, pretty soon, in a frenzy of popping veins and screeching voices, they were ranting and raving about the drug problem, the dismal economy, biological warfare, and how, in general, the entire planet was boxed into a horrible, inescapable corner.

"That's all fine and well, but *none* of it concerns me, since I won't be around." Lila Mae hopped up, then punched the swinging door into the kitchen as hard as she could. Everybody watched the wooden panel as it slammed against the maple butcher block and shuddered back and forth. When Lila Mae disappeared, she heard Irene Gaye ask, "What the hell was *that* all about?"

Just thinking about all the unfinished business got Lila Mae worked up. She grabbed another chocolate cherry and massaged the back of her sweaty neck with a lemon-soaked cotton square. How in the world could anybody blame Lila Mae for writing down her own funeral details? It wasn't all that eccentric. You'd think she was asking them to do something nutty like sprinkle her ashes over the White House lawn or stuff her, dress her up like a rodeo queen, and bury her in a pink Cadillac.

Becky Jean's standard line was, "You're not *sick*, are you, Mother?" as if to say, "If you're not on your deathbed, don't bother me with this nonsense right now."

Lila Mae wasn't *sick* sick, that much was true. Although she had her share of aches and pains and technical difficulties, it wasn't her body that concerned her so much, it was her *brain*. It was acting funny these days, like some topsy-turvy file cabinet whose files were out of alphabetical order. Oh, the information was still in there somewhere all right. But God only knew where it was and how long it would take to locate it, and from what she gathered, she was pretty sure those were signs of Alzheimer's.

Lately, she'd forget things right in the middle of a sentence or even what she was walking into the other room for. Phrases and words like "whatchamacallit" and "thingamabob" and "so on and so forth" had become the bedrock of her conversations. More and more often, she'd see a new building going up and she couldn't for the life of her remember what had just been demolished. She'd close her eyes and try to picture the store she'd probably passed hundreds of times, maybe even traded at, but she never could. Or she'd forget something like her own niece's name, and then she'd remember it days later when she was trying to remember the theme song for "The Dick Van Dyke Show."

Remembering Jackie Kennedy's shoe size and forgetting the name of that movie were so typical of how Lila Mae's brain operated. Not that she didn't pride herself on retaining such information. It's just that Lila Mae wanted to remember details like celebrity shoe sizes *plus* where she parked her automobile.

When, in an effort to demonstrate how drastic her condition was, she confessed to Carleen that she couldn't even remember the name of Becky Jean's second husband, Carleen said, "Big deal . . . Becky Jean has blocked it out, too." She even said, "Ha, ha—everybody thinks they've got that" when Lila Mae finally blurted out she thought she was getting Alzheimer's.

It just burned Lila Mae up that they wouldn't give her the satisfaction of acknowledging the condition. Why, there were millions of unsuspecting people who had Alzheimer's, so why couldn't she be one of them? Lila Mae supposed she'd have to become a blathering idiot or worse, collapse in a heap, and die right in front of everybody before they'd believe there was anything seriously wrong with her. She wondered if even that would do it. Whenever Lila Mae didn't answer the phone or doorbell right away, Becky Jean would joke casually, "Gee, Mom, for a minute I thought you were lying in a pool of blood or something."

Slipping her amber earring off, Lila Mae switched the telephone to the other side, massaging her sore earlobe. She looked at her little brass clock. It was 7:10 P.M. already. Although Becky Jean expected everybody else to have the patience of Job, if the shoe was on the other foot and Lila Mae kept Becky Jean hanging on until kingdom come, she'd have a fit. How often had she watched as Becky Jean stood over a pot of water, waiting for it to boil, grumbling, "Come on, come on, I haven't got all day." Or she'd press and press and press an elevator button in front of a whole crowd of people who'd already pushed it.

Lila Mae shuffled to the window, dragging the telephone cord behind her. It was a thick, topaz dusk, and the fire was still raging, flames cascading down the hill toward the San Fernando Valley. The aroma of burning menthol hung in the air. Swatches of charred fields, blackened trees, and a frosting of ash everywhere she looked. Pages from magazines and newspapers, curled by the sun, were spinning and pirouetting like ballerinas across the road, story by story—Lizzie Borden, the ozone, the bowling champion, the missionary couple. A huddle of firemen—faces sooty, hats tipped back on their heads—were eating sandwiches at the base of her driveway, gigantic hoses swirled around them, poised for combat.

Lila Mae wondered if she should make a run for the freezer. A big bowl of Neapolitan ice cream would sure hit the spot. With her luck, though, Becky Jean would return to the phone at that moment and think Lila Mae had hung up on her. Or, worse yet, she'd ask, "What are you eating, Mom?" Then she'd start harping on Lila Mae's cholesterol level. Since Becky Jean herself was so picky about what she ate—no dairy, no alcohol, no sugar, no salt, no red meat—she made a person who ate normal food feel like a criminal.

It almost took the fun out of going out to dinner with her. The last time, the waiter asked if anybody wanted dessert and before Lila Mae or Carleen could answer, Becky Jean said, "No thanks, we'll just take the check, please." Lila Mae pretended she didn't care for dessert, either, but it just killed her that she didn't get a slice of key lime pie, particularly since she'd spent the entire meal gazing at the dessert cart. When she got home, she ate a whole box of Pepperidge Farm Chantillys and a quart of butter pecan ice cream to make up for it.

Reaching into her bedside drawer, she pulled out the rest of her magazines, skimming the story about the woman who claimed some fellow wined and dined her just to get her brother's kidney. When he got what he wanted—at least according to the scorned woman—he dumped her. In the *Star* she read about the French poodle who had held its owner hostage for three whole days and a stunning story claiming there are mermaids in the Pacific. It included a quote from a sea merchant who said, "They're a common sight," and an artist's rendering depicting the creatures sunbathing on rocks. "Surely, that can't be right," Lila Mae muttered, and held her magnifying glass to the drawing.

She was a million dreamy miles away when Becky Jean said, "Mom? Are you still there? Sorry . . . It's like Grand Central Station around here." A florist was at the door, a Spanish-speaking plumber talking gibberish was on the other phone, and Ava was hollering for Becky Jean to make her popcorn like she promised. "Is it all right if I call you back?" Becky Jean swore she'd only be a few minutes.

"Just one quick thing, honey. I can't remember the name of an old movie. It had a soldier with hooks for arms who had a tough time handling the ring during his wedding ceremony. You remember it, don't you?"

"Gee . . ." Becky Jean seemed stumped and anxious to get off the phone at the same time. "Was it *House of Wax*?"

"*House of Wax*?" Lila Mae shrieked. "You must be kidding! That was a horror picture with Vincent Somebody in it. Oh, dern it all. I thought you'd know."

"Well, you can't think of it, either. At least I know Vincent Price's last name. . . . Mom, I'm really sorry, but I've got to go. . . . I'll call you back."

"Take your time, honey. . . . I know you're busy. Besides, I'm not going anywhere."

"Okay, Mom. Take care—love you." Becky Jean's voice drifted away like the last few notes of a song.

Lila Mae gently hung up the phone, then slipped off her shoe and scratched the back of her calf with her big toe. She swatted a mosquito against her forearm and flicked it off with her pink opalescent fingernail. It was what Becky Jean always said—that she'd call Lila Mae back in ten minutes. But . . .

by the time one phone conversation was finished, Becky Jean's doorbell would buzz, then another phone would ring, and she'd seemingly forget that she'd even talked to her mother at all. It used to be that Lila Mae would wait and wait, sometimes for hours, sometimes even rearranging an appointment or cancelling an engagement. But now she didn't wait anymore.

Carleen and Irene Gaye told Lila Mae not to take it personally, that Becky Jean, who was on quadruple overload, did the same thing to them all the time, too. Not that anybody wanted her opinion, but Lila Mae thought there was way too much commotion in Becky Jean's life: a design career; a young daughter to raise; a busy, successful husband; save-the-universe charity work; a novel she was finishing; one house here, another house there—houses all over the place, in fact. One week she'd be in New York, another in Los Angeles, and then she'd scoot off and Lila Mae wouldn't even know she was gone until she called to say she had returned.

Just keeping up with the Los Angeles place alone—which needed ten people to look after it—was enough to drive a person to an asylum. Something was always breaking down or being spruced up, like a woman who spent all of her time in curlers and face masks but was presentable only once in a blue moon. And Becky Jean was such an organization nut that every item in the house was photographed and inventoried and arranged in some special way. Pantries were lined with silver and Baccarat crystal and English porcelain, and there were special closets fitted for luggage and sporting equipment. There were enormous his-and-hers closets with Savile Row suits and Italian shoes in one room and Becky Jean's Christian Dior dresses and vintage Balenciaga cocktail gowns in another, all hanging according to color and season. So much stuff that Lila Mae wondered if all those inventories could even keep track of it.

Every time Lila Mae visited Becky Jean, she had to dodge workmen with ladders or gardeners with machinery strapped to their backs blowing leaves every which way. Three or four

fancy foreign cars were scattered at odd angles across the driveway while men wearing blue jumpsuits rubbed the chrome
work with special wax, patting the fenders like they were expensive racehorses. With all the racket going on, Becky Jean might
as well have been living in a construction zone, even though
that main house had been finished for several years. The last
time Lila Mae was there, she'd glanced at the security TV screen
and waiting at the gate was a suspicious-looking fellow in a
turban holding some statues. The maid picked up the intercom
and told him to state his business, but Becky Jean said to buzz
him in, he was the man delivering the fake owls and floating
snakes designed to scare away the birds that had been snatching
the fish out of their koi pond. Just thinking about all that turmoil made Lila Mae bone weary.

But her daughter, the hurricane in motion, seemed to thrive
on it. She ripped through the landscape like a gazelle, her
straight, tawny-velour hair flying behind her, her emerald eyes
like laser beams, scanning her surroundings for mistakes, things
to do, changes to make.

And there was no denying that seeing her daughter in action
was a sight to behold. Lila Mae had visited Becky Jean's new
beach house, her latest remodeling endeavor, and she watched,
slack-jawed, eyes popping in disbelief, as Becky Jean, a mere
squiggle of a woman, dressed in faded jeans and Timberland
boots, turned into a battering ram. The construction workers,
a herd of strapping, burly men with tool belts slung around
their waists and hands like shanks of meat, stood like gentle
lambs as Becky Jean—practically foaming at the mouth—paced
and hollered and rattled her finger at them for botching something up or for being behind schedule.

Lila Mae was nervous for her daughter, thinking, Oh,
they're not goin' to like that! But Becky Jean shrugged it off,
saying, "I know, it'll be a miracle if I'm not held up at gunpoint
before this job is finished." The next thing Lila Mae knew, the
entire batch of them—Becky Jean smack dab in the middle—

were sitting cross-legged on the floor of the unfinished living room eating pizza and cracking jokes with one another. Becky Jean even pulled out a recent tabloid article for them to take a look at. The heading said, BLIND BUT THEY'RE BUILDING THEIR OWN HOUSE!, and the accompanying picture showed an elderly couple—blind as bats, according to the story—crouched on their roof installing shingles. Congregated around the article, the men whooped and hollered in laughter as Becky Jean cajoled and teased, "You're not going to let *them* show you up, are you?" Soon, the men were back to work, smiles on their faces, sparks flying from their equipment, they moved so quickly.

Then, a mere two hours later, Becky Jean, wearing a Chanel suit and a diamond brooch, her face skimmed with carnation-white powder and her wrists dotted with two drops of Bal à Versailles perfume, was the very picture of sophistication and charm as she attended a movie premiere. Lila Mae often gaped at Becky Jean as if she were a Martian, as if the same gene pool that had constructed the rest of their family couldn't possibly have been involved in the creation of her oldest child.

But it didn't do any good to tell Becky Jean to simplify her life. One day Lila Mae urged her to take a break and she was shocked when her daughter said, "Yeah, you're probably right." Lila Mae should have known there'd be a catch, that she wouldn't be able to fix an ordinary cup of coffee without rigmarole, and she didn't. First she ground French-roast coffee beans by hand, filling an Italian coffeemaker with imported Swedish water. While the coffee was brewing, she collected her antique Battenburg linen and lace napkins, an oversized sugar bowl containing cubes of Brazilian brown sugar and petite slices of sugared fruit. Then—just as if she were expecting Queen Elizabeth and Prince Philip—she arranged it all on a fancy sterling silver tray with ivory handles, then poured the coffee into hand-painted Limoges cups so delicate that Lila Mae was afraid to drink from them.

And there was hell to pay if anybody else approached it differently. Becky Jean had almost gone off her rocker when she caught her housekeeper using ordinary tap water for the coffee. "Honey . . ." Lila Mae pulled her daughter aside. "You shouldn't holler at her like that. You'll hurt the poor girl's feelings." Becky Jean, though, said the tap-water incident was simply the straw that broke the camel's back, that she had told the dumb girl time and time again to do one thing or another and she continued to foul up. "I've had it—just *had* it!" She'd thrown a dishcloth against the sink and marched out, leaving the tire tracks of her anger behind for Lila Mae and the woman to sort out. The whole escapade embarrassed Lila Mae no end, but it seemed to roll right off the housekeeper's back. The young woman, a Guatemalan named Lupe, simply said, "I'm sorry, Mrs. Rebecca," then picked up the dishtowel, folded it across the sink, and snapped on the disposal.

At the time Lila Mae thought, This is all she needs. Lila Mae already felt sorry enough for the woman, whose husband had recently been mauled by an alligator. The family had gone to the Florida Everglades to visit relatives and the poor man had come back missing the tip of his pinky finger and the skin on his left cheek. When Lila Mae said, "Isn't that just the most horrible thing? Imagine being viciously attacked like that!" Becky Jean told her not to get too choked up, that yes, she did feel bad for the housekeeper and her children, but the guy it happened to was a "nincompoop." She told Lila Mae that he'd brought it on himself, paying twenty-five dollars and signing a release for the opportunity to wrestle with the alligator. "He knew full well what he was getting into. Ask Lupe. *She* even begged him not to do it." Although Becky Jean had a point, the incident was no fault of the girl's, so Lila Mae slipped her a ten-dollar bill.

"Well, sure," Irene Gaye had snorted sarcastically. "The housekeepers are probably used to all the abuse by now." Becky Jean could be like that one minute, like a screeching, out-of-control car, then just as easily turn around the next minute and give the maid an armload of expensive clothes and accessories that Lila Mae herself wouldn't have minded having.

It was hard to discuss the touchy subject without feeling like a traitor to Becky Jean. Carleen simply sloughed it off by saying, "Rebecca's a classic triple-A personality" but if you asked Lila Mae, "type A" was too simple a term to describe such a complicated situation.

And Irene Gaye was so envious that she turned Becky Jean's every quirk into a federal offense. "Every time I offer to help with something—well, take your birthday party, for example— she's gotta do it all by herself. According to her, she's the only efficient person alive. If I hear her say 'I did the Louvre in twenty minutes!' one more time, I'm going to choke. Yeah, like that qualifies her to run the country or something."

"You shouldn't talk about Becky Jean that way," Lila Mae admonished Irene Gaye. "Besides, if your sister's habits are so irritating, then don't borrow money from her." ("Especially since you never pay her back," Lila Mae added under her breath.) She also happened to know Irene Gaye had used the last "loan" for collagen injections in her lips instead of for the cancerous moles she supposedly had removed.

Naturally, Irene Gaye, the one-woman disaster zone, who left the refrigerator door open, lingerie dangling from bureau drawers, bathroom doors ajar, would be jealous of anyone who was halfway organized. Why, it wouldn't surprise Lila Mae if she'd even drive off with the car door wide open. The girl was like an absentminded professor, except Lila Mae didn't know if that applied to someone who had dropped out of high school.

Lights were starting to bloom—crystal-clear and Coke-bottle-green squares and geometric shapes dotting the hillsides. A fan-shaped sprinkler moved slowly back and forth on her neighbor's front lawn, and a glossy aluminum plane darted above the thicket of power lines, dumping the special chemicals on a sphere of red flames.

Standing at the window, Lila Mae remembered black-magic nights like these . . . little sunburned stars, the crazy wind making newspapers and tree limbs whip across the sky . . . when the aroma of jasmine was so thick that it was both intoxicating and nauseating, and the hot gusts of canyon wind slapped across the city. Often, she'd tell Roy she had to run to the market for bread or milk; then she'd take a jaunt along the scenic, winding curves of Mulholland Drive. It was practically the first thing she did when they moved to California. She wanted to see the panoramic views she'd heard so much about and (although she didn't tell anybody), the scene of Caryl Chessman's crimes, where he'd raped all those innocent young girls. Now, though, the scenic road was infested with gangs who went on deadly joyrides and spray-painted graffiti on the stone-gated mansions and road signs or who cut the throats of motorists driving expensive cars. Lila Mae wondered if beauty and the beast were yoked together, if every town in the country, regardless of how wonderful they used to be, had gone to seed like Los Angeles.

A vintage candy-apple-red Corvette careened around the hairpin curve below Lila Mae, its wheels squealing against the mushy asphalt. From her lofty perch, Lila Mae could see the young couple, seemingly returning from the beach, clad in bathing suits, beach towels and Styrofoam coolers stored in the backseat. The radio was so loud that the song practically exploded, the car speakers distorting the notes. It was a familiar song, a tune from a Broadway play—*Cats,* maybe? No, that wasn't it. . . . Maybe it wasn't a play, after all. She wished the car—tumbling down the road, going way too fast—would slow down so she could hear more of the song. She hummed a few notes until she got to a part she remembered. "I recall the yellow cotton dress floating like a wave . . . da da da da da . . . melting in the dark . . . all the sweet green icing . . ." "MacArthur Park"! That's what it was—"MacArthur Park"! "That's a good idea. . . ." She suddenly jumped up and bounded into her sunroom.

On the shelf where she kept her eclectic record collection, she flipped through her old albums, looking for *Donna Summer's Greatest Hits*. She slipped it from the cover, stacked it on the metal pin sticking in the middle of the old-fashioned turntable; then she added records by Ray Charles, Frank Sinatra, and the Beatles to the heap.

"At least get a cassette or CD, Mom," her kids teased her. "Those albums are as old as the hills." But Lila Mae didn't care; she liked her records just the way they were. Plus, she didn't want to learn how to use another piece of complicated equipment.

What a lesson she'd already learned with that ridiculous satellite dish. The kids told her the setup was as easy as pie, that anybody who didn't have one was a Neanderthal and that any idiot could work it, but Lila Mae still couldn't get the gist of it. She knew all about the Chinese stock market and had memorized the 800 number to purchase the Ginsu knives; she had seen *Gidget Goes Hawaiian* three times and Carmen Miranda in *Doll Face* at least a dozen. But it was only after three different clickers and forty channels that she finally got to Tom Brokaw, even then she had to watch him through a mist of static. No thanks.

Lila Mae shuffled into the kitchen and fired up the tea kettle, peeking through her dining-room curtains on the off chance she'd catch sight of Rose in her den. Except for a thin shot of fluorescent light under the garage door, the Bancroft place was dark. "For cryin' out loud," she fussed. "What is going on over there?" As she bent down to sweep up a cornflake under the dinette table, her knee creaked and locked in place. When she was crooked over, she remembered she never told Ava about Jackie Kennedy's shoe size. . . . Or had she already remembered that she'd forgotten?

Oh, well. She took a Formosa Oolong tea bag from her ceramic ginger jar and dunked it into the steaming water. "See ya later, alligator—After while, crocodile," she hummed.

Just as she opened the freezer door and reached for the Neapolitan ice cream, she remembered her luggage and those shoeboxes were still outside. "Gee whillikers, Lila Mae. Why in the *world* don't you write this stuff down? You know you'll forget if you don't!" Between the boxes and Jackie and who knew what else that had slipped by her, she figured she'd forget her head if it wasn't attached.

Grabbing her flashlight, she ambled to her car, twisting her ankle as she tried to drag her Samsonite suitcase up the staircase. The bag, which had one clasp unsnapped to begin with, knocked against her stone steps and flew open. An avalanche of mementoes tumbled onto the driveway—letters and photographs wrapped in twine and rubber bands and old shoelaces. "Lord!" she griped, wrestling with the flyaway pictures and correspondence and suitcase. "Get back in here, you blankety-blank-blank old stuff." As she fumbled to collect everything, patting the ground and pawing through the quince, she glanced at one picture, then another, and in no time she was upstairs furrowed into her brown corduroy couch, a wheel of snapshots and souvenirs fanning around her.

"My, my, what have we got here?" Lila Mae sorted through the small metal box where she'd filed brittle envelopes with tiny gnarled enamel lumps, the accumulation of dozens of lost baby teeth. She had almost forgotten about the teeth, and Roy used to tell her she was off her rocker to save such things, but now she was thrilled to have these souvenirs of her children's childhood. On each envelope Lila Mae had scribbled the name of the child and the date of the tooth loss: "Billy Cooper, 6 yrs.," "Carleen, impacted wisdom—14 yrs." . . . In a square white box that smelled of ancient, faded roses were more packets, containing slices of gold or mahogany hair from the children's haircuts plus pictures of the kids sitting on Santa's lap, framed in ivory cardboard and inscribed with the Stewart's Department Store insignia.

Inside a big leather scrapbook were tassels from Carleen's majorette outfit, Billy Cooper's third-grade report card, and an old program for Becky Jean's high-school performance of *The Crucible*. Letting a spoonful of ice cream melt slowly on her tongue, her eyes skimmed the credits until she got to the fourth line, which read "Elizabeth Proctor played by Becky Jean Wooten."

When they finally made it to California, Roy had been furious that all Lila Mae had to show for their trouble were those boxes of hair and teeth, the clothes on their backs, Becky Jean's *50,000,000 Elvis Fans Can't Be Wrong* album, and a car sitting in a filling station in Arizona that cost more to fix than it had ever been worth.

At the bottom of the box was her white zippered Bible. She lifted it up, rubbing off the pomade of dust. Billy Cooper had given it to her when he was eleven years old, a bonus for selling the most candy canes door-to-door for St. Agnes's Home for Wayward Girls. That boy had been such a go-getter! Inside the Bible, pressed between waxed paper, was a mustard-colored rosebud and fern from Clora Dee's funeral, a gummy index card with a recipe for sour cherry pie, and a blue ribbon from the 4-H Club.

All the way in the back, wedged in the concordance pages, was a photograph. Fetching her glasses, Lila Mae wiped them against her black knit top and slid them onto the bridge of her nose. "Well, don't tell me . . . is this what I *think* it is?" It seemed to be the souvenir photograph of the Grand Canyon, the picture they'd had taken of them on the Route 66 trip. Adjusting the spectacles, she held the photograph at arm's length, studying the brigade of people. "This is it all right."

Just a few months before, Becky Jean had asked Lila Mae for this very photograph and it was nowhere to be found. Lila Mae had hardly remembered it existed, but now, as she looked at the snapshot of herself, her four children, and Juanita and her son, it was all coming back to her. Lined up in a little crescent, high, puffy clouds hovering over them: the picture looked more like a group mug shot than a souvenir photograph.

There they were, Lila Mae sighed, the husks of their former selves . . . Becky Jean, ever the huffy teenager, cut a curvaceous line in her red sack dress and lamb's-wool cardigan and pearl sweater clip. Although she had a sweetheart face, her eyes, smoldering with an expression that bewildered Lila Mae, seemed to knife right through the camera lens. She had her arm looped around Carleen, who was wearing her favorite outfit—an oversized, hand-me-down felt skirt decorated with 45-rpm records. Clutched tightly to her chest was her Tiny Tears doll, and her stringy legs were crossed in front of her. Beneath her saw-toothed bangs—which looked like they'd been snipped with pinking shears—were sad turquoise eyes.

Old photographs of Carleen always made Lila Mae's heart twitch. With that shy, rubber-band smile of hers and the skinned knees, she reminded Lila Mae of an injured Raggedy Ann doll. For all that, she had grown into a vivacious beauty with gleaming baby-blue eyes and a wide, friendly smile. Year after year, Carleen took top sales honors at Bay Sign Company, and recently, she had landed her own newspaper column. Her modest daughter played it down, saying the column, which dealt with community issues, was little more than a license to complain, and the paper's circulation was "less than the attendance at the local Little League game." Although it certainly wasn't what she wanted to do for the rest of her life, Carleen admitted she was thrilled to finally have "one foot out of limbo."

"And look at Baby Sister," Lila Mae muttered. Nestled in a receiving blanket, Lila Mae was holding her high in the air like she was Exhibit A in a courtroom presentation. On her forehead was a curly wave like one swift lick of a paintbrush, and she looked so innocent, so angelic, like a small sugar cube.

Now, though, she'd changed her name to Iggy, had spiky, jelly-bean-colored hair, black dagger fingernails, and wondered why she couldn't hold down a job. She reminded Lila Mae of that crazy fifties song "One-eyed, one-horned, flying purple people eater." But Irene Gaye looked like the First Lady compared to that boyfriend of hers. Darrell—Lila Mae thought the hoodlum's name was—was the type she could picture with a butcher knife in his hand: albino-white skin, tar-black hair, and slitty, tranquilized eyes swimming in their sockets. When Lila Mae asked the boy what he did for a living, he said he was a freelance embalmer.

"Oh, dear," Lila Mae fretted. "What's that?" Irene Gaye gave her a little snap of an answer: "What do you *think* it is?" Obviously, Lila Mae knew what an embalmer was; it was the freelance part that stumped her. It wouldn't surprise her one bit if the boy was on something, but she was probably better off not even thinking about it.

Tipping the linen lampshade, she stuck the photo under the naked bulb and took a very close look at Billy Cooper. One pant leg was tucked into his tooled red cowboy boot, and his skinny arms were wrapped tightly around Lila Mae's leg, like a chimpanzee clinging to a tree branch. Through the closed shutters of her eyes, she could still picture him as a soft, chubby bundle with merry blue eyes and swirls of fine blond hair covering his head. Lila Mae remembered when Billy Cooper started to turn—like food that was getting bad: the lopsided snarl of a grin, the small jabs of sarcasm, the nights he never came home, the day he showed up—Bible pressed in his hand—preaching fire and brimstone. But in the photo, he was still a pure, care-free little boy, the only one who had an ear-to-ear smile on his face. If someone had asked Lila Mae which one of her kids would be successful, her money would have been on Billy Cooper. But now she just didn't know what made that boy tick.

The most exotic sight of all was Juanita Featherhorse. In those kaleidoscopic Gypsy skirts with the rickrack and jangling

Indian jewelry stacked on her arms and threaded through her earlobes, she was an absolute spectacle. At the time, Lila Mae didn't think she'd ever met anyone quite as colorful or unusual as Juanita. Now, with all the oddballs in Hollywood (the women with pierced, Ubangi lips or the men parading around in kilts and purple eye shadow), the Indian woman and her son looked downright ordinary. Juanita's personality was often hard to take, and the kids blamed Lila Mae for hitching up with such an unlikely travel partner, one who was a total stranger to boot. But in the end, Juanita turned out to be a good-hearted soul, giving Lila Mae her last cent to help the Wootens get to California.

Standing several links away from the chain, and making Becky Jean look like Miss Congeniality, was Juanita's son. What a character, that boy! There was so much about him she re-membered—his square, strong fingers hoisting her furniture, the fruity smell of his hair oil, even the pink, stinging imprint of Juanita's hand on his cheek when, all too often, she'd beat the tar out of him . . . but what *was* that boy's name?

Although Lila Mae used her trick of going through the al-phabet, letter by letter, to see if one of them rang a bell—A . . . B . . . C . . . D . . . E . . . nothing clicked. "Well, dern it all, anyway." F . . . G . . . H . . . Wait a second . . . B—B, that was it! She scooted up an inch. But B what?

The television wasn't helping any, so she turned off *Fiddler on the Roof* so she could concentrate. "Hold on a minute!" Something caught her eye, so she turned the set right back on. The oldest girl, who wanted to marry a poor young tailor in-stead of the butcher they were trying to set her up with, was bawling her father out for arranging the marriage without her consent. When they got to the scene with the butcher, a jolly man named Lazar Wolf, he was standing next to a slab of beef swinging from a meat hook—and all of a sudden, Lila Mae remembered that the name of the film with the handicapped actor, the one with hooks instead of arms, was *The Best Years of Our Lives*!

"*House of Wax* my foot," Lila Mae grunted, a triumphant, sarcastic snort of a noise. "Becky Jean's as bad as I am." With the name of the film out of the way, it occurred to her that she also didn't know the name of the actor who was in it, although for some reason—and luckily for Lila Mae—the man's identity didn't seem to be as important to her.

"Well, one down and one to go," she said cheerfully. "I've always got something on my chest."

Closing her eyes, she pictured Juanita's boy, but for the life of her, she still couldn't remember his name. She went through all the vowels. B-A, B-E—that rang a bell, too—B-E-A, B-E-B, B-E-C, B-E-D . . . "Now don't tell me I'm gonna have to call one of the girls." Lila Mae crossed her legs quickly, irritated. Checking the small, oval face of her Elgin wristwatch, she wondered if Carleen would be working on a column or if Irene Gaye was out of bed yet. Knowing Becky Jean, who was usually up until the wee hours of the morning, she was just getting started. But Lila Mae didn't want to call at midnight and disturb everybody else.

Finally, she got to the B-E-N and practically leapt up. Benjamin! That was it! Benny Featherhorse!

My goodness, he was a strange one, that boy.

Whenever she thought about the trip, she couldn't believe she was the same Lila Mae Wooten who'd packed up every stick of furniture and stitch of clothing they owned and driven all that distance. At the time, she was so naive and inexperienced that the journey didn't seem like a big deal. How could she have anticipated that she would get so far off the track, and how could she have known that a few little innocent side trips would create that fiasco out in God knew where?

Through the years, she and Juanita had kept in contact, calling or writing to one another at Thanksgiving or Christmas. Lila Mae would cook up a batch of divinity, wrap it in red cellophane and sprigs of holly, include a Christmas card with a drawing of sleigh bells and a message that said: "From our family to yours." Then she'd ship it to Juanita. For no reason at all, Juanita would sometimes send Lila Mae a ring or necklace, and each year on Lila Mae's birthday, Juanita sent a money order for one hundred dollars, insisting that she splurge on a gift item for herself. Usually Lila Mae had utility or grocery bills to pay, so she fibbed to Juanita about some trinket she'd bought with the cash.

As for Ramon, that hotheaded husband of hers, Juanita never gave Lila Mae explicit details, only that after their separation she had managed to keep him "at bay." For all Lila Mae knew, Ramon was just a threat to his family, an abusive, pistol-whipping husband who acted like a model citizen around everybody but his own kin. But then one day a manila envelope arrived containing a bundle of newspaper articles wrapped in a rubber band. Attached to the clippings was a note from Juanita: "Didn't I tell you he was no count??" Lila Mae's eyes popped open as she scanned article after article about Ramon Feather-horse. The papers called him a "ruthless killer," a murderer who had shot down Luther Hancock, a Protestant minister, in cold blood. Now he was cooling his heels on Death Row, scheduled for the electric chair! Juanita had circled that particular reference and next to it had jotted "Good riddance." The *Albuquerque Outlook* featured an exclusive prison interview with Ramon in which he claimed, "I'm as innocent of the crime as Lyndon Baines Johnson."

Lila Mae had showed the photos to Becky Jean and Carleen and said, "He actually looks awfully nice, doesn't he? Wouldn't it be something if, after all this, the poor man is really innocent?"

But when Lila Mae called Juanita to get the lowdown, Juanita set her straight. "Innocent my big, fat foot. I ask you, have you ever heard of a criminal who *isn't* innocent?"

Then, a few years ago, when Lila Mae dialed Juanita for

their yearly chat, the man who answered told her it was no longer Juanita's phone number, that Juanita was dead and that's all he knew. By then she was a well-known artist who owned the Featherhorse Gallery in Santa Fe, New Mexico, where she showcased Indian blankets, pottery, and her custom jewelry. One evening Becky Jean had called her from New York and exclaimed, "Mom, you're not going to believe it—I saw some of Juanita Featherhorse's jewelry in Bergdorf Goodman!" And then another time she'd seen a Saks Fifth Avenue advertisement in the *New York Times* that said: "Here in Person—September 19th—Juanita Featherhorse, the Nationally Acclaimed Jeweler." If, when they were hanging around those snake cases in New Mexico or hollering at the helicopters to come get them, someone would have told Lila Mae that Juanita would be featured in a fancy department store or an important newspaper like that, she would have sized them up as straitjacket candidates.

Lila Mae inhaled deeply, releasing her breath in a fluttery sigh. Her own life certainly hadn't been any picnic, always robbing Peter to pay Paul, sometimes even scraping together the kids' lunch money from the shabby cushions of their living-room couch. But Lila Mae's problems seemed inconsequential compared with Juanita's ordeal. A husband like that, a sick girl, a boy who didn't seem all that bad to Lila Mae but who rubbed Juanita the wrong way. Rosita had died of tuberculosis or polio—she didn't remember which one—shortly after Lila Mae met Juanita, that much she knew. But Lila Mae really wondered what had become of that boy.

Holding the photograph closer, she picked up her ivory magnifying glass looking for the ghost of the young, pretty woman with a heart-shaped face, a head of healthy, wavy hair, and a slim, sturdy body. A shiver of recognition shook Lila Mae as she peered at the image, but all in all, the young face seemed to belong to a stranger. People used to tell Lila Mae that she resembled Hedy Lamarr, but those days were long gone. She placed her splayed hand on her thigh and studied the oatmeal flecks, the raised garnet veins, and the honeycomb of lines, wondering what had happened to the little fists that curled around a tricycle or the tapered, creamy fingers she had held out to Roy when he slipped her solitary diamond engagement band on.

It seemed to Lila Mae that she had skidded downhill in unexpected spurts. One day she'd check her shopworn image in the mirror and ten years and thousands of heartaches seemed to have settled on her face overnight. She'd study the gray complexion and carved trails in her forehead and tell herself that she hadn't slept well the night before or that she hadn't eaten properly. Or she'd blame it on the silvery light of the department store dressing room, whitewashing her face like that! With some pampering, she assured herself, the rosy flush in her cheeks and the sparkly glaze in her eyes would bloom once more. In her heart of hearts, though, Lila Mae knew that no matter how many expensive creams she used or beauty pointers she followed, the glow was long gone, like the taillights of some fanciful dream.

Little by little, her life had become a cavalcade of mechanical problems—cataracts, stiff joints, benign tumors, outpatient procedures for this and that . . . and more and more cracks and crevices. Lately, she'd found herself paying more attention to commercials advertising the Clapper and Medic Alert. Pretty soon, Lila Mae thought, she could be the next member of the Death-of-the-Month Club.

From time to time, Lila Mae complained that she resembled a basset hound and her girls would roll their eyes and insist, "Oh, Mom . . . you look like nothing of the kind," which is exactly what she wanted them to say. But the last time she brought it up, Irene Gaye snapped, "Well, Mom, *do* something about it, if it really bothers you. Everybody does—not just celebrities, either." How well Lila Mae knew that, the unspoken law in Los Angeles being that if you had the gall to live past fifty, you should at least have the common decency not to look like it.

Lifting both hands to her cheeks, Lila Mae pinched the loose, papery skin to her earlobes, wondering what she'd look like if she had some work done. She turned left, then right, cocking her head to study the possibilities. If she pulled the droopy skin as tight as it needed to be tugged to get rid of the Churchill jowls, she ended up with a wide Felix-the-Cat grin. "It ain't no use . . ." She sighed, letting her face drop back down to its mooring place.

Lila Mae just didn't know where the years had gone. Oh, she knew the hours led to days, days to weeks, weeks to months, and so on. It was all mathematics, she guessed—just an equation that could be figured out in a few moments with a sharpened pencil or a calculator. But somewhere in all those minutes and hours and weeks and months, something mysterious happened that was more than the sum total of it all.

Looking down at the fabric of her dress, the pale, tiny hooked hairs on her arms, she then touched the angle of her cheekbone and jaw. Everything was so three-dimensional, so tangible, that it was hard for Lila Mae to believe that someday she wouldn't be bumping into her furniture, complaining about her kids, keeping tabs on a brush fire . . . exist altogether. "See you later, alligator," she hummed. "After while, croco— . . . See you later, alliga—"

Lila Mae slipped the Grand Canyon photograph into a small ivory envelope and stuck it in her handbag, thinking she'd take it to be processed tomorrow. Even though Becky Jean wouldn't admit it if you asked her point-blank, it seemed to Lila Mae that she was going through a childhood-appreciation phase. Recently she had pumped Lila Mae for ancestral information and family pictures, and each time Lila Mae gave her an old snapshot, she'd kiss her mother's cheek and say, "Thank you, Mom. This is just great!"

Becky Jean was also gung ho about taking the Route 66 trip

again, and she even wanted to drag everybody along with her. "Oh, come on . . . it'll be fun," she coaxed. When they didn't turn cartwheels right away, she planted her hands on her hips and accused them of being "point A to point B" types who didn't have a thimbleful of adventure in their blood. In a rapture of zeal, she whipped her arms in the air, preaching to them like an evangelist trying to convert heathens.

"The country is being overrun by mini-malls and skyscrapers!" she thundered. "One day, not too far in the future, the big cities won't even have a normal sky. The air will be so bad, the ozone so depleted, crime so hideous, that the government will create controlled environments with big domes to cover everything. Metal detectors will be installed in every restaurant, school, and office building to keep all the crooks out."

When everyone was rolling their eyes and drumming their fingers, wondering where all this doomsday chat was leading, she managed to tie everything in with the urgent need to take the Route 66 trip. "Pretty soon there will be nothing to see, nothing at all—so don't you want to visit whatever is left while we still can?"

Knowing her relentless daughter, she'd use this latest Grand Canyon picture to ignite her campaign. In a few days, a messenger would show up at everyone's door with a framed copy of the photo with a clever little note attached and a calendar with possible dates circled just to break down their resistance. Yes, yes, that Grand Canyon picture would just egg Becky Jean on.

Lila Mae sauntered to her antique secretary, the big walnut piece with cubbyholes and drawers with ivory pulls. In each pigeonhole was a memento—pink and white seashells, a four-leaf-clover paperweight, a heart-shaped ceramic dish that Billy Cooper made at Boy Scout camp. In this—her favorite spot in the house—she could sit for hours on end gazing at the city. Skewered by a shaft of blue light from the stained-glass panels of her sunroom and surrounded by wisteria, she could stare at the diorama of cypress trees. Her eyes could follow the cobblestone pathways that cut through Japanese bonsai gardens and the ribbons of pavement as they wove past the huge, flashy movie billboards on Sunset Boulevard and ended at the stone headdress of downtown Los Angeles.

Picking up the metal skeleton key, she shoved it in the slot, the green silk tassel swaying back and forth as she opened a skinny compartment. Tucked inside the cracked leather folder, the aroma of deep, dark red roses coating them, were sheets of parchment paper, each page marked "Lila Mae Wooten's Final Arrangements." Whenever she saw the words, she pictured some hazy, futuristic time when her kids would flap back this dusty curtain on a secret corner of her life.

How and when it would happen was anybody's guess. Perhaps Lila Mae would be the type she'd read about—a reliable person who didn't show up for this or that. After a day or so, friends or relatives would become concerned about foul play. Or maybe neighbors complained of a putrid odor and called the authorities, who would beat down her door with an ax or call in a locksmith.

"The body of Lila Mae Wooten, a longtime resident of Los Angeles and native of Blue Lick Springs, Kentucky, was discovered today . . ." the brief notation in the *Los Angeles Times* would state. Maybe Becky Jean was right and they would find Lila Mae in a puddle of blood. Regardless of the circumstances, after they read Lila Mae's instructions, they'd undoubtedly think she was a crackpot. But crackpot or not, by the time they found out, she'd be dead and gone, and it would be too late to yell at or humiliate her.

The way Lila Mae saw it, she didn't have any choice in the matter. The fear that she, once again, would be cut off in mid-sentence made her return to this desk to pore over more details, to issue more instructions, or to fiddle with the individual letters she was writing to each child, to wallow in the aroma of her failures and indecision. She knew only too well what consequences there were when you had no advance warning. If her situation with Roy wasn't the perfect example of that, she didn't know what was.

After all this time, it just killed her to know that out of all the thousands of words and gestures she'd exchanged with her husband, nothing counted except their last conversation at the Blue Note. Years later, she was still galloping right behind Roy, trying to catch up with him like she was chasing after one of her kids with a forgotten mitten or homework.

Squeezing her eyes shut, her head twirling in the wreckage of activity, she'd see a blurry slide show against her burning eyelids: the evening that began with dinner at the Steak Pit, then the St. Patrick's Day gathering they'd attended at the Blue Note, its window lined with flickering lights and strewn with construction-paper shamrocks. As if it were yesterday, she could still picture Roy doing the two-step with Dottie Orson, the coquettish cocktail waitress on her break. She could still remember the eruption of anger and jealousy as she watched Roy and Dottie with her leprechaun green skirt that barely covered her rear, swishing around when Roy spun or twirled or dipped her. Lila Mae had stared at the hussy's cap of vanilla hair and moist, heart-shaped lips, thinking how unprofessional it was for an employee to be dancing with a customer, coffee break or no coffee break. Even if it was St. Patrick's Day! (Lila Mae even marched up to the manager to report Dottie, but nothing ever came of it.) Yes, it was true that earlier in the evening Lila Mae herself fox-trotted with Ray Anderson, but that had been different. Ray was a solid family man with three kids and a loving wife with a sprained ankle who had encouraged Lila Mae to dance with her husband. Dottie Orson, on the other hand, was a lively divorcee who always made a beeline for Roy, giving him free refills on his beer and asking him if he could repair some on-the-blink appliance of hers.

Lila Mae had glowered at her husband and the little saucebox, twisting her whiskey-sour glass against the soggy napkin until she dug a round hole in it. Then, as her husband and

Jezebel danced their crazy legs off to a Johnny Cash song, she slipped into the restroom, studying her colorless face and the cracked lips in the cloudy mirror. As Lila Mae stood under the harsh bulb, a nimbus of bleached light hovering above, her hair looked like wisps of white chiffon. The sags and furrows on her face reminded her of driftwood, as if she'd dragged along all the nicks and scrapes of her adventures right there for the world to see.

For years Lila Mae thought positive thinking and willpower were the keys to vitality, that the sheer determination to stay young was the sole element necessary for preservation. But here she was with dozens of I-won't-let-myself-grow-old pep talks under her belt . . . all to little avail. She winced as she pictured Dottie—separated from her, at that very moment, by a flimsy plywood partition—with her pouf of buttery hair, her poreless skin, and her tanned, muscular legs swaddled in fishnet hose.

Lila Mae peeked out the restroom door, watching as Dottie—her break finally over—pulled a pencil out of a grotto in her bubble hairdo and scribbled down drink orders. Waiting until the waitress was navigating through the crowds, and balancing a tray of martinis high in the air, Lila Mae marched up to Roy and told him she wanted a trial separation.

"Oh, come on, Lila Mae." Roy, a veteran of his wife's childish, attention-getting outbursts, swatted his hand playfully. "After almost forty years? What's gotten into you?" Fanned across his face, and amplifying the amused gleam in his eyes, was the rainbow glow of the jukebox. He dropped a quarter in the slot and selected a Louis Armstrong song. "Don't be so immature."

"Immature? I'm fifty-seven years old," Lila Mae snorted. "Almost fifty-eight."

Roy, his mouth curled in a half-moon smile, told her one thing had nothing to do with the other. "How many times do we have to go through this? Dottie's just a friend. She likes you just as much as she likes me." He grabbed her shoulders and steadied her. "You know I love you."

"The hell you do." Lila Mae shimmied away from him.

"My God, Lila Mae!" Roy bobbed his head left to right and sighed. "You're not kidding, are you? You know good and well that Dottie's not interested in me. She's just a young, friendly girl. And you know as well as I do that she's getting married to Jack Deevers."

"Huh! That certainly didn't stop Liz Taylor and Eddie Fisher!" When Roy chuckled and ruffled her hair, Lila Mae reared back and said it was no laughing matter.

Roy tried one last time, his fingers creeping across the table for Lila Mae's hand. "Come on, honey, let's dance to this." On the jukebox, Louis Armstrong was singing "What a Wonderful World," but Lila Mae jutted her chin forward and, like a prim schoolgirl, said, "No, thank you!" And so they sat at the square metal table and stared at the halo of dull light shining on the empty dance floor as they listened to one of their favorite songs.

They drove in silence through the deserted streets, a lemon moon dangling above them, Lila Mae with her arms braided tightly in front of her. She drew her mouth into a hard, grim pucker. Roy kept trying to make small talk, and once he touched her thigh and said, "Lila Mae . . . honey bun . . ." but Lila Mae just muttered, "Don't 'honey bun' me" and scooted away and hugged the car door.

The next morning Lila Mae heard the crow of their neighbor's pet rooster and the muffled clatter of Roy as he padded down the hallway and turned on the shower in the spare bathroom. Drifting through the air was the scent of Lifebuoy soap and menthol shaving cream and the bacon and eggs frying in the skillet. Before he left, Roy crept into the bedroom, plucked the sleeve of her flannel nightshirt, and whispered, "Lila Mae?" but Lila Mae didn't budge. He smoothed a stray blade of her hair, tucking it behind her ear, and tiptoe out. She waited until she heard him turn the ignition of his truck and reverse out of their driveway. Then she popped up and dashed to their bedroom window, pulling back one panel of the floral drape, just in time to see the red taillights of the Chevy and hear the rattle of his toolboxes as he puttered down the road.

Still drowsy, Lila Mae stumbled through the house, dragging along the hazy memory from the night before. Her anger, already turned down a few notches, was resuscitated when she reached the kitchen. In the sink was a crooked spire of egg-encrusted plates and saucers and practically every pot and pan they owned. "Well, who in tarnation did he cook for? The U.S. Marine Corps Marching Band?" Coffee grounds and a pink grapefruit rind were dumped haphazardly in the garbage disposal, and to add insult to injury, he hadn't left her one drop of coffee. Plus, he'd used all her good wedding china. "I guess Melmac ain't good enough for Roy Wooten!"

Bending over, she threw away the wadded-up napkin and wiped an anthill of coffee grounds from the floor. "Just look at this pigsty. Ain't it just like a man to do things halfway," she wisecracked. Even when they volunteered to do the dishes, they'd leave the pots and pans soaking in cold, greasy water, then expect a Congressional Medal of Honor for supposedly cleaning up after themselves.

So now that her husband was on his merry way, Lila Mae would have a grand ole time sloshing around in a basin of cold animal fat. She had a good mind to leave the mess for him and see what it felt like. Maybe Dottie Orson wouldn't care; maybe she'd wait on Roy hand and foot with never a complaint. "Well, just let the little Delilah have him." Lila Mae kicked a cabinet door shut, making a small black rubber mark with her shoe.

Well, she wasn't about to lollygag around all day. She placed her *Best of Ray Charles* album on her stereo, turning the volume up just to jump-start the morning. Then she pushed up her sleeves, fishing around the dishwater for the sponge, singing along with Mr. Charles. As she belted out, "Hit the road, Jack, and dontcha come back no more, no more, no more, no more!

Hit the road, Jack . . ." she was amazed that the tune seemed to have been written with her situation in mind. She pictured the miserable, mismatched couple cooped up in Dottie's little efficiency apartment in a seedy neighborhood of the San Fernando Valley. The waitress, smoking like a three-alarm fire, would apply her streetwalker-red lipstick and slip into her black silk stockings every night and disappear until dawn. One day Roy would realize what a fool he'd been to throw so much away. He would beat on Lila Mae's car window, howling and pleading with her to let him see his kids (even though they were already grown up and not the toddlers that were more convenient for her operatic scenario), but the damage had been done, he had made his choice.

After finishing the dishes, doing a load of laundry, and waxing the bathroom floor, Lila Mae was still singing along with her Ray Charles album, only now she found herself crooning along with the "I Can't Stop Loving You" track. The more she sang, the more she realized that these words also seemed to describe her circumstances. Not that she would come right out and admit it—*yet,* anyway—but she could see that a lot of last night's episode was her fault. She even wondered why she acted so juvenile, why she had been flying off the handle lately. Maybe it's them dumb hormone pills, who knows? As for Dottie, she wasn't so great, either—hairier than Godzilla, with two goatees hanging from her armpits and legs that were so bowed that she looked like a walking wishbone! When she opened the freezer, she tried to guess which one Roy would rather have for dinner—chicken or pork chops. Maybe she'd make mashed potatoes with real butter and apple pie—warm, just the way he liked it—with a slab of French vanilla ice cream. . . . Well, she couldn't blurt it out that it was *all* her fault, and if he called, she certainly wasn't going to tell him she was thawing meat for supper, but she supposed they *should* patch things up. She'd just follow the same system as she always had—pretend she was still sore and then let Roy talk her out of it—and pretty soon things would be as good as they'd ever been.

By the time the phone rang in the early afternoon, Lila Mae had the formula all figured out. If it was Roy calling to sweet-talk her, which it probably was, she would go ahead and give him a piece of her mind. He had some nerve, she'd tell him, calling her like nothing was wrong. "Who do you think you are, to pull a stunt like that?" Just to let him know how peeved she was, she even used her most impatient, irritated voice to say "Hello." But it wasn't Roy on the other end at all. When Lila Mae heard a woman's voice, her anger—like a cat with nine lives—unexpectedly jumped back into the picture. She said, "Dottie, is that you? Don't start this now!" She almost hung up in a huff, but finally the woman said, "Ma'am, this isn't Dottie, this is Ivetta Teagues from Halstead Construction. I'm trying to tell you that your husband's been in an accident at work."

"An accident?" Lila Mae's heart thumped. When she asked the woman, "What *kind* of accident?" Mrs. Teagues said, "A *serious* accident." It went on like that, the woman hemming and hawing until, finally, Lila Mae told the woman to just cut the comedy. "Tell me *right now* what hospital my husband's in or put someone on the line who will. I mean it now!"

"Ma'am," Ivetta Teagues answered like an impatient robot, "I'm trying to tell you your husband's not in the hospital. He's already dead."

"Dead?" Lila Mae lowered herself into a wooden chair, her heart pressing against her rib cage. "That—that can't be. . . . You—you just said he was in 'a serious accident.'" A *serious* accident meant something else entirely. It meant she could still rush to the hospital with Roy's Old Spice, his sheepskin bedroom slippers, his *Field & Stream* magazines. How dare Ivetta Teagues throw her off the track like that! Death was an accommodating time zone, a series of hours or days or weeks in which she could address unfinished business and tie up loose ends.

One last look at the peacock-blue eyes, the chiseled curve of his jaw . . . Death wasn't a robber who with one swift poke of a weapon whisked it all away. Lila Mae cradled her forehead and hyperventilated. She murmured "I hate you . . ." to Teagues. Then she dropped the phone on the tile floor.

Dead. She remembered all those funerals when the minister would make some sad or poignant remark and she and Roy would trade knowing looks and squeeze one another's hands and perhaps in the privacy of their hearts renew their appreciation for one another. They would picture a time—a faraway time, on some different planet, even in a strange galaxy—when the subject matter would be one of them. But it was always a foggy, pastel watercolor of a scene. . . . Sometimes they even haggled over which one of them would go first. Lila Mae always thought she would, but Roy said no, no, he'd be first, he could feel it in his bones.

"Hey"—he'd even punched her ribs playfully—"wouldn't that be something? If the last thing I say to you is 'Didn't I tell you I'd keel over first, Lila Mae.' Lila Mae told him he shouldn't say such things, but Roy had always been a big joker, discussing morbid topics and the weather report in the same tone of voice.

How in the world could Lila Mae break the news to her kids that their poor father spent his last night on earth sleeping on a lumpy rollaway bed in the guest bedroom with Ava's Snoopy beach towel covering him and a gallery of celebrity criminals hanging on the wall above him? What would they think if they knew that inside his briefcase was an official letter from the Contractors' Board with information about how to get his license reinstated when nobody even knew it had been revoked? Or how could she admit that she still had his entire wardrobe . . . that she'd rushed back to reclaim every stitch of clothing that Roy owned, every shirt and pair of trousers that they'd recently delivered to the Salvation Army to be given away to the poor? Someday, Becky Jean would accidentally wander downstairs into the sewing room. She'd open the big wooden closet that smelled of mothballs and mildew and stiff gabardine and see her father's print shirts and the brown leather jacket and that horrible powder-blue leisure suit that Roy caught Lila Mae trying to throw away time and again. Lila Mae could hear Becky Jean now: "Mother! What's all this stuff doing in the closet?"

In her desk drawer, she still kept the dented fruitcake tin where she stored Roy's dogtags and Air Force wings, his dime-store reading glasses—still smudged with his fingerprints—the rubbing compound he used for his arthritis, even the crumpled breakfast napkin he'd used the morning he died.

With her Schaeffer fountain pen, Lila Mae scratched two thick lines under "Music to Be Played," pressing so hard that the point cut two trenches on the paper. Music was important, *very* important, certainly not the type of thing funeral parlor personnel should decide. There were so many songs Lila Mae loved—way too many, in fact. And just to complicate things, there were two categories of music: favorite and appropriate. A few songs, like "Battle Hymn of the Republic" and "Amazing Grace," qualified in both categories. (She'd give the world to have the Mormon Tabernacle Choir sing some of her selections, but if her family couldn't swing it or if the choir didn't do that sort of thing, the kids would feel guilty for the rest of their lives.) There were more unusual tunes, though. The Beatles numbers that she just loved: "The Long and Winding Road," "Yesterday" . . . Even movie themes such as "The Last Time I Saw Paris," and maybe even the main song from *Phantom of the Opera*. Boy, the organist would probably butcher that one, if she didn't come right out and refuse to play it. She even liked that Diana Ross song "Do You Know Where You're Going To?"—the one she sang in the film *Mahogany*. There was a heavy-metal group too, Guns n' Roses, who had a great song— "Sweet Child o' Mine," or some such. She'd been baby-sitting Ava one day and found herself humming along with a rock-and-roll station. When she'd told her granddaughter to "turn that up some, honey," Ava looked up from her Scarlett O'Hara paper dolls, wrinkled her freckled nose, and said, "You *like* that song, Grandma?"

Lila Mae could see her friends and family now, row after chapel row, trading confused what-gives glances as the organist played one unlikely tune after another.

Although she flipped to the page marked "Tombstone," the paper was empty. If the truth be known, she wouldn't mind one of those gaudy things made out of Italian marble and decorated with flowers and angels and engraved with something gushy and dramatic. As for the inscription, Lila Mae had leafed through *The Best Loved Poems of the American People,* scribbling lines from Kipling and Robert Frost for something poetic and appropriate. But she decided to give the children some leeway on these two issues.

One thing that was out of the way was her burial plot—although had she known the end result, she might have left well enough alone. But because of a chain of circumstances that even she couldn't completely remember, she got trapped. It was the very day she finalized Roy's arrangements, and she had barely finished picking out the coffin and hymns when Mr. Ray, the director of services at Forest Hills, said Lila Mae should think about killing two birds with one stone.

When he saw that Lila Mae didn't know how to take his comment, the man cleared his throat and teeter-tottered on his heels. "What I mean to say, Mrs. Wooten, is that you should think about your *own* affairs, as you make the arrangements for Mr. Wooten. Believe me, it will lighten the load on your family." Mr. Ray, a stalky fellow in a shiny gray suit and a satiny white tie, had a khaki complexion and miniature whirlpools of black hair growing in his ears. When he talked, his false teeth were like clicking castanets.

"You don't want to put your family through the same agony that you're dealing with, do you, Mrs. Wooten?" The man fixed his eyes on Lila Mae and in a lead-the-witness motion shook his head no.

It was a sizzling-hot day, and the bitter sting of smog and car exhaust filled their lungs as they strolled the Forest Hills grounds in search of the two ideal plots. They rambled through a garden of shrubbery and classical statuary, past Cupid fountains and a prim white chapel with arched stained-glass windows.

Finally, Mr. Ray ducked into a gazebo and patted the curved cement bench next to him. He wanted to tell Lila Mae what she was up against. "So many of our locations are in the sun. Your morning sun's okay. . . . But you see the white stucco building over there?" Mr. Ray swiped his forehead with a hankie and traced an arc in the sky, showing Lila Mae the sun pattern and how it moved across the grounds. "From noon on, you get blinding, blistering, scorching-hot sun, full force ALL THE LIVELONG DAY!"

"Yes, yes, I can see that." Lila Mae knotted her brow, her worried eyes following his fingertip. "That's not advisable, I suppose?"

"*Weeeellll,*" Mr. Ray brayed, "there are always exceptions to the rule. Some families want their deceased to rest in the sun—lately we've been getting some South Americans who have chosen that course." Was it possible that Roy Wooten was in that group? The man put his big square head a few inches from Lila Mae's small white oval one and lowered his voice. "If that's the case, it would be an advantage to you, Mrs. Wooten, since those are the . . . uh"—he cupped his hand and looked from side to side—"less expensive sites."

"You see . . ." Lila Mae stared at the square toe of her shoe and twisted her handkerchief. "My husband, in the last years of his life, spent almost every day workin' in the hot sun. I worried about him, Mr. Ray, I really did. His forehead was sprinkled with little dark patches and a precancer spot. . . . Why, just a few weeks ago I got on him about makin' an appointment with the dermatologist. 'Roy,' I said, 'now I'm not goin' to have to call that doctor myself, am I?' "

"Well, then . . ." Mr. Ray waggled his eyebrows and waltzed Lila Mae toward the more expensive shady area. "I'd say that settles the sun issue."

When Lila Mae heard the word "settle," she was hoping that was it, but after making the decision between sun and shade, Mr. Ray said, "Uh-uh-uh, not so fast!" and pulled a pamphlet from his breast pocket. "There's also flat terrain versus rolling hills. We've got plots near the front gates for easy entry and exit, plots on the knoll with more privacy . . . then there's the area behind the brick sanctuary. . . ."

"Gee, it sure isn't as cut and dried as it seems, is it?" Lila Mae fretted.

"No it isn't, Mrs. Wooten." The man's head was wiggling in agreement, thrilled that the sales pitch was now in the hands of the buyer. "No it *isn't*."

So, after they chose a location, Mr. Ray escorted Lila Mae into a room with fancy oak moldings, a domed skylight, and the vapor of musty funeral bouquets hanging in the air. Oil paintings of angels and religious poems decorated the walls, and a spike of dusty pink light bounced through the window. Lila Mae sat in a burgundy leather chair studded with brass upholstery tacks while Mr. Ray took his place in a chrome chair that tilted back and forth like a seesaw. Officiating over it all was a large colored portrait of E. Wallace Hinkman III, the founder of Forest Hills. For the next thirty minutes, Lila Mae and Mr. Ray—over a pot of hazelnut coffee and sweet rolls—finalized the arrangements for one of the very few places left in the entire cemetery that had two acceptable plots that weren't in the sun and were right next to each other.

As Lila Mae drove home, she was plagued by a banquet of emotions, a mixture of relief and anxiety and an assortment of other undefined feelings. The worst thought of all, the one that finally twisted its way through the confusion, and the one that made her slam the brake right in the middle of rush-hour traffic, was the idea that maybe neither she nor Roy should be buried in Los Angeles at all, that it would be much more suitable for them to end up in Kentucky.

Am I losing my marbles? Lila Mae wondered. Why in the world didn't it occur to me before? She pictured the Blue Lick Springs Cemetery with its ancient tilted headstones, sitting at the end of a bouncy country lane, with the fresh bouquets of daffodils placed there religiously by loving families after Sunday school and fried-chicken dinners. They would be back to square one, Lila Mae Stalker and Royce Clarence Wooten, returned to the farmhouses and tobacco barns, magnolia trees, and the mantle of creamy clouds of humidity draped over it all. They'd be one piece of the mosaic that made its imprint on time two hundred years ago and hadn't changed since then.

If all that was the case, that Roy would rather be buried in Kentucky—and she believed it was based on something Roy had mentioned not too long ago—then it was a fine time for it to have dawned on her. (Roy's comment was that after all these years, he still didn't think of Los Angeles as home, that he felt like "someone wearing a suit of clothes too big for him.") In any case, the funeral was two days away, and how in the world could she change it now? Plus, she could just imagine that her kids' rationale—a solid one—was they wouldn't be able to visit their father in Kentucky, not that she could ever visualize them making a trip to the cemetery a weekly occurrence.

In any event, when she told Becky Jean about her business dealings with Mr. Ray, she fired up like a blowtorch. " 'Lighten the load' my foot. That's the biggest gimmick in the book. Dad's not even buried yet and he's bringing up your death. . . . I told you I should go with you. . . . Trying to sell you something at a time like this . . . Oh," she'd snapped, a thick, lilac vein throbbing in her neck, "this just irks me no end!"

"Now, honey, don't get so upset. Nothing's really been finalized yet. . . . You can't blame the man for tryin'." While Lila

Mae was giving her daughter a calming pat, she was wondering how she was going to admit that things weren't still up in the air at all. Not only had she already signed what she believed was a binding agreement, she had even written Mr. Ray a deposit check, and he'd stuck a neon-red sold flag on the two plots.

"Nobody else is beating down the door for the spot next to Roy Wooten, believe me," Becky Jean said. "Get the one plot, then at least wait until after the funeral for the other one. . . . My God, those vultures!"

The more Becky Jean talked, the more idiotic Lila Mae felt. Gullible she was—at least from time to time—but she certainly wasn't as unsophisticated as Becky Jean insinuated. Nonetheless, she realized it was better for all concerned if she didn't rock the boat, at least for now. As much as she dreaded it, Lila Mae had no choice but to go back to Mr. Ray and try to wiggle out of the situation.

"My daughter is against it." Lila Mae had toyed with the clasp on her black calf handbag, unable to meet Mr. Ray's tarnished gray eyes. "She says I should wait until things calm down. I'll keep the plot as is for my husband. But . . . I need to get the check back . . . uh . . . for my plot anyway." She was waiting for him to have a conniption fit as per Becky Jean's prediction. "I just feel so *bad* about this."

"Pleeeease, Mrs. Wooten." The man slapped one flat hand against his desk, as if the tables were now turned and he was trying to convince *her*. "These things happen." He opened a drawer and retrieved Lila Mae's paperwork. She stretched out her gloved hand to take the check, but he placed it facedown on his ink blotter and trapped it under a crystal paperweight. "The last thing in the world I'd do is cause domestic trouble, especially now. I'm here to help, not hinder."

"I know that, Mr. Ray. But to fully understand the situation, you'd have to know the person I'm talkin' about. It's my oldest daughter—you met her that first day. Well, she gets these ideas and there's no changin' her mind. Won't she be surprised when I tell her how simple it turned out. She had me thinkin' there'd be some big song and dance involved, maybe even small claims court—who knows these days?" Lila Mae kept eyeing the man to see if he was going to hand over the check, but so far he hadn't.

"Court?" Mr. Ray said. "Why, that's absolutely *absurd!*" He gave his tie an indignant tug and cracked his knuckles. At long last, he picked up the contract and check as if he were going to return them. Instead, he rubbed his whiskers in thought and said, "Before we cancel the whole shebang, I am wondering if you might want to check out some of the cheaper possibilities for the future? That'll give you something *definite* to mull over. . . ."

Although Lila Mae had already decided to stick to Becky Jean's advice and wait a few weeks and then purchase the plot next to her husband, she didn't want to be rude. So she told Mr. Ray that she didn't see the harm in looking at a few more spots. Once again, he steered her by the arm across the wet lawn. They ducked under the hanging, feathery branches of the willow trees and strolled past the groomed flower beds and even pitched a copper penny in the wishing well.

After he'd shown her a few reasonably priced plots in what seemed like miles away from the main area, one of which was barely separated from a strand of fast-food restaurants and the Pussycat Theater (a business of ill repute) by a webwork of spindly fig trees, Lila Mae was totally pooped. Plus, they were right back where they started: the clapboard chapel that sat on the velvety hummock next to the spot where Roy would soon be buried.

Mr. Ray clutched Lila Mae's arm as if for dear life and said in a dramatic whisper, "I don't want to rock the boat, Mrs. Wooten, or contradict your daughter. And it certainly isn't our policy here at Forest Hills to push. But *this* is a valuable plot.

I'm honestly afraid it's going to go like *that!*" He snapped his fingers with a little pop.

"Do you really think so, Mr. Ray?" Lila Mae gazed at him, her eyes huge, pleading, innocent bulbs.

"I don't *think* so, I *know* so. In fact—this will sound like a come-on, but somebody else has their eye on this *very* spot." Ray's filmy serpent eyes lanced right through Lila Mae. "I'd hate to see you spend eternity next to some stranger, Mrs. Wooten, I really would."

"I don't want that any more than you do, but what can I do, what *can* I do? . . . I'm so disgusted with the whole kit and caboodle, I could just scream! Oh, dear . . . I'm sorry to drag you into all this, Mr. Ray." She told the man that she had half a mind to ignore Becky Jean's advice and just get the derned plot on her own. The man said, "That might not be such a bad idea."

But in the end, Lila Mae had hemmed and hawed, frightened to take the final plunge. Plus, she'd even begun to wonder if Becky Jean hadn't been right after all. It was rather odd, wasn't it, that the new plot cost almost quadruple what they asked for Roy's?

And what about Becky's observation that every single person who worked at Forest Hills had a last name that was really a first name, like kindergarten teachers? "Mr. *Ray?*" Becky Jean had snipped sarcastically. "Pleeease!" Although Lila Mae failed to see the big-deal aspect of it, when she checked the name tags of other employees—there were a Mr. Joseph, a Mr. Earl, and a Mr. David—Becky Jean seemed to be on to something. Although it *was* possible that all those could be last names, too, it did seem odd that there were no Smiths or Joneses in the bunch. Becky Jean claimed they had phony last names so you couldn't look up their home phone numbers in the telephone book and chew them out for being gypped. Whether there was any validity to that theory or not, it did seem fishy that they didn't want you to know who they were. And if that was the case, there might be other things, too.

Several weeks later, Lila Mae and Becky Jean had a good roaring laugh over lunch. "Just think about it, Mom . . ." Becky Jean chortled. Forest Hills had been there for decades, and if the plots were selling as quickly as Mr. Ray insinuated they were, then the cemetery would have used up all its available land ages ago. "Why, half of Los Angeles would be overrun with headstones if people were buying plots and dying as fast as that snake-oil salesman claims."

"You're right, honey . . . you're right." Lila Mae had been laughing so hard, she took a sip of water to clear her throat.

"Besides, Mom," Becky Jean said, "now you're in an ideal position to bargain. It's not the money, it's the idea that they go in for the kill when your resistance is low. What was it he said—'kill two birds with one stone'? That's real subtle. I'm glad you've taught them a lesson."

It was true, what Becky Jean said about the money. Why, that girl had evening bags and perfume atomizers that probably cost more than both plots put together. Plus, Lila Mae couldn't add up all the countless thousands Becky Jean had spent on her mother for this and that. So she wasn't a cheapskate, nosiree-bob! "I'm sorry I gave you such a hard time, honey. . . . You're smart about these things." Lila Mae stroked her daughter's hand. "Mr. Ray, or whatever his name is, will just have to find himself another sucker to play games with!"

The next month, when Lila Mae visited the cemetery, she was cruising up the hill, the bouquet of jonquils on the car seat, and the booming of a preacher's benediction in the background, when she spotted some huge commotion. At first she couldn't be sure of the exact location or what was going on. But as she drove closer to her destination, she could see a massive group of people attending a gravesite service.

She jumped out of the car and slammed the door and dug into her purse, fumbling for her glasses. She was trying to see just how close the ceremony was to Roy's plot. She marched straight ahead. As she approached the top of the knoll, she began to trot, her heart throbbing in anxiety, her palms slick with perspiration.

When she reached the plateau of the grassy hill, she filled her lungs with air. She scanned the crowd, trying to see through the standing easels of carnations and gladioli and the litter of bodies. There were men in newly purchased polyester suits and women in spring hats, a bellowing, pewter-haired preacher, and an ancient, Lilliputian woman whom several people were fussing over.

It seemed like the crowd—which was so thick it covered up half a dozen plots and made it impossible to see what was what—would never budge. But finally, the mourners formed a line, scooping up tiny handfuls of dirt. In a moment, she spotted triangles of bright sunlight bouncing off the bronze casket which was being lowered. When she looked immediately to the right, she saw—just as she'd dreaded—the small, brass temporary marker for Roy.

"STOP! PLEASE, PLEASE STOP!" Lila Mae shouted, her head spinning, terror crawling its way through her lungs. "STOP!" Several mourners crooked their heads to see what the hubbub was about, and one woman even pressed her finger on her mouth and said "Shush."

As the people filed past the open plot, flinging little fistfuls of soil onto the coffin, Lila Mae began to sob. Some intruder, some complete, total stranger named Luella Judge Hood, was resting in the plot right next to her beloved husband. How could it be? Oh, how, how could it be?

Mr. Ray, huffing and puffing, caught up with her, rubbing a large circle on her back and casting his dark, moody eyes to the ground. "I know, Mrs. Wooten . . . I know. I debated and debated with myself, wondering if I should call you one more time, but . . ." His sympathetic voice trailed off, mixing with a gust of rock-and-roll music from a passing car and the howling of Luella Judge Hood's mourners.

"I wish you would have . . . oh, I wish you *would have!*" Lila Mae stamped her foot. A heavily draped mourner with varicose-veined legs and rolled garters sniffed into a tissue, then sized up Lila Mae and Mr. Ray. Lila Mae gave the woman a dirty look although she knew the situation wasn't really her fault. "*Now* what am I going to do?"

"Dear me . . . Well, let's see now." Mr. Ray scuffled around and fiddled with his Masons ring, turning the sapphire-and-gold band around and around his finger. Reaching on his tiptoes, he scanned the grassy contours of the cemetery, hoping for an elixir for the dilemma. "You *have* heard of the film actor Errol Flynn, haven't you, Mrs. Wooten?"

"Well . . . yes, yes of course . . . but . . ." Lila Mae was baffled, her forehead a battleground of wrinkles.

"Well, you take a look right over there." Mr. Ray, a big, phony smile stretched across his face, pointed up the hill to a strip between the chapel and a Victorian pergola. "That's where Mr. Flynn is buried. Now, I could put you four spaces from him . . . *or!*"—Mr. Ray snapped his fingers—"I'll tell you what . . . I've got something only two rows up from Carole Lombard!"

Although Ray announced it as if that was the end-all–be-all of plot locations, and Lila Mae even said "You could?" as if she was willing to go along with it, at the time she hadn't even been sure which actress Carole Lombard was. Of course she knew Lombard was the one married to Clark Gable and that she died in a plane wreck, but when she tried to picture the woman, she always got her confused with Jean Harlow. She played along anyway, since Mr. Ray was so worked up about his remedy.

Pulling out a small diagram, the man scrambled to verify his findings, making little choo-choo noises as he scanned the paper. "Look! You'd only be three aisles from Mr. Wooten."

"But I don't want to have to crane my neck," Lila Mae pouted. "I wanted to be right next to my husband, Mr. Ray."

"I know you did . . . I know. But, Mrs. Wooten, as you can see, I just don't have it. . . ." He turned his palms in the air like a game-show host pointing out a washer and dryer. "I just *don't* have it."

The only other option was to relocate Roy, but Lila Mae couldn't bring herself to do that, either. So, in the end, she joined Mr. Ray in his office as he reworked the papers. She scribbled her initials in the small spaces where the changes were made, and gave him a down payment check for the plot southwest of Miss Lombard. When she made her monthly payments of $68.02, she soothed herself with the notion that she and Roy were "together in spirit."

Oh, after the damage was done, Becky Jean called Nelson, Carleen's husband, and asked him if there was some legal loophole with which to snag the Hoods. When he retorted, "Like what?" she said she didn't know, that he should think of something underhanded—after all, he was the lawyer. When she could see Nelson didn't have any bright ideas, she called the Hoods herself to see if something could be worked out. They strung her along, asking Becky Jean, "What did you have in mind?" But when everything was said and done, they didn't want to transfer Luella anymore than Lila Mae wanted to relocate Roy.

Of course, this wasn't how Becky Jean remembered the situation at all. "Mom, I feel horrible, just horrible. But please don't blame me," she said, claiming that Lila Mae had a way of twisting things. "All I told you was to wait until Dad's funeral was over. . . . You make it sound like I don't want you to be buried next to him. You admitted I was right the day we had lunch at The Ivy."

"After you made me feel like a nitwit." Lila Mae wiggled around and adjusted her belt and shoulder pads and brassiere strap. "And there's a logical reason why your dad's plot cost less, Becky Jean. If you would have just listened to reason you'd know there are subterranean root systems, natural irrigation and topical debris and—and other geological situations to consider. Your father's grave is right under some sort of undesirable exotic tree or some such thing. I forget what it is now, but the closer you get to it, the lower the price."

"Oh, Mom . . . what do you know about subterranean root systems except what that salesman told you? How could you fall for that stupid widow's sales pitch. Oh, I just *hate* talking about this stuff."

"It's not any joyride for me, either," Lila Mae answered. "Don't think it is." Sometimes Lila Mae just couldn't figure Becky Jean out. Lila Mae could mention some little thing in passing—like her television was on the fritz—and lo and behold, a deliveryman would show up with a new set the very next day. Or if she happened to tell her she was having a hard time figuring out what to wear to a certain event, she'd have a load of outfits sent over. And then, with something important like funeral arrangements, she was as stubborn as a mule and as slow as molasses. To an outside person, the whole fiasco probably seemed ridiculous, a situation that could have been easily avoided if Lila Mae had put her foot down like she planned. But after all these years, she still hadn't learned how to deal with Becky Jean. Plus, the girl was so high-strung it just didn't pay. What good would it have done to exchange cross words only to have something horrible happen? Then where would that have put them?

Outside, there was a loud commotion. Some stray eucalyptus branches were tangled in the telephone wire, and the wind swatted them against her house. Stretching out her bedroom window, hooked over the geraniums in her flower box, she rubbed the grainy patina that coated her arms. It felt like dried saltwater. Her ribbed aluminum garbage cans had somehow ended up in the middle of the road, clinking and pinging and backflipping like nimble Ringling Brothers acrobats. She supposed she'd have to go fetch them before they caused a freak accident and some busybody traced their ownership and slapped a lawsuit against her. There was always something to keep a person on edge.

As she opened the front door, the wind—muscular and wild and blustery—practically scooped her up, smacking her body against the lamppost. Tree branches somersaulted and twirled in midair and rushed across the road, disappearing into an empty canyon lot. A bird flitted from the pitch of her roof to a bough of her Japanese maple tree. "Bob Whiiite! . . . Bob Whiiiiiite! . . . Bob Whiiiiiite!" It was too late to retrieve those trash cans of hers. They were already tumbling out of sight, headed south of the border.

Leaning against the wooden railing on her patio, her hair lashing across her face, she gazed at the moon, a murky orange halo. The stars looked like dull, smoky pearls. Now and then, a coyote would howl, and the clay wind chimes that hung from a brass hook on her front porch played a jangly, discordant tune. There was still a cavalcade of fire trucks all along Mulholland Drive. In the air was the sound of sirens, sirens, and more sirens.

Through the umber haze, she traced the constellations, looking for the Big and Little Dippers. On hot summer nights in Kentucky, they would take tubs of popcorn and orange Kool-Aid, then spread quilts on their front lawn. For hours the whole family would stare at a wild yellow moon and the stars and the planets and the rumble and flash of heat lightning. They'd listen to the tinkle of the ice-cream truck and the chirrup of crickets and cicadas, all the sounds of a magical Southern summer. They would breathe in the sweet aroma of the bluegrass and the honeysuckle that tumbled in wild bunches across their property. Roy, who knew all the constellations by heart and had been the first one in their neighborhood to pinpoint Sputnik, would guide them through the black-and-silver wonderland above them, pointing out Ursas Major and Minor and Cassiopeia.

It was Billy Cooper who loved those evenings the most of all. He'd even dream up his own constellations and imagine beautiful objects up there. "Sky jewelry," he called it. "Look, Mommy!" He'd shake her sleeve with his warm, dimpled hand. There would be grime and sweat in the little creases in the palm after playing outside all day. "It's a diamond tiara!"

"MacArthur's Park is melting in the dark . . ." Lila Mae sang. "All the sweet green icing flowing down . . ." Above her was one strand of smoke like a long, gossamer scarf curling slowly into the sky. "Someone left the cake out in the rain . . ." In the bushes, there was a rustle of movement and the rattle of a dog-collar chain. "I don't think that I can take it . . ." She jumped up, sitting ramrod straight, and listened. Whatever it was had run off. " 'Cause it took so long to bake it . . ."

If they *did* take that Route 66 trip—not that Lila Mae thought it was a good idea or that she was even in a position to go along with such a harebrained scheme—maybe she would find Juanita Featherhorse's grave. If she was lucky, perhaps she could locate Juanita's boy and see what he was up to, or track down that prissy little girl who made them all feel like heels when she shooed them off her plantation, or she could even look up that nice black man who repaired their car toward the end of their trip. Wouldn't that be nice, now? She didn't know what made her think they'd still be alive except that Lila Mae still was. Or who knew if they even remembered her, even though she still remembered them?

Lila Mae took a deep, shivering rattle of a breath. How did that work? she wondered. Why was it that other people always made more of an impression on her than she did on them? Why was it that even with her horrible memory she could still remember Mrs. Hull, the third-grade teacher who had a shrub of fire-hydrant-red hair and who wore a brooch of acorns on her shoulder and who always called on Lila Mae when she didn't know the answer to a question and completely ignored her when she did?

And why was it that for years Lila Mae had bought bouquet on top of bouquet of fresh flowers from Josie's Flower Cart in Hollywood but the old battle-ax with the sickle eyebrows and coronet braid who stood behind the counter had never remembered her? Another customer had bought one lousy ivory rose and got treated like royalty. Once Lila Mae had watched in utter disbelief and frustration as the owner asked the customer if she wanted baby's breath with the rose, then wrapped it in clear cellophane and tied it with a gold cord. To boot, they even gave the customer a gift card and a packet of additives that would keep the flower fresh longer.

When it had been Lila Mae's turn to pay, she figured she'd warm the clerk up and establish herself as a repeat customer, so she had said, "I just can't thank you enough. That bug spray you suggested last week certainly did the trick. . . . I'm the one who had aphids on my American Beauty roses, remember?" The woman had glanced at her with thin, translucent eyes and simply said, "Oh, hi," and that was that. Lila Mae just didn't get it.

When she had told Roy about the situation, he gave her arm a gentle pat, trying to shake it off. "People are preoccupied these days, that's all. Believe me, it's not *you*, honey. It happens to me, too."

If that was true, then how come her own children sometimes made her feel like a heel? Everytime Lila Mae made a comment, even in public, they'd sigh and roll their eyes as if to say, "Don't mind her." To this day, Becky Jean still circled Lila Mae like a border patrolman, inspecting her before they went out to lunch, making a run in her stockings or a chip in her nail polish a federal crime.

Jeanine and Roger Fullbright were still playing tennis. She could hear the pong of the tennis ball as it plopped back and forth on their clay court. There was the splashing in a swimming pool, the giggling and shrieking of small children. "That's not fair, Daddy . . . he cheated." a little girl cried. Her eyes closed, Lila Mae rolled her head back against the chaise longue. The night-blooming jasmine and the smoke had made her dizzy; her head boomed in pain.

"MacArthur's Park is melting in the dark . . ." Lila Mae sang softly, not wanting her voice to carry through the deep canyons the way sounds did. "All the sweet green icing flowing down . . ." How was I to know, Lila Mae thought to herself, that I wouldn't see him ever again? "Someone left the cake out in the rain . . ." I'm not a fortune-teller, for Pete's sake. "I don't think that I can *take* it . . ."

How on earth *would* I know, Lila Mae whimpered, that everything I'd ever wanted to say to him had already been said? "'Cause it took so long to *bake* it . . ." Lila Mae's voice bellowed, the notes and instruments seeming to vibrate from some secret hollow deep inside her own body. "And I'll never have that recipe again . . . Oh no . . ." Or that his body would be so mangled that Mr. Ray would tell her that an open coffin wasn't advisable? *"Oh, nooooo!"* She realized that her voice was carrying, but she really didn't care who heard her, not the firemen across the street, not even her neighbors. Maybe, just maybe, she could scream loud enough to reach Roy. Because it was Roy and only Roy that she had to get through to.

Oh, if only she could jump into her car, jam the accelerator to the floor, and just keep driving and driving and driving forever into the rose fire glow of dusk. Somewhere hot and humid, someplace where she could sit at a small table at a lively outdoor cafe, sipping iced cappuccino and scribbling postcards. Then she'd shove the car in gear and drive someplace else. Drive to some quaint country towns where there were rambling farmhouses surrounded by white picket fences, flowering dogwood trees, and yards of deep blue sky and white clouds. She wanted to visit New Orleans and stroll along Basin and Bourbon Streets and listen to the jazz while sipping mint juleps. Or maybe have her fortune told by a Creole voodooist and take a carriage ride through the Garden District. Then she'd visit the Café du Monde for hot beignets sprinkled with powdered sugar, just like the ones that Becky Jean had brought her the mix for when she'd gone to the Mardi Gras.

And what she wouldn't give to visit one of those South American countries, one that was always on the brink of a revolution. A place where the air crackled with tension—air redolent with lemon verbena, and the pungent smells of the jungle, maybe even the threat of cholera epidemics. Flamenco guitars, cabaret dancers with petticoats and flashing white enamel teeth clinched around one red rose. Soldiers with guns strapped to their chests, marching through the streets, their eyes cesspools of violence. She'd probably be scared stiff if she was actually there, but all that turbulence seemed so exciting. There was just so much territory out there that she'd never seen. There were little parcels of her own property she'd probably never set foot on, let alone sections of her neighborhood. That didn't even include Los Angeles or California or the rest of the world.

The wind made all the twinkling lights twinkle even brighter, and all the cars and buildings fluttered as though they were floating under water. Wouldn't it be something, Lila Mae thought, as she leaned against her crossed arms and stared at the vast maroon-and-black sky above her, if her children were looking at those same stars right now? It made her feel sad to think that somewhere, under this same sky and moon, they were scattered. Becky Jean, a night owl, was probably editing her novel, the centerpiece in a swirl of papers and coffee cups and reference books. At this hour Ava would be nestled in the cool white sheets of her bed, sound asleep. And David, if he wasn't off on a film location someplace, would be coaxing Becky Jean to get to bed. It was no telling what Carleen was doing—maybe moving furniture and accessories or writing a gripe column on zombie airline stewardesses or highfalutin sales clerks who thought they were too good to wait on customers. And Casey, with her sheet music propped before her, would be practicing "Lady of Spain" on her accordion. Nelson would be where he always was—baby-sitting his laptop. Undoubtedly (and unfortunately) Irene Gaye was getting gussied up to go carousing with the Darrell guy. Those two were regular Dracula types, cruising the town at midnight, just revving up when everyone else was bone tired. Or maybe Darrell was lugging some dead body into a dark rented room somewhere, fixing to do whatever it is freelance embalmers do to corpses. And Billy Cooper . . . gee whillikers, who could tell what he was up to? Sometimes, when he was locked up somewhere, she wouldn't hear from him for a while. Then he'd surprise them all by calling from a street corner in San Francisco or popping up during a holiday. This time it had been almost a year since Lila Mae had heard from him.

And then Lila Mae wondered about Bill Corn, that nice man who'd given them a map at the beginning of their trip, and that girl who sent all those bedspreads that got her in trouble with Roy. She just wondered what in the world they were doing. Not what they were up to in general but what, as Lila Mae listened to the swishing of her eucalyptus trees and a wild dog howling somewhere over a mountaintop, they were doing at that very moment.

It was still ninety-five degrees when she switched off the porch lantern. Ash flurries drifted through the sky, landing here and there, like lazy, injured butterflies. A helicopter snaked across the sky, carving long, sinewy trails. Then it fluttered away like a firefly, plunging into a wall of black thickness. The air was so heavy with smoke, parts of the sky so orange, that it seemed like the whole world was on fire.

As she stumbled down her hallway, she noticed that the wallpaper—pink and yellow and dark red Roosevelt roses—needed rinsing down and that the lamp bulb in the second bedroom was burned out. Plus, she'd completely forgotten that Leona's photograph still could use a good dousing with Windex. On television, Channel 7 flashed the latest string of losses—a caravan of charred X rays showing the rubble of houses and buildings and machinery. She wondered what was going on with those zebras and lions and tigers that were still roaming around.

In the bedroom, she caught a glimpse of herself in the mirrored closet doors. In her black robe, with the halo of snow-white hair and camellia skin, Lila Mae looked like a photo negative. Resting on her vanity footstool, Lila Mae removed the frosted stopper from her White Shoulders bottle and placed one fleck on each wrist. Then she dug her fingers into the porcelain jar of her cold cream, smearing one cheek, then the other. Quickly, she tissued it off, wadded up the paper into a ball, and threw it at the waste can. It tottered against the metal lip of the basket before tumbling to the carpet.

It was midnight when she slipped into her pink cotton nightgown. She twisted the top on her pills and pulled out a long wisp of cotton, shaking the pellets into the palm of her hand. Before she turned back the cool, embroidered sheets on her bed, before she swallowed the canary-yellow tablets, she picked up her bedside telephone. Just as she did every now and then (usually in the evening, when it was likely that both Sid and Rose would be at home), she called next door. There was always the off chance that Rose would pick up. Or when Sid answered, maybe, just maybe, Rose would cough or make some telltale noise in the background.

Lila Mae pressed the familiar digits, her heart throbbing. There was one ring, then another. "See you later, alligator . . ." She waggled her bare foot, then stopped suddenly. On the fourth ring, Sid, his voice groggy and irritated, picked up.

"Hello . . . Hello . . ." He sighed. "Who's there? . . . Not again . . . *Pleeeaasse!*" Lila Mae pinched the receiver to her ear, taking very shallow breaths. She sat stone still for a second, her eyes clamped shut. Then she slowly, carefully hung up the phone. Quickly, she darted to the window and peered through the network of trees. Coming from their bedroom window was a wafer of gray light. She tugged the blind and began to shudder. Her stomach felt queasy. She'd been so careful to turn off all her background music, and she'd definitely stopped humming that stupid alligator song before the fourth ring. She'd even held her breath when Sid picked up. But for some reason—even though he couldn't *possibly* know, and even though it was much more likely that the Pinkertons (with whom Sid wasn't even on speaking terms) were the responsible parties— Lila Mae felt certain that Sid knew exactly who had been calling and hanging up. She just couldn't put her finger on why, and even though she was going to try not to call over there ever again, she really, truly did want to know if Rose was dead or alive.

Acknowledgments

So many people gave me invaluable support, assistance, and inspiration. A million thanks to Karen Butler who seemingly set aside everything to read the various drafts and give me pointers. My sister, Peggy Sandow, the funniest and very best person I know, who filled in so many blanks. My UCLA classmates and lifelong friends: Vanda Warden, Nancy Lipsky, and Ashby Jones; the Walnut Groves Farm gang; Amy Dean and KristieAnne Reed; also Bob Bookman; Michael Lynton; Clare Ferraro; Elaine Koster; the inimitable Jake Bloom; Lynn Nesbit, my wise and wonderful agent; and Danielle Perez, my editor.

Finally, I owe more thanks than are possible in a lifetime to Allie Aschbacher, my century-old grandmother, in whose living room I spent many memorable moments just soaking up her sunshine.